SNOWFLAKES AND APPLE BLOSSOM

A Benjamin Bradstock Tale

ALEXANDRA JORDAN

Acknowledgements

With sincere thanks to all who have made this book possible, including the Writers' Village International Novel Awards who shortlisted this novel in 2014.

Also to the members of my family who are the inspiration behind this story, and to all who have supported and encouraged me – a never-ending thank you.

FOREWORD

Mattie Payton, the main character in this story, is now a very dear friend of mine. Hers is a tale that must be told. To illustrate, I would like to quote a famous 20th Century visionary and innovator:

'I adopted the theory of Reincarnation when I was twenty six. Genius is experience. Some seem to think it is a gift or talent, but it is the fruit of long experience in many lives. Some are older souls than others, and so they know more. The discovery of Reincarnation put my mind at ease. If you preserve a record of this conversation, write it so it puts men's minds at ease. I would like to communicate to others the calmness that the long view of life gives to us.' Henry Ford.

I trust you will bear this in mind as you read Mattie's amazing story.

Benjamin Bradstock, Edinburgh

CHAPTER 1

Folksbury Lincolnshire

THERE was something about that particular Monday afternoon. A kind of premonition, a foreboding of things to come. Don't ask me why, it's a feeling we women get sometimes.

I was busy at the kitchen sink, washing sweaters, thinking about the conversation Rob and I were about to have. I wanted another baby and he didn't; not yet anyway. But my body clock was ticking, losing time

1

with the speed of a tachyonic particle, and we needed to talk.

I looked up, out through the window. It had become dark suddenly, long fingers of November rain hammering against the back door. Thomas, our four year old, was playing in the garden. Still in my slippers, I yanked open the door. A vicious gust of wind ripped at my hair just as a pool of water appeared at my feet.

'Shit...'

I ran out, towards the patio where Thomas played, round and round on his blue trike. But it was empty, his trike beside the fence, abandoned like a sinking ship.

'Thomas!' I called, my eyes searching furiously.

He always came in at the first drop of rain, the first millilitre.

And he hated the dark.

So where was he?

'Thomas!'

Suddenly fearful, my heart thumping, stomach churning, I continued. To the bottom of the garden, to the tall leylandii, to the fence with the honeysuckle.

'Thomas!'

But the wind blew my words straight back.

I returned, past the kitchen and up the drive to the gate, wooden with an iron latch. The latch was undone, the gate swinging like a noose in the wind.

'Thomas!' I screamed.

I carried on, up the street, panic reinforcing every stride.

'Thomas!'

My baby.

'Thomas!'

I reached Mrs Wilson's, our next door neighbour's. Her gate was open, too. I rang the doorbell frantically, shivering from the cold, all the while knowing she must be out; no car, no lights. No reply.

Returning to the path, I walked on, calling, shouting, berating myself for leaving Thomas, for even thinking of having another baby.

I came to the end of the street. There was nowhere else to go; he wouldn't have crossed the road by himself.

Unless someone was with him.

Oh - my God.

Turning back, I searched frantically with my eyes - every nook and every cranny of every garden I passed. A couple of houses had lights on, yellow and cosy and warm. But all the gates were shut tight.

The storm stopped then, as suddenly as it had begun.

'Thomas!' I screamed again.

My wet hair clung to my face, tears choked my throat. Angry suddenly, at myself, at Rob for not being there, at Thomas for going off without telling me, I kicked our open gate.

But a sudden squall of wind tugged at me, pulling me back, stopping me in my tracks.

And I knew. I knew where he was.

The shed. Mrs Wilson's shed.

Of course.

Sprinting as if my legs had wheels, I ran back. The shed was to the rear of their house, opposite the back door. Her husband had used it for his fishing gear. When he was alive.

Shivering with fear now, afraid I might be wrong, that it might just be wishful thinking, I pushed open the creaking door. The scent of creosote rose up to hit me.

'Mummy.'

Thomas's face, lit by an old flashlight balanced upon the shelf, looked up, his tiny hand reaching out.

'Thomas. Oh, darling.'

Pulling him to me, relief surged through my body, and I sank against the wall.

*

Radio Two babbled quietly in the background. I stirred at the thick, pungent sauce I was making for the spag bol, its aroma of red wine and garlic a tonic for the senses.

Turning down the gas, I opened the kitchen drawer, pulling out my pills. Microgynon 30. Little pills of Heaven.

To some.

I smiled quietly. What if ...

What if I don't take it? What if I don't take the pill for just one day? Miss just one day? I picked up the instruction leaflet, thinking it might help me decide.

Instead, it was having a good old laugh. In big bold analytic letters.

How your body gets ready for pregnancy.

'I'm sorry, Mummy,' I heard.

Thomas looked up at me with his big blue eyes, cheeks rosy from the cold November air. His soft thick curls, the colour of cocoa beans, had already dried in the heat of the kitchen. Wrapped in his dressing gown,

4

he was perched on a tall stool beside the worktop, a finger of Kit Kat in his hand.

Warm tears filled my eyes. 'It's okay, darling. But why? Why did you run off like that?'

'Sorry, Mummy.'

I hugged him to me, wanting never to let go. 'It's okay. Just promise me, faithfully, you'll never do that again.'

'It was the lady that told me to hide in the shed,' he protested. 'I only wanted to see the puppy.'

Alarmed, I stood back. 'Lady? What lady? Mrs Wilson?'

'No, she was out, I rang-ed her bell. But I couldn't see the other lady because it went too dark.'

A handful of cold ice slithered down my back. 'Just promise me – promise me you'll never wander off like that again. You must always tell me where you're going.'

'Okay. But I did see a snowflake.'

'Did you? Well, it's cold enough, I'll say that.'

The phone in the hall rang then, and I dashed to answer it. Picking up the receiver, I peered at my face in the mirror. I'd wrapped my long dark hair in a towel and changed into dry clothes, but my cheeks were still burning hot.

'Hi. Mattie speaking.'

'Hi there.'

I could hardly hear him, but the horrendous cacophony of traffic screeching and banging in the background told me it was Rob; I could practically smell the diesel. He'd be sitting in his van at the edge of some dual carriageway. And I knew exactly why he was ringing.

5

'Hi, Rob.'

'Sorry, can't talk long – just to let you know we need to stay and get finished. We've got Louise Bates's first thing tomorrow. Is that okay?'

My stomach churned. The face in the mirror turned suddenly pale.

There was a loud, impatient sigh. 'Come on Mattie, I need to get back.'

His question was clearly rhetorical then.

But what could I do but agree to his request? What could I do but swallow back my hurt, my disappointment? Because, despite all my entreaties, all his promises, he was still working late, still spending precious evenings away from home, from Thomas. Hours lost forever in the archives of time. And there'd be no conversation tonight after all.

I nodded at the mirror.

'It's okay with me, but just so you know – Thomas ran off this afternoon. In all that rain. I didn't know where the hell he was, Rob. He could have been abducted for all you care.'

'What?'

'He ran off – went to see Mrs Wilson's new puppy. I found him in her shed.'

'Why weren't you watching him?'

'I was only in the kitchen. He was playing on his trike.'

'What was he doing in her shed, then?'

'It got really stormy. I think it scared him. I don't know.'

'Listen, Mattie, I'm sorry, I really need to get back. Loads to do. Sorry.'

'You'll come home as soon as you can?'

'Obviously.'

'I'll explain to Thomas.'

There was a pause. Silent, yet loud as thunder.

'Sorry Mattie, but you know what it's like.'

No, actually, I don't. I don't know what it's like. What *is* it like – getting home every night after your one and only son has gone to sleep? What *is* it like – never having time to chat to him over dinner, help brush his teeth, read a bedtime story, cuddle and kiss him goodnight?

'I know,' I said, my huge sigh letting him know I didn't. 'See you later, then.'

*

Thomas, our four-year-old going on forty (unless we refused him sweets), hair damp from the bath, blue SpongeBob pyjamas fresh from the drawer, patted his bed.

'Come on, Mummy – come and sit down.'

'Coming.'

The storm had returned with a vengeance. I drew the curtains together, replacing the dark night with a sunny blue rainbow picture. Plumping up Thomas's pillow, I sank into it, stretching my legs out along the bed.

Thomas opened his new book, a huge, glossy, colourful inspiration, with a flourish, his eyes shiny as flying saucers spinning in the sunshine.

'Is it good?' I asked.

He nodded enthusiastically, his face open and fresh, his milk teeth pure and white. 'It's Red Riding Hood. Did Nannie send it me for Christmas?'

'No, it's not Christmas yet. I think she saw it in the shop and decided to buy it. Just for you.'

7

'Shall we ring and say thank you?'

Delaying Tactic Number One, I thought.

'No, darling, it's bedtime. But we can ring her tomorrow, after school. So come on, or you'll be yawning all day.'

Snuggling his head against me, we sat, safe and warm, the vanilla scent of Johnson's Baby Bath in the air, the storm raging outside. I turned to the first page.

'Right, are you sitting comfortably?'

He nodded quietly.

'Then I'll begin.'

I paused for effect. A silly routine really, but one we seem to have had forever, a leftover from my own childhood, my own mother.

And so I began. 'It was once upon a time that there lived a little girl. I say she was little. She was in fact seven years old, so you could say she was a medium-sized girl if you wanted to.'

Thomas giggled infectiously.

'Anyhow, this girl was named Red Riding Hood because of the cloak she wore. If you look at this picture of her, you'll see what I mean.'

'Let's look.'

'You've already looked once.'

'But we've got to look - it says so.'

I grinned. 'Anything to delay bedtime …'

He scanned the page briefly. 'Okay. Ready.'

'Red Riding Hood lived with her mother in a small cottage in the middle of a large forest.'

'No, she didn't.' He sat upright, his arms crossed defiantly.

'What?' I stared, unconvinced by this new Delaying Tactic.

'No, she didn't. It was the Granny that lived in the middle of the forest, not Red Riding Hood.'

'It might say that in another book, darling, but in this one it's Red Riding Hood who lives there. It's a different author and the author decides where everyone lives, yes?'

'So if I did a story about Red Riding Hood, she could live in my pink house with my little girls?'

'Yes, she could live in your pink house with your little girls.'

Thomas had been making up stories about a pink house ever since he could talk. It unsettled me sometimes; he spoke as if the place actually existed. But then lots of kids, especially those with no siblings, make up imaginary friends. All the more reason for a baby brother or sister, another life of sweetness and charm, of whispered secrets and dirty knees, to help while away his childhood. Pulling him close, I kissed his damp curls affectionately.

'Good,' he replied.

'So - Red Riding Hood lived with her mother in a small cottage in the middle of a large forest. One fine summer's day, as the birds were singing and the squirrels were running about between the tall oak trees, Red Riding Hood's mother baked a most delicious apple pie. The pastry was crisp, the apples were soft, and there was the most wonderful scent coming out of the oven. But the wonderful scent from the oven escaped out of the small cottage. It escaped out of the doors and out of the windows. It escaped out between the tall oak trees. It escaped all the way out into the forest itself. The birds could smell it. The squirrels could smell it. But who else do you think could smell it?'

Thomas squealed delightedly. 'The big bad wolf!'

*

I kissed Thomas's forehead, running my hand through his hair, now dried into a soft bundle of curls.

'Night-night, darling. Sweet dreams.'

'And Blue Bear, Mummy.'

Blue Bear is a washed woollen-blanket bear from Thomas's baby days; he was nearly as big as Thomas at the time. I kissed his nose.

'Night-night, Blue Bear.'

'And Jeremy Bear.' Its dark fur worn away, its claws reaching out, a faded red ribbon around its neck, this bear is a relic from Rob's childhood, bequeathed to Thomas by Rob's mum.

'Goodnight, Jeremy Bear.' I kissed him too. 'These aren't new Delaying Tactics, are they, by any chance?'

'No.' He screwed up his face inquisitively. 'Mummy?'

'Yes?'

'Is Daddy going to work at night-time forever?'

'No, I hope not. Soon he'll be home every night, just in time to tuck you into bed. You wait and see. He just needs to get his new business going, so we can go on exciting holidays like the one we've just had, and so we can have a nice home and lots of yummy food to eat.'

'I know.' He nodded, his face a caricature of *Yoda*, the brow furrowed, the eyes large and appealing.

I stroked his hair. 'Daddy does love you, you know.'

'I know.' He closed his eyes. 'Night-night, Mummy.'

'Night-night, darling. Love you.'

10

Planting a kiss onto his tiny nose, I hesitated, suddenly reluctant to go, needing more time with him, aware our time together would be all too short before he'd be off on his own, living his own life, buying his own place. I really should have another baby before he's too old, I thought, before he considers babies smelly, piddling things to be ignored while he gets on with the real business of climbing trees.

He opened his eyes again. 'Mummy?'

'Yes?'

'When *will* Daddy be home?'

'When he's ready. I'll get him to come and say night-night, promise. Now – sleep.'

Downstairs, the brass pendulum in the hall clock rocked gently, to and fro. Apart from that, the only sound was the angry storm raging outside. Clearing the dining table, I carried dirty pots through to the kitchen, its cupboards covered in splashes of primary red, yellow and blue. Thomas's paintings from school.

Switching on the radio, I pulled my pills from the drawer, placing the green foil blister pack onto the worktop. The word MON stared at me in big, black letters. Monday. Still unused. Still unsure.

Tidying up, I wiped a damp cloth over the cooker, rubbing hard in my attempt to wipe away the storm, the dark shadow of glass at the back door, my unusual melancholy. And as I rubbed, my mind raced back to our summer holiday, to the heady scent of sweat and suntan lotion.

Rob had resigned from Central Carpets that June, intending to set up on his own, become his own boss, rich and all powerful. Prior to setting up the new business, however, we wanted to take Thomas island-

11

hopping in Greece, before he started school and holidays became inflexible and too expensive. It was something we'd talked about for ages. So we booked flights to Kos, packed our belongings into two huge rucksacks and, as excited as kids with a barrel of toffee sauce, set out for the Dodecanese, its sea a sparkling landscape of turquoise, its tiny grains of sand like Californian gold-dust upon my warm skin.

Sighing, I rinsed my cloth under the tap, dejected at being on my own. Again. Holidays were all very well, I mused, but they hardly made up for the fact that Rob was never at home the rest of the year. Why did he never manage to finish work on time? Why couldn't he delegate to Luke?

The phone rang again, echoing through the house. I dashed to rescue it.

'Hello?'

'Mattie …'

It was Mum, her voice a grey shadow in the corner. My heart missed a beat.

'Mum – you okay?'

'Your father's crashed the car. We're in A&E,' she sobbed.

'Oh, my God. Is he alright?'

'A bit of concussion, that's all.'

'Are you alright; where are you?'

'We're in Grantham Hospital, but I'm fine – don't worry about me.'

I frowned at the mirror. 'Grantham?'

Mum and Dad live in Baslow, Derbyshire – two hours' drive from Grantham. It's where I was brought up, where they ran the village newsagent's until their recent retirement.

'Oh, you know what your father's like, love. He had to go and see one of these Audis he's been on about. We were just on our way home – stopped for fish and chips.'

'Where's the car? Shall I come and get you?'

'It's been towed away. But it looks like they're keeping him overnight, anyway, what with his age and everything.'

'I'm coming over, then.'

'Well, only if you're sure.'

'It's fifteen minutes, Mum. Thomas is in bed, but I'll get Becca round.'

'Isn't Rob there?'

That accusing tone. Again. She never wanted us to get married in the first place.

'No, he's out working. But it's fine; Becca won't mind.'

*

Becca's my closest friend; we've known each other since Mums and Toddlers. Chloe, her daughter, is the same age as Thomas, only a few months between them. I remember meeting her in the church hall, watching her play with Chloe on the huge rug, her long blonde hair catching at the wool of her navy sweater. Pale, delicate skin, tall and slender. The very antithesis of me. People say I'm pretty and I suppose I have nice blue eyes, but I've always thought of myself as a bit dumpy, really. Okay, my addiction to chocolate doesn't help.

I came to discover, however, that Becca is not only stunningly good-looking, but also highly talented. She was a top graphic designer for the BBC in London, earning loads of money, but gave it all up to look after

Chloe. When she discovered she was expecting, she and Alan bought this gorgeous farmhouse in Pepingham, a tiny village near Grantham. According to her, however, there was so much mud on the floors she couldn't understand why the previous owners had needed a farm; a few seeds scattered around the furniture legs would have done it. But now they've made the place their own, with trendy antiques from Newark Market and shabby chic pieces from the High Street. The place is a total delight. I love it.

And I had to drag her away to babysit.

It was nearly midnight by the time we got back. Becca and Chloe had gone home and Rob was working on his laptop in the dining room.

'Hi Rob,' I called. 'Just putting the kettle on.'

Dad hobbled through behind me, perching himself carefully onto a barstool, Mum guiding him with her hand.

'Eeh, Mattie, what a day we've had,' he moaned.

'The main thing is, you're both alright.'

Mum, dressed in a black sweater beneath tweed jacket and trousers, placed her huge leather bag onto the worktop and sat beside him.

'But it was awful,' she moaned. 'I'm so glad we had those huge golf umbrellas in the car.'

'Let's just forget it, Winnie, put it right out of our minds,' Dad replied. 'What I need right now is a decent cup of tea and a good night's sleep.'

I grinned. 'I think we can arrange that for you. I'll change the sheets on our bed so you can sleep in there.'

'But what will you and Rob do?' asked Mum.

14

'We'll use the sofa-bed. It'll be fine. I'll dig our sleeping bags out; it'll be like being on holiday.'

Rob walked in, his face pale and tired. 'Did I hear my name?'

Rob. My gorgeous husband. Overworked and underpaid, in the hope that one day he'll hit the jackpot. His thick strawberry-blonde hair needed cutting desperately, but he'd not had the time. I looked up at him, my heart reaching out.

'Hi there.'

He kissed me. 'Becca told me what happened. Everything okay?'

Mum nodded. 'We're alive.'

But Dad grinned ruefully. 'Apart from the car. Bloody thing's in the garage. Looks like it'll be a couple of weeks an' all.'

*

The hospital had only allowed Dad to come home if we promised to keep an eye on him. He got up a couple of times during the night to visit the loo, but that's normal. Otherwise, apart from a bruised knee, he was fine. Upset about his car, of course, but fine.

Mum was her usual self, too. Not a hair out of place, not a crinkle in her clothing. I offered to lend her some pyjamas and they had to be my newest pair, my blue ones from Next. But at least she slept well.

It was Mum who found my pills, still on the worktop, the following morning.

CHAPTER 2

HARINGEY'S always reminds me of an old-fashioned sweet shop. Which is exactly what it was when Mr Haringey bought it, thirty-six years ago. Now a thriving estate agency in Folksbury, its clients are a mixture of tourists and locals, some wanting a small village school, some the bargain of a tumbledown cottage, and some a tranquil retirement property.

I only worked for Haringey's part-time, Mondays and Tuesdays. Today was Tuesday, but the phones were quiet, silenced by icy, roaring winds. Well, no-one wants to move house in the depths of winter.

This particular branch of Haringey's has an unusual quality for a modern-day shop. The deep woollen carpeting, leather armchairs and vintage oak desks all reflect the building itself, stone with Georgian bow windows and bulls-eye panes of glass. The great red door, situated between the windows like an outstretched pillar box, is the original from 1838, the year of Queen Victoria's Coronation. The Haringeys have never replaced it, instead filling in the woodwork and carefully painting over. The pampering of a majestic lady with Botox and Max Factor.

That Tuesday morning Emma, the full-time negotiator, had already rung in sick, my coffee had gone cold, and the remainder of the double chocolate chip muffin I'd bought from the Deli next door was cold and crunchy where it had been warm and oozing. Suddenly the shop bell, the old-fashioned kind that coils above the door on a rusty spring, clanged loudly.

I stared guiltily at the muffin. Gathering up its white paper case, I slid it into my drawer. I am of course fully aware that eating four hundred and fifty calories at ten in the morning is not a good idea, and my waistline has never been the same since having Thomas. But I'd already walked off breakfast taking him into school, and the only thing of sustenance in the *bijou* kitchen at work was a pack of soggy Digestives.

An elderly woman in a smart grey coat was outside, struggling with the door. Her shopping bag, scarlet to match the beret perched upon her head, had become caught in the gap between the door and frame. Rushing to help, I pulled it back, ice-cold air slapping at my cheeks like wet newspaper.

'Sorry about the door,' I murmured.

She smiled her thanks, her deep brown eyes crinkling at the edges.

'It's okay, my dear. Cold again today.'

Wiping her shoes on the doormat, she stepped onto the carpet, a geometric Axminster of cherry, blue and turquoise. Newly fitted by Rob, its opulent scent filled the room. I guided her past the shiny brochure display towards the rear of the office, warm and cosy. Patting

17

the armchair facing my desk, its buttons forming deep recesses in the green leather, I smiled.

'Here we go, a nice comfy chair.'

'Thank you.'

We made ourselves comfortable and she settled her heavy bag onto the floor beside her.

'Now then, how can I help?' I asked.

'Well, I want to buy a house, my dear.'

Her voice was warm and kind; I detected a touch of Cockney. Heavy golden hoops adorned her ears, the hair around them a carefully-dyed auburn. She looked friendly, intelligent, a little mischievous, an Angela Lansbury-type character.

I completed her contact details onscreen; name, address, phone number.

'And what type of property are you looking for, Mrs Phelps?'

'Something small. I am used to bigger, you see. Me and my husband, we've been running a guest house, a bed and breakfast, for years.' Her eyes filled with sorry tears. 'But my Peter has gone now and I need to sell up. Can't run the place on my own, not now I can't.'

'I'm so sorry to hear that, Mrs Phelps. When did he die – have you been on your own for long?'

Her eyes widened in shock. 'Oh no, he hasn't died, my dear. Goodness, it would've been easier if he had. No, he went off with one of the guests, a Mrs Lucy Conanby. No, if he'd died, I wouldn't have to sell the house, now would I? I'd be able to live off the insurance.'

I wasn't at all sure how to respond to this. 'It – it must all be very upsetting for you.'

Pulling a carefully-ironed handkerchief from her pocket, she produced a small brown bottle. Twisting the lid, she allowed three drops to fall onto the white cotton.

'Just frankincense with a little sweet orange. It helps me feel better. I mix my own, you know.' She breathed in deeply. 'Been a few months now, it has. Time I was getting over it. Anyway, I thought you were going to choose me a house.'

'Of course. So, any type of property.' I ticked the boxes. 'What's the maximum you wish to pay?'

The spicy, peppery scent was making its way to my side of the desk. I couldn't help but breathe in. And as I did so, a vision of Thomas filled my head; my baby, dark swansdown covering his head, and the delivery room, Rob arriving breathless at the very last minute. The joy, the overwhelming joy of having my warm, pink baby in my arms at last, my adoring husband grinning by my side.

'Well, it really depends on how much I get for mine,' Mrs Phelps was saying.

Pulling my thoughts back into the room, I caught her watching me carefully.

'I need to invest some of it, you see, to live on,' she continued. 'My Peter says he doesn't want anything. Doesn't need it, not with what she's got. Left loads by her husband, she was. He won't need to work no more, that's for sure. Run a B and B for years together, we have. Brought up our kids on it, we did.'

On the verge of tears, she began playing nervously with the large black button at the neck of her coat.

I smiled. 'How about if we have your house valued? Our surveyor, Andrew Whirlow, could come and see you. He's very nice.'

There was a weak smile.

'We have a slot a week on Thursday,' I continued.

But I looked up to find her crying softly, the handkerchief fulfilling its original purpose.

'How about I make you a nice cup of tea, Mrs Phelps? We're not very busy today; the run-up to Christmas, I think.'

'That would be lovely.' She glanced at the nameplate on my desk. 'You're very kind, Mrs Payton.'

'Call me Mattie, please.'

'Thank you. And I'm Enid, of course. Lovely name, that. Short for Matilda, is it?'

'Yes, after Great Aunt Matilda – my grandma's sister.' I headed towards the tiny kitchen to the rear of the office. 'I'll put the kettle on then.'

One cup of tea and two soggy Digestives later, Mrs Phelps was chatting away.

'I gave up nursing to marry my Peter, you know. Left home when I was sixteen to join the QA's, the Queen Alexandra's Royal Army Nursing Corps, in Aldershot. Loved it I did, but I wanted to be with him.'

But the phone rang suddenly. Mouthing an 'Excuse me' I pulled on my headset.

'Good morning – Haringey's. Mattie speaking.'

'Hi, Mattie.'

'Hi, Rob.'

'Listen, I know I said I'd try to get back on time tonight but …'

'You can't.'

'Sorry.'

I was at work; I couldn't argue. 'It's okay. I'll explain to Thomas.'

'Thanks, Mattie. See you later then.'

'See you.'

Suddenly despondent, I hung up. 'Sorry about that, Mrs Phelps. Now then, where were we?'

She placed her empty cup onto my desk. 'Thomas your son, is he?'

'Yes.' I smiled. 'He's only just started school, which is why I took this job. And the fact that he saw the notice in the window and dragged me in here. But I couldn't stand the thought of rattling around the house by myself all day.'

Her eyes were sympathetic, knowing. 'It is an enormous wrench – best to take your mind off it. I take it he's your only one?'

'Yes. For now, anyway. He does get lonely sometimes, makes up imaginary friends – you know what kids are like. It'd be nice to have another one before he's too old. But Rob's so busy at the moment he hardly has time for Thomas, let alone another …'

I stopped myself abruptly. Why was I telling her this? Why was I telling her, a perfect stranger, all this?

'That is a shame,' she said. 'What does he do, your husband?'

'Flooring and carpeting. Self-employed. It's a brand new business and what with the recession – I mean – I try to understand.'

She blinked away the sudden concern in her eyes. 'Things might change, you know. Once he's established. You'll see. Give it time, my dear. Give it time.'

*

Becca rang that evening. I'd just got Thomas off to sleep and was starting on a huge pile of ironing. So any excuse for a girlie chat.

We'd been talking for around ten minutes, organising coffee, discussing holidays, the dreams we all have, of long lazy beaches and glorious sunshine, when I started moaning about Rob's hours. I knew he was lucky to get work at all in the current economic climate, but still I felt he was staying out too late, working too hard. Constantly grumpy, he'd begun nit-picking at every little thing.

'I wouldn't be surprised if he was having a fling with that Louise Bates or whatever her name is', I said. 'He seems to prefer spending time there instead of here with me.'

'Did you know seventy-five per cent of men would have an affair if they thought they'd never be found out? Seventy-five per cent?' asked Becca.

I laughed. 'Typical.'

'Do you think men find it easy to have affairs?'

'Depends on the man, I suppose.'

'No, really. Do you think men take their vows seriously, you know, when they get married?'

'I think so. It's not all like Coronation Street, you know.' I paused then, my mind working overtime. 'Are you alright, Becca?'

Her reply came quickly. Too quickly.

'I'm fine, just ignore me. Been a bit down just lately, that's all.'

Something was wrong. I knew it.

'I mean, are you and Alan alright? You know, with him working away and everything?'

Alan, a self-employed advertising executive, hired himself out to various well-known companies. He worked hard, with meetings all over the country, but the money was good.

Becca sighed loudly. 'Mattie, I'm fine, there's not a problem. Just tired, fed up of Alan being away all the time.'

*

I rang Mum immediately afterwards; the ironing could wait.

She and Dad had arranged a hire car that morning, arriving home just in time to watch Dad's favourite programme – you've guessed it – Countdown.

Dad was fine, relaxing with a good book, she said, and she was getting ready to go round to her friend Carol's for a natter.

But then the conversation became slightly awkward.

'Mattie,' she said.

I knew what was coming. 'Yes, Mum?'

'You know I found your pills in the kitchen this morning?'

'Yes,' I sighed.

'Is it an old packet?'

'No, Mum. I forgot to take it yesterday, that's all. I got them out ready, but when you rang from the hospital I completely forgot.'

'Oh.' Disappointment echoed through her voice.

'What is it, Mum?'

'I was hoping they were old ones, that's all, that you might be planning a nice little surprise for us. After all, Thomas isn't getting any younger. And neither are you.'

I was thirty. 'Thanks, Mum.'

'You know what I mean.'

'Sorry, but we're not planning a nice little surprise. It's not really a good time at the moment, not with Rob's new business and everything.'

'Well, don't leave it too late, you know. If you wait until he's properly established, it might be years.'

'I know. And it is something we need to discuss.' If he ever gets home in time to discuss anything, I thought. Before time runs out. Before my body shrivels and dries into a wrinkled chronicle of regret.

'Well, you look after yourself, and that little boy. He's a real sweetheart.'

'I will. Give my love to Dad, and tell him to stop driving round like a boy-racer.'

'Mid-life crisis, come late.'

I laughed. 'Do they ever grow up?'

*

Later, in the quiet of the kitchen, I stared at my pills, at the bold lettering on the green foil backing. MON - still unused. TUE.

If I missed TUE as well …

I'd read the leaflet, looked up what would happen if I missed a pill. If I missed only one, my contraception was still intact. But if I missed two ...

24

CHAPTER 3

VERY early the next morning, Thomas tiptoed into our room, Blue Bear held by one ear, and threw himself onto our bed.

'Mummy-Daddy!'

His elbows caught my shins, and I yelped in pain. Rob groaned, rolling away towards his side of the bed.

'Thomas, that hurt,' I whimpered, rubbing my legs.

It was dark, but I could sense his cheeky grin. 'Sorry, Mummy.'

'Just be careful, please. Come on, come and have a cuddle.'

Nestling beside me, he lay as still and quiet as dew on a spider's web. I tucked the edge of the duvet around him and softly closed my eyes, trying to recapture the dream I'd been having - something to do with chocolate, I think.

After what seemed like a mere glimpse of time but was in fact thirty minutes, the alarm clock, like a Harrier jet, exploded into the silence. Rob put out a hand to silence it, his hair forming a fringe at the edge of the duvet.

'Don't know why we bother with that thing. Get woken up anyway,' he grumbled. 'I'm knackered. I'm always bloody knackered.'

Taking a deep, calming breath, I stared at the ceiling. 'What do you expect, Rob? Doing your accounts until one in the morning doesn't exactly help.'

'Some of us have to keep the wolves from the door.'

His hair disappearing once more beneath the duvet, he hid himself from the world. From me. My eyes filling with sudden tears, I swallowed hard, dreading yet another conversation about my only working part-time, about not being able to afford another baby just yet.

Thomas tugged at my hand. 'Come on Mummy, time to get up.'

'Come on then, pest.' I smiled at him, my heart filling with love, my reward two arms around my neck.

'I'm not a pest.'

'Yes, you are. How do you spell pest?'

He pronounced the letters phonetically. 'P E S T. That right, Mummy?'

I poked my feet out of bed. 'It is. You are a clever boy.'

Shrugging into my dressing gown, I followed as he hopped and skipped his way downstairs. Blue Bear slid down the banister.

'Are you coming to work in school this morning?' Thomas asked.

'It's not really work, is it? I don't get paid. And yes, you'll see me all morning.'

26

The kitchen, a haven of light oak panels, was warm, the heating already on. I filled the kettle, made tea for myself and hot chocolate and cereal for Thomas. He stood beside me, cuddling Blue Bear, watching intently.

'Right, a question for you,' I said.

'What?' he asked.

'What do you think Mrs Webster would like for Christmas? Chocolates or flowers or hand cream?'

He screwed up his button nose. 'Why are we getting her a present?'

'That's what you do at Christmastime. It's our way of saying thank you.'

'Oh.' He shrugged nonchalantly.

Taking his cereal bowl and hot chocolate to the dining table, I asked again. 'So - what do you think?'

He jumped onto his chair, giggling gleefully. 'Cream.'

I laughed. 'What? Ice cream?'

He looked at me, his expression instantly serious. 'Don't be silly, Mummy.'

I put his hand onto the spoon, encouraging him to eat. 'Okay, hand cream it is.'

'Why do you buy so much cream, Mummy?'

'I didn't realise I did. And I didn't know you knew I did.' Smiling, I preened my hair. 'But well, we've got to do something to stay beautiful for Daddy, haven't we?'

*

I kissed Thomas goodbye, leaving him to queue with the other kids in the playground. The deep layer of sparkling frost on the ground had been sprinkled with grit by the caretaker, reminding me of icing sugar and squashed demerara cubes.

Making my way to the classroom, I breathed in deeply at the earthy scent of fresh poster paint. A thrill of nostalgia seared through my veins, my own childhood a lively round of painting, singing and hopscotch.

Mrs Webster, her silver hair recently grown into a fashionably smooth bob, looked up.

'Good morning, Mattie. Nice to see you.'

'Morning, Mrs Webster. How are you?'

I slipped off my coat ready to hang behind the door, but she shook her head at me.

'I'd keep it on if I were you. The heating's not working again. Mr Hunter's trying to sort it out, but you know what it's like.'

'Well, these old village schools - what can you expect?'

'As it happens, I expect Government funding.' She rearranged the papers on her desk. 'But well, I suppose if we can manage a Reception class five days a week, we can put up with old pipes.'

I hung up my coat anyway. 'Is there anything I can do?'

'I'm fine at the moment, but if you could take the children up to the library this morning, that would be a huge help. They need to choose their books?'

'Of course, no problem.'

Suddenly, like a swarm of bees, children poured through the door, chatting excitedly, their noses pink from the ice cold air. Mrs Webster clapped her hands together.

'Five, four, three, two, one. Quiet, please!'

Her firm but gentle voice calmed completely, a soft blanket of swansdown settling upon them. Thomas sat at the red table, his tiny hands placed neatly together. He smiled at me, and my heart roared with love.

The literacy hour was always the first lesson on a Wednesday morning. Mrs Webster would read from a giant storybook, pointing to each word with an old snooker cue. I guided groups of children to the library at the other end of the school until playtime arrived, when they rushed outside, energy bursting from them like an explosion of cartwheels.

Mrs Webster smiled appreciatively. 'Thanks for all your help, Mattie. I'll see you in the staffroom. Won't be long.'

The staffroom was near the school entrance, beside the secretary's office. Its shelves bowing under the weight of faded books and folders, it was already a hustle-bustle of teachers, classroom assistants and other parent volunteers. Chatting away, they swapped local gossip, put right the state of the economy, discussed their offspring.

Pouring a coffee from the tall green pot in the corner, I smiled at the friendly faces around me, but for some reason felt on the outskirts, at the edge, unsettled, a seed in the pit of my stomach waiting for the rain.

*

The bell rang for lunch, and I made my way home. Piles of leaves littered the pavements, a palette of burnt sienna, crimson and gold, slippery like paint. I recalled how they'd been frozen solid on the way into school that morning. How quickly things change, I thought. Kicking at them, my thoughts turned to Becca, to our

29

brief conversation of the day before. I kicked even harder.

I walked steadily on through the leaves, my mind a circle of confusion. Becca and I were meeting in the Deli for lunch that afternoon, and I knew there was something wrong. Should I ask her? But there again, did I want to know? Becca and Alan had always been so happy. A strong couple, a good marriage.

Unless … he had been working away an awful lot. But I didn't want to think about that either. I didn't want to think about people splitting up at all.

Passing Mrs Wilson's, I reached the gate of our own 1960s semi. Unlocking the door, I threw it open, eager for warmth. But even my own home felt cold, hostile; the face of the bank manager discussing an overdrawn account. The pictures on the wall, of Thomas, of me and Rob, of us as a family, seemed odd, distant, from another lifetime. Having stepped over the pile of letters on the floor, I went back to gather them up, carrying them into the kitchen. Pulling the biscuit tin from the cupboard, I took out a ginger crunch covered in thick, black chocolate, devouring it hungrily as I looked through the mail. There was a magazine from a children's clothing firm I'd never heard of, but the others, addressed to Payton's Carpet and Flooring Ltd, I perched onto the hall table.

It was then that I noticed the blinking of the red message button.

Mattie, I tried your mobile, but it's not answering. Could you ring me as soon as possible? Thanks.

Becca. Probably cancelling lunch. I rang back.

'Hi, Becca, sorry about my phone. I've been in school …'

'Mattie?'

It didn't sound like Becca at all.

'Are you okay?' I asked.

A cry, strange and ethereal, found its way down the line.

'Becca, what's wrong? Not Chloe?'

'No.'

'What then?'

There was no reply.

'Becca?'

'It's Alan. He's gone,' she sobbed.

'I'm coming round. Be two minutes.'

I'd known there was something wrong.

*

The grey stone of Becca's kitchen floor was smooth with age. Three pine dressers lined the far wall, the appealing clutter of brightly-coloured pots, fine white china and the odd piece of warm copper testament to her creative energy. Radio Two was a murmur behind me, Jeremy Vine discussing VAT. There was the tang of cinnamon and melted butter.

Becca was sitting at the huge pine table in the centre of the room. Twisting her hair compulsively, her eyes red and swollen, she gazed at the box of tissues before her, a pile of used ones beside it. A huge white mountain of sorrow.

The kettle on the Aga rattled suddenly. Having felt as useless as a clown at a funeral, I dashed to rescue it. Two minutes later, I placed a mug of hot, sweet tea onto the table.

'Right, missus, I want you to drink this, then you're going to start again. I've hardly understood a word you've said so far.'

31

'Sorry.'

Her words were a groan, a resonation from the heart, a huge sigh. I pulled up a chair to sit beside her.

'Come on, let it all out.'

'I've known about it for ages, Mattie. But I've not told anyone, not a soul. I thought it was just a fling, you know?'

Her words, at first a whisper, a trickle, became a torrent, a dam releasing its load.

'I thought maybe he'd been lonely one night. You know, working away from home and all that. I thought she'd just bloody well go away and - and we'd carry on as normal.' She shook her head in disgust. 'Stupid.'

'You must have been through hell. I can't believe I never noticed anything. Why didn't you say something?'

'I didn't want to put upon you. I probably shouldn't be telling you now, but I - I need to tell someone, and I know you'll understand - that you'll listen. And yes, it has been hell, pretending everything's alright, waiting until Chloe's in bed before I can cry myself to sleep, lying to Mum every time she asks how I am, then waking up the next morning knowing I've got it all to do again.'

I felt awful. Worrying about my own little world while Becca was going through all this.

'You should have told me,' I said. 'What would you have done if you'd had a breakdown or something? What would have happened to Chloe then? I mean, we all like to think we've got perfect lives, and it can't be easy to admit when things go wrong. But it doesn't do to keep it all inside.'

She shook her head listlessly. 'It's not that, not really. I suppose I thought if I didn't say anything, that when he got fed up of her, we'd just carry on as normal. I mean, to the outside world nothing's changed really. He's just the same old Alan, we're just the same old couple. And I thought it would make it easier if no-one else knew. You know?'

I didn't know. Not then. But I understood.

'Becca, no-one shall hear it from my lips. Not even Rob. I promise. So if you did want to start again ...'

A weak smile brightened her lovely face.

'It's been awful. Ever since I found that bloody ... for some reason, for some bloody stupid reason, Mattie, I decided to clean the cars. Back in June, it was. A beautiful day, good exercise, fresh air. Alan was at the gym, Chloe was playing at Abigail's, and I was having a clear-out, you know?' She shook her head. 'It was in Alan's car, the ribbon. There was a ribbon in the boot. You know, the chocolate-box kind. Brown, with a little gift-tag.' She demonstrated with long, slender fingers. 'I was about to throw it away. To be honest, if it hadn't been for the Hoover, I wouldn't even have seen it. It was stuck between the carpet and the side of the car, but the bloody Hoover sucked it out. Oh God, I wish it hadn't.'

I was puzzled. 'What?'

'The tag - the bloody gift-tag. You want to know what it said?'

I nodded quietly.

'To my darling Alan. All my love forever. Susie baby. Hah! Can you believe that? Susie baby! I thought maybe it was a present from one of his mates, having a laugh. Or even some girl at work trying to get her hands on him. I never thought for one moment - like I said, he was the same old Alan, *my* same old Alan.'

Anger bubbled up inside me, her pain pressing upon my heart like a carbuncle.

'So what did he have to say for himself?'

'I never told him.'

Silence.

Silence as I tried to understand.

'What?'

'I threw it away. Never told a soul. It would have made it too real. I know it sounds stupid, but I thought if I never said anything, if no-one knew about it, life would just carry on as normal, you know?' Closing her eyes, she sighed heavily. 'Talk about denial.'

My stomach rumbled with hunger, but I couldn't have eaten a thing, not even a warm double chocolate chip muffin. The radio murmured in the background as I sipped my tea, finally understanding Becca's recent moodiness. This self-deception, this denial of the truth, had made her irritable, short-tempered, a wave constantly pounding against the sea-wall. She'd become obsessed with her looks, spending hundreds on new clothes, shoes, cosmetics, even talked about having fillers done. In *her* face.

But then a thought struck me.

'Sorry, Becca, but I'm lost. If you didn't tell Alan, then what happened? Why has he left?'

She studied the tissue in her hand carefully. 'I told him I'm pregnant.'

'What?' I stared stupidly. 'Why?'

'Because I am.'

'What?'

'I know, I know. Something else I've managed to keep quiet. The thing is, with him working away, he loses track of time, doesn't take much notice of things. I'm pregnant, Mattie. Nineteen weeks.'

'What?' Reality hit me with the thud of a house-brick. 'Oh my God, I'd absolutely no idea.' Dumbstruck, I stared at her.

'No, you weren't meant to. Nor was Alan. Not yet. But he's had meetings in Grantham this week, been at home, taken more notice, caught me pouring my wine down the sink last night. He knew.' She smiled ruefully. 'Should have been more careful, shouldn't I?'

'But he was going to find out some time. It's not exactly the kind of thing ...'

'I know, I know. Anyway, he put two and two together, asked if I was pregnant. I said of course I wasn't, that he was being ridiculous, I just didn't like the wine. Cheap and nasty, I said. But then, this morning - he'd obviously been thinking it over - and it all came out. I admitted I'd found that bloody stupid gift-tag, that I knew he was having an affair, that he'd been deceitful and - and everything.'

'Oh, Becca.'

'He went mad, said I'd lied, said it was me being deceitful because I should have been on the pill.' Unable to continue, she sobbed, burying her head in her hands.

'He's definitely seeing this woman then?'

She looked up. 'Mm. But he's right. I am deceitful.'

'No, you're not. He's the one having the bloody affair.'

'You don't understand. I did it on purpose. I got pregnant on purpose. This baby was a ploy, a ploy to stop him going off with 'Susie baby'. Just how deceitful can it get?'

I was stunned. They'd seemed like the perfect couple. Could this really be happening? What had gone wrong? What can go wrong? A shudder of fear, an ache of foreboding, ran through me.

But I pushed it aside.

*

Driving slowly along the High Street, I switched on my lights. The sky had darkened rapidly, suddenly. But the quaint old shops, strong and steadfast through two world wars, pollution and the threat of nuclear annihilation, shone their calm, orange glow invitingly. Christmas trees, heavy with coloured bulbs, swayed to and fro. Metal signs creaked above the shops dangerously. Cocooned in my blue Golf, however, I drove on, oblivious to the icy, weaving wind and the dried leaves dancing on the road behind me.

Drawing up outside the school gates, I hurried into the playground to find Thomas huddled near the doorway, his face white with cold. Mrs Webster held tightly onto his hand.

'Hi, darling,' I said.

'Mummy!' He threw his arms around me.

'Sorry I'm late.'

Ruffling his hair, I looked up to thank Mrs Webster, only to find her walking away without a word. Guilt tugged at me and I rushed towards her, calling out against the storm.

'Mrs Webster! I'm really very sorry.'

She turned, smiling only with her mouth, her eyes as silent as stone.

'It's okay, we've not been waiting long,' she said. 'I think Thomas was getting worried, though.'

'I really am sorry, Mrs Webster. I've been visiting a friend. She's going through a pretty bad time at the moment. I didn't realise the time. Sorry.'

Smiling with her eyes this time, she accepted my apology.

'It's okay. And Thomas has done extremely well in school today; he really is a clever boy. You should be very proud of him. Now get yourselves home, out of this awful weather.'

I smiled back. 'We will, and thank you.'

Hurrying to the car, I fastened Thomas in. Pushing into first gear, I drove away, glancing into the rear-view mirror.

'Had a good day, darling?'

'You know what, Mummy? Joe threw his football out of the window and it fell on Mrs Turner's plant pot. And when Amy said she didn't want to go to the toilet she did really, because she wet herself. And Mrs Turner was *not* a happy bunny!'

I giggled. 'Well, she's enough on her plate looking after you lot, without having to mop up after Amy.'

'But then she started crying, and Mrs Turner said she could go to the quiet corner and read a book, and I went with her to cheer her up. Mrs Turner said I could.'

'You are a nice boy.'

'I know.'

Grinning at my wonderfully precocious son, I relaxed a little, relieved my head was no longer full of Becca, pregnant and alone. I'd spent the whole afternoon there. After her revelation, we were like currents on the breeze, weaving in and out, chatting, consoling, eating leftovers, giggling over the silliest things. Particularly after her mother rang to ask what she should wear to the Barristers' Chambers' Christmas Lunch, husband number two being a barrister of some standing. Blissfully unaware of her daughter's plight, she'd gone on and on and on, until Becca had a sudden fit of giggles, unable to speak. Excusing herself quickly, she'd rung off to find me sitting there, tears rolling down my own face, wondering why it was all so funny.

I signalled to turn right, my mind like a plane circling the runway, unsure of how to land.

The thing is, I was thinking – if Becca can have a baby at the drop of a hat, then why can't I?

I'd taken my TUES pill after all. I couldn't see myself lying to Rob; it would have been too obvious, and I'm not the world's most natural liar. But something had to be done. We needed to sit down and talk.

*

Nine o'clock. I popped my head round the sitting room door. The laptop was shining its light onto Rob's rugged face as he typed up invoices.

'Cup of tea?' I asked.

'Mm, please.'

But the ringing of the phone muffled his reply. Anxious not to disturb him, I rushed to answer it.

'Mattie Payton speaking.'

'Mattie …'

It was Jenny. Instantly recognising her soft Scottish brogue, I smiled, sitting onto the bottom step. Jenny and I go back a long way. We shared rooms at

Edinburgh Uni, both of us studying French and Economics. A few years older than me, she'd had the experience of life that I lacked. And it showed. While she went on to teach French in a private school, I dropped out after a year to marry Rob. Much to my mum's unwavering displeasure.

'Happy Birthday for yesterday,' I said, smiling.

'Thanks, Mattie.'

'Did you have a good day, then?'

'Lovely, it was. Chris took me for a meal at this new place up the road. Very posh. We were so stuffed we had to take Angus for a walk afterwards. At midnight, would you believe?'

I laughed. 'I believe.'

'Anyway, I'm just ringing to say thank you for my pressie. They are so delicious.'

I'd sent her a box of rose and violet creams, the ones you order online. It didn't take much thinking about, but I knew she'd like them.

'It's a pleasure. What else did you get, then; anything exciting?'

'A new watch from Chris. It's gorgeous. And Mum and Dad bought me a year of facials for the beauty room at Jenners. I'm really looking forward to that.'

I smiled. 'That's a brilliant idea. I suppose it must be difficult to know what to buy you nowadays. I mean, you must have nearly everything you could possibly want.'

There was a long pause, a gap, a balloon that's burst, leaving only the air from inside. I felt dreadful. Had I said something I shouldn't? I had the distinct feeling there was something Jenny wanted to say, but couldn't. Or wouldn't.

39

'Jenny? Sorry, Jenny, I didn't mean it like it sounded. You know what I mean.'

'No, it's okay. Sorry, I was just daydreaming. But listen, we were thinking - how do you fancy coming up here before Christmas? I thought a nice, cosy weekend. I know it's short notice and everything, but what do you think?'

I hesitated, wondering if Rob would want to go. Rob leaving work to go away just before Christmas would be like making cherry pie without the cherries. He didn't have enough time as it was. But maybe he needed a break; *we* needed a break.

'Mattie?'

'It does sound fabulous. Could I let you know? I just need to run it by Rob first, with it being Christmas and everything.'

'Yes, I suppose he'll be busy. But it's only a weekend, isn't it? Tell him Christmas in Edinburgh is extra special. Thomas will love it. Jenners have a brilliant Father Christmas, and there's ice-skating in the Gardens. Anyway, just make sure you talk him into it. Maybe a bit of gentle persuasion?' she asked brazenly, releasing her infectious laugh.

I smiled. 'Maybe.'

'You thinking of having any more kids?'

CHAPTER 4

I looked anxiously at my watch. A few minutes late into work, but it couldn't be helped. Emma had a hospital appointment, so I'd agreed to work Friday morning for her. Turning the key with icy fingers, I unlocked the great red door of Haringey's, rushing through to disable the alarm.

Making coffee, I filled the icy kitchen with swirling steam and the aroma of Carte Noire. Wrapping my hands around my warm mug, I settled down to work, expecting an easy morning. But the phone seemed alive, never stopping, like a baby goat crying for its milk.

Osborne House, built in Pepingham in 1923, was in desperate need of renovation. A shell, an apple without its core, it was today the centre of attention. Having suffered a fire in the early Nineties, it had been left, deserted, its apathetic owner a doctor living in

Hong Kong. He'd recently died, however, leaving the house to his one and only son, who had immediately put it up for sale. I'd expected to hear from rich property developers and builders, but it was middle-class housewives who were ringing the phone off its cradle.

Then Emma rang from the hospital at eleven.

'They want me back in for the test results this aft. Are you okay holding the fort for a bit longer?'

'It's really busy, but yes, no problem. Is everything okay?'

'I think so. They've cut it out and are doing a biopsy as we speak.'

She'd had a large mole on her forearm that had kept bleeding.

'I hope everything's okay, Emma.'

'Thanks, sweetie. Listen, why don't you ask Andrew to cover lunchtime if it's busy? He does the same for me when I'm on my own, so I don't have to close up.'

'Okay, thanks, I will.'

Andrew Whirlow was a senior partner of Haringey's and surveyor for the Grantham area. I rang him and he agreed to be there at twelve on the dot.

But twelve o'clock came and went, and by half-past I was so hungry all I could think about was chocolate. By one o'clock I decided I'd waited long enough and went to get my coat. Suddenly, however, the bell clanged and Andrew's tall frame filled the doorway, his green eyes crinkling around the edges.

'Andrew - thank goodness. I'd given up on you. I was going to close up for five minutes and pop next door.'

'Sorry.' His hair was dark, wavy, and very messy. Threatening to fall across his eyes, he pushed it back nonchalantly. 'I got caught up with the North Street house. They wanted to chat, as usual. Anyway, you get off, and not just to the Deli either. I'll see you in an hour's time and not a minute before.'

'Thanks, but it's okay, I only need a sandwich. I'll be half an hour.'

'Listen, seriously. An hour's lunch is what you're entitled to, and an hour's lunch you shall have. Don't worry, I won't frighten the customers away.' Pulling off his jacket, he sat at my desk, picking up a pen and studying it carefully. 'Anyway, you should relax more, take a little time for yourself.'

I grinned. 'You sound like a woman's magazine.'

'Huh.' He screwed up his nose, aquiline and bronzed from a recent holiday. 'No, seriously, I really do think you should chill out a bit more.'

Puzzled, I became slightly alarmed. 'Why, is there something wrong? Is my work not up to scratch?'

'No, it's just - you. You always seem to be rushing around. It's not good for you.'

'Really?'

'You should come along to my yoga class some time, you know. We're at the gym in Grantham. I highly recommend it.'

'*You* do yoga?'

'I trust that's not a sexist comment, Mattie Payton.' Feigning hurt, his pale brows knitted together. 'I'm surprised at you. I actually run the classes. Two a week.'

'Oh, so that's it.' Suspicion dawned, a glimpse of the rabbit in the magician's cloak. 'You're trying to

43

promote your own yoga class. Well, I'm surprised at you too, Andrew Whirlow.'

'No, really. It's an excellent form of self-discipline. The union of mind and body. That's what yoga means. It'd do you good, put some colour back into your cheeks, relax those tense shoulders.'

'I suppose a yoga class would be rather nice.' I shrugged my shoulders animatedly. 'I did go to a few once, at uni. It's difficult though, getting into town in the evenings. Maybe if there was one in the village.'

'Look, you can practise at home. If you've already been to classes, you should know what you're doing, and I've got an excellent DVD. I'll bring it in. There's a book on meditation that comes with it.'

'Oh, I don't know about that.' I folded my hands together in prayer, bowing gracefully.   'All that omming ...'

He laughed. 'No, seriously. It's more about deep breathing, calming the mind. You'd enjoy it, I know you would.'

'You've only known me a couple of months. How do you know if I'd enjoy it or not?'

Shocked, I suddenly realised I was flirting with him, teasing him.

'Well, seeing as you're asking, I think I'm a pretty good judge of character.'

Quickly, very quickly, I pulled on my coat. 'Okay, I might give it a go, but right now I'm starving.'

*

The phone finally stopped ringing. Alone in the office, my thoughts turned to Jenny's invitation. I'd tried my best to persuade Rob, but in my heart of hearts had known from the start he wouldn't go. And he'd made such a fuss. Too busy to take time out, too concerned about the loss of business, too worried about how much it would all cost. He was in such a mood that, even though I did my usual seduction thing before going to bed – hair up and messy, sexy body lotion, waltzing round in a slinky nightie – it didn't work. He stayed up for ages doing his stupid accounts.

Tidying the envelopes in my desk drawer, I pushed aside my disappointment, tried my best to understand that his business, our main source of income, must always come first. But when I considered the state of Becca's marriage, I did wonder whether it was all worth it. Surely it's better for couples to take time out, have fun together?

And that poor, unborn, baby. A bargaining tool. A trap.

Dejected, I put the kettle on for tea, rubbing at the tension in my neck. Then stopped. Andrew was right. My shoulders *were* tense. I *could* do with a break. A rapid thudding against the kitchen window made me jump and I looked up to find balls of ice, hailstones nearly the size of quail's eggs, bouncing against the glass.

Suddenly and decisively, I'd made up my mind.

*

Emma rushed in at exactly three twenty, droplets of rain splashing from her umbrella, a bright fuchsia pink that had seen better days.

'Hi, sweetie. Sorry I took so long, love, but you know what it's like. Bleeding hospitals.'

'That's okay, don't worry about it. Everything okay?'

45

'Yes, thank God. Not skin cancer, just a weird kind of wart thing. Got me worried, though, I can tell you. I think I must have kept catching it.'

'That's great. I'm glad you're okay.' I pulled on my coat. 'Sorry, Emma, but got to dash. Mustn't be late for Thomas.'

'No, that's fine. Thanks for covering. See you on Monday.'

I ran into the rain, torrential, grey, never-ending. My feet splashed along the shiny ground as I held my coat above my head and raced along the High Street, past shops, cafés and the village green, until I reached the school gates, breathless and completely dishevelled.

'Here, share my umbrella,' said a voice behind me.

I turned to find Annie Murdoch offering her coal-black umbrella, sturdy and serious enough for a city gent. Her daughter, Holly, was in the same class as Thomas.

'Thanks.' Shrugging on my coat, I stood beneath it. 'That's better.'

'I've got a PTA meeting tonight, so I need to dash once Holly comes out. I'm afraid.'

'That's okay.' I turned, surprised. 'I didn't know you were in the PTA.'

'Only just. And we're up to our eyes in it. Jumble sale, shoe boxes, Christmas Fayre.'

'Well, if you ever need any help, I do happen to have some experience in that department. I used to help with Mums and Toddlers. Give me a ring.'

*

Thomas was his usual chatty self all the way home. I nodded and smiled, looking ahead to the weekend, to

46

spending time with Rob. Maybe I'd get him to change his mind about Edinburgh. At least, I could discuss me and Thomas going on our own. And maybe we could discuss making a baby – at least make some kind of plan – an *in ten months' time we'll start trying* kind of a plan.

The phone was already ringing as I opened the door.

'Mattie Payton speaking.'

'Hi, I – I didn't think you'd be in yet. I was going to leave a message.'

Rob. My stomach sinking in disbelief, I groaned inwardly. But I didn't know whether to feel angry or sad, and there was a pause, deep, and pregnant. Unlike me.

'Mattie – you there?'

'Yes.' I wrapped the telephone wire around my fingers, as if strangling my thoughts.

'Had a good day?' he asked.

'I've been at work, filling in for Emma. You?'

'I'd forgotten you were working today. I've had a great day, been really busy. So I – I'm going to be late home again. Luke's gone and cut the power supply, bloody idiot, so we're waiting for the electrician. Sorry about this, Mattie.'

Suddenly, like a slither of glass revealed by the lightning, I did know how I felt. Angry. Downright angry. So I retorted, but quietly, aware of Thomas in the kitchen behind me.

'Can't Luke wait for the bloody electrician? It is his fault.'

'Mrs Butler's really upset. I can't just leave Luke with her – she'd never employ us again. No, I need to stay here, let her know we're professionals.'

'But Rob – it's Friday night!'

'I know, I know, I'm really sorry. I'll be home as soon as I can, promise.'

And I believed him.

'Okay, but make it as quick as you can. See you later.'

'Mm, see you later.'

I put down the receiver, shocked to find hot tears, raging torrents of despair, rolling down my cheeks. Wiping them away, I forced a soft smile, checking myself in the mirror. Droplets of rain sat like diamonds in my dark hair. My eyes, deep blue, stared fixedly at their own reflection, searching for answers. But none came. I wasn't even sure of the question. After all, he had a business to run, didn't he? Blinking back new tears, I searched my bag for a lip gloss, running its moisture across my lips, dabbing a little onto my cheeks. There. Better.

A warm smile, a mannequin's grin, on my lips, I walked into the kitchen. Thomas, busy running a toy car up and down the worktop, looked up.

'Mummy? You feeling sad?'

Not for the first time could I see how very perceptive and caring my darling son could be. He reminded me so much of my beloved Grandma Beattie. At the mere thought, my smile fell, warm tears filled my eyes, and an ache, thick and swollen as sodden wood, rested itself inside me.

I was thirteen when my mother, her face swollen and red from crying, led me quietly into the sitting

48

room. To talk, she said. The sitting room was sacrosanct, a place away from the hustle and bustle of our newsagent's shop. We always discussed family matters, schoolwork, and business in the shop, while Mum and Dad cashed up, sorted through papers, or did the stocktaking. But today, in the peace and quiet of this Friday afternoon, with deep snow covering the ground outside, I was to be told in the sitting room at home, a grand display of yellow roses on the hearth.

Grandma Beattie had cancer of the liver, and nothing could be done to make her better.

Looking back, I've realised I was the wrong age. The wrong age at which to lose my maternal grandmother. Just starting to mature, desperately needing a mentor, someone to trust, someone not my mother, someone willing to talk about anything, even – especially – boys. Oh yes, Grandma Beattie knew all about boys. She met Grandad at the beginning of the war after he and his brother Michael, evacuees from London, were sent kicking and screaming to her village school. Grandma Beattie and Grandad became childhood sweethearts, devoted to each other for over forty years. Oh yes, she knew all about love and passion. She understood a teenage girl's yearning for adventure, for romance, when all my mother wanted for me was university and a good career, my rapidly maturing body rarely mentioned, and then only when she thought it absolutely necessary.

Even now, the resonance of a strong but feminine laugh, the notes of *The Yellow Rose of Texas* (Grandma Beattie's favourite song), or the sweet touch of her apple blossom perfume, flood me with precious memories, spinning my thoughts around like the turning of a cartwheel.

Picking up Thomas, I hugged him tight. Fighting hard not to cry, I swallowed at the lump in my throat. I remembered how, just a few weeks earlier, I'd driven him to a school-friend's birthday party. A delightful child, charming parents, the kitchen table heavy with food. Butterfly buns, strawberry tarts, chocolate muffins, cream horns, tiny chocolate chip cookies, sandwiches oozing jam, glass bowls of raspberry jelly. No cold pizza, no slimy ham sandwiches, cheese on sticks or bits of apple. Nothing at all to satisfy the appetite of parents in this age of healthy eating. No. The food was there for the children and for them alone. I stood there, stunned, unable to move, as memories of Grandma Beattie's kitchen table came flooding back.

A shiny yellow oilcloth splashed with pretty pink roses protects the table, plates heavy with buns made just today. Decorated with hard cherries, or pirouettes of chocolate icing sprinkled with hundreds and thousands. Homemade biscuits too. Ginger, raisin, chocolate. Strawberry jelly and ice cream if the weather is warm, toasted teacake and hot chocolate if not, the burners on the gas stove alight for warmth. The sweet scent of apple blossom perfume, teeth yellowed with age, smiling, joking. The same. Just the same. No ham sandwiches, no tiny grapes, not even cheese and onion crisps. Just sugary delights, the finest ingredients, all made with Grandma Beattie's own fair hands.

'Mummy?' Thomas tugged at me, his warm arms around my neck.

'Sorry, darling.' I pushed the memories away. 'Come on, let's do something nice for tea, shall we?'

50

Tired, unsettled, my stomach a tight knot, I poured myself a glass of Sainsbury's red, carrying it through to watch TV. But I couldn't concentrate. The sight of Rob's dinner, cooling, coagulating, had filled me with a strange uneasiness. I sipped at the deep purple liquid. Warming, soothing, its bouquet of blackcurrants and butter filled my senses while I watched *Coronation Street*. It entertained me for half an hour, but then I'd had enough. Switching off the TV, I took my empty glass back to the kitchen. A low, heavy sigh echoed along the walls. My own, I realised with a start. The house was quiet, eerie, the only sound the ticking of the clock in the hall. Placing a tablet inside the dishwasher, I turned the knob. Click, click.

Then a new sound startled me. Rob was in the hallway, the front door wide open, pulling off his trainers. My melancholy vanished like raindrops in the sun.

'I didn't hear you come in.'

'I was trying not to wake Thomas.'

My arms encircled him as we hugged, kissed, smiled. Then, without my agreement, without my knowledge, like silent fingers reaching out, my eyes looked up to his, deep and dark as the ocean. And searched.

He grinned. 'What you been up to today, then?'

I blinked, looked down, pulled away. 'You've already asked me that. On the phone, remember?'

'Yes, sorry, I forgot. How *was* work?'

'Busy. Everyone just wanting the one house really. Osborne House. You know the one, in Pepingham?'

'Mm.'

Picking up his mail, he carried it into the kitchen. I followed, pushing his shepherd's pie inside the microwave.

'The market's definitely slowing down, though. People running scared with the recession. Self-fulfilling prophecy some of the time, I think. The papers tell us the market's slowing down, so we all panic and hey presto - the market slows down.'

'Oh well, so long as it doesn't affect my business.'

'Cup of tea?'

We watched a documentary on the BP oil disaster, the pictures lurid, disconcerting. Rob ate his dinner from a tray. I sipped at my tea. Both of us thoughtful, silent, a soft cloud hanging in the air between us. As the programme ended, he switched it off with the remote, picking up the newspaper instead.

Abruptly the silence became awkward, a huge yawning gap to be jumped across. I tried to break it.

'So how was work? Did you manage to get finished?'

Wrapping both arms around my knees, I snuggled back into the sofa. A sudden energy surged through me, a pulse, a shiver of delight, and I smiled coquettishly. But he didn't notice.

'Only just. The chap had to work by torchlight, so it took a while. By the way, have you got anything planned for this weekend?'

'Sainsbury's in the morning. I missed my slot online again.'

'Good. Because I've got a load on. We're at that new vet's and I don't know what time we'll finish.'

He looked up, gauging my reaction, testing me.

'That's okay, don't worry about it.' I smiled persuasively. 'Actually, while I have your attention, could we talk about Edinburgh?'

'What about it?'

His look now was one of derision. We'd already discussed it, so what was the problem? Yet I continued to smile. Like a clown.

'I really would like to go. I could do with the break. I mean, I know you're busy and everything, but would you mind just this once if we went without you? We could go up on the train.'

'Mm?' His eyes had glazed over suddenly.

'Edinburgh?' I leaned forward to gain his attention. 'Would you mind if we went on our own? Please, Rob?'

He blinked, smiling apologetically. 'Well, I suppose you might as well. It'll be nice for Thomas and you've not seen Jenny in ages.'

My arms were around him before he could finish. 'Thank you. I'm really looking forward to it. You don't know how much I could do with a break. And - Rob?' I decided to broach the subject again while he was in a good mood.

He looked down, and I noticed the beginnings of wrinkles around his eyes. Tiny spidery lines eating up the membrane of his body. Too many late nights, too much work.

'Yes?'

'Thomas is five in June. We really ought to be thinking about ...'

Anger flashed through him, a lightning bolt of impatience. 'Mattie, can't it wait? I need to get on. I've got measurements to work out and, and ...'

'Neither of us is getting any younger, Rob.'

'Mattie? Please? Not now.'

I dropped my arms obediently. 'Okay. Sorry.'

'Maybe this weekend. We'll talk about it this weekend.'

*

The tight knot in my stomach revealed itself to be more than just tension. My period started. Just before bedtime. I sobbed, quietly, into the bathroom sink.

It was only later, as I lay in bed, frustrated, lonely, body-clock ticking away, a fresh tampon inside me, that I realised Rob had been just a bit too enthusiastic about us going to Jenny's without him.

Had my clowning-around conversation with Becca really been a clowning-around? Was I, somewhere deep in my sub-consciousness, my psyche, worried he *was* having an affair? Or was I becoming paranoid, a silly little woman with too much time on her hands, nothing better to do than worry about her marriage when her husband was putting in every hour God sends?

But then, who wouldn't worry?

Becca. Mrs Phelps. Two lovely, attractive ladies. Both with cheating husbands. Why would Rob be any different?

CHAPTER 5

THOMAS pushed his nose against the sitting room window, his tiny fingers gripping at the sill beneath. Huge snowflakes, each one different, each a tiny miracle of creation, tumbled gently to earth, already hidden by a deep crust of sparkling diamonds. A huge mountain of powder snow suddenly dropped with a whoomph from the roof to the garden below. Jumping back, Thomas laughed in delight.

Britain was buried beneath the most significant spell of late November snow in years. Schools were closed, cars abandoned, airports on standby. Today, the first Saturday in December, there was still no change in the weather. Not that Thomas minded. Rob had found it impossible to get out and about in the van, so had stayed home, grumpy and withdrawn, a soccer player without a pitch. But then Thomas had nagged so much he'd finally consented to sculpt two snowmen, male and female, carve an igloo for them to live in, sledge down the only hill in the village, and generally have fun with the crisp walls of snow at their disposal.

Farmer Bob and his son Jeffrey were working on the street outside, their snowploughs pushing and heaving, creating great banks of snow either side of the road. Having spent Friday clearing the main road out of the village, they were now working on the hill that led to our cluster of semis.

Once the road was clear, Rob dug out the van and we all climbed in. Supplies were low in the village. Milk and eggs had managed to get through from local farms and bread was freshly baked in the bakery, but other essentials – tinned food, toilet rolls, cereals – were in short supply. We needed a Sainsbury's shop. And before everyone else got there.

Rob started up the engine. 'Glad I'm back on the road. I need to get to Sleaford this afternoon, pick up that Karndean so I can start on the Winstons' kitchen. Be nice to start earning some money again.'

*

Becca's lane was treacherous, the snow having softened and hardened again overnight. Not risking the van, Rob dropped us off at the end of the lane. Treading carefully, a heavy rucksack on my back, I held onto Thomas tightly. We reached the farmhouse a precarious ten minutes later, our faces glowing with exertion, a ghostlike mist pouring from our lips.

The sweet scent of strawberry jelly hit me as I pushed open the kitchen door.

'Hi, Becca, sorry we're late.'

Becca grinned, stirring at a great pan of glowing yellow custard. 'I'm glad you could get here at all. It's horrendous out there.'

I heaved my rucksack onto the table, pulling off my coat. 'I've brought some bits and bobs to help out. The main roads aren't too bad now, so we managed to get to Sainsbury's. It was busy though, everyone stocking up just in case. Anyway, I got what I could.'

'Thanks, Mattie, you're a star.'

Pulling out a small box, wrapped in pink tissue paper and fancy ribbon, I handed it to Chloe. 'Happy Birthday, Chloe. I hope you like it. Thomas helped choose it.'

'Cool. Thanks.' Opening it excitedly, she picked out the silver chain, a purple butterfly hanging from it, its glittered surface sparkling in the light. 'It's beautiful - thank you.'

Thomas grinned. 'I said you'd like it. I like butterflies too.'

'Here, let me.' Pushing aside her long blonde hair, I fastened the chain around her neck. 'There.'

*

I placed a tray of sandwiches and juice onto the playroom table, the room itself a haven of sparkling pinks, deep plums and purples.

'Here you go, you two. Don't spill.'

'Thank you,' Chloe replied. 'We're going to watch a film.'

'Okay, have fun now. Be good.'

But I returned to the kitchen to find Becca beside the dishwasher, pale, shocked, hands gripping at her back in agony.

I rushed towards her. 'Come on, sit down. I'll empty the dishwasher.'

She collapsed into a chair. 'Thank you. I keep getting this, had it with Chloe.' She grinned weakly. 'I don't know what I'd do without you sometimes.'

'Don't be silly, you'd do the same for me.'

I pulled out two plates, holding them up high. 'Have you ever thought how much more convenient it would be if you had two dishwashers instead of one?'

'No.'

Placing them onto the dresser, I pulled out two more. 'Well, you use the same pots and pans every day, don't you?'

'Yes?'

'So what you do is – you fill Number One dishwasher with dirty pots. You run it so everything's clean, but don't empty it. You just take a clean plate from Number One dishwasher. Then, when it's dirty, you put it into Number Two dishwasher. When Number Two dishwasher is full, you run that. Then Number Two dishwasher becomes Number One dishwasher and the whole process starts again. Do you see? It cuts out the middleman. No more having to empty the dishwasher and put everything away.' I rolled my eyes. 'It's such a bore, don't you think?'

She laughed, her back pain forgotten. 'Mattie, you're mad. It is a good idea, though. Always assuming, of course, you've got enough room for two dishwashers.'

'And enough money. But I'm always looking for a gap in the market. I could invent a dual dishwasher. You know, one on top of the other, a bit like a washer dryer. Or I could go into business extending kitchens. I've always fancied doing a bricklaying course.'

'Oh yes, I could just see you humping a great big wheelbarrow round, Mattie Payton.'

'I don't know, I'm stronger than I look. Besides, I'd like to get my teeth into something. Maybe I will do a bricklaying course. I'd introduce you to any gorgeous young students, of course.'

She giggled. 'What are you like?'

*

Soft finger rolls covered three huge plates. Layered with cheese, boiled egg or ham, decorated with cucumber, cherry tomatoes, or sliced grapes, some of them were smiley faces. Bowls of crisps, tiny punnets of pomodorino tomatoes, and cocktail sticks of fresh pineapple chunks and black grapes added colour to the table, and two glass jugs of fresh orange juice stood like sentries beside the pile of paper plates and Ikea beakers.

I dried my hands on a soft white towel. 'There, I think we're done.'

Becca had recovered, her face glowing, her back upright. 'Brilliant.'

'By the way, Thomas hasn't left one of his teddies here, has he? I've looked all over the place and can't find it anywhere.'

She shook her head. 'I don't think so. What's it look like?'

'It's light brown with little claws and a red ribbon. It was Rob's when he was little.'

'I've not seen it, but I'll keep a lookout. Do you know, I've not stopped all morning? And Chloe's been

59

so excited, but then of course her dad had to bloody well call round.'

Tears filled her eyes, yet they refused to fall, droplets of glittering ice on a windowsill.

Astonished, I stared at her. 'Alan called round? Here?'

She nodded miserably. 'We'd not even had breakfast. I mean, I've not seen him since … he's rung occasionally, but …'

Their calls, she said, brief and to the point, had been mere conveniences. To discuss Chloe, the bills, the house. They'd had nothing to say. Yet everything to say.

'I should have guessed he'd come round, but I wasn't thinking properly. I mean, it is Chloe's birthday. But I just opened the door and - there he was.'

'So what did he have to say for himself?' I asked.

A tear escaped, but she brushed it away. 'Sorry, I keep crying all the time. You must think I'm an idiot.'

'No, I don't. You're in love with the man and you *are* pregnant.'

'I should have faced it.' Her voice distorted with rage. 'I should have admitted it to myself. Why didn't I? I'm such an idiot.'

'Becca …'

But she threw her words like knives across the floor. 'And then of course I go and get myself pregnant! How idiotic is that?'

'You were only trying to save your marriage. None of this is your fault. *You* didn't go running off with someone else.'

'I sometimes think I should have. I could have done, you know, lots of times - let him know what it feels like.'

'But would it really have bothered him?'

'You're implying he's no longer in love with me, but that's where you're wrong, my dear Mattie. He's never said he's not in love with me. He is, I know it. I mean, if I'd known he was on his way here I'd have made myself beautiful. But there I was, still in dressing gown and slippers at ten o'clock, making strawberry jelly. God, what must he have thought? His floozy was probably in full makeup and designer linen by then.'

I glanced at the antique carriage clock on the dresser. 'Becca, what time does this party start?'

'Two.' She checked her watch. 'Bugger - I must look a sight! Put the napkins out, would you? I won't be a minute; just sort myself out.'

'You've got ten minutes ...'

'Your son, by the way - wonderful imagination. I heard him talking to Chloe about his pink house. You think he'll be a writer or something?'

'Becca, you've got *nine* minutes ...'

CHAPTER 6

SNOW-LADEN trees swapped places with misty fields, the scenes playing like a motion picture outside our carriage window. Inside the train, though, it was warm and cosy as we whistled happily through the countryside towards Edinburgh.

Swallowing the remainder of my ham roll, I wiped my buttery fingers on a white paper napkin and smiled at Thomas sitting opposite, an egg mayo sandwich clutched between his hands. Sheets of paper, bright felt pens and empty paper cups littered the table between us. Across the aisle an elderly gentleman, engrossed in his newspaper, tut-tutted every time a young girl ran up and down the carriage, hair plaited across her head like Heidi.

But the train's motion, as soothing as an old rocking chair, was making me sleepy, and my mind turned to Rob, busy at work, earning his daily crust. Our daily crust. Maybe his concern about having to work this weekend had been genuine. Maybe he was the sensible one in the relationship and we really did need to look after the business, earn the pennies. Or maybe he just wanted time on his own, no nagging wife, no child running around. The thought hit me with a chill. Shaking it off, I determined to relax, enjoy myself. Reaching into my bag for the magazine I'd bought especially, I flattened it onto the table with the palm of my hand. The cover, an inviting shiny red, proclaimed *Prepare Your Body Now for Summer.* Snuggling back into the warm velour seat, I turned the page.

*

Thomas was calling out. I shook myself awake. Kneeling at the carriage window, he held one hand against the glass, as excited as a kitten with a ball of wool.

'Mummy, Mummy, you've got to look. Look, it's like my pink house. Look!'

My eyes drowsy with sleep, I saw a rose-pink house, a sugar lump soaked in grenadine, nestling into the snow-covered hillside. A slight mist lay upon the scene, two tall cypresses providing an impressive backdrop.

'Do you like it, Mummy? It's just the same.'

'Yes, darling, it's beautiful.' I fought crazily to wake myself up.

'The parlour window - that's where my little girl fell out.' He shrugged with the self-assurance of a French diplomat. 'She broke her humerus, but she got better really quickly. Children do, you know.'

Fully awake now, a slither of electricity ran down my spine and, without thinking, I questioned him.

63

'Where is your pink house, darling?'

But he shook his head, his initial enthusiasm turning to panic, a dark desperation filling his eyes. 'I don't know. I keep thinking about it, but I can't remember. Why can't I remember, Mummy?'

Hastily, I let go of my question, allowing it to float away. It would not be asked again. I patted the seat beside me.

'Come on, let's forget it. Shall we do some more drawing?'

I smiled, but my thoughts were racing. Parlour? Humerus? From a child? What was all this? Maybe my mother was right. Maybe Thomas's stories were something to do with reincarnation. She'd once read that children only remember their previous lives until about the age of five. And yes, Thomas was now talking about it less frequently. But he *was* still talking about it. Did this mean there was something in it - that it wasn't all his imagination, a fantastic work of fiction come to life?

I'll admit I did find it rather disturbing. Although I had wondered about the concept of reincarnation. Haven't we all? What other explanation could there be for so much injustice in the world? And why was I born into a loving, middle-class family with food, clothing and education, while others suffer the most horrific poverty and violence? If we were all given the same chances at birth, then having only one life to live would make sense. But through no fault of our own, some of us are born into poverty, violence, war. Forced into lying, cheating, stealing, prostitution. Just to feed ourselves. Our need to survive is inherent. Whichever deity one believes in, whatever holy being one prays to, surely if He is a truly loving being He would give us all the chance of living at least one good clean life. Equal opportunity for all.

Wouldn't He?

*

Thomas was fast asleep, his head on my knees, his hair shining like blackcurrants in juice. The train shuddered noisily as we pulled away from Durham Station. Long, shivering icicles hung beneath the huge green sign like shards of glass. Excited suddenly, I couldn't wait to reach Edinburgh, to see Jenny and Christopher again.

But the old chap across the aisle was coughing to gain my attention.

'Er, excuse me.' He folded his newspaper, resting it upon his lap.

'Yes?'

'Would you mind very much if I sit opposite, now your son has moved? It's so much easier with a table to lean on, isn't it?'

'That's okay, no problem.'

I pushed the pens and paper to one side. He placed his coat onto the vacant seat, his newspaper onto the table, and sat down heavily. I caught the scent of washing powder.

'Thank you so much,' he said. 'It's very kind of you. I didn't think there'd be a train running at all today, what with this awful weather.'

'I think it's just the flights that are having problems. Too much ice and not enough de-icer,' I joked, feeling there was some ulterior motive here.

'I hope you don't mind,' he said. 'I don't mean to be rude or anything, but I couldn't help overhearing your conversation. You didn't used to live in that pink house back there, did you?'

His voice had a lilt, an accent that brought back childhood holidays in Cornwall, sandy shores, cream teas. I noticed the worn edges of his tweed jacket, the crookedness of his reading glasses, the soft light in his blue eyes. He reminded me a little of the old professor from The Lion, The Witch and The Wardrobe.

'No,' I replied. 'Sorry, we didn't - never have lived there. My son just likes making up stories sometimes.'

'Oh, well. As children do.' He leaned forward conspiratorially. 'Sorry - again. I'm not being nosey, but does he often make up such - intricate stories? I'm afraid your conversation *was* rather interesting.'

I shrugged as if to say it didn't matter, although I couldn't for the life of me understand why he found it all so fascinating.

'I suppose he does. Thomas has a very vivid imagination, but then I think most children do.'

He dismissed himself with a wave of the hand. 'Sorry. Just ignore an old man's curiosity. It's because I live on my own, you see. No-one to talk to.'

I squirmed, feeling suddenly guilty. 'No, *I'm* sorry. It's just I don't think people always understand Thomas's behaviour. It can seem a bit odd at times.'

'May I attempt to hazard a guess, my dear?' Removing his glasses, he looked directly into my eyes. 'You see, I'm rather good at understanding children - some of them, anyway. I've met children with extremely vivid imaginations before. They're lovely children, and very special.' He winked at me, the skin around his eyes crinkling with delight.

'I'm sorry, I don't quite understand.'

He sat back comfortably. 'Well, my guess is Thomas often talks about things that at his age he should know nothing about. Am I correct?'

'Well, yes. Yes, he does.'

I did wonder where this was leading.

He tapped the table with a long bony finger. 'Well, don't you go worrying your wee head now. It's quite normal for some children to talk about a past life at this age.'

I stared at him, not knowing what to think, what to say, my heart thudding with anticipation. Yet I sensed a weight lifting from my shoulders, like wings taking flight.

I held out my hand. 'I'm sorry, I haven't introduced myself. Mattie Payton.'

'Very pleased to meet you, I'm sure.' His hand was warm and soft. 'I'm Benjamin Bradstock. I'm from Edinburgh, just on my way home now.'

I smiled. 'I love Edinburgh.'

'It's a beautiful city. But tell me - have you read much about reincarnation?'

'No. My mother has. I have to say I'm quite sceptical about the whole thing. And anyway, I'm much too busy to read these days. Apart from when I read to Thomas, of course.'

'But you should make time. It broadens the mind. I like to keep an eye on the papers, too.' He patted his newspaper, still folded upon the table. 'Apart from anything, I can watch my stocks and shares. Not that I have many, but it can be quite fun.'

'Really?' I laughed, visions of him in Wall Street, smart collar and tie, hair smoothed down with oil, filling my mind. 'I might invest myself then, once I've made a few million.'

'You can jest, but the time may come. Never underestimate your own talents. Use them. Respect them for what they are. Each of us is different and we all have different roads to travel.'

Amused, I could only smile.

'You'll see,' he continued. 'As you get older, you come to realise that we go through many lifetimes. And I'm not just talking about reincarnation here. In this one lifetime you will lead many lives - we even become different people sometimes - and we should take each life by the throat and embrace it. Each one changes us, develops us, makes us who we are. The same applies to our existence as a whole. We have many lifetimes through which we must travel.'

I didn't quite know what to say, so said nothing.

He looked at me carefully. 'Sorry. I'm embarrassing you. It's just, as you get older, you come to see things from a different perspective. You wait. You'll see. But tell me now - does Thomas talk a lot about this past life?'

I wondered if he'd heard the bit about my being sceptical. 'He did used to talk about it much more than he does now.'

'Yes. They lose the memories after a while.' He looked suddenly sad.

'Mr Bradstock …'

'Benjamin – please.'

'How do you know so much about these things?'

'I have a great interest in the subject, a great interest. I'm an accountant by trade, but I had to take early retirement a few years ago. I was a bit lost at first, didn't quite know what to do with myself. Then I saw this hypnotherapy course advertised in the local rag and - well, I suppose I've always had a keen interest in the subject. But it was practising hypnotherapy that led to my discovering reincarnation. It does have its roots in science, you know.'

'Does it?' I couldn't help the cynicism in my voice, a harsh jangle of a sound.

But he appeared not to notice. 'Energy cannot be created or destroyed. It can only be changed from one form to another. Yes?'

'Yes.'

'Think of a raindrop. As it falls, it becomes a completely separate entity from the clouds above, lives a life of its own, then dies, so to speak. Its essence evaporates, rising back to be absorbed into the clouds again. Then when the time is right, a new raindrop forms and the cycle begins all over. The new raindrop may be different, but it still contains the essence of the earlier one that had lived and died.'

'Yes, I can see that.'

'Good.'

The little girl with the plaits was running up and down the carriage again.

Benjamin lowered his voice. 'I only wanted to help people, you know. Stress, smoking, drink, drugs. But not long after I'd set up in practice, this young lady - we'll call her Jacqueline - came to see me. She'd been suffering flashbacks after a very bad childbirth and was severely depressed. It was affecting her relationship with the baby.'

'Oh, that's sad.'

'It was. So I put her under, but - and I still can't quite believe this myself - instead of merely relaxing she became childlike, small, not like herself at all. I assumed, naturally, she was returning to her childhood days as a kind of security blanket. But no, she'd gone back to a previous lifetime, said her name was Millie, her dad was a miner and they lived near the Clyde.'

I nodded sympathetically; anyone could make that one up.

'According to what she told me, she lived right through the First World War, only to die from the 'flu in 1918, at the age of nine. Well, as you can imagine, I couldn't believe what I was hearing. I truly thought she was having me on, just as you are now.'

I blushed. 'Sorry.'

'It's fine,' he smiled. 'You see, I came to realise the details were too realistic, the wording too authentic. Just like Thomas earlier.'

'Really?' Now I *was* interested.

'Luckily, it all made her feel so incredibly relaxed she wanted to come back. And I made very sure to do some research before she did, in case the same thing happened again. And it did. She brought up another name.'

My eyes opened wide, great pools of curiosity. 'Did she?'

'Ann.'

I grinned. 'Wow.'

'We never found out exactly what this woman did, except she'd been brought over from Ireland to live in Glasgow, and she died in 1821 giving birth to her first child.' He rubbed his eyes emotionally. 'It was amazing. Truly amazing. It explained all the problems she's been experiencing in this lifetime - giving birth and so forth.'

'Unbelievable. Did it help with her flashbacks, too?'

'The result was immediate. Giving birth in this lifetime had brought the memory of her previous experience back. Subconsciously, of course. Digging out that ancient memory helped clear away the dread of giving birth. She's fine now, had another child, no problems whatsoever. It is a wonderful treatment, you know, for the right people.'

I looked down at Thomas, his fingers curled into a tight ball.

'These children who remember their past lives - what makes them forget them?'

'I think when they're born, whatever it is that usually prevents us from remembering our previous life hasn't quite blocked it out for them. They recall it as if it's quite normal to do so. But after a while those memories fade into the background as newer, more exciting, memories take over. I have to say, though - the children for whom this happens tend to be quite remarkable. They're often very bright, very mature for their age, and supremely confident. They know things they've never had the opportunity in this lifetime to learn. It's usually quite obvious to people with an open mind that they've been here before.'

'Goodness,' I exclaimed. 'You're describing Thomas to a tee. If I'm honest, though, and I hope you don't mind my saying this, I do find the whole thing a bit weird. People think you're strange if you start talking about your child in that way.'

'Well, as I said - they need to have open minds. As you have, Mattie. I can tell just from looking at you.'

Thomas opened his eyes, stretching out his arms. 'Mummy …'

I looked down. 'Hello, you. Had a nice sleep?'

*

The driver warned of our imminent arrival.

'Please mind the gap when boarding or alighting from this train. This train is for Edinburgh Waverley.'

I caught a glimpse of Arthur's Seat, the craggy cliff-side of an extinct volcano. Covered in crisp white snow, it formed a monochrome silhouette against the darkening sky.

'Come on, Thomas - nearly there now.'

The cold air hit as I lifted him from the train amidst the hustle-bustle of passenger announcements, doors slamming, whistles blowing, and the odour of hot coffee mingled with a century of grime.

Thomas pulled my hand excitedly. 'Jenny! It's Jenny!'

Her tall slim figure, clad in black cashmere, pushed its way through the crowd.

'My goodness me, it's Jenny Mills,' Benjamin murmured, helping me with my case.

'Do you know her?' I asked.

'She's in my Book Club. My, my, what a small world.'

'We were at uni together. A long time ago.'

'Well, well. Edinburgh, wasn't it?'

'Yes.' I wriggled with embarrassment. 'I only managed my first year, though. I left to get married.'

He smiled sympathetically. 'Never mind, it wasn't meant to be. Some things just aren't.'

Jenny had a smile on her face that could have launched the Queen Elizabeth.

'Benjamin Bradstock,' she exclaimed. 'What are you doing here? Do you two know each other?'

I laughed. 'We do now. We just met on the train.'

She grinned. 'Well, well, it's a small world.'

Benjamin shook my hand. 'It's been lovely to meet you, Mattie. But I must dash, get myself home. Have a lovely weekend. See you on Thursday, Jenny.'

As he left, she turned to hug me. She smelt of schoolrooms, university halls, fun nights out, tears and laughter. 'It's so lovely to see you.'

'You too,' I grinned.

She ruffled Thomas's curls. 'And how's my little godson, then? You're a proper wee boy now, aren't you? You'll have to stop feeding him, Mattie.'

Thomas glared in horror. 'No. I'm always too hungry for that, aren't I, Mummy?'

Jenny laughed. 'You're a cheeky wee rascal and no mistake. But come on, let's get home. I'm freezing.'

There was a loud pitter-patter suddenly, a shower of hailstones onto the iron roof above.

We all looked up. 'Just listen to that,' I murmured. 'Come on, let's get out of here.'

We threaded our way through the other passengers, heading out into the dark afternoon. Tiny balls of ice littered the frosty pavements. Huddling together against the biting wind, we walked tentatively so as not to slip. A speeding fire engine in the distance echoed through the empty streets.

Our route took us along East Market Street, its ancient cobbles hidden beneath deep layers of snow. Reaching New Street, we walked quickly through the underground car park, trying not to focus on the rusty old cars and caravans that lay there, dotted around like dead soldiers on a battlefield. I'd been here before, but could never understand the reason for this strange phenomenon. Was the place being used as a repair shop or had the owners just parked up and never returned? And if so - where were they? My imagination running riot, I shuddered, clinging tightly onto Thomas.

'Bit scary, this place,' I said. 'Was the other one full again?'

Jenny nodded. 'It's being renovated. It should be finished soon, though.'

Reaching her shiny black Volvo, we sank gratefully into the warm, leather seats. Sighing contentedly, Jenny turned the key, paid her two pounds at the exit barrier, and pulled rapidly away.

*

Located in the millionaire's hotspot of Morningside, Jenny's magnificent Georgian home was exactly as I remembered. The heavy door with its stained glass panels, the spacious hallway, the tall ceilings, the magnificent airiness of the place. Yet still homely, inviting, like a hand-knitted tea-cosy.

Fatigued by our journey, Thomas and I followed Jenny quietly, past the sitting room, the dining room, down three steps and on into the kitchen. A warm tang of sugar and spices filled the air. A large Airedale terrier, spread out before the iron-black cooking range, lifted his head sleepily.

'Angus!' Thomas ran up to stroke his head.

Angus, opening his warm brown eyes, licked Thomas's hand sleepily.

'He's a bit tired right now, aren't you, Angus?' said Jenny. 'Jack next door took him for a walk earlier.

Chris is in Glasgow until tomorrow. But come now, Thomas, what will you have to eat - a wee snack before dinner?'

He ran up to the table, his eyes lighting up. 'Yes, please. I'm hungry.'

'Just as I thought. So let's see what we have in here, then.'

Pulling open a small oak door in the wall, she stretched into the pantry, producing a large plastic cake box. Removing the lid, she revealed a deep cake, lovingly covered in thick milk chocolate and decorated in white chocolate bears.

'Wow,' gulped Thomas.

*

Two pieces of chocolate cake later, Thomas was snug and warm in bed, listening intently as I reached the end of his bedtime story.

Jenny had made up a small bed in the guestroom, its silk lamps throwing a soft light onto the raspberry pink wallpaper. Deep, overflowing bookshelves lined the walls on either side of an enormous gilt mirror. Jenny herself was slouching lazily across an old red armchair, faded pink by the sun, her arms wrapped around a tartan cushion.

I was perched on the end of the bed. 'And Baby Bear shouts …' I waited for the others to join in. Sleepy, giggling, eyes sparkling, we all shouted, 'I want my mummy!'

Minutes later, having kissed and cuddled our goodnights, Jenny and I made our way downstairs.

'Why don't you go sit yourself down, and I'll bring through a glass of wine?' she suggested. 'Did you manage to get through to Rob, by the way?'

'I left a message. He'll be working hard, probably left his mobile in the van. But you know what it's like. He'll be fine.'

I smiled, to convince myself more than Jenny. Maybe I was becoming paranoid. Maybe I had good reason.

'Well, as long as he knows you've arrived. Now then, red or white?'

'Red, please.'

'Right you are.'

Treading lightly across the rustic oak flooring in my thick socks, I pushed heavily upon the sitting room door. And gazed. An ivory marble fireplace dominated the far wall, a home for the small log fire that nestled there. Two sofas, shrouded in cream damask, faced each other, separated by an enormous blood-red Persian rug. Three lamps of white alabaster provided a low light. To the right of me sat a beautifully-carved camphorwood chest, upon which rested a silver quaiche. Filled with dried roses, its delicate perfume filled the air. The very air in this room whispered – like a hypnotist before his audience – *relax*.

Obediently, peacefully, I sat down and closed my eyes.

CHAPTER 7

Morningside, Edinburgh

SOME people may not see it the way I do, but for me the Royal Mile is the very best part of Edinburgh City. It's always fascinated me, running between Edinburgh Castle and Holyrood House as it does, with its cobbles, intersecting wynds and closes, and its tall buildings with their air of mystery.

Despite the cold air, there were lots of people out, crowding round the effervescent entertainers, stamping their feet to keep warm, filling the scene with colour. There were singers in bright blue, mime artists in silvery-black, and sword-swallowers in dark crimson. Vivacious woollen hats, warm scarves, bright gloves, spots and stripes, reds, blues, yellows, greens, all added to the ambience, to the party atmosphere.

No-one could be unhappy in such company.

Our morning was filled with memories to be treasured forever, like a child's first shoes. Jenny,

Thomas and I walked slowly up the Royal Mile and along to Princes Street. We browsed the shops, clapped our hands at the artistes, and took Thomas to see Father Christmas, a pensioner with rosy cheeks and a too bright smile. But Thomas loved him. When we finally settled down, exhausted, to a lunch of haggis, neeps and tatties, he chatted away, enthusing over everything; the enormous Christmas tree rising up through the centre of Jenners' department store, the kilted pipers on every street corner, buskers playing instruments, violins, guitars, flutes, with ice-cold fingers, and magicians floating balls through the air.

'But my favourite thing is the beautiful lady,' he insisted. 'Can we go and see her again?'

A mere girl, a drama student earning money over the Christmas break, was performing a mime routine outside Jenners. Tiny, ethereal, dressed in white netting and sparkling beads, she was the image of Truly Scrumptious in Chitty Chitty Bang Bang. Her mime routine was similar to the one in the film, the doll in a jewellery box twirling slowly round and round, each movement a minutia. At first Thomas thought she was a doll and pushed his way through the crowd for a better look. But when her eyes followed him, he saw that she was real. Beautiful. Delicate. Perfect. Amazed, awestruck, he stood, watching carefully. Until their eyes met, and she smiled. He was smitten.

'How on earth does she do it?' I asked Jenny. 'It's freezing. She's barely moving and she's hardly a stitch on.'

This beautiful creature, this Christmas fairy, forced countless shoppers, huddled inside their coats and hats, hands aching with shopping bags, to pause in the midst of their feverish flurrying, to stand still for just a few minutes. To enjoy, to be transported, to another Christmas, a Christmas where time stands still. A Christmas of joy, of peace. Pure and white, she was like freshly fallen snow, a barrier, a buttress, if only for a minute or two, against the constant rushing around and getting ready, the headaches and the backaches. Against the twenty-first century's concept of Christmas.

*

Jenny's clear voice filled the bedroom.

'And past the great clock tower of Big Ben. Peter laughed with glee as he pointed up into the sky. *There it is, Wendy - Never Land. Second star to the right and straight on 'til morning.* From high up in the sky, they finally spotted the land of their dreams.' She closed the big blue book. 'And there, young man, we shall leave it. Time for sleep.'

I yawned sleepily. 'Thanks, Jenny. That was lovely, wasn't it, Thomas?'

'Mm ...' His eyes were already closing.

Jenny kissed his forehead. 'Night-night, Thomas.'

Christopher leant across too, patting Thomas's hand tenderly. 'Night-night, Thomas. Sleep well.'

Jenny and Christopher tiptoed out, pulling Angus after them.

'Night-night, darling. Love you,' I whispered.

Looking up, he held out Blue Bear. 'And Blue Bear, Mummy.'

'Night-night, Blue Bear.' Kissing his nose, I tucked him in beside Thomas.

'Mummy?'

'Yes?'

'Why didn't Daddy come with us?'

I hesitated. Why hadn't Rob come? Really? And why hadn't he answered his phone last night? He'd rung this morning with some vague excuse about having been in the shower when I rang, that he'd only just got my message, had left his mobile in the van. Why didn't I believe him? Why hadn't he rung me to check we'd arrived safely? Why *was* I becoming paranoid?

I cleared my throat, my heart pounding, my nerves shreds of cotton wool. But I smiled for Thomas.

'Well, he's very busy with his new business, you know. And Christmas is a very busy time of year.' I sighed heavily. 'The thing is, I'm sure he'd much rather be here with you instead of working. But that's what he has to do.'

He nodded sleepily.

Guiltily, I asked, 'You miss him, don't you, darling?'

He nodded again.

I stroked his hair gently. 'Who loves you?'

'Mummy and Daddy.'

'Yes, we do. We both do. And don't you *ever* forget it ...'

*

The table flickered with seven tall, white candles.

Christopher, his lean face still tired from the crawl home from Glasgow, passed a cooled wine glass to each of us. Dessert.

'Here you go now.'

My face flushed from too much wine, I was relaxed, the fresh air and good company like Valium to my jangled mind.

'These look amazing, Jenny,' I enthused.

Each glass was full to the brim with clear jelly, decorated with a swirl of syllabub cream and embellished with the tiniest of frosted green grapes.

'Thanks. They're only champagne jellies and syllabub cream. Really easy to make.'

I scooped some up, letting it melt onto my tongue. I tasted lemon, wine, evenings in the sun, warm Mediterranean air, a sweet deliciousness.

'It's gorgeous. Is it real champagne?'

'Yes. And there's a reason ...' Glancing at Christopher, she looked suddenly shy. 'We have something to celebrate.'

There was a tension in the room, the silent gasp of an audience as the trapeze artist falls from the high wire.

'Come on then, what is it? You're making me nervous.'

Christopher stood, his tall frame towering above us, and coughed pretentiously.

'Unaccustomed as I am - no, no.' Pushing back his hair nervously, he raised his glass. 'A toast then, to our future. Jenny and I are adopting.'

'What?' Astounded, my voice was much louder than I'd intended.

Placing a finger to his lips, his next words were a whisper. 'And it's twins.'

Amazed, I found myself crying, silly tears rolling down my cheeks.

'Twins? Two of them? At the same time? I can't believe it! It's the most fantastic news ever. I'm so happy.'

'Mattie, you okay?' asked Jenny.

Standing up, I raised my glass importantly. 'I'm fine. Actually, I'm fantastic. So here's to you then - both of you - and your new family.'

We sipped at the cool, clear liquid.

'So - when do you get them? Did you ask for twins? And how old are they? Boys, girls, or one of each?'

I stared at Jenny as her eyes twinkled in the candlelight, tiny stars of wonder in the night sky. The wine, her obvious relief at finally being able to talk about it, and the look of shock on my face, all took their toll. Happy tears streamed down her face.

She brushed them away. 'Sorry.'

I grinned. 'But it's the most absolutely wonderful thing I've heard in ages.'

'Come on, you two,' Christopher scolded. 'The champagne jellies are getting warm. Make the most of it. You'll be eating leftover rusks before too long.'

Jenny took a deep breath. 'Sorry - too much wine. We had a wee glassful or two before you got home.'

'But you still haven't answered my questions,' I scolded.

'Okay. You win,' Christopher replied. 'I'll start from the very beginning.' Sitting back, he stretched out his long legs and toyed with the stem of his glass. 'Well, we've been trying for a family for a few years, but unfortunately, obviously - no luck.' He looked at Jenny affectionately, and her coy smile filled the room. 'So we took ourselves off to see Doctor Sargeant, the best fertility specialist in Scotland. We discussed IVF and all the implications - of which there are many. And I think we'd have gone for it, even though our ages were against us.'

'No, Chris, it's *my* age that's against us.' Jenny shook her head, candlelight highlighting the specks of gold in her dark brown eyes. 'Don't try taking the blame. Charlie Chaplin fathered a baby in his eighties, remember.'

'Okay, darling.' He shrugged generously. 'Well, anyway, what with uni and our careers and everything delaying things ...'

'More likely the fact I'd have got married at twenty-seven and had kids then, if I hadn't found out the pig was a two-timing ...' She paused dramatically.

Christopher grinned. 'Without which ...'

She blushed. 'Without which, I'd never have met you.'

'Anyway, we'd both left it a bit late to start trying. Time was definitely against us, so we decided to head straight for adoption. We put our names down at the agency ...'

Jenny took up the story. 'But they were taking ages. It was all red tape, one interview after another. I was starting to give up hope, to be honest, but then one day I was out shopping on Princes Street. And I happened, by pure coincidence, to bump into the mother of a girl I used to teach. Well, we got chatting and, long story short, Mrs Howden's niece, who lives the other side of Glasgow, was pregnant. To the first boy she'd ever slept with. She'd taken a year out to tour Europe, as they do, and met him there. Lovely boy, he is. But her mother was distraught and after much soul-searching, said she'd bring up the child so Charlotte could continue with her education. She'd been offered a place at Newcastle, you see. But when the first scan revealed twins, she knew her parents just wouldn't be able to cope. They both have full-on careers. So by the time I met up with Mrs Howden they were considering adoption.'

'This got us to thinking,' continued Christopher. 'We rang Charlotte's parents and arranged to meet up so we could discuss the whole thing. They got in touch with the adoption agency and well, the rest is history, as they say.'

I was curious. 'I know I shouldn't even suggest this, but if they knew pretty early on, why didn't she just have an abortion?'

'Catholics. Very strong. They go to church every Sunday. The whole family would have been gutted.'

'That's understandable, I suppose. So - just when are these babies due?'

'April. April seventh or thereabouts.' Jenny released her infectious laugh. 'But who knows? It could be any time. Apparently, twins are notorious for arriving early.'

I smiled. 'In that case, we'd better start shopping. There'll be two of everything to buy.'

CHAPTER 8

I opened my eyes, searching for the clock Jenny had placed there. Seven forty-five, and still in bed. I stared at Thomas's bed, amazed he hadn't woken me. Empty. He must have crawled out of the room, a silent mouse scurrying quietly through the door.

Putting my feet to the floor, I yawned, stretched, my body coming alive, my blood pumping through my veins like petrol through an engine. I pulled my soft blue dressing gown from the armchair and placed it around my shoulders. As I did so, however, a book caught my eye. It was on the shelf, sandwiched tightly between two ancient Thomas Hardy paperbacks. Intrigued by the cover, I pulled it down. The title, *The Art of Meditation - from illusion to reality in four simple steps,* made me think of Andrew Whirlow, his bright green eyes clear and honest. He never had brought me that DVD.

Perched on the edge of the faded armchair, my bare toes curling in and out, I thumbed through the pages, yellow and crinkled with age, and delicate as rose petals. The text was easy to read, simple to follow, so I tried the breathing exercises.

Sit in a warm comfortable place. Having sat down, ignore any distracting thoughts of business, relatives, disease, worry, and doubt. Do not fight such thoughts, but as they arise, gently as it were, look at them as though they did not belong to you or concern you. If you fight them violently back, they will only intensify and take away your concentration.

Instead of giving consideration to them, mentally project a thought of well-wishing towards all living beings in front of you, to infinity. This thought must not be directed at any particular individual, but must be all-encompassing, as if rays of goodwill were emanating to all beings ahead of you. On no account must the rays be visualised as returning to oneself.

I sat back, placing the book onto the chair arm. Stifling a yawn, I closed my eyes, relaxing, visualising warm thoughts, orange rays of light, emanating from my forehead, my third eye. But as I sat, this array of colour changed from warm orange to cool white. Sunset to sunrise. Calming. Pacifying. After about a minute, I opened my eyes, picking up the book again.

When you are satisfied that the thought has projected without any feeling of self-interest, the same procedure should be enacted to the right side, without turning the head. Then, still looking ahead, the thought should be projected to the back, then to the left. Next, beneath one, and lastly, above.

I concentrated hard, visualising rays of goodwill floating away from me, before reading on.

Stage 1: Counting the Breaths. *Breathe gently and slowly to a mental count of FIVE. Breathe in to ONE, breathe out to TWO, in to THREE, and so on. After the FIFTH breath, begin again at ONE and repeat the process. Fix the attention on the breaths going in and out of the nostrils, concentrating on the point just under the nose where the breath enters and leaves.*

I followed the instructions.
'One. One two. One two three. One two three four ...'
My stomach rumbled loudly. I lost concentration, but tried again, focusing on my nose.
'One. One two. One two three. One two three four. One two three four five ...'
As I counted to five maybe nine or ten times, I became oblivious to my surroundings, cut off from the outside world, from my past, my future, every thought I'd ever had. My mind was completely still, a rock surrounded by the storm.
It felt wonderful.
Finally opening my eyes, I felt light, airy, not really there, my shoulders relaxed, my mind calm. Sleeping Beauty awoken by the prince after a hundred years. Closing the book carefully, I placed it back onto the shelf. Removing my dressing gown, I stood before the

mirror and wound my hair into a chignon, ready for the shower.

But the door flew open behind me. It was Thomas, with Angus at his heels.

'Mummy, you're awake! Been a long time, you have. It's snowed again, look.'

Running to the window, he pulled at the long, velvet curtains. The row of Georgian houses, crisp snow covering the roofs, tall chimneys peering out like white pillar boxes, was the exquisite image of a Victorian Christmas card.

'It's beautiful, Thomas.' Picking him up, I hugged him tight. 'Good morning, you. But where've you been? You were very quiet.'

'I tiptoed, didn't I? I've been downstairs with Jenny and Angus. We made chocolate buns.' He grinned, that cheeky smile he'd acquired since starting school. 'We have left some for you.'

*

Our journey home was uneventful. Lulled to sleep by the warmth of the train and the constant swaying of the carriage, we slept most of the way. Rob picked us up from the station in the van and we drove back through dark starlit streets.

But I hardly recognised our small sitting room. A beautiful Christmas tree, tall and dark, filled an entire corner. Some of its needles were already a small heap of forest on the carpet, but I breathed in deeply. This was Christmas to me. The fruity, spicy aroma of the cake in the oven, mulled wine simmering on the hob, oranges, cinnamon, ginger, cloves, and pine trees.

Rob called from the kitchen. 'Dinner's in the oven and the tea's mashing.'

Thomas dived beneath the spiky branches, needles catching on his hair. Pulling back quickly, he groaned, disappointed at the lack of presents. Running to the sofa, he jumped up and down noisily.

'No, you don't,' I chastised. 'You know that's naughty.'

Swinging him up, I sat down with him on my knee. He smelt of the frosty air outside – an earthy scent, the fragrance of ginseng tea.

Rob brought the tea through. 'Here we go.'

'Thanks, darling.' I smiled up at him. 'Just what I need.'

'Dinner's in five minutes.' He gestured wildly to our suitcase in the hallway. 'You haven't spent all your time shopping, have you?'

The look on his face was one I had never seen before, his jaw set like iron teeth in stone.

Shocked, dismayed, I blushed. 'No, not really. Well, maybe a bit. But they're only Christmas presents, Rob. We did want to go and see Dynamic Earth, but by the time we got there we were running out of time and it wouldn't have been worth it …'

Thomas chipped in, his voice high with tension. 'But we did have a nice time, Mummy, didn't we?'

I kissed the back of his head in thanks. 'We did. It was freezing, though, and it snowed again last night. We didn't even know if the trains would be running.'

Nice change of subject, I thought.

And the bait was taken.

'Mm, I heard. Edinburgh Airport not flying. Gatwick and Heathrow, too. The whole lot, by all accounts.'

'I know, and all those poor people trying to get away for Christmas.'

Thomas climbed down, skipping out of the room. I could hear him, *plod, plod, plod,* making his way upstairs. I sipped my tea, relaxing into the cup.

'But Rob, you've not heard the best news.'

'What's that, then?'

'Jenny and Christopher are adopting twins. Can you believe that? They're not even been born yet. Twin babies. Isn't that absolutely wonderful?'

'Well. That is a turn-up for the books. I always thought they were the ambitious types, lived for their careers and all that.'

'They've been trying for a while, apparently. The mother's a cousin of one of Jenny's old pupils. She got a place at uni, took a year out, then found she was pregnant. It is the most marvellous news, though, isn't it? I'm really happy for them.'

'I suppose it is.' He moved to the fireplace, standing with his back to it, hands on hips, master of all he surveyed. 'Nearly ruined the girl's career though, didn't it? Bit stupid, sleeping around when she's got good prospects like that.'

'I suppose, but these things happen. And she wasn't really sleeping around – she's not that kind of girl. He was her first proper boyfriend.' I watched him carefully over the rim of my cup. His face was grey, drawn, a cotton sheet left too long in the rain. 'Did *you* have a good weekend, anyway?'

'Yep. We did a house in Pepingham – flooring, carpets, the lot. Only got finished this morning, so I called at the garden centre on the way back. That tree cost an arm and a leg. I got the decorations down from the loft, then made dinner. Oh, and I popped into Sainsbury's, got those things you asked for. I remembered to use your Nectar card, to get the points. Here, you can have it back now. Thanks.' He pulled it from his pocket.

I'd needed a few bits, and there was a big blue tin of Buzz Lightyear chocolates Thomas had seen that I wanted to buy for Christmas. Taking my card, I looked up, realising suddenly how very much I'd missed my husband.

'You okay?' he asked.

'I'm fine. The tree's beautiful, darling, worth every single penny, thank you. Thomas loves it, too.'

Putting down my cup, I wrapped my arms around him. His brown woollen sweater was soft beneath my fingers. We kissed gently, his skin smooth against my face. His kiss was warm and tender. Too tender. I tried to melt into him, remove the angst from his face, become one, become us. But the fireworks were gone. Where was the passion, the excitement? Hadn't he missed me, too?

Whispering seductively, I looked up. 'How do you fancy making another one like him – another Thomas? Tonight? I can stop my pill and …'

'What?' He pulled away, shock reddening his face. 'We've been through this before, Mattie.'

My pulse raced in horror. 'But Rob …'

'You know we can't take on another child. I'm only just setting up …'

I couldn't bear to hear more. 'It's okay, I'm sorry.'

Pulling away quickly, I turned to the door.

'Mattie?'

91

Confused, my mind in turmoil, my nerves like broken guitar strings, I ignored him.

In the bathroom, I swallowed back hot tears, trying to understand. Maybe he was tired after his hectic weekend. Maybe he was genuinely worried about money. Maybe he'd just lost interest. Taking a deep breath, I pushed away my thoughts, the ones at the bottom of the lake that no-one ever sees, the ones threatening to drown me, to pull me down, and smiled for Thomas.

He was in his bedroom, chatting away to his toy donkey. Shiny cars littered the floor. Lego pieces had been fashioned into a red and blue petrol station.

Sitting cosily at the edge of his bed, I determined to seduce his father that night. To show him how much I'd missed him.

And how much he should have missed me.

CHAPTER 9

Folksbury, Lincolnshire

SMILING sweetly, Sally ushered us through the violet-blue door into the wide hallway of her Victorian semi.

'Hi, Sally.'

'Morning, Mattie, come on in. How are you?'

Huge windows displayed bright fluorescent paintings, stridently advertising Sally's child-minding business. They were beguiling, but Thomas wasn't interested in any picture. He clung so tightly to my hand I could hardly feel it.

'Mummy ...'

Pulling my fingers gently away, I knelt down. 'I'm only just around the corner, darling. You'll be fine. You'll have a lovely time playing with the other children, I promise.'

Sally took his hand, dimples making deep hollows in her smooth skin. 'We're making tree decorations today, Thomas, all ready for Christmas. Would you like that, do you think?' Nodding at me, her eyes told me to go, and quickly. 'Say goodbye now. Mummy will see you later, okay?'

Unable to speak, he merely nodded, his tiny fingers waving.

I waved back guiltily, a huge lump in my throat. 'Bye, darling.'

It took one minute to walk to Haringey's. And it was Christmas, the phone as silent as a snow blizzard at night. Sipping hot coffee, I checked my emails and typed up replies. But my mind was elsewhere. Spinning round and round, turning upside down, inside out, round and round and round. Analysing. Doubtful. Fearful.

Edinburgh. For three whole days. Any other time Rob would have missed me, wanted me, been desperate for me, just the touch of my body an aphrodisiac, like kerosene lighting the flame of his torch. Yet he'd fallen asleep as soon as his head had touched the pillow. And I wasn't sure he hadn't been pretending.

I sighed loudly, wondering whether I was just losing my touch. Or my looks. Reaching the last email, I thumped the Delete button.

Today was Emma's official Christmas Shopping Day, an extra holiday, a perk of the job. I didn't usually mind working alone, but today I could really have done with the company. Especially Emma, who's always good for a laugh. So I watched the minutes tick by – like a line of soldiers marching through treacle – and my thoughts turned to Thomas. He'd only been to Sally's once before, at half-term.

Poor kid.

Yes, that's what I'd do, I decided. I'd take him out for lunch as a Christmas treat. Christmas, my favourite time of the year. Time spent with Rob and Thomas, my two most favourite people. Opening presents, playing games, cementing the bond between us so Thomas would have the memories I have, of wonderful childhood Christmases, of warm mincemeat and cold chocolates and cake with crisp, sugary icing. And this year my parents were coming to stay. I just couldn't wait.

I dialled Sally's number and arranged to pick up Thomas for lunch. Then, deciding to make myself useful, I tidied drawers, straightened property leaflets, washed my coffee cup. I was still in the kitchen when the great red door opened, the bell clanging against it.

'Hi ...'

'Andrew.' I smiled, glad of his company. 'How are you?'

'Fine. Fine, thanks. Apart from this lousy weather. It's very pretty and all that, but hell when you're driving round.' Placing his laptop case onto Emma's desk, his smile became a lopsided grin. 'How are you, anyway? Did you have a good time in Edinburgh?'

'Yes, thank you. Marvellous.'

'Did you get to see all the sights, then?'

'Not really – shopping mostly. But it *was* fun. I didn't want to be dragging Thomas round the sights, anyway. He's a bit young yet. Besides, it was absolutely freezing.'

'It would be.'

'Would you like a coffee?'

'I'd love one, thanks.'

'Did you get to see Mr and Mrs Thompson?'

'No, it was the daughter again. They're still at their Spanish apartment. But I've told her straight – they're not likely to sell Stoneleigh, not at that price. She's tried her best, but they won't see sense. They'd be better off letting it out over the winter, then trying again next year. Apparently, they've also got a place in Bexhill, so they spend summers there and winters in Spain.'

I spooned coffee granules into two mugs. 'Wow. Not a bad life, is it?'

'It obviously does them good. You should see them – both in their seventies and bundles of energy.' He paused thoughtfully. 'I've just remembered something.' Returning to his case, he handed me a crumpled plastic carrier bag. 'I brought you this – Happy Christmas. Sorry it's taken so long.'

'Thanks.' Pulling out a Barbara Currie DVD and a white ring-bound book on meditation, I smiled. 'Actually, I did try some meditation up in Edinburgh.'

'Really?' He sat on Emma's chair, swivelling round to face me, stretching out his long legs, expensive grey suede brogues flattering his feet.

'I found a book on it at Jenny's, the friend we were staying with.'

He leaned forward with interest. 'And?'

I shrugged, suddenly embarrassed, a child caught with an illicit sweet.

'To be honest, I only did it for about ten minutes.'

His smile warmed the room. 'Yes?'

The child realised it didn't matter; it was only a sweet.

'It was easy, *very* relaxing. It just seemed to take me out of myself – which is what I could do with at the moment.'

'That's great, Mattie, really great. Well done. Keep it up.'

The phone rang suddenly, and I pulled on my headset.

'Good morning, Haringey's. Mattie speaking.'

'Good morning, my dear. It's Mrs Phelps, of twenty three Dunleary Lane.'

I remembered her immediately, the lady with the red beret and matching bag.

'Enid – lovely to hear from you. How are you?'

'I'm very well, thank you. And you?'

'I'm fine, getting *very* excited about Christmas.'

Her voice was a smile. 'Well, you will be, with a little one running about. Now I'm ringing because your young man there came to value my house for me.'

'Yes, I remember. I have the details just here.' I searched for the property.

'Well, that's what I'm ringing about. I've decided I'm definitely selling, but after Christmas, when all the snow's stopped and folks feel like coming out a bit more.'

'That's alright. Mr Whirlow just needs to call and measure up, and take some photos.'

'Of course. When do you think he could come, then?'

I consulted Andrew's diary. 'Would tomorrow be any good?'

'That'd be lovely. Any particular time?'

'I'll just check.' I pressed the mute button. 'Andrew, it's twenty three Dunleary. Mrs Phelps wants to put the house on the market after Christmas. You've got space tomorrow. Could you call round then, do you think?'

He stared at me, a mystified look on his face, as if seeing me for the very first time.

'Did anyone ever tell you you're the image of Elizabeth Taylor?'

'What?' I exploded.

'In her prime, of course.'

Unable to believe we were having this conversation in the middle of a call, I ignored him, pointing at my headset. 'Mrs Phelps?'

'Yes, tomorrow's fine.' His eyes crinkled attractively.

I ignored that too. 'Ten-thirty?'

'Ten-thirty's fine,' he replied.

I released the mute button. 'Hi, Enid. Would ten-thirty be alright?'

'Yes, my dear, that'd be lovely. Tell him I'll have the kettle on, and I'll make some currant biscuits. I know he doesn't like buns. But he's such a lovely man, so understanding. But then you know that, don't you, my dear? Of course you do.'

'Yes, Enid, I'll tell him.' An inexplicable heat rose through my body, and I found myself blushing. 'Ten-thirty it is, then. Andrew will see you tomorrow. Thank you for your call. Bye, Enid, and Merry Christmas.'

'Merry Christmas to you, too.'

I removed my headset.

'What will you tell me?' Andrew asked.

'Just that she'll have the kettle on and is making currant biscuits. I think she's got a soft spot for you.'

'How did she know they're my favourites?' He shook his head. 'Very strange. She is quite fascinating, though. Did you know her grandparents were Romany gypsies? Travelled the length and breadth of Ireland. It was her father who came over to England looking for work.'

'Interesting.' I was busy typing up his diary.

'I'll do the diary, Mattie, you go for lunch. After all, that is why I'm here.'

I looked at the time. 'Oh no! Got to dash.'

*

At five o'clock, I locked the great red door of Haringey's and made my way to the Post Office. Old Mrs Fleming, as she's known throughout the village, filled the entrance to the greengrocer's across the road. Wrapped in numerous old cardigans, a coat, two scarves and a brown woollen hat, she was emptying a bag of potatoes into the old wheelbarrow. She waved at me with gloved fingers. Waving back, I smiled.

I breathed, filling my lungs with fresh, cold air. Dragons of smoke poured from my lips as I paused occasionally, admiring the arty cupcakes on display in the baker's window, the delicate stitching of stuffed elephants in the craft shop, and the jewelled colours of a life-size nativity scene in the churchyard. The village always came alive at Christmas. Posting Haringey's mail through the letterbox, I walked back to Sally's house. Thomas, his hand strangling the top of a white carrier bag, was already at the door.

I hugged him. 'Hi, you - had a good afternoon?'

He took hold of my hand quietly. 'Mm ...'

Standing behind him, Sally winked. 'He's fine, really. He just wants his mummy.'

'Well, can't complain about that, can we? Thanks anyway, Sally. We'll see you tomorrow.'

'You will,' she said.

As we walked away, Thomas pulled a huge paper snowman from his bag. Its arms and legs bounced around as he released them, like ricocheting limbs on a trampoline.

'Look what I made, Mummy.'

Relieved he'd had such a good time, I paused to admire it. 'That's brilliant, and what a big, smiley face. Aren't you a clever boy? It'll look gorgeous on our Christmas tree.'

He looked up, suddenly thoughtful. 'Mummy?'

'Yes?'

'Have you seened Jeremy Bear anywhere? I looked for him again this morning. He'll be lonely all by himself.'

I felt dreadful. I'd completely forgotten to look. 'No, darling. Sorry. You've not taken him to school, have you?'

'I've not taken him to anywhere. He always sits on my bed.'

'I'm sure he'll be fine. I bet he's having a wonderful time exploring the house while we're not there. But I'll have a good look round.'

*

Rob's dinner sat cold in the kitchen, congealing like raw blood. Thomas had been in bed an hour. A glass of Rioja was balanced on the hearth. The sitting room floor was a sea of shiny red wrapping paper, the pile of presents growing by the minute. I sat cross-legged before the fireplace, wrapping, sticking, labelling, watching TV, an old James Bond film with Pierce

Brosnan. Yet all the while my stomach churned. Rob had not even had the decency to ring this time, had merely texted, giving me no opportunity to chat, to ask questions, to plead.

Even Thomas was starting to ask questions. Why isn't Daddy home yet? When will he be home? He never kisses me goodnight, Mummy.

I was tired of making excuses, yet could see how overworked he was. He was exhausted, irritable, moody. Reaching for my wine, I sighed. Maybe I should let him off the leash a little, give him some space. The last thing any man wants after a hard day's work is a nagging wife. I just wished - I wished that when he came home he made me feel cared for, that he'd missed me. Guiltily, I put down my glass and pulled off more sticky tape, convincing myself that, really, I was very lucky. At least I still had a husband. Unlike poor Becca.

Holding up a shiny Buzz Lightyear annual, I smiled, imagining Thomas's happy, bubbling face on Christmas morning.

CHAPTER 10

THOMAS, his face rosy pink from the fresh air, his pearls of teeth a wide grin, bubbled over with excitement. There were finally presents under the tree, bright red and shiny with curls of silver. Just like Father Christmas.

I rang Sally's doorbell. 'Here we go, Thomas.'

Sally opened the door swiftly, a flood of warm air greeting us. 'Hi, you two, come on in.'

The scent of Play-Doh, nostalgic and all-consuming, filled my nostrils. 'Are you ready for today, then, Sally? I'm afraid I have one rather excited child here.'

'I'm used to it, don't worry. And today's a special day, isn't it, Thomas? We have Mr Nosey coming to see us, and who knows - we may have a few little presents as well.'

I grinned. 'Can I come?'

*

Emma, breathless and slightly dishevelled, arrived for work exactly twenty minutes late. Pulling off a blue woollen hat, she shook out her mop of bleached blonde hair.

'Sorry, ducks, missed the bus. It's my own fault, I know. Couldn't seem to get out of bed this morning, what with the boys being off school.' Pulling an upside-down face, she hung up her coat and hat.

'It's okay, don't worry about it. I'm just glad you're here. Coffee?'

'Yes please. At least I remembered mince pies. And only the best.' She pulled a bright red M&S box out of her shopper.

'I take it you had a good day's shopping, then. You get plenty done?'

'To be honest, I didn't really have much to get. Steven and James are at their father's for Christmas, though why he wants them I've no idea. Takes him all his time to see them the rest of the year.'

Ever the pacifist, I shrugged. 'Maybe he's trying to change, realises they're growing up.'

'More likely he's wanting to impress the bloody girlfriend. He's buying them Ipads too, and have you seen the price of them? Mind you, the money he's making, he can afford it.'

'So what are you doing for Christmas?'

'Llandudno. Mum's place. Assuming I can get there, what with the snow they've been having. Our Tracy's going too, with her kids, so it should be good fun. I'll miss my two, though.'

'That's sad. I'd hate to spend Christmas without Thomas.'

'I'll be fine, really. Anyway, how was Edinburgh?'

103

'Fantastic. Thomas absolutely loved it.'

'So how was Rob when you got back? Okay without you?'

'Of course. Why?' I watched her carefully.

'Just wondered.'

I felt suddenly sick. 'That's a strange kind of question. What is it, Emma?'

'Just checking. I thought it a bit strange he didn't go with you, that's all.'

'He's just busy, what with Christmas and everything. I told you.'

'I know. I just thought ...' She shrugged animatedly. 'You know, if he's going off the boil, there's always Andrew.'

'What?' My question hit the ceiling, reverberating around the room.

'He really likes you, you know.'

'Don't be ridiculous, Emma. I'm a married woman. And anyway, he's old enough to be my - my ...'

'Your big brother? He's what - ten years older?'

'It's enough.'

'Sorry, ducks. It's just he's always talking about you. And he is gorgeous, you have to admit. I mean, I think he *really* likes you.'

*

I smiled into my headset.

'Thank you for calling, Mr Teasdale. Goodbye now.'

Emma was still at lunch. Andrew, having called in for some paperwork, was in the kitchen.

'Tea or coffee?' he called.

'Tea, please. Thanks.'

'The kettle's boiling.' Lounging in the doorway, he folded his arms casually. 'Last day for you today, isn't it? You all ready for Christmas at your house, then?'

'Just about. I've still got to pick up the turkey, but other than that we're done. Thomas is *very* excited.'

'That's what Christmas is all about though, isn't it – kids?'

'Mm, I think so, too.' Quickly and succinctly I changed the subject, a sore point. 'How did you get on with the B&B?'

'It's a lovely house, but sorely neglected. Such a pity. A touch of paint here and there and it'd sell quite well, no problem. She'd have been better off selling it as a going concern, of course, but they've let the business slide. Old age, I suppose.'

'She's so lovely, too. I don't know – what are some men like? How could he just run off and leave her in the lurch like that? She doesn't even look capable of painting a few walls, bless her.'

'You're right,' he agreed. 'She is lovely. In fact, she said exactly the same thing about you. She even asked if I'd let you go round some time for a cuppa. How about that, then? I knew we'd employed you for a reason. You do seem to impress the punters.'

'Thank you, kind sir.' I bowed my head towards him.

But then a vision of Enid sitting alone in that empty house over Christmas filled my head.

'Actually,' I said. 'I think I will call round. In fact, I'll arrange it now.'

CHAPTER 11

BECCA breathed in deeply. 'Your house smells good enough to eat.'

'That'll be the mince pies,' I said, pouring water into coffee cups. 'Or it could be Thomas's gingerbread men. He decided he didn't want mince pies after all, once we'd finished making them.'

I yawned, my mind a shroud of thick syrup after a miserable few hours' sleep. Rob hadn't bothered to ring at all last night, and turned up at nine-thirty without a word of apology. And I hadn't asked.

The dining table was covered in felt pens and bits of paper. Pushing them to one side, I replaced them with coffee, gingerbread men and warm mince pies. The scent of cinnamon, coffee and ginger filled the air like soft balloons nudging for space.

'Sorry, I've not had time to tidy up. Help yourself to a mince pie – they're still warm. I love them when they're just out of the oven.'

Becca shook her head. 'No thanks.'

'Gingerbread man, then?'

'I'm not that hungry at the moment. Sorry, it's not long since I had breakfast.'

I studied her carefully. 'You are eating properly, aren't you? You do look as if you need feeding up, now I come to think of it. Pregnant women aren't supposed to be slim, you know. Is that baby behaving itself?'

'It's fine. Worse luck.'

Shocked, I couldn't believe what I was hearing, couldn't believe she didn't want what I wanted so desperately.

'How can you say that? You wanted this baby.'

Her eyes filled with sudden tears. 'I know, I know. But maybe I made a mistake. I mean, I might be able to start all over again with one child, but who's going to want to take me on with two children tagging along behind?'

Now I *was* furious. 'That's silly. You must know how absolutely gorgeous you are. There'll be thousands of men wanting to take you on, with your children. You come as a package. And besides, you can't regret making this baby. Some women would die for one. All these couples paying a fortune for IVF, and you just go and fall pregnant at the drop of a hat. My friend Jenny in Edinburgh can't have kids, so they're adopting. But I know they'd much rather have had their own.'

She wiped her eyes. 'Sorry. You're right. It's just – I think it would have been easier if it was just me and Chloe.'

'Hey now, you're going to be fine – you'll see. It's not easy to see it now, but if Alan can do this to you, then he's just not worth it. He's obviously not the man you thought he was.'

'But he is. You don't know him, not like I do. We're soul mates, everyone says so. And I love him, and he loves me. I know he does. It's just this woman who's led him astray. He'll realise, you wait and see. He'll realise what he's missing, and then he'll come back. He *will* come back. I just need to be patient, that's all.' Pulling a tissue from her bag, she wiped her nose daintily.

'Maybe you're right. I hope you are. But could you ever trust him again? If he's betrayed you once he could do it again, you know.'

She jumped up, a screech of disbelief echoing across the room. 'How can you sit there and say that? I thought you were my friend, Mattie. Don't you want me to be happy?'

The children appeared suddenly, just at the wrong time. Chloe ran straight to her mother, where there was a fresh outburst of tears.

'Sorry Mattie – I – I need to go home,' she cried.

I felt dreadful, couldn't believe what had just happened.

'Sorry, Becca, I didn't mean it the way it sounded. Of course I want you to be happy. I just …' But I couldn't think of the words to say, the excuse that would make everything right.

Grabbing her bag, her sobs echoing through the house, she and Chloe stormed out of the door.

*

I felt wretched. And watching Thomas pick at his lunch was like watching sea evaporate. I thought about ringing Becca, but decided I'd done enough damage for one day. What a fool I'd been.

'You alright, Mummy?'

'Just upset about Becca.'

'I know. She was upset as well, wasn't she?'

'Sorry. I spoilt your day, didn't I?'

He mashed a fish finger with his fork until there was hardly anything left. A wrecking ball on the end of a crane. Total obliteration.

'Why *was* she upset?' His eyes moved from his plate to my face slowly, accusingly.

'Eat your lunch, Thomas. We need to be at Mrs Phelps' house for two, and it's ten past one now.'

We drove into Pepingham exactly an hour later.

'Mummy, it's there. Look, Dunleary Lane.'

'Thank you, darling.'

I indicated left, turning carefully up the hill, the fresh layer of early morning snow still evident. Number twenty-three was easy to find, the last one in a long row of mid-nineteenth century houses. A green sign, frosted around the edge, announced *Bed and Breakfast, No Vacancies.* Parking up, I took Thomas's hand and walked along the narrow path to the door. A wooden pew, grey with age and bathed in weak winter sunshine, nearly filled the small garden. I knocked on the door nervously, not really knowing what to expect.

109

But I needn't have worried. Enid Phelps was a delight, an inspiration. She opened the aged olive-green door with a flourish, a large black cat curling around her ankles.

'Hello, my dears.' Picking up the cat, she stroked the thick fur behind its neck. 'Don't mind Genevieve, she's just saying hello. But come on in. More snow today, but not too much, thank goodness, not like last time. But it's good to see you again. And this is Thomas, is it? Lovely to meet you, Thomas.'

He smiled shyly.

She led us into her spacious sitting room. 'In here now. It's nice and warm, so make yourselves at home.'

I twirled round slowly at the centre of a huge Chinese rug, faded pink. Green dragons, pink peonies and Chinese wealth coins rose up out of the soft, deep wool. My feminine mind took in the room's detailing, its simple coving, its picture rails high up on the pink flocked wallpaper.

'I just love your house, Mrs Phelps. It's gorgeous.'

'My dear, I've told you before - if you're going to come visiting for tea and cake, you must call me Enid. Mrs Phelps makes me sound so old.'

*

Enid's Victoria sponge cake was delicious. Buttery and moist. Once we'd finished eating I asked if I could take a look round the house.

'It is in a bit of a state, Mattie. But I can't do it on my own, not properly anyway, and people like to do their own decorating, don't they? Your Mr Whirlow says it'd sell better if it was done up a bit. But what can you do?'

'Don't worry about what I think, Enid. I just love old houses.'

'I'll just have to take what I can for it, won't I? Anyway, have a look round if you want. Thomas can stay here with his Lego.'

Sprawled across the Chinese rug, a battered cardboard box by his side, Thomas was in his element, fastening together the colourful plastic pieces once belonging to Enid's son. Genevieve lay stretched beneath the radiator, watching his every move.

He looked up, his smile a shaft of sunlight. 'It's alright, Mummy, I'm going to make a helicopter.'

'Okay, but be good.'

'He'll be fine, my dear. The front door's locked, he won't be going anywhere, and Genevieve will keep an eye.'

We wandered through the house into the kitchen, a mess of worn cupboards and bleached worktops. There was a herb-like scent about the place, strong, nose-tickling.

'Oregano oil,' Enid explained. 'I always use it in the wintertime. It acts like a disinfectant, good against the flu. I used to grow all my own herbs, you know, but last winter was so cold I couldn't keep them going.' She shook her head. 'Maybe if I had, things wouldn't have turned out so bad.'

Puzzled, I shook my head. 'Sorry, I don't understand.'

She looked away quickly. 'Sorry. I get morbid sometimes, just ignore me.'

Taking me through the kitchen, she described how she and Peter had extended the property to provide not only guest accommodation, but living space for

111

their growing family. The original house, built in 1865, featured a short hallway, a sitting room, and a long dining hall leading to a small kitchen. A small lobby led off, and here they'd added the extension - a lounge/dining room, a spiral staircase rising up to a narrow landing, a tiny bathroom, and three small bedrooms.

I felt as if I was going back in time, to the Seventies, to long flowery skirts and Led Zep. The decade before my birth, but I know all about it. Brown and orange flowered wallpaper in the lounge, avocado suite in the bathroom, oak-effect wallboards on the landing.

Enid took me into the main bedroom. 'Not very big, I know, but big enough for me and my Peter. He never used to have them big ideas before he met her, you know.'

The room was small and tired, miserable, a bare light bulb hanging like a forgotten martyr.

'Well, I suppose you needed somewhere to live, away from the guest accommodation, and this is ideal. I admit it could do with a bit of updating; Andrew's right. It would sell better if it was cheered up a bit.'

'I know it's a bit run-down, but we spent all our time on the bit of the house people could see.' She looked anxious. 'You do think it'll sell alright, don't you?'

'Let's see what the rest of the house is like.'

Briefly surveying the remaining bedrooms, I followed Enid downstairs. Checking on Thomas, I found him engrossed, a tiny helicopter, simple but effective, on the floor beside him.

Enid beamed. 'What a wonderful helicopter, Thomas. My, you are a clever boy.'

He grinned. 'Thank you.'

'We're just going back upstairs for a minute, darling,' I said.

The wide, graceful staircase of the original 19th century house was thickly carpeted. Its broad, glossy banister curved upwards to a broad landing, the rich cream walls and beige carpeting adding their touch of opulence. Running my hand along the smooth, rounded surface of the banister, I followed Enid upstairs.

'This is the Four Poster room,' she said, proudly.

She turned on the light to reveal a large room, tall and wide. Deep coving ran around the ceiling, its gold leaf matching the rose at the centre. Now dull and lustreless, it was nevertheless still very appealing, and I knew a wipe with methylated spirits would bring it out beautifully.

'Sorry about all the clothes on the chest,' she said, indicating the oak drawers in the corner. 'I'm sleeping in here now. Well, I might as well.'

'I don't blame you. It's beautiful.' Mesmerised, I couldn't help but stare at the ceiling.

'It's made out of tin. They put it up in panels in those days, in big squares, can you see?' She pointed to show me the edges. 'The ones downstairs are proper plaster, but they used to make bedroom ceilings from tin because it was cheaper. They've lasted, though.'

'That's incredible. I never knew that.'

'Now, when I was a girl my old dad would plaster ceilings and walls, wherever we went. That's how he made his living. We were travellers, you know. But we were always honest, made our own way in the world.

Just think, though, we'd have been destitute if they'd all had tin ones like this.'

I studied the ceiling carefully. 'I'd never have thought it was made from tin. Very clever. And just look at the four-poster.' A canopy of heavy cream silk hung above the bed like an angel's wing. 'It's beautiful.'

Two tall windows looked out over the ancient village of Pepingham, but the dark sky revealed only a few stone cottages and shops, their windows filled with orange light and the coloured bulbs of Christmas trees. A layer of snow covered the roofs.

'It is lovely isn't it?' she sighed. 'Been here thirty-four years, we have.'

'It'll be hard to leave, won't it, Enid?' Able to use her first name quite naturally, I suddenly realised how fond of her I was becoming. 'I bet you thought you'd be living here forever, didn't you?'

'I know we've let the business go over the past few years.' Bravely, she brushed away a sudden tear. 'I think my Pete was getting a bit fed up then, truth be told. Seemed to lose interest after the kids left home. I think he missed them.'

I patted her arm gently. 'Come on, let's finish up here and go back downstairs. I'll make you a nice cup of tea.'

But as I made the tea, Enid fussing behind me, an idea formed slowly within my mind and took root, the grain of sand becoming a pearl.

Excited, inspired, I turned. 'Enid?'

'Yes, my dear?'

'I've had a bit of a thought. I've a bit of time on my hands at the moment, now Thomas is at school. And

I've been thinking - I'd like to help you get this place up to scratch. That's if you don't mind.'

She shook her head emphatically. 'Now you don't have to go doing that. But thank you. I'll get what it's worth, no more and no less.'

'But there's not really that much to do. I think it might sell better with just a few licks of paint here and there, and if maybe the extension was updated a little, with new wallpaper and so on. Please, Enid, I want to.'

'Oh, I don't know ...'

Her face a contortion of indecision, she brought a small brown bottle from her pocket, poured a few drops onto a handkerchief, and breathed in deeply. Looking up, her features were suddenly calm, secure, anchored.

'Rosewood, for making a decision,' she said.

It was filling my nostrils, too, sweet and woody like nutmeg. 'So?'

'I - I'll think about it.'

But she was coming round to the idea, I could tell.

'Really Enid, it won't take a lot of doing. It shouldn't cost too much. Just a few tins of paint, a few rolls of wallpaper. I'd do all the work. And you'd make thousands more towards your next house.'

Thoughtfully, she twisted the hankie between her hands, her skin soft and wrinkled like a sweet over-ripe apricot. Then she smiled.

'Well, my dear, this is a turn-up for the books. To be sure.'

*

I tried ringing Becca later, but there was no reply, just the answer-phone. Disappointed, I replaced the receiver. But then the phone rang, making me jump.

'Mattie Payton here.'

'Mattie. Hi.'

Rob. And I knew exactly why he was ringing.

'Hi, darling, how are you? Had a good day?' I asked.

'Well, we're getting there, but I'll be home about nine-ish, I'm afraid. We've still loads to do. Will that be okay?'

Anger stirred at me like the spoon in a witch's cauldron.

'To be honest, Rob, I'm getting used to it. Thomas isn't, though. He's only little, he doesn't understand.'

'Mattie, I'm sorry. I'll make it up to him, I promise.'

'When? When will you make it up to him? When he's eighteen and ready to leave home?'

'You know I need to do this, Mattie. There's only the two of us, and we're still building up the business. It's not easy for me either, you know.'

Desperately, I swallowed my anger.

'It's okay. I'll see you later, then.'

'And Mattie - don't make me any dinner. I'll grab a McDonald's or something.'

*

Keen to become 'an estate agent like Mummy', Thomas was adamant that playing Monopoly was the way forward. It was he who suggested the game after dinner. But then balked at the result.

'That's not fair - *I* wanted Park Lane.'

'Oh no, you don't.' Laughing, I pulled my hand away as he tried to snatch the card from me. 'You should have bought it while you had the chance.'

'But I didn't have enough money.'

116

'Then you shouldn't buy every property you land on, should you? How about we do a few swaps, and then at least we can both buy houses?'

'Alright. But please let me have Park Lane?' He smiled at me sweetly, his dark hair a shiny ball of tousled curls. 'Please?'

Laughing, I threw the card at him. 'Alright then, just this once. You'd better not win, though.'

One hour later, sprawled on the floor with Blue Bear, Thomas had three rows of cherry red hotels.

I stared at my tiny hamlet of green houses. 'Right, that's it. Bathtime.'

He sat up quickly. 'That's not fair. Just 'cos I'm winning.'

'No more Delaying Tactics, Thomas. You're tired out, look at you. Come on, let's add everything up.'

Quickly calculating the value of our property, I discovered that once again Thomas was the winner.

'Clever boy, aren't you?'

'Mummy …' He looked up from beneath his lashes, his eyes shiny bright with fatigue. 'You want to know something?'

'What?' I packed the game away, houses and hotels into one compartment of the box, cards and banknotes into another.

'Well, when I lived in my pink house and I played this game with my little girls' mummy, *she* always used to win. So I must have practised a lot, mustn't I?'

I drew him onto my knee. I never encouraged him to talk about his pink house, knowing if he were to talk to other people about it they might react badly, unsettling him, damaging his innate self-confidence. The concept of my sweet, unblemished child having

117

lived a previous life had always sent shivers down my spine, but lately, after meeting Benjamin Bradstock, I'd found myself coming to terms with it. I hugged him close.

'You're a very clever boy, and yes, you have practised a lot, haven't you? But then, we've played Monopoly lots of times while Daddy's been at work, haven't we?' Sighing, I thought of all the hours Rob hadn't spent with his son.

He pushed his head into my shoulder. 'Don't be upset. Daddy will be home soon.'

*

I closed *Winnie the Witch*, placing it onto the bedside table and tucking Thomas into bed.

'A good story, isn't it?'

'Mummy, did you found Jeremy Bear yet?'

'No, sorry, I haven't found him.'

'I keep thinking 'bout him.'

'We need to have a really good look over Christmas, don't we? I've not told Daddy yet, though. It was his teddy and he might be upset.'

'Okay.' His eyes closing briefly, he yawned.

'Cover your mouth, Thomas, please.' But he ignored me, too tired, too interested in dreaming about ships and starlight and adventure. 'Night-night, darling. Night-night, Blue Bear.' I kissed them both.

Reaching the door, I turned to find Thomas already asleep. Switching off the light, I felt instantly dejected and lonely. Tiptoeing downstairs, I dialled Becca's number and left a message. I just needed to say sorry.

*

Rob walked through the door at exactly nine-thirty. Expecting him to be tired, irritable, I was surprised to find him in a very good mood.

'Cup of tea, darling?' I asked, smiling, happy that the house was a home again, complete. Mother, Father, Baby.

'Yes please.' Placing his arms around me, he kissed me on the cheek. 'Sorry I'm so late. Everyone wants everything doing yesterday, and it'll be the same tomorrow, I'm afraid. Luke won't be working. They're driving down to his parents for Christmas.'

'It's okay.' I snuggled into him, his thick sweater soft and warm. 'I'll be busy, anyway. I want to get as much done as possible so I can spend Christmas Eve with you.'

'When are your mum and dad arriving?'

'Friday. They want to be here Christmas morning. Oh, I'm so looking forward to it.' I looked up at him excitedly. 'Hey, let's forget the tea. How about a glass of red? We could take it with us and - and drink it in the bath. Like we used to? Bubble bath? Candlelight?'

'Sorry, Mattie.' Alarm filled his features like a sideshow tent hiding its wares from prying eyes. Yet he shrugged nonchalantly. 'I really have got the accounts to do. I'll be up 'til midnight as it is, and if I don't get my invoices out now, there'll be no money in February. Tea will be fine.' Pecking me on the cheek, he carried his briefcase into the dining room.

But the thought of spending just one more nanosecond by myself; I followed him.

'I'll do the ironing in here then, shall I? It's just - I'm a bit lonely - on my own nearly every night.'

119

'Of course. I'm fine with that. Just as long as I'm not distracted.'

Confused, hurt, I sat across the table from him, a lump forming at the base of my throat.

'Rob? Is everything alright?'

Opening his laptop, he avoided my eyes. His own were deep shadows of silt.

'Yes, of course. Why?'

I hesitated, unable to describe my emotions, unwilling to admit to the sudden gaping hole in our marriage, a lit match put to nylon.

'You just seem a bit preoccupied at the moment, that's all.'

Now he looked at me. Now the deep shadows scurried away, replaced with blue skies. Now he smiled.

'Sorry. We've just been so busy. But you'll see - it'll be worth it in the end. When we're up and running.'

I murmured acceptance. 'It's okay.'

With a heavy heart, I made tea in huge mugs. We drank the warming liquid slowly, me at the ironing board, Rob at the table.

But my mind, exhausted after a busy day, darted back and forth. To Enid. To Thomas's pink house. To Jeremy Bear. To Becca. To last night ...

I am awake. My eyes gaze at the wall, sweeping back and forth like the headlights of a car. I finally fall asleep. But I sleep too heavily, a mannequin stuffed with straw. Until a dream, floating, surreal, envelops me.

We are making love. Not in bed, not at home. Some other place, I'm not sure where; I see everything as if through a curtain of gossamer. There is no bedding, no clothing, just a breeze, warm and soft, stroking our bodies this way and that. Rob is kissing me, his head inching slowly down, his every motion finding me, loving me, his lips as delicate and perfumed as a rose petal. A delicious fluttering begins inside, an awakening. Raw, yet majestic, complete. My body arcs in response. My stomach contracts in delight. My eyes open as I moan aloud at the orgasm sweeping through me, convulsing, releasing. A letting go, the taking of my very soul ...

I am fully awake now. My heart is still throbbing, but my breath comes in quiet gasps. I know my dream should have satisfied, should have sent me back to sleep - peaceful, warm, fulfilled. But no. I want more. I turn to Rob. My whole being aches for him, yet I know already he is sound asleep. Warm tears roll onto my pillow, soft bubbles of fear, until sleep comes to take me again.

As Rob worked on his invoices, I pressed harder with the iron. A shot of hot angry steam rose abruptly through the air.

CHAPTER 12

I sneezed at the bathroom cleaner, ridding myself of its caustic fumes with the force of a hurricane. I was so looking forward to Christmas, to Mum and Dad's arrival. Just the bathroom to do, then I'd be finished.

But the peal of the phone sliced through my ablutions. I downed tools ready to run, but was too late. Thomas was already there, clutching the receiver with both hands.

'Hello.'

I ran downstairs. 'Who is it, darling?'

'Don't know, Mummy.' He passed it to me.

I watched as he toddled off, a *Paddington Bear* book tucked studiously beneath one arm.

'Hello?'

'Hi, Mattie, it's Alan - Alan Bradbury.'

My heart skipped in horror. If Alan was ringing, something had happened to Becca; *that's* why she'd not called back.

'Alan …' My voice was the squeak of a broken toy.

'It's okay, Becca's fine. Well, considering she ran into the back of a car yesterday. She's in the Infirmary, but it's just minor injuries. I understand from Chloe they were on their way home from seeing you - and I just got your message. Thought I should let you know.'

'Oh, my God.' I sat onto the bottom stair, my stomach churning with guilt. 'It's all my fault, it must be. I really upset her. I'm so sorry. But the baby - what about the baby?'

'The baby's okay. They did a scan. It's a boy.' His sudden emotion was like a gentle breeze, clear and pure.

'You sound like the proud father. Alan? Does this mean what I think it means?'

I sensed his broad smile. 'Well, it's early days yet but, well, it may do. It may very well do.'

'That's wonderful. I am so, so pleased for you. But how is she?'

'Well, the airbag took the brunt of the crash, but she's got a fractured wrist and a couple of marks on her face. She's okay, really - except for her blood pressure, which is sky high. I think she'll be out in time for Christmas. Chloe's okay - she's here at home with me.'

'Thank goodness for that. Give them both my love, won't you?'

*

Thomas pointed at the counter as if it were the opening to Aladdin's Cave. Brimming with bright cartoon characters, crisp packets, and giant gold coins of chocolate, it might very well have been.

'Can I have one of the nice boxes, please - that one - with Scooby Doo on?'

My feet were sore from shopping, and my head ached from tension and lack of sleep. Feeling like Willy Wonka after he's run out of chocolate, I wondered why everyone else had decided to lunch in Sainsbury's two days before Christmas. And why had I left it too late to order online? Again?

'Sorry, darling, these kiddie boxes really are a waste of money. Why don't you have something Christmassy, like Mummy? I'm going to have a turkey and cranberry sandwich. Wouldn't you like that?'

'No.' He screwed up his face in disgust.

'Why don't you try it? I bet you'll love it. It's a bit like chicken and jam.'

'Alright, then.' He still wasn't sure; his mouth said yes, but his eyes were devouring the counter.

'If I buy you one, Thomas, you have to promise to eat it.'

He looked up beseechingly, his tiny hand taking hold of mine. 'We are still going to Enid's house, aren't we?'

'Oh no, Thomas. When we go to Enid's it will be a quick visit. No eating her out of house and home. And we've not been invited, so she won't have food in anyway, not for us.'

'Okay, I'll have a sandwich,' he agreed.

'Good boy.'

A sudden *Oompah* and *Clang* reverberated through the store as the brass band at the entrance began playing. The atmosphere suddenly changed, from utilitarian necessity to festive cheer, and people began to smile.

Once in Royal David's City ...

A thrill of nostalgia ran down my spine. The woody aroma of Dad's cigar, the sweet scent of the tangerine in my Christmas stocking, the roar of the coal fire as chocolate wrappers steadily fuelled the flames. What wonderful Christmases we had, Amecia and I. Unwrapping presents in front of the fire. Comparing each one. Chocolate for breakfast, playing with our dolls, making up stories for them, undressing them, dressing them up again.

I looked down at Thomas, wondering how he'd remember his own Christmases, and how much more fun they'd be if he had a brother or sister. Rob and I really needed to talk.

We moved forward in the queue.

But no. He never would talk. He'd always be much too busy. And even if he did - eventually - I could see him putting it off another couple of years. Until the business was established. Until he had enough money in the bank. Poor Thomas would be far too old by then, would have made his own circle of friends, would have no interest in a tiny baby interrupting his life like an annoying wasp.

No. It was up to me to make the decision. Right there. Right then. Immediately.

And in the middle of Sainsbury's, too.

I expected to feel guilty, was amazed when I didn't. Instead, a glow like that of a firefly winged its way to my heart.

But as we reached the hot food counter, my conscience did begin to prick. Wasn't I only doing what Becca had done, having a baby to keep my marriage together? No. That was ridiculous. We were

125

just going through a bad patch, a dandelion in a field of roses. Everyone has them. Rob was just working too hard. Maybe in the New Year his work would become steadier, with more regular hours and a regular income. And a new baby would focus us - he'd *want* to spend more time at home.

A new baby. Just how lovely did that sound?

*

Coaxing Thomas into hiding the box of Dairy Milk behind his back, I concealed a posy of pink and white carnations behind my own.

The old door opened to reveal Enid in a baggy moss-green jumper and pink rubber gloves. Auburn flecks of delight filled her eyes.

'Mattie! What a lovely surprise.'

We followed her into the kitchen, warm and cosy with the scent of cinnamon and ginger.

'I hope you don't mind us dropping in,' I said. 'We've just been to Sainsbury's, so thought we'd call and say hello. We won't stay long, though – we're visiting the hospital. A friend of ours has been in a car accident.'

Pulling off her gloves, she threw them onto the old grey sink. A finger-length of heavy gold bangles adorned one arm.

'Dearie me - not serious, is it?'

'No, but she's pregnant and has high blood pressure, so they're keeping her in for observation.'

'Well, I do hope she's alright. Have you time for a quick cup of tea?'

'Yes, please, that'd be lovely.'

As she filled the kettle, I nodded to Thomas. Pulling gently at her jumper, he presented her with the chocolates.

'Happy Christmas, Enid.'

Surprised, delighted, her smile was a circle of sunshine. 'Thank you, dearie. Oh, but you shouldn't have.'

Then I pulled the carnations from behind my back. 'Merry Christmas, Enid.'

She breathed in their scent. 'Carnations. My favourites. Thank you so much, Mattie, you are so kind. But do you know - I had an idea you might drop in. I've been making mince pies and gingerbread men.' She indicated the large plate on the table. 'Do you like gingerbread men, Thomas?'

'I love them!'

Jumping up and down, his dark curls waved at the sky.

'But - how did you know?' I asked curiously.

'Oh, we Romanies have our ways.' Coy suddenly, a snail retreating into its shell, she changed the subject. 'But I do love to see you both ...' Suddenly tearful, her hand flew to her face.

'Enid?'

'Sorry - it's just Christmas. It's hard being on your own. I mean, I miss my Peter all the time, of course I do. But somehow it's much harder at Christmastime.'

She pulled a handkerchief from her sleeve, and a strong floral scent filled the air. This time I recognised it. I use it in the summer to deter moths from my wardrobe and Mum buys great cans of its wax for her furniture. Lavender oil.

But I was shocked. 'You're not spending Christmas on your own, are you?'

She dabbed at her nose. 'No. My Carol and her family are coming up tomorrow 'til Boxing Day. They wanted me to go down to their place in London, but I don't feel like travelling all that way on my own, not at the moment I don't.'

'No, I don't blame you. But look - if you're feeling lonely after they've gone, just give us a ring. We're not far away, you know.'

'You're so kind, but I don't want to be any trouble. You just enjoy Christmas with your own family. They grow up so much quicker than you realise. Make the most of it, my dear.'

But as we drank our tea at the kitchen table, Enid had something other than Christmas on her mind.

'Mattie …'

'Yes?'

'I've had an idea put to me, something I think may be of interest.'

'What is it, Enid?'

'Well, my friend Josie, she's had this brilliant idea. You see, I've told her you're coming to do up my house for me, and she thinks it's really kind of you. Which it is.' She smiled gratefully. 'But then she said - would you come and do up hers as well?'

Unable to hide my alarm, I wondered what kind of Pandora's Box I'd opened.

But she continued hastily. 'Oh no, don't get me wrong. She'd pay you, of course, and it'd be the going rate. The thing is, elderly women like us, we don't like workmen in the house. It makes us nervous, you know.

Now I know a young thing like you wouldn't understand that, but ...'

My mind was churning. What on earth had I started? What was I doing?

'No, I do understand, Enid. It's just that ...'

But her hands pushed my words away, her gold bangles jangling a warning.

'Just listen to what I have to say. And then you can say no if you've a mind to.'

I sighed inwardly, aware of my now very tired child, our impending hospital visit, and the food waiting in the car. Thankfully, nothing was frozen and the temperature outside was minus two, anyway. But no, I was being ungrateful. I smiled.

'Sorry, Enid. Okay, I'm listening.'

'I won't keep you long, I know you've things to do. It's just Josie says she's often wondered if there was a decorating firm that employed just women. So when I was telling her about my house, she thought you might make a pretty penny or two setting up on your own.'

'I don't know, Enid. I'm busy as it is. I work two days a week and I help out in school as well. And there's Thomas to look after. I mean, it won't take me long to do up your house, and it's something I really want to do. But to do it full-time ...'

'But that's the beauty of it, don't you see? You could work around them - work, school, Thomas. You'd be self-employed, your own boss, choosing your own hours, nobody telling you what to do.' Sitting back, she folded her arms triumphantly. 'Have a think about it. There's no rush. You might just decide it's what you need.'

Her eyes, coal-black suddenly, were burning into mine, insistent, demanding. It *is* what you need, they were saying. It *is* what you need.

I blinked, took control, and sipped at my tea.

'Well, it is a brilliant idea, Enid. And there's obviously a gap in the market, as you say. I suppose if it came to it, I don't have to go into school, although I do enjoy it and Thomas likes me there.' Realising, reluctantly, that I was warming to the idea, I let it take flight. 'And I could always give up Haringey's if it really took off.'

*

A nurse, her short spiky hair bleached white, paused on her way out of the ward. The corridor was quiet; just the occasional sound of a comedy programme. TCP hung in the air like a wet rag.

'You looking for someone special?' she asked.

I nodded. 'Room Ten. Becca Bradbury.'

'Oh yes - Becca. This way.'

I followed gratefully, Thomas trailing along behind.

She paused at the end of the corridor, pointing the way. 'There you go.'

'Thank you.'

Knocking, I poked my head around the door. The TV was chatting away, Becca watching it with half-shut eyes.

'Surprise!' I called.

'Mattie! Oh – lovely.'

'You weren't expecting us?' I kissed her cheek.

'Why? Should I have?' She switched off the TV.

'I told Alan.'

'You've spoken to Alan?' She grinned, her eyes a misty grey. 'Did he tell you then?'

'Tell me what?' Tilting my head to one side, I feigned ignorance. 'About the accident? Yes, of course - that's why we're here.'

'Well, yes. Obviously. But I didn't mean that.'

I giggled inanely.

'Mattie Payton, you're terrible.' Laughing, she patted the bed. 'Here, perch up. You too, Thomas.'

Thomas climbed up cautiously beside me.

Becca pulled a sad face at him. 'Bit silly, wasn't I? Running into a car like that?'

I pulled a box of Thornton's out of my bag, a huge silver bow adorning the lid, and gave them to her.

'Actually, it's me who's silly. I shouldn't have said all those awful things, and I'm really sorry. Here - my peace offering. They should help get you nice and plump. I trust you're eating properly now.'

'You're forgiven.' She picked up the box with her uninjured hand. 'God, this weighs a ton. I'm not supposed to lift heavy things, you know. It's bad for the baby.'

*

Rob, for once, arrived home just in time for dinner. He pushed open the front door easily, but had to struggle through the gap with an enormous bouquet of pink roses.

'Hi - I'm home.'

I rushed towards him, surprised, at his timing, and at the flowers.

'Rob!'

'Merry Christmas, Mattie.'

Long-stemmed hot-pink roses mingled with white oriental lilies and limonium, the cellophane held together with white ribbon.

131

'They're beautiful. Thank you, darling.'

Kissing him, I swallowed back my sudden tears. Warm tears, grateful tears, having been so afraid, so fearful, through all those lonely evenings, those unfulfilled nights, with tiny voices clattering in my head like the wheels of a long-distance train.

'Why the tears?' He wiped them away with his thumb.

I felt suddenly ridiculous. All those doubts, when all he was doing was working like a dog to keep the roof over our heads.

I smiled. 'I'm just happy. Ignore me - I'm being silly.'

Kissing him again, I sank myself completely into the familiar softness of his warm lips. But as we parted, he looked around. The house had become suddenly quiet.

'Where's Thomas?' he asked.

'Boo!'

He'd been watching from behind the kitchen door. Running up, he filled the hall with joyous laughter, a tiny ball of giggles.

Rob scooped him up. 'And Merry Christmas to you, too. I bet you're just the tiniest bit excited.'

His arms around his daddy's neck, Thomas nodded.

I searched for a vase in the kitchen, the aroma of grilled chicken and spicy paprika filling the air. Rob followed me in, Thomas on his shoulders, tiny hands gripping wildly at his chin.

'You have a good day, then?' he asked.

Filling a tall Dartington crystal vase with tepid water, I squeezed in liquid plant food.

'Good, thanks. We went to Sainsbury's, then visited Mrs Phelps, the lady I met at work. Then we went to see Becca in hospital.'

'Hospital?' he asked, shocked.

Embarrassed now at not having told him about Becca and Alan splitting up, I told him the whole story.

'I had a good day, too,' he said, twirling round slowly with Thomas on his shoulders. 'You remember the Foster's, Jack and Lizzie?'

'Yes?'

Arranging the roses one at a time, I stood back to admire my handiwork.

'Well, they've bought Megan Beasley's old house - up on the hill there.'

'Gorgeous. Lucky them. I didn't even know it was on the market.'

'A private transaction. The rumour is it went for a million and a quarter.'

'I'm not surprised. It's beautiful.'

'Daddy …' Bored, Thomas wriggled in his attempt to get down. Rob lowered him to the floor and he ran upstairs.

'Well, they're hoping to move in at the end of January. They want me to fit new carpet and flooring to the whole house. Isn't that excellent news?'

'It's fantastic news. Well done, darling.'

I wrapped my arms around him, pulling him to me, and we kissed slowly. His hand, finding the hem of my pale blue shirt, moved inside, gliding up and over my breast. My pulse racing, my body responded with a mad urgency.

But I pulled gently away.

'Sorry, but it's dinnertime and a certain person is not too far away. Anyway, much better keeping it for later.'

CHAPTER 13

CHRISTMAS Eve. The sky was a watercolour of pale blue, the sun a ball of orange. Thomas, dressed warmly in fleece and dungarees, was racing round and round the patio on his trike. I pegged the last tee-shirt onto the line, carrying the empty washing basket into the kitchen.

Quiet, cool air wafted in from the open door. Dirty washing was piled up on the floor. I split it into two piles - coloureds and whites - my thoughts on the previous night. A vivacious warmth, like ribbons of pink velvet, surged through me. We'd finally made love. Satisfied, replete, I'd slept afterwards like a newborn baby. Two months; never again would I leave it so long.

Picking out the whites, I pushed them inside the washing machine and poured in powder and softener, all the time smiling shamelessly. My decision, my wonderful decision made in the Sainsbury's queue had been fulfilled. I hadn't been taking my pill, had hidden the tiny green blister-pack in my bedside drawer.

I sighed, a long deep sigh, and switched on the radio. *Take That* were playing. Scrubbing the kitchen sink with a scouring pad, I sang along.

'If love is truth, then let it break my heart; if love is fear, lead me to the dark; if love is a game, I'm playing all my cards … what is love? …'

I stopped scrubbing. I needed something Christmassy. I needed my Christmas compilation. Joyous, loud, full of bells and tambourines and trumpets. I put it on every year. Rushing through to the dining room, I pulled open the CD drawer.

But there was a large gap in the usually full-to-the brim drawer. Puzzled, I looked again, couldn't decide what was actually missing. Where were they? Who could have taken them? There'd been no-one in the house, apart from Becca and Chloe. I wondered if Rob had had a clear-out while we were away in Edinburgh. I'd ask him. But I did find my Christmas CD, thankfully, and closed the drawer.

*

Pieces of Lego littered the floor. *Engie Benjy* was a murmur in the background. Thomas's tiny fingers busied themselves, designing, constructing, adding, taking away. I'd already fulfilled my female gender by assembling a bright red house, complete with blue swimming pool and jacuzzi, all set within the walls of a vivid green garden. But I was becoming sleepy.

'Well, I could do with a cup of tea. Would you like something to drink, darling?'

'Apple juice, please.' He looked up at me, one tiny hand brushing back the hair from his forehead. 'Mummy …'

'Yes?' I stood up.

'Have you founded Jeremy Bear yet?'

I was beginning to dread this question. Jeremy Bear wasn't anywhere. I'd turned over every single stone. He was the elusive Pimpernel, the real Nowhere Man; he had the Harry Potter of invisible cloaks.

I shook my head. 'No, darling, I haven't found Jeremy Bear yet. Sorry, I don't know where he can be.'

But I was rescued by a sudden knock on the window.

'Nannie! Grandpa!'

Jeremy Bear all forgotten, Thomas moved like water through a pistol. Somehow, I reached the door before him.

'Mum, Dad, Merry Christmas! We've been so excited.' I peered at the silver Audi TT parked beside the kerb. 'Very nice.'

'Thank you, love,' Dad replied. 'And Happy Christmas to you too.'

He pulled me close, his teddy bear frame filling the doorway, his checked shirt soft and warm, smelling of sugar lumps and cedar wood.

'Thanks, Dad.'

Thomas had his arms around Mum's legs, his head against her knees. I went to hug her.

'Merry Christmas, Mum.'

'Merry Christmas, love.'

Careful not to spoil her makeup, she planted an air-kiss onto my cheek.

137

'I was just about to put the kettle on. You must be psychic.'

Dad perched himself onto a barstool in the kitchen.

'Eeh, we've had a bit of a journey, haven't we, Winnie love? The whole country must be going away for Christmas.'

Mum, in red silk shirt and black trousers, sat beside him, her huge black patent leather handbag a carbuncle on the worktop.

'Well, we're here now, Ken. Mind you, it's a pity Amecia and everyone couldn't come too.' She looked round incisively. 'But then, I suppose there's not really the room, is there?'

Pouring milk into three mugs, I cringed guiltily.

'Well, never mind,' she continued. 'Maybe we can all go to Amecia's next Christmas. You haven't seen their new house yet, have you, Mattie?'

Knowing full well that my mother's memory is that of an elephant, I dismissed the question good-naturedly.

'You still taking sugar, Dad?'

'Yes I am, and yes, I know it's bad for me. But if you consider how good tea is, what with all the antioxidants and so on - well, if I didn't take sugar I wouldn't be able to drink it, would I? And then I wouldn't get all those yummy antioxidants, now would I?' He winked.

'Here you go, then.' I stirred in two sugars.

'Thanks, love. Just what I need.'

'Here you are, Mum.' I placed her tea in the small space not taken up by her handbag.

'Thank you, dear.' Sighing animatedly, she preened her perfectly coiffed hair. 'I don't know why we're sitting in the kitchen, Mattie, when there's a perfectly good sofa in the sitting room.'

I cringed again, childhood memories rushing through me like trains through a tunnel - the ink-scent of fresh newspapers and magazines, me walking in from school to the heavy aroma of lavender wax left by the cleaner, Mum always smart, Mum always on display, always preening …

'Sorry,' I mumbled. 'We just seemed to settle in here, didn't we? Let's go through, shall we?'

We made ourselves comfortable on our faded brown sofas. Thomas sat, cross-legged, on the beige carpeting.

Mum looked around thoughtfully. 'Not done much to this place, have you, love? I thought you loved decorating.'

I tried to smile, to brush it off. 'Well, we've not really had the time, what with one thing and another. Rob's going to replace this carpet, he just hasn't got round to it yet.'

'Where is Rob?' she interjected. 'At work?'

'Yes, Mum.' She'd always blamed Rob for my decision to leave uni and get married, still hadn't forgiven him. 'He's really busy, so snowed under these days we barely have time to breathe.'

At least Dad showed an interest. 'So, he's doing well then, young Rob?'

I nodded. 'He's out most evenings, sometimes even weekends. And he's got a fitter working for him now. The orders are coming in thick and fast. He's just been …'

'Nannie want to see Thomas's bedroom?' Rescuing me as usual, Thomas climbed onto Mum's lap.

'Mummy bought me a new crocodile. You've got to come and see. Please.'

*

The aroma of roast garlic, sautéed onions, peppers and tomatoes filled the kitchen. I added minced lamb, passata, and a cupful of red wine to create a lasagne sauce, piquant and succulent. Adding a few sprigs of basil, I divided it between layers of green pasta. A layer of cottage cheese whisked with egg, and a creamy white sauce sprinkled with finely grated parmesan completed my creation. I placed the dish into the oven, set the timer, turned on the radio, and poured myself a drop of wine. Then, composing a green salad with French dressing, I set the table. Cloth, cutlery, and candles. White and silver.

Satisfied, I dashed up to Thomas's room. To find Mum and Dad on the floor, playing Monopoly.

'You've got a whiz kid here,' said Dad. 'He's got hotels on Park Lane and Mayfair already, and he knows all his letters and numbers.'

Mum ruffled Thomas's hair. 'Clever boy, aren't you? But I'm spent up now and all my properties are mortgaged, so I think you've won. Anyway, what Grandpa and I need is a good cup of tea.' She looked up at me. 'I'll make the tea, Mattie. You just help me up off this floor, that's all I ask.'

'It's a deal.' I helped her up. 'Can I leave you and Grandpa to tidy away please, Thomas?'

'Er, just a minute now - who says I'm finished?' Dad replied. 'I've got some good properties here. I might just win yet.'

But he stood up, slowly, carefully, favouring his right knee and leaning one shoulder against the wall. I was filled with a deep sorrow, a gradual gnawing, knowing his ageing body would slowly but inevitably run out of time - a long corridor down which we both must run, and from which we could never escape.

Brushing the thought away like a silent, persistent cobweb, I smiled.

'I don't think you'd win anyway, not with Thomas. I don't know how he does it, but he does. Every time.'

But I should have kept my mouth shut, my thoughts to myself.

Unlike Mum.

'I told you, Mattie, he's been here before. He knows more than he's letting on. All this stuff he comes out with, about pink houses and children.'

I put a finger to my lips and shook my head, gently silencing her. 'You're just a very clever boy, aren't you, darling?'

He nodded gravely. 'Yes, Mummy. But Grandpa can win if he wants. It's alright.'

'Well, that's really nice of you, but we're just about ready for dinner. How about playing tomorrow and you can let him win then?'

He grinned cheekily, his voice a singsong of anticipation. 'Alright, but remember Father Christmas is coming. We might not have time to play Monopoly.'

We returned to the kitchen, a mess of dirty pans and scruffy spoons. Dad soon spotted the open bottle of wine. He squinted at the label.

'What's this, then? Rioja?'

'Rio - ka, Dad. You pronounce the jay as a kay. Sounds like mocha.'

'Oh, Rioja. Right. Well, it still tastes the same, I'm sure. Do you mind if we have a glass?'

'Of course not.'

The smooth liquid mingled with the warm cosiness of the kitchen as we washed up and tided away, and the conversation turned naturally to my new venture.

'There you go, Winnie,' Dad insisted. 'Always told you our Mattie would end up running her own business. Like father, like daughter. She may have left university too soon, but upbringing will out. My dad used to say that, you know. Upbringing will out, in the end.' Lifting his now nearly empty glass, he proposed a toast. 'Well, here's to you, Mattie, and your new business. Good luck to you, love.'

'Cheers, Dad.'

Mum sipped her wine carefully, inquisitively. 'Well, I must say I'm glad you're going to do something with your life, although it's not quite what I had in mind. But they say the best time to start a new business is in a recession. So good luck to you, darling.'

And I knew, as always, she meant it.

*

Thomas was in bed. Mum and Dad were in the sitting room, reading. I joined them, busying myself, plumping up cushions, tidying away toys, putting a match to the six orange candles I'd bought from the craft-shop in the village. As I placed them on the mantelpiece, careful not to put them too close to the mirror, the sweet scent of cinnamon and oil of orange filled the air.

'There - doesn't that look pretty?'

Mum smiled. 'Beautiful. Look at the reflection in the mirror.'

Dad grinned. 'You see, you need only have bought three. The reflection in the mirror would have done the rest.'

'Oh, Dad.'

'Mattie,' Mum said. 'About what I was saying upstairs. I don't think it would do any harm, you know, Thomas knowing he's been here before.'

I crossed my arms defensively. 'Look, Mum, he hasn't *definitely* been here before. No-one knows if anyone has *definitely* been here before. And anyway, if you want the truth, I was talking to someone on the train about it, on the way up to Edinburgh. He was quite an intelligent chap, and he did seem to think there might be something in it.'

She bristled. 'Did he now?'

'Yes. And, having thought it over, I think if Thomas is a reincarnation of anybody, then it's Grandma Beattie. He's just so much like her sometimes.'

'Oh no, I don't think so.' She shook her head. 'She didn't have a pink house. She did have two girls, admittedly, but the pink house - no.'

'She might have lived in one and just never mentioned it.'

'I suppose it's possible. But no, I wouldn't have thought so.' She studied her fingernails carefully. 'Although they did rent rooms when they first got married, so I suppose ...'

'They might have rented a pink house.'

But Dad interrupted. 'Mattie, love?'

'Yes?'

'I'm a bit thirsty. That whisky you were talking about earlier...'

I grinned, happy at the change of subject. 'Sorry, Dad, I forgot.'

I laughed and joked, pouring whisky for Dad, white port for Mum. Yet all the while thoughts of Rob's continuing absence nagged me. It was rude of him to stay away for so long; he knew my parents were here. So when the phone rang, I answered quickly.

'Hello?'

'Sorry, Mattie. Late again, I know. I shouldn't be too long now, be home about nine. It's my fault this time; I've gone and hit a pipe. Stupid, but not much I can do about it. I've had to switch the water off, just while the plumber sorts it. I can't possibly leave the Smithsons without water over Christmas.'

Hot anger burst through my veins. 'Rob, are you sure you're cut out to be doing this kind of work? You always seem to do something wrong.'

'Have faith in me, please, Mattie. It's these old houses. They put pipes all over the place in the olden days. Sorry, it can't be helped. Say hi to Ken and Winnie for me. See you later.'

'Bye.'

'Everything okay, Mattie? Was that Rob?' Mum asked as I walked back in.

Putting on my brave face, I nodded. 'He's going to be late. He's hit a water pipe and the plumber's sorting it out.'

Avoiding the astute look on her face, I poured us all another drink and tried to relax. Yet my mind was spinning somersaults. Dad rolled whisky around his tongue thoughtfully, succinctly changing the subject.

'But eeh, it's a lovely little lad you've got there, Mattie. Bright as a button, he is.'

'Yes, you're not wrong there,' Mum said. 'Reminds me of Mattie at that age. Well, maybe a *little* older.' My shoulders tensed dramatically as I correctly anticipated her next remark. 'It's a good thing he takes after you, though, isn't it?'

'Well, I'm sure Rob's doing his best,' Dad replied. 'He's building up a nice little business, by all accounts.'

'Although he has been coming home a lot just lately,' I admitted.

'Well, there's nothing wrong with putting the hours in. Did the same thing myself when I started out. Talking of putting the hours in, Mattie love, your mother and I are thinking of selling Grandma Beattie's old house. We've made money out of it over the years, as you know, but the Thompsons have given us notice, and we've had enough of all the trials and tribulations. People moving out, moving in, decorators, builders. So we thought if we sell up now, we can enjoy spending it.' He looked at me carefully. 'We thought we'd split the money between you and Amecia. Not that our Amecia needs it, mind.'

On the verge of tears, I didn't know what to say, and the huge lump in my throat threatened to explode.

'Oh, Dad ...'

'Now don't go feeling guilty or any of that stuff. You know we don't need the money, and it would help with your new business. So - no arguments.'

*

Ten o'clock. Two bulging Christmas stockings lay on the bed, one for Thomas, one for Mum; a ritual from my early teens. Pushing the sticky tape and scissors into a bag, I hid everything inside my wardrobe before going down to join Mum and Dad. They were busy

145

too, placing presents beneath the tree. I watched admiringly from the doorway. Mum always was brilliant at wrapping; it looked more like Aladdin's Cave than a Christmas tree.

'They look absolutely gorgeous, Mum. It must have taken ages.'

She smiled demurely. 'I do my best.'

Dad winked. 'She's offered to do the dress for the next royal wedding, you know, but they've not taken her up on it. Yet.'

I grinned. 'Look, would you two mind if I go up to bed? I know Thomas will wake us up at some ridiculous time in the morning, and I don't know about you, but ...'

'But where's Rob?' Mum's eyes narrowed suspiciously. 'You can't go to bed without him. Surely he should be home by now?'

My heart kept time with the hammer in my head. I glanced at Dad for support, but was sorely disappointed. 'Maybe the plumber took longer than expected. I'll ring him, find out what's happening.'

'Okay, love,' replied Dad. 'We'll get ourselves to bed, but let us know everything's alright, won't you?'

'I will.'

I slid into the kitchen, leaving them to mount the stairs. I didn't want anyone listening to this conversation. And the room was cosy, familiar, the wine bottle in the recycling box reminding me of last night's wine-fuelled passion. Recalling Rob's kiss, the touch of his hands, my anxiety ebbed away like waves at the seashore. Only to return the moment I heard his voice.

'Hello, Mattie.'

He sounded cool, calm. Too calm.

'Rob, where are you? You said you'd be home by nine.'

I didn't mean to nag, but sometimes my words, like new-born babies, have minds of their own.

'Sorry. The chap took absolutely ages, but it's done now, I'm on my way home. And don't worry about food, I stopped for a Drive-Thru. Be ten, fifteen, minutes ...'

And the line went dead.

Stunned, suddenly nauseous, I filled a glass with water and sipped. I could hear the tap upstairs running; my parents getting ready for bed. Busying myself, I emptied the dishwasher, but my heart was as heavy as the cast iron lasagne dish I returned to the cupboard. Guiltily, I reminded myself it was Christmas Eve and I had a beautiful and wonderfully excited child upstairs. I tried my best to cheer up, but tears kept springing to my eyes, rolling down my cheeks. Each time, I brushed them aside.

My tears were easily removed with a wipe of the hand. But the raindrops of doubt splashing the pavements of my mind could not be.

CHAPTER 14

A shriek, a screech, and Thomas scrambled onto our bed, all arms and legs and Blue Bear.

'Mummy-Daddy!'

My eyes fluttered open.

'Father Christmas has been! Mummy, look what I got.'

I pushed back the duvet and sat up, stretching out my bare arms. Shivering as the cold air hit, I snuggled down again.

'What time is it?' I asked.

'Dread to think,' Rob mumbled, burying his head beneath the duvet.

Leaning over to his side of the bed, I checked the clock.

'Thomas darling, you do know what time it is? It's five past five. The heating isn't even on yet.' Braving the cold like a female Ernest Shackleton, I sat up again, rubbed my arms, and smiled. 'Now then, what was that you were saying about Father Christmas?'

'Look what I got.'

Proudly clutching a bright red stocking embellished with Pinocchio characters, he pulled out a small bag that had at one time contained chocolate buttons.

'I've eaten them all. But look - I got a tiny teddy, and a Thomas Tank whistle, and a funny pencil, and a jigsaw, and chocolate pennies and ...' He pulled them out, one by one, piling them onto the bed, finally reaching into the bottom for the clementine. 'There.' He sighed with satisfaction.

'Well, you are a lucky boy. And you must have been a very good boy, to get all these presents from Father Christmas.'

I admired each and every gift, savoured every precious moment, even though I myself had filled his stocking only hours ago. The clementine pushed into the toe, then gold chocolate coins, toys, whistles and pencils dovetailed around each other, topped off with a soft toy, its tiny nose peeking out enticingly. Each and every Christmas the same, just as my own mother had done. Every stocking packed with care. With love.

*

Dad was busy loading the dishwasher.

'Right, love, are you sure I can't do anything else?'

Wearing an apron wrapped round the red woollen dress I insisted on wearing for Christmas, despite it now pulling in all the wrong places, I pulled the turkey tray out of the oven.

'Honest, Dad, I'm fine. You go and watch the film with Mum.'

'Okay, if you're sure now.'

149

I basted the turkey, replaced the tinfoil, and pushed the tray back in. Closing the oven door, I looked around, finding myself alone for the first time that day. Tired from lack of sleep, my mind began to wander, and the seeds of doubt already planted began to grow. I didn't want them, certainly didn't need them, but there they sat, arms folded, patiently waiting.

My head ached for other, more soothing, thoughts. Putting on my Christmas compilation again, I thought about the gaping hole in the CD drawer. I hadn't asked Rob about it yet; he'd been much too busy. But I would.

So I sang along, putting parboiled potatoes, parsnips and onions into the turkey tray, baby carrots, broccoli and Brussels' sprouts into the steamer. But my lungs became hard, constricted, separate beings, imprisoned by their own fear. Suddenly faint, I steadied myself, sitting onto a barstool and gulping in air. Breathing in slowly, deeply, to a count of one, and out to two, as I'd learned in Edinburgh, I began to feel better.

But a sudden anger replaced my fear. How could Rob do this to me? I didn't deserve all this. But - wasn't he merely doing his job - he could hardly leave customers without water over Christmas, could he? Anyway, where else could he have been? It was Christmas Eve, for goodness' sake. But this thought alone prompted another - unbidden, unwanted, a venomous snake at a midsummer barbecue. What kind of person would have their flooring fitted late on Christmas Eve?

I caught my reflection in the mirror on the wall. Pale, angry, my eyes were dark torrents of disillusionment. And suddenly, in my heart of hearts, I knew what I had to do. I had to ask him. Outright. But ask him what?

Just because Becca's husband had been unfaithful. And Enid's. Tossing back my dark, glossy hair, today like ribbons of silk, I smiled back at the doubting face in the frame.

*

Five pairs of muddy walking boots were parked up in the garage. We were tired, relaxed, having walked for miles along the river after lunch. Thomas was soporific, curled up beside Dad in front of the TV. Rob was piling toys and books neatly into a corner ready for tomorrow's onslaught. Mum made a pot of tea while I prepared a quick meal of turkey and cranberry sandwiches.

She sighed. 'You know, Mattie, it's a real pity Thomas only has us old people to play with on Christmas Day.'

I spooned cranberry sauce from a jar.

'Mum, don't start. Please. It is something I've -we've - thought about. But now is not the time, not just yet, not with my new business and everything.'

I bit my lip, my stomach churning at telling such a blatant lie, something I'd not done in years, not since taking the morning-after pill at eighteen. The pill, gleaned from a sympathetic doctor, made me so ill Mum threatened to take me to hospital. In the end, I'd had to confess. But the lying, the deceit, damaged our relationship for quite some time, making me vow to always tell her the truth, no matter what. But - how could I now? How could I tell her that even though my marriage might be on the rocks, I was already trying for another baby, and without Rob's knowledge? Especially Mum, who would only say, 'I told you so - you got married too young. I did tell you.'

'Well, don't leave it too late, you know.' She placed the tea-cosy over the pot. 'Thomas needs someone he can play with now, not when he's twelve years old and no longer interested. And as for the business, give it a year or so and you can employ someone else to do the hard work. Delegation, that's what it's all about. You ask your dad.'

'Yes, Mum.'

Tea was a quiet affair, Thomas picking at his sandwiches as if they were actually made of sand.

I sighed. 'Thomas, there's nothing wrong with the turkey. It's delicious. You can't just eat bread and cranberry sauce.'

'He's tired, poor love,' Dad murmured.

'He'll be all excited again in the morning. We're going to see Rob's parents - more presents to open.'

'We'll be off doing our usual Boxing Day Sales trip, won't we, love?' Dad patted Mum's hand affectionately.

'I just hope that suit's in the sale, and they've still got it in my size.'

I pushed a slice of turkey to the front of Thomas's plate. 'You eat that and then you can have some chocolate roll.'

'Had my eye on it for weeks, I have,' Mum continued.

'What's it like, then?' I asked.

'It's tweed, in a kind of caramel colour. It nips in at the waist - like this.' She stood, demonstrating with her hands, proud of her trim figure. 'And the skirt is straight, down to the knee. But it's just what I need, and just my colour as well.'

'What happens if it isn't in the sale, then?' asked Dad, winking at me. 'We've not got to pay full price for it, have we?'

'No, dear. I'll only get it if it's been reduced. But the House of Fraser sale is usually very good. They get rid of stuff so they can buy more stock for the New Year. Isn't that right, Mattie?'

I sighed. 'Dad, why don't you just buy it for her?'

'Well, we'll see. But it's that expensive she won't *tell* me the real price.' He glanced at Thomas. 'Mattie, love, I think Thomas needs his bed.'

Thomas was fast asleep, a piece of bread squashed between his tiny fingers. I stood, ready to pick him up, but Rob was there first.

'I'll bring him up,' he said. 'You go get his pyjamas ready.'

'Thanks.'

I put fresh pyjamas onto Thomas, wiping his face and hands with a damp flannel. He slept through it all. Holding back the duvet, I watched as Rob put our son to bed, cover him up, tenderly kiss him goodnight. My heart ached. Sudden tears threatened and a vicious lump formed at the base of my throat. Wiping my eyes, I looked down so my hair would hide my face.

But Rob, seeing the slight movement, caught hold of my wrist. 'What's wrong?'

'Nothing.' I pulled away, my voice sharper than intended. 'Why - should there be?'

He let go. 'What do you mean? Of course there's something wrong. You're crying, for goodness' sake.'

153

Wearily, I sat at the end of the bed, my thoughts spinning, round and round, a concentric whirlpool of emotion. How could I tell him all that was going on in my head? How could I? He'd think I was mad. I looked down at my son, peacefully asleep, one arm tucked around Blue Bear, cute and soft and innocent.

And so I began. 'It's just, you're never here at bedtime and we miss you. Thomas misses you the most. It used to take him ages to get to sleep, waiting for his daddy to come home and kiss him night-night.' I paused, waiting for a reply, but nothing came. 'But he's used to it now. He just goes straight to sleep.'

He sat beside me, taking my hand. 'I'm sorry, Mattie.'

I looked at him, wanting to believe him, wanting to see he really was sorry. What I didn't want to see was the sudden animosity written - etched - there, the narrowing of his eyes into tiny slits. Like poisoned arrows. What I didn't want to know was that, despite what had recently happened between us, the rosy hue that was once our marriage had turned rusty red, weak and brittle. My eyes searched his in desperation, hoping the look on his face would soften, become a figment of my imagination, be dismissed, forgotten. Yet it remained, as solid as the bed on which we sat. Unyielding. Immovable.

The sudden adrenaline pumping through my body had nowhere to go. My heart pounded. I felt sick.

Unable to meet my gaze any longer, he blinked and looked down, his face as chilled and smooth as ice cream.

He squeezed my hand. 'I really am sorry.'

Unable to believe it, I pulled away.

Anger curved his every movement as he stood up, his voice a stage whisper.

'Come on! You're being totally unfair, don't you think? You know how busy we've been. If I'd been able to come home on time, I would have done.'

My eyes searched for Thomas, my beautiful son, *our* beautiful son, long eyelashes forming shadows over his tiny button nose, and my throat tightened. I swallowed hard, looking up, saying the words I knew I had to say.

'I'm sorry, darling. You're right. I'm just being silly, I know. It's just that we miss you and …' I paused, my words choking me.

'And what?'

'It's difficult. I suppose what I'm trying to say is …' I shrugged as if to say it didn't really matter, that it was secondary to the real issue. 'I feel a bit left out too, you know. You don't seem interested in me anymore. It's all work, work, work.'

His jaw tightened. 'Christ, Mattie - don't land me with a guilt trip. It's bad enough being told Thomas is missing me without this as well!' He walked to the door, his back to me, his spine as straight as a rod. 'Listen, I'll try to get home earlier if I possibly can. I'll try to delegate more.' He turned round. 'Is that what you want?'

Weak with fear, I merely nodded.

Taking hold of my arm, he pulled me gently off the bed. 'Come on, let's get downstairs before your parents suspect something's wrong. Wouldn't want that now, would we?'

'Mm. But give me a minute. I won't be long.'

He left.

155

And as he left, the bedroom door made solid the barrier between us.

CHAPTER 15

IT was snowing. Again. We'd only just recovered from the November snow; traffic disruption, fuel shortages, leaking roofs, total chaos. And now, Boxing Day, here it was again.

Thomas watched from the sitting room window, still in his pyjamas. I stood beside him, thrilled by his questions, his innocence, knowing he would always remember this winter. His very first white Christmas.

'How big is the biggest snowflake? What happens when snow melts? Where does it all go?'

I too would remember this exquisite layer of whiteness. It would become a symbol of my new beginning, a blanket laying itself down upon my old life, before both melted quietly away. This I would recall at some time in the future, but today - today I had no future, my life shattered into tiny fragments, Thomas the only part that mattered.

When he'd jumped onto our bed that morning with his big, happy smile, I'd been awake for hours. But upon seeing him, the one thing in my life I'd done right, my melancholy lifted and I had to smile back. I'd looked over at Rob, still asleep, or pretending to be.

'Shush, don't wake Daddy,' I whispered, climbing out of bed. 'Come on.'

We scrambled downstairs to the kitchen. A white brightness leaked from the doorway, even though it was dark outside.

Thomas ran straight to the window. 'Mummy, look. Snow! It's snowing again!'

'Shush - come on - sitting room.'

Tiptoeing in, we opened the curtains and watched, fascinated, our breath forming small circles of mist on the double-glazing. I picked Thomas up so he could see properly. But as I did so, he placed his head quietly onto my shoulder.

'Are you tired, darling? Want to go back to bed?'

'No, I want to watch the snow.'

'What is it then, sweetie?'

He lifted his head and, his eyes as still as mountains, he looked directly into mine.

'You alright, Mummy?'

His dazzling intuition threw me for a moment; to gain time I brushed back his hair playfully. It bounced back into place like a jack-in-the-box.

'I'm alright. Just a bit tired, that's all. Come on, let's get some breakfast.'

But he wasn't a bit interested in food. Still in his pyjamas, he jumped down from the table and ran round and round and round, a toy aeroplane in one hand.

'Neeeyow!'

'Thomas,' I called, 'if you don't want your breakfast, why don't you go upstairs and talk to Daddy?'

'Aw, Mummy ...'

'Go on.'

'Okay.'

I had no appetite, either. Picking up my bowl, my cereal still uneaten, I carried it into the kitchen. Dad was there, making tea, his dressing gown a deep aubergine, his face a soft set of wrinkles.

He stirred at the teapot. 'How are you, love? You look tired.'

'Fine, thanks, Dad. Did you sleep alright?'

He watched me pour my cereal into the bin. 'What's wrong - not feeling well?'

'Just a bit tired, that's all.' Avoiding his gaze, I placed my bowl and spoon inside the dishwasher.

'How about some toast and marmalade, then?' He tapped the loaf of uncut bread with his spoon.

'No.'

'I'll make you some. You go and sit down. You've looked after us for a couple o' days, so now it's my turn.'

Silently, I obeyed.

Three minutes later two slices of hot buttered toast dripping in thick-cut marmalade were placed before me.

'There you go, lass - and the tea's mashing. Can't see our Mattie going hungry now, can we?'

'Thanks, Dad.' My mouth watered so much my ears hurt.

'It's my pleasure. Now - eat up.'

159

Smiling, he turned to go, but not before I saw the concern in his face. Not before I knew that he knew.

I grabbed hold of his hand. 'Dad?' The tears came now, hot and hungry.

'What is it, Mattie love?' He sat down, putting his arm around me. 'I can see you're upset about something. Come on - you can tell your old dad.'

So I wept into the comfort of his broad shoulder, the familiar scent of his crisply ironed shirt.

'Sorry, Dad.'

'Nay, don't be sorry, lass. That's what I'm here for, isn't it?'

He stroked my hair. The action was meant to soothe, to show how much I was loved, yet it only served to show me how much I was unloved, by Rob.

'Whatever it is, love, you know we're here, don't you? We're here to help, whatever's happened.' He waited for my reply, was disappointed when it didn't come. 'But you don't have to tell me if you don't want to. And yes, Thomas is upstairs, so you've no concerns there.'

I fished inside my pocket for a tissue. Wiping my eyes, I gazed at the toast and marmalade, cooling rapidly. I picked up a piece, nibbled at the edge, and threw it back down.

'It's probably all in my imagination, in my mind, I don't know.'

'Go on love, whenever you're ready.' He waits patiently, my dad, always patiently.

'It's just - I may be wrong. But I think - I'm not sure - Rob might be having an affair.'

'Oh.' He nodded, patting my hand, his reply careful, discreet. 'I'm sorry to hear that, love. But why aren't you sure? Haven't you asked him?'

'That's just it. I've tried to, but he won't talk, just pushes me away. That's why I'm not sure. But it all keeps - it just keeps spinning round and round in my head - until I think I'm going mad.'

He nodded. 'Go on.'

'He stays out all the time, comes up with one excuse after another. It's always the business - the business this, the business that. But nobody wants their carpets fitted on Christmas Eve, do they, Dad? And he never sees Thomas. You'd think he'd want to spend time with his only son, wouldn't you? And I know the business is important, but he's got Luke. Surely he could delegate if he really wanted to.'

I waited for his opinion, expecting him to be shocked, but was shocked myself when he wasn't.

'Mattie, love - I hate to say this, but your mother's had her doubts for some time now.' He watched me carefully. 'We didn't want to say anything, but ...'

'Oh, Dad.'

'The thing is, love, you need to set your own mind straight. Or you will go mad. I mean, what will you do if he is? Would you leave him, do you think?'

'I don't know.' Shaking my head, I backed away mentally, terrified of the trap I'd set myself.

But he continued. 'Well, then, let's assume your intuition is right. Let's assume the worst-case scenario, as you youngsters put it. Yes?'

I nodded.

'Right. If he is having an affair, then A - you can stay with him for Thomas's sake and to save face with

161

the village gossips. Or B - you can kick him into touch, take time to lick your wounds, and start over again.'

I was already wounded; the battle-scars were showing already. 'Oh, Dad, how could I?'

'If that's how you really feel, let's take a look at option A. You stay with him, never knowing where he is, always wondering and worrying. And he's no father to Thomas, who'll grow up living with deceit and lies. Thomas will have you both there - yes - but all he'll see is unhappiness. So - he'll grow up learning deceit and lies from his father, sorrow and pain from his mother. Is that what you want for your son? By taking option A, you'll have not only ruined two lives, but three.'

'I know,' I sighed. 'You're right, as usual.' Picking up my toast, I stared at it. 'But I don't know where to go from here. Where do I go? I don't know if I can cope without Rob. I'm not cut out to be a one-parent family.' I put the toast down. 'Even the name sounds awful.'

'Better to be a one-parent family than a two-parent 'not' family. That's what it would be, wouldn't it? No family at all. And at least you'd have Thomas. No court on earth would take him away from you.'

My hand flying to my mouth, a burning vision of hell opened up before me.

'Oh my God, I hadn't even thought of that. But no, Rob wouldn't want him anyway. If he doesn't have time for him now ...' Hot tears burned down my face. 'Poor Thomas. How could he do this to him? Doesn't he realise what it must be doing, not seeing his daddy for days at a time? He really loves him, you know.'

'He's a level-headed boy, Mattie. You've done well with him. He'll come through this - you wait and see.'

CHAPTER 16

JANUARY. My first day back at school.

Mrs Webster and I had an exceptionally busy morning, everything starting again for the new term. And there were two new pupils, sisters, who needed pegs and bags and labels. So by the time lunchtime arrived, I was ready for home.

I wandered through the village. Cars streamed by, visitors gazed into shop windows, and workmen removed Christmas trees from the walls and pavements. It was Twelfth Night, I realised. Reaching the greengrocer's, I picked out carrots, some mud-encrusted potatoes, a few apples, and some overripe bananas. My mind having been on other things, I'd forgotten to do my online Sainsbury's order again. I'd also thought about ringing Jenny for a chat and hadn't done that either.

But I had remembered to ring Enid; tomorrow would be the very first day of my brand new business. The thought sent tiny pearls of excitement rippling through me.

Old Mrs Fleming took my basket, greeting me enthusiastically, her eyes old and rusty, scarlet-red lipstick and nails her only adornment. But as she weighed the carrots, concern seemed to etch itself into her worn face.

'You alright, Mattie, love? You're looking a bit tired, if you don't mind my saying.'

Guiltily, as smooth as ice, I said, 'I'm fine. Thomas woke up extra early this morning, that's all. So excited about going back to school.'

'First day back, isn't it?' She weighed my potatoes. 'He's enjoying school, then?'

'He loves it. It is a very good school.'

'These village schools are, you know. I went to one as a lass. Just after the war it was, up in West Melton, near Sheffield. A grand little school. Mind you, it's been knocked down since ...'

That name rang a bell, loud and clear. 'West Melton?' I repeated. 'You went to West Melton Primary?'

'I did,' she replied. 'Why, do you know it?'

'My grandma went there.'

She placed my purchases inside a green carrier bag. 'Did she now? Well, well, it's a small world.'

'It would have been before your time, though. It was during the war.'

'What was her name, then, your grandma?'

'Beattie. Beattie Baxter.'

'Yes, I did know of some Baxters. Mrs Baxter – yes. Husband got killed, didn't he? My mum used to talk about it. All very tragic, it was.'

'That's right – a pit accident.'

'Mind you, if he hadn't got killed down the pit, he'd have got killed in that bloody awful war.'

I paid for my purchases. 'What a coincidence. Amazing.'

'It is, Mattie. It is.'

Weighed down by my shopping, I walked slowly. My eyes were focused not on my immediate surroundings, but on the fields rolling gently in the distance. A cloud of mist nestled there, pale and ghostly. Only an occasional tree, bare and lonely, broke the monotony. Shivering inexplicably, I pulled my scarf up over my mouth and forcibly lengthened my stride.

*

Still dressed in my coat and scarf, I slid an egg into moss-green olive oil. The frying pan was already hot, so it didn't take long to cook, and I made a sandwich with thick wholemeal bread, smothering it in tomato ketchup. Starving hungry, I ate greedily.

Warm now, and satiated, I removed my outer clothing, hanging my damp scarf across the hall radiator and my coat onto its hook, and made hot tea. It was only as I carried my cup into the sitting room that I realised I'd forgotten to take down the Christmas tree.

'Damn, completely forgot,' I muttered. 'Bad luck otherwise. And we don't need any of that.'

Pulling two cardboard boxes from the under-stairs cupboard, I paused at the doorway to gaze reflectively

165

at the tree, remembering my joy upon seeing it when we came home from Edinburgh, beautiful and proud. Looking at it now, its branches pale and spiky, its needles a dark green circle on the carpet, my eyes filled with sorry tears. Bits of silver foil hung like limp lettuce leaves, and a layer of dust lay across the tinsel. The coloured baubles and tiny wooden toys looked lost and lonely without the fullness of the branches to cradle them.

But the phone rang suddenly, startling me.

'Mattie Payton here.' I sat onto the bottom step.

'Hiya, Mattie.'

Amecia. My sister, her husky voice immediately recognisable. Always a magnet to the opposite sex until they realised she smoked thirty a day.

'Mecia, what a lovely surprise,' I replied. 'How are you? Happy New Year.'

Our sisterly ritual of ringing each other at midnight on New Years' Eve had long since died.

'Thank you, the same to you. Did you have a good one?'

'Not bad. We just stayed home, really. It's impossible to get babysitters on New Years' Eve.'

My stomach churned guiltily. I'd omitted to mention Rob had only come home at half past eleven. I had decided to confront him this time, but by the time he'd arrived I was much too tired, much too overwrought, and couldn't face an argument. Plus - my period had just started.

'Oh, we don't bother with babysitters,' Amecia was saying. 'We get the neighbours over here. They bring their kids round for a sleepover, and we party, party, party. Tremendous fun.'

Not quite in the mood for tales of how the other half lives, I changed the subject.

'We did have a lovely Christmas, though. Mum and Dad came over for a few days. Thomas loved it. Spoilt to bits, he was.'

'I know; I spoke to Dad last night. Speaking of which, Mattie ...'

'What?'

I listened to her breathe in deeply, and out again, and imagined cigarette smoke hanging in the air. A carcinogenic balloon.

'Well, I'm really ringing to see if you're alright, whether you need to talk or anything - you know.'

'No, Mecia.' Smelling a rat, my voice hardened perceptibly. 'I don't know.'

'Mattie, don't make this any harder for me. You know I don't mean to pry.'

'What are you doing then?'

'Alright, I'll come clean. Dad told me you and Rob are having problems and I ...'

'Did he now?' Fury rushed at me. 'Well, he'd no need! It's not your business, nor anyone else's, for that matter.'

'Mattie, calm down. Okay, he didn't exactly tell me. I guessed. We were just chatting and it was more his tone of voice. Dad can't lie, never could - you know that.' She paused, breathing in and out again. 'A bit like you, really. Oh, honey bun, I'm so sorry. I'm just worried about you, that's all. Please don't be angry.'

My anger turned immediately from red bull to blue kitten, and soft tears trailed down my face. 'Sorry, it's not your fault. I just - I'm not sure. Dad knows I'm not sure. Rob - he stays out so late - says he's working, but it never seems to ring true. And I don't know whether to believe him or not. But he won't discuss it with me, so what am I supposed to think?'

'Mattie, I'm so, so sorry. But, to be honest, you should be able to tell if he's having an affair, don't you think? I mean, I'm no expert on these things, but I'd imagine it would become a bit awkward - you know - in the bedroom department.'

'Thanks, Mecia,' I groaned. 'You really know how to come out with it, don't you?'

Her childish giggle took me back suddenly, to scrunched-up notes in school, warm cider behind the tree in the park, illicit squirts of Mum's *Coco Chanel*.

'Well, no point in beating about the bush now, is there? Come on then, spill the beans, sweetie.'

'Well, things haven't been brilliant. But then, I'm so tired all the time. I can't sleep, not with all this going on in my head. And Rob, he's working every hour God sends. Although -well, we did have a bottle of red one night, just before Christmas and - you know ...'

'Well then, things can't be that bad, can they?'

'Yes, but it was ages before that, and not much has happened since. And - I know this sounds paranoid, but I'm starting to think that maybe he was feeling guilty - you know? I'd kind of asked him if there was anything wrong, he said there wasn't, but then went and bought me the most gorgeous bouquet of flowers and took me to bed.'

'Oh. Now that does spell trouble. Flowers, when it's not your birthday.'

'Well, they were supposed to be for Christmas, I suppose. Oh, I don't know - I've been going from one thing to another, round and round in my head, and

168

coming up with no answer. Well, none that makes any sense.'

'Have you checked his phone?'

'I have. No names, no messages, no calls, nothing. And before you ask, I've checked his pockets as well. Nothing.'

'None at all? No messages or calls? He runs a business, for God's sake. In that case he must have deleted everything. Why would he do that?'

'It's called good housekeeping. I delete mine when I get a minute.'

'Mm, I suppose so. But, you poor thing, you should have rung. Why didn't you? That's what sisters are for, you know.'

I felt rotten. Amecia always manages to make me feel guilty.

'Sorry.'

'I've just had a thought. Doesn't he have a guy working for him now?'

'Why?'

'Well, he'd know if there was something going on, wouldn't he? I mean, if he's working evenings too, then Rob'll be working when he says he is. But if he goes home at six or whenever, then Rob's either doing the job on his own, or he's up to something. What do you think?'

Thoughtfully, I played with my hair, watching my reflection in the mirror. 'I've not really thought about that. Maybe I should get in touch.'

'Is he married?'

'Engaged.'

'Then it might be easier to ask her. I mean, he might not want to tell on his boss - it might get him the sack or something. But a fiancée might be a bit more forthcoming.'

'No, no, I wouldn't like to ask Lizzie - that's unfair - and anyway, I don't know her that well.'

'That's a pity. It might have set your mind at rest. So what exactly are you going to do? Just carry on, not knowing?'

'I do need to find out, don't I, one way or another? I mean, I thought we were happy - I mean *really* happy.' The muscles around my throat tightened like a noose.

'Don't cry, Mattie, please. God, I can't even begin to imagine you and Rob not being together. You even left uni to marry him.'

'Mecia - don't. I hope it doesn't come to that. I'm sure we just need to sort things out - maybe see a counsellor or something?'

'I really, really hope it works out for you, honey bun. Keep in touch, though, won't you?'

*

My long chat with Amecia had forced Rob to leave a message. Sighing, I pressed at the red button.

'Sorry Mattie - late home again - much too busy. Really sorry. See you later.'

Desperately unhappy, I ignored the Christmas tree. I needed to place an order with Sainsbury's before the slots were all full again. Switching on the laptop, I waited impatiently for the connection. Logging on, I booked a delivery slot, then searched for 'My Favourites'. Scrolling down the list, I ticked the box beside each item, missing out the things I didn't need and adding a few others.

Reaching the last page, however, I was surprised to read *Milk Tray 500g £4.99, Posy of Christmas Carnations*

£3.99. Then I remembered they were the ones Thomas and I bought for Enid. Realising for the first time that the list includes items bought in store as well as online, I scrolled down. There was the *Buzz Lightyear Chocolates Tin* - the one I'd asked Rob to buy for Christmas, when he'd used my Nectar card.

But if I was surprised by the chocolates and flowers, I was amazed at the last two items. These were a definite mistake. *Green and Black's Organic Luxury Assortment 800g £15.99, Bollinger Vintage Champagne, Grande Annee Brut 75cl £54.99.*

I deleted them hastily. Nice try, Sainsbury's.

CHAPTER 17

SPARKLING frost adorned the old bench. Small clouds jumped through the sky like iridescent frogs. I pressed the doorbell, rubbing my hands together against the cold, and silently thanked my mother for her passé gift of a black thermal vest.

Enid pulled open the door, smiling apologetically.

'Come on in, Mattie. Sorry, my dear, I was just in the kitchen. These old legs don't carry me as fast as they used to. Come straight from taking Thomas to school, have you?'

I nodded. 'Thought I'd make an early start. We've got to get this house on the market.' I carried Rob's old blue tool-bag and a tin of white emulsion into the sitting room, Genevieve watching my every move. 'This room only needs a bit of wallpaper and a quick lick of paint to brighten it up. But I've got everything in the car. Hope you like it.'

'Mattie, don't start now,' she pleaded. 'Sit and have a cup of tea with me instead. You must be frozen through.'

'Okay then, put the kettle on. But I'll carry on working, if that's okay.'

She smiled happily. 'I understand. It's just nice to have company, I suppose. I mean, I know I've got Genevieve, but it's nice to have human company. Getting a bit lazy in our old age, aren't we, Genevieve?'

Genevieve, curled beneath the radiator, stared at us demurely before stretching out and closing her eyes.

'We'll have a nice cuppa, then I'll pop to the village,' Enid continued. 'Thought I'd make us some jackets and a bit o' salad. I do love my jackets.'

'Sounds delicious, Enid - thank you.'

'Right then, that's settled. Good.'

*

It was too late, afterwards, to realise I should have been more careful. The stepladder wasn't high enough to reach such a tall ceiling; I should never have tried. Losing my balance, I fell back, pulling the roller and paint pot with me. So there I was, in a heap, my left arm throbbing like mad, Genevieve sniffing at me. Cursing, I pulled my phone from my pocket and dialled 999.

The ambulance was still there when Enid came running up fifteen minutes later.

'Mattie - oh, Mattie - I had this terrible feeling - I came straight back ...'

They carried me out on a stretcher. Frantic with worry, Enid questioned one of the paramedics, a stout bodybuilder-type with short ginger hair, his voice unexpectedly soft and feminine.

'She's okay, love. Looks like a couple of broken ribs, but she'll be fine.'

Distraught, she turned to me. 'I never should have left you on your own. What was I thinking?'

'It's my own stupid fault. I've spilt some paint as well.' I grinned through the pain. 'Good job I'd put the dust sheet down ...'

*

I was in a room all by myself, its large window looking out over fresh, green fields. I'd done my best to focus on an article in Hello magazine, but the painkillers they'd given me insisted I go to sleep. No longer able to fight them, I closed my eyes.

'Mummy, Mummy!'

I forced my eyes to open as Thomas barged through the door.

'Hello, darling.' I smiled, patting the bed. 'Come on - up here. Did they let you out of school specially?'

'Daddy came to get me.'

I hadn't noticed Rob in the doorway, the most beautiful bouquet of baby pink carnations and white oriental lilies across his arms.

'How are you?' he asked, placing the flowers onto the bed. 'I've rung your parents. They send their love.'

I indicated the flowers. 'Thank you, Rob, they're beautiful.'

'Here - we brought you some chocolates to munch on.'

He produced a large box of Green and Blacks Organic Luxury Assortment.

Suddenly I was awake. Excruciatingly awake. Coincidence? I stared at the box in disbelief.

'We called in at Sainsbury's on the way.'

174

Picking up the bouquet, I breathed in its delicious perfume in an effort to stop myself from spinning out of control, from drawing ridiculous conclusions, unproven, dark shadows of doubt. It had to be pure coincidence. Even so, I did feel slightly sick.

Rob sat down, the faux leather armchair creaking beneath him.

'I'll get someone to put them in water on my way out. How are you, anyway? We've spoken to the nurse - she says two fractured ribs.'

Nodding, I looked closely at my husband, shocked again at the sudden creasing around his eyes, the way he seemed to have aged suddenly.

'My arm and shoulder feel the worst. They really hurt. They'd have let me come home today, but I went a bit dizzy earlier, so they're keeping me in for observation. I'll probably be home tomorrow, though. Which reminds me - Sainsbury's are delivering tonight. Can you be there?'

He nodded. 'Of course. No problem.'

But Thomas was more interested in my chocolates. 'Mummy, aren't you going to open them?'

I broke through the sticky tape at the edges. 'Here, you open them, darling. Give one to Daddy.'

Nestling the box on his knees, he removed the lid carefully. 'Here, Daddy.'

I watched Rob pick a dark chocolate from the edge of the box. Without once glancing at the contents list. I had never, ever, seen him choose a chocolate without checking first - he loathed sugary centres. Confused, puzzled, I checked the list myself, picking out a chocolate almond.

'Thank you, darling.'

But Rob was not happy. 'You're in a right old state, aren't you, Mattie? How the hell did it happen? That Mrs Phelps said the stepladder fell over ...'

Still in a daze, I shook my head. 'I know. I was stupid. You don't have to say it. But they're really high ceilings in that part of the house. I could have done with a bigger stepladder. It just seemed to topple over. To be honest, I'm not sure quite what did happen.' I smiled ruefully. 'Poor Enid. I'm delaying the sale of her house.'

He shook his head mournfully. 'Just because she's a nice old lady doesn't mean you have to go round doing favours for her, half killing yourself into the bargain.'

'I'm not doing anyone any favours, Rob.' Anger settled onto me, spreading across my shoulders like a dark cloak of midnight. 'It's a business venture. Well, I'm not charging Enid, but it's good experience and she's introducing me to all her friends.' Taking a deep breath, I calmed myself, smiling gently. 'It's okay for you to have your own business, is it - but not me?'

'Come on, I've only got your best interests at heart.' Going to the window, he stared at the view before turning, acquiescing unexpectedly. 'Well, okay, if it's what you really want, then fine. But please don't go killing yourself. Thomas needs his mummy.'

*

Enid arrived that afternoon, bringing a bagful of luscious green grapes, pink carnations and a bunch of bananas.

'Bananas?' I queried.

'They're herbs, you know, full of tryptophan. The body converts it into serotonin, the feel-good chemical, so it helps you relax. They're good at reducing swelling, too.'

'Wow. I've never heard that one before.'

A nurse, brunette and petite, fussed around Enid as she sat onto the armchair beside my bed.

'Thank you, my dear,' she smiled.

The nurse picked up my carnations. 'I'll find some water for these, shall I? They're beautiful.' The scent of *Chanel No 5* filled the air as she walked away.

'How are you, Mattie? I rang at lunchtime but they said you were asleep.'

Munching on grapes, I gave her the grizzly details.

She smiled. 'Oh, you'll mend soon enough. Made out of rubber, you young things are.'

'I'm not so sure about that one,' I grimaced.

'Anyway, first things first.' She patted my hand. 'Now, you're not to worry about selling my house, because it'll keep. I'm better off selling it in the summer, anyway. People won't smell the damp so much, will they?'

Her sudden laughter was so infectious I had to hold my ribs. 'Don't, Enid. It hurts.'

'It's true enough, though, isn't it? I'm much better selling in the summertime, when everything's nice and dry and my geraniums are out.'

I felt awful, a silly girl who's taken on more than she can chew. Why is life so complicated?

'I'm so sorry, Enid. I only wanted you to get a really good price, and now look what I've gone and done.'

'Like I just said - don't you go worrying yourself. You've got enough on your plate without my house to contend with. Now then, the nurse said they should be letting you out tomorrow. But you're to rest, you understand? So now it's my turn to help you. Anything I can do, you just have to ask. You got that?'

I nodded weakly. 'Thank you, Enid. I can't believe it - what a start to the New Year.'

'Listen, it just wasn't meant to be. I'm meant to stay in that house for a bit longer, that's all, and maybe you're meant to have a rest. These things happen for a reason. Now, the more you stop worrying about it all, the sooner you'll get better.'

'I know.'

My eyes threatened to close again. I could have slept for a year.

'I'm not staying long, Mattie. I promised to call on old Beth, see how she's getting along. And she might be putting some business your way, when you're ready. So get some rest, and if you need me to collect Thomas from school or do some shopping, you just ask. It don't take me long to get in on the bus, you know.'

CHAPTER 18

MY mind soothed by painkilling drugs, I slept peacefully all that night and most of the following morning. The troubles of the past few months became tiny atoms of dust in the recesses of my mind; I felt able to blow them away with a whisper of breath.

But a gentle tugging of my hand startled me, and I awoke to find Becca, the aroma of warm food pervading the air around her.

'Hi, Mattie.'

Offering a weak smile, I tried to sit up.

'Don't get up. You need to rest. Sorry I woke you, but the nurse said it would be okay - it's nearly lunchtime.'

'I'm fine, Becca, really.' My body wanted to stretch out, my arms to reach up, but I knew it would hurt. 'I've had a lovely sleep. I feel quite refreshed.'

She smiled. 'I don't know, Mattie Payton, what are you like? First day of a new job, and you try to kill yourself.' Perching herself onto the armchair, she placed a gold heart of Thornton's chocolates beside me. 'These should cheer you up.'

Amazing what chocolate can do. I sat up - no problem.

So, giggling like two schoolgirls at an end of year party, we munched our way through the entire box.

'Becca,' I said, biting into a *Cappuccino*. 'I know I shouldn't be asking you this - particularly after what happened last time - and I don't want you to be upset. But I am genuinely curious. There must be something in your relationship that makes you think Alan will never stray again. What is it?'

A dark shadow fell across her face. 'The truth is - I don't really know for sure, do I? I mean, maybe when the thrill of the baby has worn off ...' She rubbed the smooth bump beneath her cornflower-blue sweater dress. 'Who knows? But if I can't trust him, then I might as well give up now. I *need* to be able to trust him, don't I?'

I lowered my voice. 'But don't you ever think about him - you know - in bed with *her*?'

'Of course.' She lowered her lashes becomingly. 'But he slept with other women before he met me - and vice versa. I don't think about that, do I? I try to think of it as a brief interlude, where we weren't actually married for a while. I know it sounds hard, but I have to put it into another box, compartmentalise it. And if I wasn't able to do that - to be honest, I'd have just gone to pieces.'

'Have you ever thought about marriage guidance - Relate or whatever they call it?'

'We have discussed it.' She reached for another chocolate. 'But at the moment, I don't want to push it. I mean, sitting there, pulling the whole thing to pieces with a complete stranger. And we're so happy together. It's like we lost one another for a while and now we've found each other again and, well, we realise what we'd lost.'

'That's so ... I'm so happy for you.' Shocked at the tears hurtling down my face, I brushed them away. 'Sorry. Must be the painkillers.'

'Mattie, what on earth's wrong?' But her mind was racing ahead. 'It's not you and Rob? Mattie, no ...'

I reached for a tissue. 'You'll probably think I'm going mad. I mean, I don't know anything for certain. It's just ...'

'What?'

'I don't know,' I sobbed. 'I - I think he might be seeing someone.'

Her eyes wide with fear, she took hold of my hand. 'Not him, too.'

'He's good at bluffing his way through it, though. He's late home nearly every night, says they're running late, they've damaged something, need to sort it out, or some other ridiculous excuse. But I don't believe him anymore.'

'Well, it could be true, you know. Don't let what happened to me affect the way you see things. Maybe he *is* snowed under at work. It's not easy setting up a business from scratch, is it? And in a recession?'

'It's not just that. He's different, doesn't seem bothered about me any more - I can't explain it. And he bought me the most enormous bunch of pink roses just before Christmas. The only time he's ever done that is before we got married. I think it's because I'd started asking questions - he was trying to put me off the scent.'

Doubt clouded her face. 'Have you asked him about it?'

'On Christmas Day.' I stared at my tissue. 'He didn't admit to anything, but then he didn't deny it either. Becca, I know it's not right - there's something ...'

She nodded. 'I know. I know what you mean. With Alan it was all cut and dried - no doubt whatsoever. But I can somehow see Rob wanting to have his cake and eat it too.'

'A good analogy. Considering the chocolates.'

'What?'

'The chocolates. He borrowed my Nectar card just before Christmas so he could call into Sainsbury's and pick up some bits for me. But well, on Wednesday I was ordering my Sainsbury's online. Did you know they put stuff on your Favourites' list even when you've bought it in the store?'

'Yes?'

'There was a bottle of Bollinger on my list. Bloody champagne, fifty-five pounds worth. And a box of Green and Black's Luxury Assorted Chocolates.'

'You think he bought them and used your Nectar card?' She shook her head. 'No, not Rob.'

'He won't know they put it all on your Favourites. *I* didn't until this week. When I saw it, I thought it was a mistake, so I ignored it. But then, in he came yesterday with a bunch of flowers and - and a box of Green and Black's Luxury Assorted Chocolates. The same make, the same weight, the same box, everything. He *never* buys the most expensive of anything. It's usually a box of Dairy Milk or something. But look, it's here,' and I showed her the empty box. 'Now is that coincidence, or what?'

She stared. At the box. At me.

'It could be, you know.'

'No. The more I think about it, and I have thought about it - more than you'll ever know - the more sure I am he bought these for someone at the same time as the champagne. And it wasn't for Luke, before you suggest it. He'd never buy a bottle of Bollinger as a Christmas bonus. In fact, I know he didn't. He put an extra thirty quid into his wage packet. Not exactly the last of the big spenders is Rob, so it must be someone damned special if he paid that much for a bottle of sparkling bloody wine.' The words hit me like a felled oak tree, and my face crumpled into hot, heavy tears.

Becca hugged me, her voice hoarse with grief. 'Mattie, don't ...'

'Ironic, isn't it? Just a few months ago, you were sitting there in your kitchen telling me just the same thing.'

'And I don't know what I'd have done without you. But, Mattie - you've no evidence, have you? I mean, he may actually just be working very hard. And he might have bought champagne and chocolates for a customer or something.'

'I know what you're saying but - it's just this gut feeling I have - you know?'

'I know. But look, I think you should ask him. Ask him outright. Make sure. Don't just sit there imagining things. It's not doing you or your marriage any good.'

183

'I know. It's just - I'm scared, Becca. What if he says he is having an affair? Do I really want to know? Because then it really would be over, wouldn't it?'

'Not necessarily.' Rubbing her tiny bump, she held her head high. 'Look at me, girl. I've been through hell and back, but look at me now. I've survived. Just.'

'I know.'

'Really, Mattie - you need to know. One way or the other.'

CHAPTER 19

ROB poked his head around the sitting room door.

'There we go. Thomas in bed, pots in the dishwasher. I just need to ring Luke and see how he's getting on.'

'Okay.' Unable to get comfortable, I wriggled around on the sofa. Moving a cushion, I pushed it behind my back. 'Would you pass me the remote first, please? This stuff's boring.'

'There's probably nothing on, anyway. Saturday night.' He handed it to me. 'You want me to get you a film from the shop?'

'No.' I hesitated, wondering at his real reason for wanting to escape. 'Thanks, I'm okay with the telly.'

'Right then, I'll just ring Luke, then I'll make us a cuppa.'

'Thank you.'

I waited patiently, just a few seconds, before lowering the volume on the TV. But I couldn't hear a thing. Silence. I couldn't understand it. He'd said he was ringing Luke. A gust of cold air brushed against me, and I realised the front door was open.

An ice-cold glove pulled at my heart. Suddenly knowing, suddenly certain, I bounded out of the room, all pain forgotten. Peering outside, the driving rain shielding my vision, I could see him in his van, the glow of his phone against his cheek, talking animatedly. I ran outside with only socks on my feet.

Yanking open the van door, I knocked his phone to the ground.

'You bastard! You absolute, bloody bastard! Who is she? Come on - out with it - I need to know!' I grabbed hold of him, pulling him out with a strength I never knew I had, pounding my fists against his chest like mallets, my voice hoarse with fear. 'I - want - the truth!'

'Mattie! Off!' He pushed me away, steadying himself against the van.

'Who is she, Rob?' I went to hit him again, but he held my arms.

'Steady on! You're supposed to be injured!'

Sobbing, the emotional pain so much greater than any broken ribs, I twisted free.

'Just tell me, Rob - just tell me. Who is she?'

'Come on.' He took my hand, his voice gentle, as if to a child. 'Let's discuss this inside, shall we? We don't want the neighbours knowing all our business.'

Back inside, I sat down, soaking wet and sobbing. 'Rob ...'

'Sorry, Mattie.' He hovered just inside the door. 'You weren't meant to find out like this.'

But I covered my ears, not wanting to know, not wanting to hear, even though I'd known, deep down inside, for months.

'Rob - no ...'

'I'm so sorry.'

He sat beside me, taking me into his arms.

'No.' I pulled away, my ribs screaming with pain. 'Leave me alone. How can you even touch me?'

Standing up reluctantly, he moved to the door. 'You wanted to know ...'

'Who she is? Who the whore is? Go on then. Who is she?'

'Mattie ...' His voice was a whisper. 'I - I can't talk to you like this. I need some air. I need to go.'

He left then, the front door closing with a click.

CHAPTER 20

THE empty space at my side was enormous, the throbbing in my heart gargantuan. I switched on the bedside lamp. Mascara stains trailed like a child's writing across my pillow. I rolled back, wondering desperately how to get through these next few hours, these next few days, this lifetime. I checked the clock - on Rob's side - to find it was still only five o'clock. I lay there for a while, staring into nothingness, quiet tears rolling down my face.

Suddenly angry, I sat up, straight as a rod.

'The bastard. How could he do this to me? To us?'

Struggling to breathe, I threw myself down again, my tears hot and hungry, and sobbed uncontrollably, dreading today. And tomorrow.

*

Thomas bounced onto the bed, Blue Bear tucked under one arm.

'Where's Daddy? Is he in the toilet? I didn't hear him.' He stared at me. 'You okay, Mummy?'

'Oh - darling ...'

Hugging him to me, I sobbed and sobbed, until the wife - the lover - in me took a step back, and the mother took her place.

'Sorry, darling.'

'It's okay, Mummy.' But dark concern filled his eyes. 'What's wrong?'

Wiping my face dry, I readied myself to tell the truth.

'There's something I have to tell you, darling, and you must listen because it's very important.'

His face crumpled in anticipation. 'What?'

'You do know Daddy loves you, don't you? Very, very much.'

He nodded imperceptibly, his small body tensing. 'Yes.'

This was by far the hardest thing I had ever had to do.

'Well - even though Daddy does love you very much, he doesn't love Mummy anymore.'

Tears rolled down the soft curves of his tiny nose. 'Yes, he does. He does, Mummy. I know he does.'

'You don't have to try and make me feel better, darling. You're a wonderful, very special little boy, and we both love you very much. But there's nothing you, or anyone else can do, to help.'

'Where *is* Daddy?'

'He's gone to stay with a friend. He doesn't want to live with Mummy any more, but I'm sure he'd still like to live with you, and maybe soon we'll arrange it so you can go and stay with him sometimes.'

He shook his head. 'No. I don't want to stay with him. He doesn't kiss me goodnight anymore, does he?' He pushed Blue Bear into my arms. 'And Blue Bear and me like to be kissed goodnight.'

'Oh darling, he's not always able to kiss you goodnight. He's been very busy working.'

'I don't think Daddy was working. I think he went to see his friend.'

Stunned, I was unable to comprehend. 'What?'

'You know - Sonia.' He tilted his head to one side enquiringly. 'Is that the person Daddy's gone to stay with?'

'What?' I asked again.

Astonished, astounded, I wondered what else he knew. I looked closely at him, my child, my son, my protector.

'I'm so sorry, darling. I didn't realise you knew so much about Daddy's friend.'

'That's okay. But I don't think she's a real friend. She's making you sad, isn't she?' He threw his arms around me, burying his head into my shoulder. 'Don't cry, Mummy - please. You can keep Blue Bear if you want. He'll look after you.'

*

Sleep being the wonderful healer it is, I awoke with a smile. I'd forced myself out of bed earlier, showered and dressed, but had fallen asleep again on the sofa. My smile faded, however, as I recalled, like a slice of midnight that refuses to become day, the previous evening. Groaning loudly, I sat up.

'Mummy ...' Thomas ran up, threw his arms around my neck and hugged me. 'I love you, Mummy.'

Tears rolled down my sorry cheeks. 'I love you too.'

'Don't cry.'

I looked around. The floor was covered in Lego bricks. Wracked with guilt, I checked my watch. Twenty past ten.

'You must be starving,' I said.

'No, I founded some chocolate biscuits, and look ...' Running back, he picked up a sheet of paper, holding it out to me, his eyes full of concern. 'I made you a picture.'

Beautifully drawn in cherry red and deep blue, the colours mixed in places to make purple, he'd shaped a beautiful butterfly.

My aching heart unfolded. 'Oh - Thomas.'

'It's a butterfly, Mummy, and a tiny chrysalis - here in the corner. Do you like it? I drawed it 'specially for you. It's you, Mummy.'

'No - it's *for* me, darling.' I corrected. 'But thank you, it's beautiful. You really are a clever boy. But, seeing as we've missed breakfast, what shall we do about food?'

He sat beside me, all grownup suddenly, his hands clasped together. 'I can do it.'

'Thank you, that's very kind of you.' I nodded gratefully, visions of burnt toast and spilt orange juice filling my head. 'But I'll help, shall I? How about Weetabix, then toast and jam? That'd be easy, wouldn't it?'

Jumping down, he took hold of my hand. 'Come on. I'm hungry.'

After eating, I took another shower, long and hot, and dressed in jeans and my favourite yellow tee-shirt.

I felt better, brighter, but every now and then the name Sonia floated before me, teasing me, hurting me. Killing me. I wondered where she lived, whether she was local or not. Surely I'd have heard the name before.

Restless, fidgety, I desperately needed company, but was not yet in the mood to talk - not to anyone. Suddenly, however, I wanted to ring Rob, needing to talk to him, to hear his voice. My heart pounding, I dialled his number, but there was no answer, not even voicemail. A greater part of me was relieved. It would have been a mistake - we'd only have argued. Putting down the receiver, I turned away, wondering whether to text instead. But suddenly the phone rang - too loudly - and I turned back.

'Mattie Payton speaking.'

'And how's the invalid?'

Becca. I wished I'd not answered.

'I'm fine, thank you, much better.' But my voice, still rough and hoarse from crying, betrayed me. Like DNA at a crime scene.

'What is it, Mattie? What's the matter?'

'Sorry - I must be starting a cold or something.'

But her disbelief cartwheeled along the airwaves.

'How can you tell such a blatant lie to me, Mattie Payton?' She paused. 'It's Rob, isn't it?'

CHAPTER 21

FASTENING Thomas into the rear seat beside Chloe, I kissed him goodbye.

'Thanks for taking him in, Becca. I really appreciate it. See you later.'

'No problem. Bye, Mattie. Take care.'

And her Lexus disappeared into the distance.

I closed the front door. The house was empty, silent, save the ticking of the clock. Rushing through to the kitchen, I turned on the radio, welcoming the banter of Chris Evans. Busying myself, I tidied away Thomas's toys and dusted and cleaned, completely ignoring the fact I was on sick leave. Becca had been amazing. I don't know what I'd have done without her. I hadn't been able to sit still for one second, could barely eat, could hardly think.

And my poor dad. Even though he knew we were having problems, he'd still been very upset. Mum too.

She'd been wonderful, offering to put us up for a while until I'd sorted out my head. Although it was totally impractical, with Thomas being at school.

Switching on the kettle, I pulled a cup from the drawer. Rob had ignored every text and every call I'd made. I had no idea where he was. He definitely wasn't at his parents' house, so I could only assume he was with this 'Sonia'. Could she be one of his customers, I wondered suddenly? If she was, and if Thomas was right about the name, then she might just be somewhere in Rob's accounts.

Switching on the laptop, I carried it to the table. Finding the accounts, I studied each name in turn, not really expecting to find anything. But then …

An invoice, addressed to Mrs Sonia Stephenson, The Old Bakery, Back Lane, Pepingham. Dated 28th August. Only a few weeks before Rob began staying out. Building up the business, as he called it.

I choked, anger tearing at my throat. I wanted to scream, to shout, to throw something. But there was no-one to throw at.

'The bastard …!'

But the peal of the phone interrupted me.

'Mattie Payton ...'

'Oh. Rob here ...'

Scared suddenly - of what he would say, of what he would do - my heart raced, my body trembled. Nauseous, I collapsed onto the bottom stair. Then a sudden anger flashed across my face like an untamed hurricane, black and relentless.

'Hello, Rob.'

My voice was solid, deep, a bottomless pit of strength. His was like a child's after being told off at school.

'I just wanted - I need to come over - pick some things up. And I need my laptop - for work. If that's okay.'

'What?' The untamed hurricane was unleashed. 'What did you just say? You need to come over and *pick some things up*? You've left me here all weekend, not knowing where the hell you are, ignoring my texts, my phone calls, while I'm wondering what the hell's going on! And now you want to come over and *pick some things up*? Pardon me, Rob, but I think there's slightly more to do here than pick some things up!'

'Mattie - I - I'm sorry. I didn't know what else to do. It's difficult.'

'Too right it's difficult. But you know what's really difficult? Having a husband who goes off with another woman every night and can't even tell the truth. Not to his wife or his precious son. Not that you'd know what the word precious means. And you know what else is difficult, Rob? I really loved you. Completely. Utterly. I gave up uni for you - my career, everything. And how do you repay me? By going off with some tart. What is it? She rich or something? Or does she think *you're* rich because you run your own business? There's got to be some kind of attraction ...' I paused for breath.

'Mattie, calm down. I'm sorry. Listen, I'm coming over for my stuff tonight. And - I'd like to see Thomas as well.'

'Oh, no. Oh, no. Thomas will be fast asleep in bed, I'll make damn sure of it. If you couldn't be bothered to see him at bedtime before, then you sure as hell aren't going to see him now. And you can forget about custody as well. I'll fight you tooth and nail.'

'I won't take him off you. I wouldn't do that. I know he needs his mother. I just wanted to see him, that's all.'

'You can come and get your things.' The tears came then, thick and fast. 'I'll pack them for you. But I don't know about Thomas. I'll see ...'

*

The doorbell awoke me from my slumber on the sofa. I stretched out, checking my watch. Twelve-fifteen. Lunchtime.

I opened the door.

'Emma.' I grinned, pulling at my hair, a tousled mop of sleepiness. 'What a nice surprise. Come on in, it's lovely to see you.'

'Did I wake you up? Sorry. I should have rung, but it was really a spur of the moment thing. Here, I've brought you some flowers - from me and Andrew.' She handed me a beautiful posy of freesia, carnations and roses, set amongst green tissue paper and tied with string.

'They're gorgeous, Emma - thank you.' I hugged her. 'But come on through. Would you like a coffee or something? I'm ready for one - I'm not sleeping that well at the moment. My ribs hurt every time I turn over, so I snatch an hour or so whenever I can.'

'Coffee would be lovely, thanks. I've got permission to take as long as I like. Andrew's covering for me.' Perching herself onto a barstool, she looked around. 'Mm, nice kitchen.'

I filled the kettle. 'Thank you. It's just as we bought it really, not done much at all.'

196

Cupping her chin with her hands, she placed her elbows onto the worktop, her eyes dancing cheekily. 'So - how are you, anyway?'

'Getting there.' I spooned coffee out of a jar. 'Feeling much better than I was, though. Biscuit?' I offered her my tin of chocolate gingers.

She picked one out. 'Rob been waiting on you hand and foot, then?'

I froze stupidly.

'What? What is it?' she asked.

Warm tears flooded my eyes, great big globules of water.

'Come now, lovey, don't cry.' Placing her arm around me, she sat me down. 'You rest, I'll finish the coffee.' Quickly, she made two fragrant cups of coffee. 'Now then, tell me all about it. But only if you want to. I'm not the nosey cow everyone thinks I am.'

*

The doorbell rang again at six o'clock. Busy in the kitchen, I stood, frozen to the floor, fear clutching at my stomach. The thud of Thomas's feet running downstairs echoed through the house.

'It's Daddy!'

I shook myself. 'I'll get it. You go and play in the garden.'

'No, Mummy.'

I pushed him gently outside. 'Please do as I say. You can see him later.'

Opening the front door took all my strength, and not only because of my sore ribs. Rob, still in work-jeans and trainers, stepped inside.

'Hi.'

Unsure of himself, he stood there, his hands clutching an empty holdall. I crossed my arms like an old fishwife.

'So, you can finish work on time now, can you? Running out of customers, are we?'

He stared at the floor. 'Sorry. Sorry about everything. It wasn't meant to turn out like this.'

I recalled Becca's words - *I can somehow see Rob wanting to have his cake and eat it too.*

'Just how was it supposed to turn out, then? Were you supposed to have a quick passion-filled fling with your floozy before returning home to your cosy little nest? To your nice little wifey? Was that it?'

He shook his head. 'Mattie, I wouldn't have hurt you - not for the world.'

'Really? That's a pity because, believe it or not, you have. Now, get your stuff, say hello to Thomas, and get out. Your fancy piece - Sonia, isn't it? - will be waiting with your slippers nicely warmed, no doubt.'

He turned, shocked. 'How do you know?'

I smiled, mentally scoring a 'tick' on the chalkboard.

'I know her name, that's all. And that's all I want to know. But I *can* tell you that any woman who can take another man's wife is not worth all this. Tart!'

Shamefaced suddenly, his shoulders drooping, he picked up his suitcase and laptop, already packed. 'Thanks for doing this. You've saved me a job.'

'I didn't do it for you. I just wanted you to be in the house, and out again. Oh - and I'm changing the locks, so please don't try to get in while I'm out.'

'There's no need for that. I won't be a nuisance.'

'Too right you won't.' I blinked back my tears. 'If you want to see Thomas, he's in the garden.'

Leaving the cases in the hallway, he went outside. A short while later, they came in together, Thomas's tiny hand curled inside his father's.

'Mummy, is it alright if Daddy gets to see me sometimes? When I'm not at school? Will it be alright?'

'I'll see what the solicitor says about access.' I glared at Rob. 'But this is for Thomas, not you.'

'Does that mean he can, Mummy?'

He looked up at me, and my heart creased with pain. Such a beautiful child. How could any man do this to his own son?

'Yes. We'll have to work something out, won't we?'

Rob picked him up, tears in his eyes. 'Thanks, Mattie. I won't make it difficult for you, I promise.'

'More than you already have, you mean?' My own tears felt dry and bitter. 'We could have had everything, you know - the whole world. But you had to spoil it, didn't you? Was I just not good enough?'

'We can't discuss this here. Come on, Thomas, it must be your bedtime soon. Time to say night-night.'

Kissing his forehead, he lowered him gently to the floor. But Thomas, suddenly realising the finality of it all, clung to his legs, his eyes bright and shiny.

'Daddy! I don't want you to go! Daddy!'

I pulled him away, my tears huge, thick spoonsful of syrup. 'Come on, darling. Daddy's got to go, but you'll see him again soon.'

'No, Mummy! No!'

Picking him up, I hugged him to me, my arms around his legs as they kicked out. 'Go on, Rob. Just go.'

He nodded briefly, his face shiny with tears. 'Sorry …'

So I watched him leave, taking with him his bags. And my heart.

CHAPTER 22

DAD pulled me close, and I was a little girl again, safe, secure.

'My goodness me, lass, what a time you've had,' he murmured.

Mum wheeled the suitcase from the car. 'Shall I take this up to the spare room?'

'I'll do it later, Mum. Just leave it there for now while I put the kettle on.'

'Here, I thought you might like this.' It was a Morrison's carrier bag, flat and folded. 'I found it when we were clearing out the loft at Grandma Beattie's.'

Curious, I peeked inside, pulling out a pile of papers, the edges yellowed with age. 'It looks like some kind of diary.' I glanced through the first page. 'It's Grandma Beattie's?'

'There,' she beamed. 'I knew you'd like it.'

'Thanks, Mum.'

'It was at the bottom of that old trunk in the corner of the loft. Not touched in years, by the looks of it. And to think of all the tenants we've had in since she died - it could so easily have been thrown out.'

'I can't wait to read it.'

'Mattie love, how about that there cuppa?' Dad closed the front door behind him. 'Tell you what, I'll do it. You rest - get yourself back on your feet.'

'Honest Dad, I'm fine. I'm better off keeping busy.'

'Now I can understand that.' As I made tea, he studied the paintings on the cupboard doors. 'How's young Thomas doing? Can't be easy, especially him being a boy. Boys need their fathers.'

'He's managing. He does miss him, though. We need to sort out some kind of routine so he can see him regularly.'

'I'm so sorry it's come to this,' Mum said, sitting down and re-applying her lipstick. 'But you're a strong girl. When one door closes, another opens, you know.'

'I know.'

'We're a strong lot altogether, us Sedgewicks. Look at my gran - left all on her own when her husband died down the pit. Life wasn't easy for a woman on her own in those days. And she had your Grandma Beattie and Great Aunt Matilda to look after. If she could do it then, Mattie, you can do it now.'

'There's one thing I've never understood about that. Why didn't Great Grandpa have to go and fight in the war, like everyone else?'

'Well, miners were still needed, you see. The coal helped make steel for the ammunition and planes. After he died, Gran had to go and work in the glass factory to earn money. Not something she was used to, not by any means. And even then, after the war ended, she had to sell their beautiful home. Great Grandpa's dad had left it to them in his will - he was a market gardener, you know. Very well to do, he was.' She preened her hair.

'It didn't happen to be a pink house, did it, Mum?'

'Do you know, love, I've asked myself the very same question. But I have no idea. All I do know is it was a beautiful cottage, and it broke her heart having to sell it.'

I was enthralled. I've always loved hearing about my ancestors, but this time the story acted like soft polish on wood, refreshing me, enthusing me.

'She must have gone through hell, mustn't she? It's not as if he was killed outright, is it?'

'No, love. He was in hospital nearly two years before he died - practically paralysed, he was. His brother Joe, too - your great uncle - same thing. Uncanny how it happened. Both of them injured the same week, but in different pits. Spinal injuries. They lay in hospital together, side by side. Grandad was moved to Nottingham after Uncle Joe died. Their mother lost two sons. Such a sad time.'

'Dreadful.'

'And Gran not only had to look after Mum and Aunt Matilda, she had to travel all the way to Nottingham to visit her Benny each weekend. And she didn't drive, you know - it was all buses and trains.' She smiled, memories flashing across her face like doves in the wind. 'She used to tell me, when I was little, how they'd play Monopoly in hospital for hours on end. It was only just out, you know. Brand new game, it was. That's where I think Thomas has got it from.'

'What?' Puzzled, I shook my head.

'All this playing Monopoly.'

'But he never knew them. How could he have picked it up?'

'You know what I'm talking about, Mattie.'

'Oh – right. Reincarnation. Only don't go telling Thomas, will you? It's not something I want to worry him with.'

'What do you take me for? You've already asked me not to. What time's he home from school?'

'Becca's bringing him home, so it'll be just before three. She's been amazing, Mum.'

'I know, love – a true friend.'

I stirred at the teapot. 'Well, I suppose if I'm going to be following in Great Gran's footsteps, I might have to set up in business sooner than expected.'

'It's to be hoped Rob will be paying some maintenance,' said Dad. 'But you won't need to worry about the mortgage. You can buy Rob's share and pay it all off with the money from Grandma Beattie's house.'

'Thank you - both of you. I am *really* grateful. But I don't know if I want to keep this house. Too many memories at the moment.'

'Well, we'll see. There's a lot of water to go under the bridge yet, love. But you know - if you need any help with anything …'

'As it happens, Dad, do you think you could help me with the business side of things? You know, like registering the company and advertising - that kind of thing?'

'Eeh, you don't need to ask twice, love. You know I'd love to help. Anyway, I'd enjoy it – it'd get my brain going again. Wouldn't it, Winnie?'

*

Tired, exasperated, my teeth were gritted together like glue.

'Thomas, eat up your fish fingers. Then Grandpa might just read you a nice story.' The phone rang suddenly. 'Mum, would you mind feeding Thomas for me?

Picking up the receiver, I sat onto the bottom stair.

'Mattie Payton here.'

'Hi, Mattie, it's Annie Murdoch.'

Annie with the black umbrella, from the playground. I smiled.

'Annie – how are you?'

'Fine, thanks. I'm just ringing to see how you are - I heard about the accident.'

I tried to make light of it. 'I know. Stupid or what? It's only a couple of fractured ribs, though. I got away with it quite lightly, I think. I could have broken my arm, and then I'd have been in trouble.'

'Well, at least you're cheerful enough. Mrs Webster told me about it this morning, and I wondered if you needed help taking Thomas into school or anything.'

'That's really good of you, but a friend's taking him in for me.'

'Oh, right. So - second question. When do you think you'll be up and about again?'

'I'm not sure, really. Why?'

'It's just - your offer of helping with the jumble sale. We've got one coming up in February and I wondered

205

whether you'd like to help out. It'd be brilliant if you could.'

This was just what I needed – to get involved, to help someone else. Instead of everyone helping me. I smiled.

'That's brilliant, Annie. I'd love to. I should be fine by then. I've a friend who might like to help out as well - if that's okay.'

'The more the merrier, I say.'

*

I rang Becca about the jumble sale. Thrilled, she agreed to help immediately.

But there was something else I needed to know.

'Becca, do you happen to know anyone in your village called Sonia Stephenson? She lives at The Old Bakery?'

'Sonia Stephenson? Well, I've heard her name mentioned once or twice, and I know the address. Why?'

'What do you know about her?'

'Well … oh, it's not *her*, is it?'

'I found an invoice dating back to August.' My voice cracked suddenly. 'I think it's been going on all that time.'

'But how do you know it's her?'

'Thomas told me. Children know so much, you just don't realise, do you? He might have overheard Rob talking to her - maybe - I don't know. But August is when he started working late, so it all fits in.'

'I'm so sorry, Mattie.'

I swallowed back the huge lump in my throat. 'Come on then, what's she like?'

'I only really know what I've heard. I know she's been married, I think for quite a while. But she got divorced recently.'

Surprised, I'd expected her to be young. 'How old is she, then?'

'Not young, that's for sure.'

'I thought she'd be a spring chicken, Becca – not some old boiler. I wonder what the attraction is, then?'

'Mattie, please don't go torturing yourself. It's Rob's problem, not yours.'

'So - what else do you know?'

'Mattie ...'

But I insisted, the force of a tsunami behind my teeth. 'Becca, I need to know. Please.'

'Well, she was married to a lorry driver.'

'A lorry driver?'

'Yes.'

'It's not her money he's after, then?'

'Cynic. Careful now - don't get all bitter and twisted.'

'Sorry.'

'Having said that, there is money there. She was left some kind of inheritance in her early twenties. She's always jetting off somewhere or other. She moved into Pepingham when she got divorced - I suppose it'd be about June last year - and that's when all the gossips started. I'd never heard of her before that.'

'Have you seen her? Do you know what she looks like?'

'Lizzie Woodhead pointed her out to me once, at the Village Gala.'

'Well - go on then. Describe.'

'You *are* going to torture yourself.'

'I'm not, I just want to know. Please, Becca.'

'Well, I wouldn't be lying when I say she's nothing like you to look at. You are such a beauty, Mattie. Long dark hair, those *lovely* blue eyes ...'

Exasperation made me frantic, a snake hungry for food. 'I want to know what *she* looks like?'

'Well - lots of wrinkles ...'

'Becca - the truth!'

'Really, it *is* the truth. Too much sun, I think. Top heavy, too. Her boobs were on display for all to see, couldn't exactly miss them. But I suppose she's attractive in a tarty kind of way, nice clothes and all that. She probably has men queuing at the door. Rob won't be the first, and he probably won't be the last.'

'So she's taking him for a ride.'

'Don't go feeling sorry for him. He's made his bed and he must lie in it.'

'What a waste. He had everything, and he's given it all up for that – that tart.'

'You *are* torturing yourself.'

'Becca, you're a wonderful friend, but I truly believe if they can do it once, they can do it again. I know you've forgiven Alan and I pray he never does do it again. But I really can't forgive Rob. I'd never be able to trust him, not ever. So it's over. I know it.'

CHAPTER 23

Baslow, Derbyshire

SUNDAY morning, two weeks later. What happened during those two weeks, I shall never know.

The ancient Grandfather clock chimed eight o'clock. Looking round at the heavy, old-fashioned furniture, dusty from two weeks of neglect, at the old clock ticking away behind me, at the magnificent pink orchids on the sideboard, newly brought from the supermarket, I sighed with pleasure. How I loved growing up in this house.

Then I recalled the many times I'd been chastised - here in this very room - for being naughty. The times Amecia and I had been made to sit on chairs at opposite ends of the room, forbidden to make a sound. For half an hour. Pure torture. We'd resort to sign language, giggling silently, unreservedly, until Mum came out of the kitchen, nearly catching us at it ...

As if reading my thoughts, Dad smiled. 'Glad you came back home with us, love?'

'Yes, thanks, Dad. It's doing me the world of good. I'm pretty much worn out from doing up Enid's place.'

'I know, love, I can tell.'

'It is looking good, though. Even if I say so myself.'

'Well - once it's done, you'll be able to start earning some real money.'

'That's true. Can't wait ...'

We'd awoken to sparkling frost and sunshine, to the scent of fresh coffee and toast. We ate breakfast in the dining room with the French doors ajar, to the sound of birds singing, the promise of Spring on its way.

Thomas ran outside as soon as we'd finished eating. It was only after he'd gone that I noticed his sweater on the chair.

'Look at that - Thomas's fleece - and it's chilly out there. I'll just pop it out to him.' Snatching it up, I ran outside, searching for him, calling him.

I'd always loved that garden. Huge, sprawling, unkempt. A child's paradise.

Suddenly, I caught sight of Thomas - a brief glimpse as he brushed past the red berries of the holly hedge. 'Thomas, your fleece,' I called.

Following him into the orchard, its trees knotty and bare, I called again. 'Thomas! Thomas - it's naughty, running away like this. What have I told you before?'

There was a giggle, then footsteps.

'Thomas ...'

I ran through the orchard into the clearing at the end of the garden, pausing at the old grey summer-house, now sad and neglected. Dead leaves and branches crunched beneath my shoes.

Pausing to catch my breath, I listened carefully. But there was only a deathly quiet. A snowflake tumbled down, all by itself. Then, the sweater still dangling from my fingers, I thought I heard something. I thought at first it was a radio, yet knew it couldn't be; the house was surrounded by woodland. Then it became louder for a second, and I caught what I thought was music. Yes, I was sure now. It definitely was music. It had to be a radio. But no, I decided. It was more like someone singing. A young girl. Singing.

There's a yellow rose in Texas, that I am going to see ...

Suddenly, there was the distinct scent of apple blossom perfume. No, it wasn't my imagination. It really was there, surrounding me, enveloping me. Sweet and memorable.

Grandma Beattie's perfume.

The snowflake. She'd always loved the snow, could never wait for it to come.

I expected to feel afraid, was surprised when I wasn't. At peace suddenly, calm, my mind was as still and solid as a rock, lapped by waves at the seashore. And I knew, implicitly, as sure as I could feel the blue fleece dangling from my fingers, that everything would be alright, that my beloved Grandma was there. That she was taking care of me.

The gentlest whisper of a strong but feminine laugh confirmed my insight. And I wept softly at the knowledge.

Reluctantly, slowly, my heart as light as helium, I returned to the house. Thomas was already there, in the kitchen.

'Thomas, where were you? That was naughty, running away like that.'

211

'Sorry, Mummy.' But his cheeky smile gave him away.

'I should think so. I only wanted to give you your fleece.'

Mum was busy, scraping cake mixture out of the Kenwood bowl, flavours of sugar and vanilla wafting gently through the air.

'Thomas,' she chastised. 'You must do as Mummy says, you know. It's naughty not to come when she shouts. It could be about something very important.'

His face crumpling, he began to cry. 'Sorry, Nannie.'

I hugged him to me. 'I think you've had your own way a little too much just lately, haven't you? Well, never mind - it's probably just what we both needed. It's not been easy, has it?'

Mum passed him the bowl and spatula. 'Here, Thomas, you can lick this clean for me.'

The tears all gone, I watched him scrape the bowl clean.

'Mum?' I asked.

'Yes?'

'Did Grandma Beattie like coming here, to our house?'

'She loved coming here. She and Grandad used to come all through the summer holidays, and at Christmas. They looked after you and Amecia when you were little, so Dad and I could run the shop. Don't you remember?'

'I think so ...'

I could vaguely remember ice cream and strawberry sauce and paddling in the stream, holding tightly onto Grandad's hand.

'Why do you ask?' she said.

'Oh - I just wondered.'

'Have you read her diary yet?'

'No, I've not really had time. But I will when we get back.'

CHAPTER 24

Folksbury, Lincolnshire

BORED silly, I actually relished the ringing of the phone. It was the second week of February and the temperature was minus three. People were sitting beside their fires, cosy and warm, instead of looking around houses.

Mrs Witheringham's taut tones echoed down the line. 'Hello, Mrs Witheringham here, of Tall Trees.'

I groaned inwardly. 'Good morning, Mrs Witheringham. How are you today?'

'Very well, thank you. Would it be possible to speak to Emma?'

'Sorry, she's off sick. Can I help at all?'

'I'm just ringing to see what's being done about my survey for The Cottage. I've not heard a thing in ages.'

'I'll just take a look for you.' I quickly checked the notes for her property. 'Emma's been onto the solicitors a couple of times now, but they're still chasing it up, I'm afraid.'

'It's just not good enough, tell her. My solicitors are all ready to go. Could you ask her to ring as soon as she gets back?'

'I will. It'll be tomorrow, hopefully.'

'Well, thank you for your help.'

'Thanks for your call, Mrs Witheringham. Goodbye now.'

Pleased I'd got away with it so lightly, I checked my watch for the millionth time. It was hard to believe it was only five to eleven. Time for another coffee. Obviously.

But I'd only just put the kettle on when the doorbell clanged. Poking my head out of the kitchen, I was delighted to find Enid standing there, her scarlet beret and shiny red shopping bag brightening up the freezing cold day.

'Enid, what a lovely surprise. Tea or coffee?'

She grinned. 'Must have been able to smell it, mustn't I?'

The coffee was delicious, warming, and we settled down to a cosy chat.

'Now then, what have you come to see me about on this awfully cold day?' I asked.

'Well now, I thought seeing as how we're nearly done with decorating my house, maybe I should finally put it on the market. I've seen these lovely apartments for sale, just round the corner from Josie's.'

Just then, the bell clanged again. This time it was Andrew Whirlow, wrapped in a dark woollen coat and scarf.

His smile lit up the room. 'Hi there.'

215

'Morning, Andrew.'

Closing the door behind him, he nodded to Enid and placed his laptop on Emma's desk.

'Morning, Mrs Phelps - nice to see you again. Putting your house on the market at last?'

'I am,' she replied happily. 'Mattie's just about finished with the decorating and suchlike. She's done a wonderful job, you know.'

'I'm sure she has.' He beamed approvingly. 'It was an excellent idea. Although nearly breaking her neck in the process wasn't such a good one.'

'I can assure you it won't happen again,' I replied.

'Seriously, she's quite a special lady, our Mattie. We'd be devastated if anything happened to her.'

Enid's eyes lit up like lanterns at midnight. 'Mr Whirlow - I know exactly what you mean.'

*

I tucked the duvet carefully around Thomas.

'Night-night, darling. Sweet dreams.'

'And Blue Bear, Mummy.'

'Night-night, Blue Bear.' I kissed Blue Bear's nose.

Leaving the door ajar, I tiptoed downstairs. The pendulum in the hall clock was rocking gently, to and fro. The rumble of the dishwasher echoed along the kitchen walls. Making a cup of tea, I returned to the sitting room. The doors were locked, the TV switched off. I'd already brought the Morrison's carrier bag from its hiding place in my wardrobe. Carefully pulling out the loose sheets of Grandma Beattie's diary, I gazed at the first page. Embellished with faded drawings of stick-men and flowers, it was thin as onion skin.

Wednesday 19th November 1941

This is the diary of Miss Beatrice Mary Baxter, Beattie for short. I'm exactly ten years and one month old. I live with my mum and Matilda, my little sister, in a cottage in West Melton - eleven miles from Sheffield.

But I wish we didn't live in West Melton. There's a pit here, a coal-mine. All the men work there. It's all there is for them to do, apart from the factory, but that doesn't pay as much. You see, if there wasn't a pit my dad would still be here with us. He was down the stupid pit when a slab of coal fell and broke his back. Last year, it was. They took him to the hospital in Sheffield for a few months, but then he got sent to the spinal unit in Nottingham. Mum took us to visit at weekends and in school holidays, which wasn't easy, what with bus-times and air-raids and suchlike. But I'm really glad we went now. And I loved the nurses, with their starched pinnies and their hair all fastened up under beautiful white bonnets. I want to be a nurse. I want to look after people like my dad and Uncle Joe. I want to be able to help people.

Mum says the doctors told her right from the beginning that Dad would die from his injuries, but she never told me and our Matilda because she didn't think it would be for years and years. So when the telegram arrived on Monday, she just collapsed in a heap, right there on the front step. The telegram boy had to fetch Auntie Betty. We were at school, so I didn't find out until I got home.

I really love my dad, even though he was scary sometimes with his coal-black face and his eyes peeking out like big, shiny green marbles.

Uncle Joe was Dad's brother. He's dead too. Last year it was. And it sounds like too much of a coincidence, but it's absolutely true, I swear it. A slab of coal fell on him too, the same week, four days after Dad's accident. It was a different pit though, because after he got married to Auntie Maud they moved away. What a job, being a miner. And they say it's good because you don't get called up. But it isn't good, not really. You're just as likely to get killed down the mines as out fighting the Jerries, I think.

Mum's calling me from the yard. She's having to get dressed all in black for the funeral tomorrow. I'm dreading it. Our

217

Matilda and Gyp, my dog, are going to stay with Mrs O'Mara up the street, but Mum says I can go to the funeral because I'm ten and old enough to understand what's going on. I'm not sure I am, though. I mean, why did it have to happen in the first place? Why has God taken away my daddy? He did nothing wrong - he was just working so we didn't have to go and steal our food. No, my daddy was a good man, always kind, coming home with a great big grin on his face, holding out his arms for me to run into. I never would, though, not until he'd been through the bath, our great big tin one that hangs on a nail out the back. He'd drag it into the parlour and sit it in front of the fire, ready for Mum to fill with hot water. Afterwards, while he chatted to us girls, Mum would scrub it clean with Vim. It was always black-bright.

Mum's really shouting now. Got to go.

She was furious, asking where I've been all this time. I haven't told her about my diary. It's to be my secret, a place where I can scream and shout if I want to. And at the moment that's all I ever, ever want to do.

When Mum had finished with the shouting, she held out this frock. It's got short puffed sleeves and a wide sash belt, and is supposed to be black but has been washed to a dark grey. I knew straightaway it was a hand-me-down from Cousin Alice. And I was right.

Cousin Alice is nearly all grownup now. She's Auntie Mary and Uncle Jonathan's girl. Auntie Mary's my dad's sister. I envy Cousin Alice. She's really pretty, with big blue eyes and bright red lips, although Mum says she does that with lipstick, and she shouldn't be wearing such things at her age. But she does look kind of inviting. Enticing. The older boys in the village hang around her like mice around a lump of cheese.

I threw the lousy dress onto the table and put my arms around Mum. I'm dreading tomorrow. That's why I'm writing this diary - well, partly. Mrs Cooke, my teacher, says it's a good idea to write a diary every day because it helps with your English. But I also need somewhere to put my thoughts, somewhere no-one else can see, somewhere private.

Mum let me hug her for a moment, then pushed me away. White as a sheet, she was. I thought she was going to faint, so I *helped her to the old armchair in the parlour (we still call it the parlour - it's always been the parlour - this cottage has been in our family for two generations now). I was shaking like a leaf and didn't know what else to do, whether to get Auntie Betty or someone. In the end, I just stood there, stroking her lovely dark hair. She was talking about the dress, but I could tell she was trying her best not to cry. I wanted to cry too, but I didn't, even though my throat hurt lots. She looked so vulnerable, sitting there, my mum. She's usually so strong and sturdy, with her solid, black leather shoes and her flowered pinny that she wears just for housework, but hardly ever takes off.*

Then suddenly she sat up straight and smiled. "Sorry, Beattie, I shouldn't be upsetting you, talking about funerals and suchlike. It's not for little girls to worry about. You've enough on, losing your father."

But it didn't work, not with me. "I'm not a little girl. I'm ten. And it's all right, you can talk about anything you want to. I don't mind. Really." She smiled properly at that, so I knelt beside her, taking hold of her hands. "I miss him too."

I couldn't speak after that, my throat felt so tight. It hurts now, just thinking about it.

Tearful, I paused to sip my tea, unable to believe what I'd just read; the bringing to life of Grandma Beattie's very own thoughts.

Thursday, November 20th

I'm back at school tomorrow - for a day, anyway. It's easier being at school, although I do miss our Gyp. But I love my school. I can switch off from what's happening at home. I have to concentrate really hard though, even in Maths, which I love.

Bertie Willie Coughdrop is our Maths' teacher's name. Mrs Cooke is our class teacher, but she doesn't teach us Maths, I don't know why. Bertie's real name is Bertram William Holt. But after he caught a bad cold from fire-watching once, his false teeth fell out when he sneezed. So we re-named him. I think his teeth must be too small for him, and we really shouldn't make fun. He's an old

219

man. He'd actually retired from teaching, but then after war broke out and Mr Cooper went off to fight, they dragged him back in again. But it's so, so funny when he sneezes.

The funeral. I don't want to say much. It was cold. Dry. Apart from the thousands and thousands of tears.
Dad. My daddy. I love you, Dad.

I reached for the tissue box, sincerely hoping this diary wasn't going to make me sad all over again. I'd only just stopped crying over my own rotten life.

Saturday, November 22nd

Our Matilda is a twaddle! Honestly! I came downstairs this morning to find her and Mum arguing like cat and dog. Here's how it went:

Matilda: "I want Weetabix, Mummy."

Mum: "You'll get Weetabix when the Co-op gets some in, but until then it's bread and marg."

Matilda: "But I want bread and jam - I don't like just bread and marg."

Mum: "You'll have bread and marg and like it, young lady. There's plenty of children in Africa who are starving for lack of a bit of bread and marg. In fact, truth be told, there's children in this country who are starving."

Matilda: "I won't eat it!"

Mum: "Right. Off to your room. There'll be no playing out for you today, not if you can speak to me like that."

Matilda spent an hour in her room, which is a long time for Mum to be angry. It's usually only five or ten minutes where our Matilda's concerned.

I ate my breakfast - you've guessed it - bread and marg. Cousin Barbara calls it 'bread and scrape'. You scrape the marg on, then scrape it off again. Margarine is rationed. I do love bread and jam, though. But there's a war on. That's what everyone around here says - "Don't you know there's a war on?"

Mum always used to make her own jam. We've a garden full of gooseberries, and there are blackberries out on the lane in the Autumn-time. But with visiting Dad in hospital for the past year, and being the only one looking after me and our Matilda, she's not had the time. Maybe I ought to start learning what to do. We're supposed to be 'digging for victory', but after Dad broke his back we never got round to it. It's all in aid of the war effort. There are notices everywhere - 'Dig For Victory'. You're supposed to get rid of the flowers in your garden and replace them all with fruit and vegetables. You see, the ships that bring us food from abroad keep getting attacked by the Jerries, and there's no point in them putting themselves in danger when we can grow our own food, is there? Uncle John did offer to come round and do our garden for us, but Mum wouldn't hear of it. I think she was hoping, deep down somewhere, that Dad would get better and be able to do it himself.

Maybe gardening's another thing I ought to learn to do.

Mrs O'Mara from up the street came round just now. She says there's a job for Mum if she wants it, at the glass factory, Hale and Brown's. Mum's never worked a day in her life - well, not worked away from home, anyway. So I don't know how she'd cope. And how she'd manage to get me and our Matilda ready for school, then herself to work, then come back home and make our dinner and do all the housework, I don't know. I suppose I'll have to help, but I move up to big school the year after next. Mrs Cooke says it'll probably be the Grammar. I do hope so. And according to her, I'll have loads of homework to do. I certainly won't have time for my diary. Sorry, Diary.

After our Matilda ate her bread and marg (yes, Mum always wins) we went off to the Co-op. Mum makes us a shopping list, gives us the money with the ration books, our gas masks and a couple of shopping bags, then off we go. It's not far – just along our street, up past the farm, and then left onto Fitzackerley Street. It's Mr and Mrs Standen who run the shop. When I first started going, I remember the shop counter being nearly twice as big as me, but now I can see over the top. Me and Matilda only go there on a Saturday morning. It gives Mum a break and anyway, she says we need to learn the value of money.

Mr Standen took our shopping list and ration books off us as soon as we walked in, even though there was a queue of people already there.

"Come along now, duckies," he said. "Let's not keep you waiting, aye?"

I hate to say this, but I think he was trying to be nice to us, with our dad having just died. But I'd much rather he was just normal. I don't want to be reminded all the time. I just want to get our lives back to normal – well, as normal as they can be. I mean, I suppose we'd got used to Dad not being there when he was in hospital. And that was hard enough, but now we know he's never going to be there, ever, ever, it's just awful. Empty. Hurting. Right in the pit of my stomach.

Anyway, Mr Standen weighed out our rations for us, one at a time, clucking away like old Gertie, Uncle John's goose.

That's another thing. Uncle John gets extra cheese rations because he's a miner. They must have decided that miners need the extra protein to keep them strong. And Mum always used to give me and our Matilda lots of cheese to help us grow strong, before the rationing came in. And I sometimes wonder - if we'd given our cheese to Dad, would his back have been stronger, and would it not have broken so easily? I suppose what I'm trying to say is, if me and our Matilda hadn't eaten so much of the cheese, would Dad still be here now?

I like watching Mr Standen weigh out the butter. 'Best butter' he calls it, I don't know why. They keep a great big slab of it beneath the counter, a solid, slippery, slimy block of yellow fat. He cuts tiny chunks off it, so much per adult, so much per child, then slides it onto a square of greaseproof paper, already sitting on the scales, before wrapping it up and marking it off in our ration books. The same goes for the margarine and cheese. Sugar and flour, though, is weighed out into little blue paper bags. Which are all right until they get wet - so we have to empty everything into tins when we get home. It's a big job, and our Matilda's not very good at it yet, so I have to do it. I don't dare spill a grain, or Mum goes up the wall. We managed to get strawberry jam this week, much to Matilda's pleasure. We got Weetabix and porridge oats, too.

222

After I helped Mum rinse the washing in the scullery and hang it out, I took Gyp with me to see Cousin Barbara. She's a laugh, always up to something. Today, she was sheer disaster:

"Come on, Beattie, I've said I'll pick nettles for Mum's soup."

"Oh, Barbs, I hate the allotments. What about old Gertie?"

"Oh, we'll be all right. She'll be cooped up with the hens. Don't be such a scaredy-cat."

Well, I won't say it (well, I will), but I did warn her. Cousin Barbara has a definite mind of her own. People say she's a bit like me, two peas in a pod. But I'm not too sure about that. At least I'd have the sense to learn from my mistakes. Not our Barbara. In she dives, feet first. Always has.

The allotment belongs to Uncle John. Uncle John is Mum's cousin. He's married to Auntie Betty. They've got Barbara, who's the eldest, and little Jack, who's six and always up to mischief. Just like their Barbara really.

The allotment is a good-sized piece of land, full of carrots, potatoes, parsnips, cabbages and all sorts of other good things. Uncle John keeps hens and geese there as well. The geese are for Christmas dinner. But one of them, old Gertie he calls her, has managed to escape Christmas dinner for some time now, I don't know why. I think she's become more of a pet. Anyway, she's old now, about fifteen by all accounts, and is becoming very cantankerous. She reminds me of old Mrs Tripp, the missionary lady at Chapel.

Barbara got to the nettles before I did. "Here, Beattie, there's loads!"

"I'm coming." I patted Gyp's head. "Gyp! Stay!"

I was being really careful not to nettle my legs. I only had ankle socks on – the shorter the better, as far as the war effort is concerned, and in November, too. When I got near the nettles, Barbara pulled this old piece of sacking out of the bag she'd been carrying. It looked like she'd picked it up off the ground from somewhere - covered in petrol it was, all blotchy. She was already piling torn nettles onto it when I got there.

"Come on, Beattie."

I looked enviously at her red woollen gloves.

"Barbara, how am I supposed to pick nettles? I've not brought any gloves. You're all right - you came prepared."

She stopped in her tracks. "Well, all right, you can hold the cloth still while I pile them up."

Leaning forwards, I placed my hands either side of the sacking. But it wasn't easy, doing that and trying to avoid the nettles, all at the same time, and my gas mask kept swinging around my neck, getting in the way. So I decided to hold the sacking in place with my feet instead. I think it's all my messing about, and Barbara shouting at me to stand still, that attracted old Gertie. Because the next thing I knew, she'd escaped the coop and was sprinting down the narrow path towards us.

Our Gyp spotted her first. It was her barking that alerted me.

I screamed, "Barbs! Run!"

I ran fast, with Gyp at my heels, towards the great big oak tree near the stream. Swinging my hands into the air, I grabbed a branch and heaved myself up, screaming for all I was worth. I looked down to see poor Gyp yelping, desperately trying to climb up the trunk. I felt awful.

Then, as if things weren't bad enough, Barbara, who was just beginning to catch up with us, suddenly tripped and fell headlong into the grass, her hands sprawling out into another nettle patch. I've never heard her scream so loudly before.

"Beattie! Help!"

Gertie took advantage and started pecking at Barbara's arm. This was really serious. Luckily, she had on the really thick jumper Auntie Betty knitted last Christmas. I know, because she made one for me too. It's lots of different colours all knitted together. She buys old jumpers at the jumble sale and unpicks them. 'Make Do and Mend', she calls it.

Well, I didn't know what to do about our Barbara. I felt sick. All I could do was swing myself down to the ground and try to shoo Gertie away. I was terrified.

"Go on! Shoo! Shoo!"

This was when our Gyp saved the day. She was terrific. She ran at Gertie, head down, teeth bared, barking for all she was worth. Brave Gyp. Gertie stopped pecking at Barbara and began to back away slowly. This gave Barbara chance to stand up. Gertie

224

was still there though, watching with her beady little eyes, her claws scratching at the ground.

Again, I screamed and shouted for all I was worth. "Shoo! Shoo!"

"Come on, Beattie, let's just run for it!" Barbara's face was white, her pupils tiny pinpricks.

I clicked my fingers at Gyp. "Gyp, come on! Follow me, girl!"

We turned and ran. And didn't stop until we were at the end of our street.

I was completely out of breath and my lungs felt like bags of dried sawdust. "Oh! Oh, Barbara, I said it wasn't a very good idea."

Our Barbara was in an even worse state. Being a redhead, from Auntie Betty's side of the family, her face was practically purple.

She gasped. "I know. Sorry, Beattie. Won't do it again."

But I know she will.

We've just had our tea, and it's nearly time for bed. I've sneaked upstairs to write this - Mum thinks I'm outside on the toilet. But I'm really worried, and Mrs Cooke says it's good to write your worries down. She says it gets them out of your system.

The fact is, Mum looks dreadful. She has the prettiest face, I think, especially for a mum. Really lovely, smashing blue eyes, beautiful smile, dark shiny hair. But the strain is beginning to tell. She's ever so pale, and her hair is all dull and knotted, as if it's not been combed in weeks. And it's not like her. It's understandable, I know, but I'm worried she'll make herself ill, and that's no good for anyone. I might have to go see Gran, although Mum would kill me if she ever found out. She's got so much on her plate, though. I overheard someone at the funeral talking. Apparently, the pit will provide Mum with a pension, but it won't be much. She'll definitely have to work to keep us all. Well, I'm ten now, so I suppose it's about time I started helping a bit more. And our Matilda's eight, so she can start doing things, too.

Placing the sheets I'd just read behind the others, I carried them all up to my wardrobe, hiding them away, safe and sound.

CHAPTER 25

I chewed the last bit of my sandwich. Cold roast veg and mozzarella. Not quite what you need on a winter's day, but it was food.

The phone was dead, Emma was still off sick with her cold, and I was bored silly. I'd been on the internet most of the morning, looking at clothes, recipes, things to do in school holidays. Not that I had much money for school holidays.

So I began to daydream, fiddle with my pen and stare through the old Georgian window from the comfort of my desk. I wrinkled my nose at the falling snow. Thick white flakes, tiny balls of kitten fur, seemed to swirl and fall, swirl and fall, forever and ever. Throwing the pen down, I went to the window for a closer look, acknowledging its quiet beauty, the absolute perfection of the scene outside. Even so, I shivered, folding my arms around myself, and thought about my poor car. It was so dreadfully cold I'd driven Thomas to school. But there was no way I'd be able to drive back again, and the thought of having to drag him all the way home after a day in school was not pleasant.

But my thoughts were disturbed by the old bell clanging noisily above me. Turning, I smiled at what looked like a very slim snowman.

'Hi, Andrew.'

Closing the door quickly, he wiped his feet on the mat. 'Sorry I'm late. Got stuck and couldn't get out. It's amazing the way some people drive in this stuff. Idiots, most of them.' Removing his coat, he shook off the snow, hanging it over the back of Emma's chair. 'Did you manage to get something to eat?'

I nodded. 'From the Deli. Roast veg and mozzarella. It was okay. I could have done with something hot, though - spicy veg soup or something.'

I looked up at him, his thick, dark hair wet with snow, his green eyes the colour of summer leaves. I was surprised, shocked even, at how pleased I was to see him. Shuffling away from the window, I returned to my desk.

'How are things, anyway?' He smiled, and his smile warmed the room. 'You must be bored stupid. I bet you've not had many calls.'

'I'm fine, really. Well, apart from the fact that my car's probably stuck in about a mile of snow. Or is it kilometre?' I grinned. 'Would you like a cuppa? I seem to have the kettle on permanently today.'

'Actually, I'd prefer coffee, if that's okay. It's a coffee kind of a day, don't you think?'

227

'I don't know about that. More like a hot chocolate kind of day, if you ask me. Thomas loves it, with squirty cream on top, and pink and white marshmallows.'

He followed me into the kitchen. 'There again, it might actually be a hot chocolate and brandy kind of a day. Excellent stuff when you've got to ski a black run and you're absolutely terrified of the thing.'

I filled the kettle. 'Do you go skiing, then?'

I'd become acutely aware of his presence. The kitchen, at the best of times small, was suddenly microscopic. And despite the cold, a sudden heat engulfed me, my heart thudding as it raced through my body. My face must surely have been the colour of the bright pink orchids on Mum's sideboard. Perplexed, confused, unable to control this sudden development, I swallowed hard, praying he hadn't noticed.

He hadn't. 'I only went the once. Me and some old pals from uni. All divorced now, every one of them. We went on this crazy, all-boys-together skiing holiday a couple of years ago. Mad, it was. But the brandy helped no end, I can tell you.'

'Sounds good to me. But sorry, the café's all out of hot chocolate today. Only tea or coffee, I'm afraid.'

Stirring his coffee, I handed it to him. But as he accepted it, our hands touched, causing me to pull back abruptly. For no reason at all. Shocked, I looked up at him, at his face, bewildered and silent.

Then he put down his cup and he took my hand. 'Mattie …'

Before I could respond, before I had chance to accept or deny him, he continued.

'I hope you don't mind, but I've wanted to do this ever since the first time - the very first minute - I saw you.'

Softly, imperceptibly, he pulled me close.

And we kissed.

His gentleness overwhelmed me. His wet hair smelt of pine trees in the rain. And I was paralysed, not wanting this to happen, not wanting it to stop. I thought about pulling away, telling him to go and never return. But the strength of his kiss became hypnotic, and I couldn't. Then it became more than that. It became longing. It became wanting. His kiss became everything, the whole world, the universe. And I could not deny him.

I heard the closing of the door as he kicked back with his foot. My mind in denial, my body throbbing with expectation, I felt his hand move lower. And as he found me, suddenly, acutely, I wanted. Without restraint, without guilt. Without Rob. As the knowledge hit, my aching body replied fervently to his. And only when he knew I was ready did he lift me onto the icy cold table, and enter.

But even though I was there with him, I wasn't. Mysteriously, the sudden vision of a churchyard appeared before me. Ice-cold gravestones. The silhouette of a church. Tall, dark oak trees. Inexplicable. Unfathomable. Except - I'd been here before. I'd known this before. Him. His hands caressing, his body thrusting, strong and hard. And young. A feral cry ran through me as I gave myself to him, and I found myself sobbing, a love I could not understand settling over me.

Afterwards, groaning, kissing me fervently, murmuring my name, he held me in his arms for what seemed like forever.

Outside, thick white flakes, tiny balls of kitten fur, continued to swirl and fall, swirl and fall.

*

The journey home had been treacherous. Andrew had insisted on picking Thomas up from school in the Land Rover, slipping and sliding as we went. He would have stayed at our house for a drink but, grateful as I was, I really wanted him to go. Partly to avoid questions from Thomas, but also because I needed to think. A lot.

Settling a very tired Thomas into bed, I went downstairs, pulled back the curtain in the sitting room and peered through the window. The snow had stopped. The street was quiet, floodlit by streetlamps, a halo of light around each one. I wandered into the kitchen, the radio a quiet whisper in the corner. Tidying away, I ploughed through the remainder of the ironing, berating myself constantly.

What *could* I have been thinking? We hadn't even take precautions; it had all happened so quickly. And at our age, too. But I knew I'd be okay; it hadn't been long since my period. I did consider the morning after pill, but knew from experience it would make me ill. But what about diseases? What about HIV? Chlamydia?

What on earth *could* I have been thinking?

And then the guilt, thickly layered. I was still legally married. I'd never, ever been unfaithful. What would Rob say? What *could* Rob say? A vision of him making love to Sonia, bangles of gold jangling at her wrists and ankles, scudded before me as if driven by a tornado. Angry, all-encompassing.

The bastard!

And Andrew. So sweet, so caring.

But what had I done? It wouldn't work. It was too soon. How could I ever work there again? How could I look him in the face? I'd have to hand in my notice, and soon. I'd say I was going full-time with my new business.

What had I done?

But then - I smiled.

How wonderful he was.

*

I nearly didn't hear the ringing of the phone. All ready to climb into bed, I dashed downstairs to catch it, but was too late.

A message flashed at me, and I pressed the button.

'Mattie, it's Andrew. Hi. I just wanted to say, I'm thinking of you. A lot. I hope you don't regret what happened. I certainly don't. And I meant what I said - I really do love you. Always have.' There was a pause. *'Anyway, I'll ring tomorrow. Sleep well - my darling.'*

Hastily deleting the message, I padded back upstairs. Happy, yet bewildered.

Was I quite ready for another relationship? Just yet?

CHAPTER 26

THE next day the snow had nearly gone. Melted away. Miraculously. Only a few scraps along the edges of the pavements. As if it had been there merely to create a cocoon, a place away from the world outside, a happening.

The phone rang just as we were eating breakfast. I dashed into the hall to answer it, my heart in my mouth. But it was only Emma to say she was feeling better and would be back at work.

Thomas whooped for joy. 'That means you'll be in school today. That's good, isn't it?'

I'd not been into school since my accident, partly to recuperate, partly to avoid the unavoidable comments of parents and teachers in the staff room. Today, however, I felt strong, in control, a totem pole of power. I'd go in, answer their questions about Rob and Sonia. Get it over with.

'Yes darling, it is good,' I replied. 'But let's eat first, quickly.'

I shooed him into the kitchen. Laughing happily, his face a great big smiling sunflower, he scrambled onto a barstool, his red school sweatshirt already covered in toothpaste.

But the phone rang again, and this time it *was* Andrew.

'Hello, Mattie.'

'Hi, Andrew.' Delicious butterflies fluttered around my insides.

'How are you today?'

I sat down onto the bottom step, my voice a stage whisper. 'I'm fine. You?'

'Wonderful.' The word was a sigh, deep and cavernous.

Despite the delicious butterflies, I felt decidedly awkward. How could I have done what I'd done? And with my boss? Licking my dry lips, I hastily changed the subject.

'Has Emma rung you yet? She's going in this morning, so I can help out in school as usual. I can't believe the snow's gone so quickly ...' I was babbling, and I knew it.

'Divine providence,' he replied, softly. 'It came especially for us.'

'If Emma had been there yesterday ...'

'And if it hadn't snowed ...'

'I know.'

'Mattie, do you think we could meet?'

'Andrew ...' Unsure of myself, of us, of what I wanted, a trickle of guilt ran down my back.

'Mm?'

'Could we discuss this another time? It's just, I'm not sure where I want to go with this.'

'Put you on the spot a little, haven't I?'

'Sorry.'

'No, don't be. And don't worry, I understand. I won't push you into anything you're not ready for. But I'll ring again some time?'

'Okay. Yes.' Thomas had appeared in the doorway. 'Have to go, Andrew. See you on Monday, maybe.'

'Okay, have a good day.'

'You too.'

'I'll be thinking of you.'

'Bye.' I put down the receiver.

'What did Andrew ring for, Mummy?'

'Oh, just to make sure we were alright. That was kind of him, wasn't it?'

*

School was bustling, hectic, everyone preparing for half-term, testing, checking, tidying. I listened to Emma, Jack and Ben read their books in the library, their voices tinny and soft, lacking confidence rather than skill.

'That's it, Emma - very good. Now let's try the next page.'

'Jack, remember magic 'e'. Rack, race, back, base.'

'Excellent, Ben. One house point.'

Pushing my thoughts - of yesterday, of Andrew, to the back of my mind - I just about managed to get through the morning.

Mrs Webster was her usual calming self. Her first lesson was literacy, the second numeracy, with plastic pizzas brought in to demonstrate simple fractions. Helping the less able children, my mind was focused, concentrated. I was not, however, looking forward to my coffee break. In the event, however, it wasn't as bad as expected. Some of them knew about Rob leaving, some didn't. Some were sympathetic, some shocked.

Mrs Webster was very sympathetic before school began. 'You come to me if you need any help with the busybodies, Mattie, any time.'

But it was Sue Jennings who brought up the subject in the staff room.

'I heard all about it, couldn't believe he'd do such a thing. And I thought you were such a lovely couple. He was doing so well with his new business, too. Shocking. Completely shocking.'

I wondered how shocked they'd be if they'd known about my day at work with Andrew.

*

Thomas and Blue Bear were fast asleep in bed.

I tried to relax, tried to ignore the myriad of questions in my head. Too many questions, not enough answers. Should I see more of Andrew? Must I hand in my notice? Why hadn't he given me a bit more time? Why couldn't all this be happening once I'd got over Rob? It had all been too soon.

Pouring myself a glass of rich, fruity Burgundy, I finally relaxed. Playing an old CD by *The Corrs*, I lazed on the sofa, sipped from my glass, and turned to the next page of Grandma Beattie's diary.

Sunday, November 23rd
Mrs Tripp was at Sunday school, waiting for me. I knew she would be, of course. It's the same thing every Sunday morning. I have to go round all the houses on our street, then Orchard Lane, Farm Street, and Fitzackerley Street, collecting money for the

missionaries in Africa, so they can teach the children there about Jesus.

I don't mind collecting the money. It's quite nice, chatting to everybody. But I do mind old Mr Carpenter. He's a miserable old so and so. Mum says it's because he's lonely, but I don't think it is that. Or else, he's lonely because he's so miserable and nobody wants to be with him. He complains like nobody's business when I knock on the door, then fiddles about in his filthy kitchen, his face like an old trout with its down-turned mouth, looking for a few halfpennies, then hands them over as if they're the crown jewels.

But this morning was different. Everyone was really kind. It set me off, to tell the truth - crying, I mean. I couldn't help it. I wish they'd been horrible, it would have been so much easier. And old Mr Carpenter actually smiled at me and rubbed my head as if I was a little girl.

Anyway, Mrs Tripp stood there in the doorway of the Bell Room. She had the big red velvet bag dangling from her hand, as usual. But, not as usual, she didn't push it into my face as I walked through the door. She just smiled, not in that sickly way she has, but kind of sweet and gentle.

"All that money you've collected for the little African children this year, Beatrice – I think you deserve to keep this week's money for your poor Mum and your baby sister. Don't you?"

I didn't speak, didn't know what to say at all. Speechless. Not like me, that. I just knew if I said anything at all, my throat would tighten up and I'd start crying again. And I didn't want that, not in front of her. So I just nodded, pulled our Matilda's hand, and ran into the room, still clutching the bag of money.

I thought Mum would be really angry when she saw it. All through Sunday school, I was trying to work out how to give it to her without upsetting her. She's so proud, won't accept charity from anybody, unless they're family. I know.

There was that time, just after Dad's accident, when everyone at the pit collected for us. You see, although the pit still paid Dad's wages, they didn't pay him for overtime or anything. So, even then, we weren't doing too well. But we're lucky, in a way. We don't have to pay rent on this house. Grandad left it to Dad in his Will, you see, so it's paid for. Mum says it's a blessing from Heaven. Grandad made his fortune as a market gardener before he bought

236

the house. He was able to buy it outright, didn't have to borrow a penny - but they were only in it about sixteen years before Grandma took ill and died. And Grandad wasn't long after her. They were very close, couldn't live without each other. I suppose Mum and Dad would have become just like that, if he'd not had his accident. Poor Mum.

But Mum wasn't happy at the amount the men from the pit sent home. It was a huge amount. She accepted it, though. It would have hurt their feelings if she hadn't. But she wasn't happy. A lot of it went into my bag for the Missionaries. Mrs Tripp's smile was the size of a barrage balloon for weeks. And I never let on.

I was surprised today, though. When I met Mum coming out of Chapel with my paper bag and told her, she wasn't angry at all, not one bit. In fact, the opposite. Clutching at our hands as if we were going to float away, she pulled me and our Matilda all the way home, with not one word between us. She opened the back door, fell onto a chair at the table, sat, her head held high, and let the tears come.

I placed my arms around her, didn't know what else to do. I couldn't cry. I'd already cried nearly all morning. My eyes were sore and my ears and throat hurt much too much. The whole thing is too painful. And besides, I'm the eldest, so Mum needs me to be strong.

I washed all the pots after dinner. Our Matilda dried them, and didn't complain once.

Monday, November 24th

Just woken up and remembered. It's as if I've forgotten during the night, and then it all comes flooding back again, like a great big ink blot filling the page. Dad, I mean. It feels like losing him all over again.

Back at school today. Didn't feel too well, think I'm coming down with a cold. I'm all sniffly, with a sore throat, and my head aches all down one side as if someone's been bashing it with a big book.

Mrs Cooke came to see me at dinnertime (shepherd's pie again, and spotted dick with custard). She said she'd heard Mum was looking for work, and had we thought about taking in some evacuees? There's a woman and her little girl coming up from

London, and the woman could probably help at home while Mum's out at work, and you get money for taking them in. She said there'd be some evacuees in the Memorial Hall on Saturday, and would I tell my mum. Well, I didn't know what to say. I mean, the last thing my mum needs right now is more people to look after. But then, I suppose if she's at work, she won't be here and they'll have to look after themselves, won't they? I don't know if I want to share our house, anyway - they might not look after it very well. And me and our Matilda might have to share a bedroom or something.

But when I told Mum about it just now, she said it was a good idea and that the money would come in handy. Then the bit I was not looking forward to. "We could put you two in together, couldn't we - that would be fun, wouldn't it? We're very lucky to have such a lovely home with three bedrooms. We could make someone very welcome."

We nodded, "Yes, Mum."

"And the lady could help around the house a bit and look after you two, so I can go out to work and earn some money. Mrs Cooke's had a great idea there."

"Yes, Mum."

"Right - that's settled, then."

So, that's it. Settled.

School was okay, apart from my sore throat. I keep sneezing all the time, and my whole head feels itchy and scratchy. Mum gave me sweet tea when I got home, and a spoonful of Parish's Chemical Food, which is thick and dark red like oil. Mum gets it out whenever she thinks we need extra iron. Yuk!

Bertie Willie Coughdrop cheered up the day, though. He lost his teeth, again! He's not done it in ages, sneeze like that. He just goes on and on. There must have been at least ten sneezes. Maybe he's caught a cold, too. Anyway, there he was, standing there at the blackboard, chalk in hand. We were learning fractions, and he was dividing up the class into halves, then quarters, then eighths, and then sixteenths. There are thirty-two of us, so that makes it easy, I suppose. Good job Charlie Russell wasn't off, because he usually is on a Monday morning - helps his mum with the washing and suchlike. They've seven children in their house.

Well, we were copying down these fractions and David Benson - he's our doctor's son, so quite posh, and you'd think he'd know

238

better - started rolling his pencil backwards and forwards on the desk. Don't ask me why. But it really annoyed Bertie. You could see it in his face. He got redder and redder, just like the huge great beetroot Uncle John brought home that time. At first though, Bertie didn't say anything, just kept on talking - I think he thought David was just trying for attention. Some boys do that, don't they? But then, you could tell, it really got to him, and he turned from the blackboard, threw his chalk at David, and sneezed, once, twice, etc. His teeth fell out after the very first sneeze, and he caught them just in time before they clattered to the floor. We were in fits of laughter, but we daren't let it out, we just daren't. He'd have killed us all. As it was, he finished sneezing, pushed his teeth back in, stood upright, his old back straight as a die, and walked out of the door.

I feel quite sorry for him now. We didn't see him for the rest of the day. Mrs Cooke came in and took over. I wonder if he'll be there tomorrow.

After school, I met up with our Barbara and Matilda, and we walked home together. Barbara's hand is still a bit sore from the nettles, but she didn't tell her mum about it, so of course it would be, because Auntie Betty's a dab hand with anything like that. She uses herbs and flowers and things. Like magic, it is. Could do with some of her stuff for my cold. I'm starting to lose my voice. At least it'll be quiet in class tomorrow. That'll please old Bertie. If he's there!

I missed out on Bible Class tonight. Mum says I need to stay home and keep warm. And she's got a job. Not at the glass factory, though. I couldn't see her working there with that lot, anyway. A bit rough and ready, the girls at the factory. You see them sometimes, hanging round outside Hale and Browns, reeking of scent and smoking Woodbines like there was no tomorrow. And sometimes there's that Mr Young, he's the foreman at the pit, standing there laughing and joking with them. I don't like the way he stares at them. Or me.

No, she was brought up properly, was my mum. She went for an interview today at the Hall. Posh, it is. Wilderwood House Hall, it's called. They're short of housemaids and parlour maids as nearly all of them have gone to work in the munitions factories or joined the Forces. So they've taken Mum on as a housemaid.

They're letting her work days, with Sundays off. I suppose it's better than having to sell the house or being hard up, but I'll miss her being around. Poor Mum, it's going to be so hard for her. But I promise you, Diary, that I shall try to help as much as I can. And I'll make Matilda help, too.

Tuesday, November 25th

Off school today. Feel dreadful. Our Matilda's livid at having to go in.

Just woken up again. Must have been asleep for hours. Mum popped round to Auntie Betty's for some kind of concoction earlier. It tasted really funny, like something our Gyp would do against a tree. Anyway, I think that's what sent me to sleep, or maybe I'm just worn out from being hot and cold all the time.

Mum's just brought me up some chicken soup. Uncle John killed a hen for me and she's cooked it to make the soup. I don't know if the Food Inspector knows about the hen or if he needs to know. I know when you kill a pig you have to have your rations deducted, and the Food Inspector comes to check on how many you've killed. I've heard Mum say that lots of people kill two pigs, then hide one of them. Can't blame them. The soup was delicious and my head's much better now.

Mum says I need to make the most of having my room to myself, because after the weekend I may be sharing it with our Matilda. I'm all upset. That sounds really selfish, doesn't it? Sorry, Diary. But I do love my room. It's a beautiful pale blue, my favourite colour. I've always had my own room, never had to share. And our Matilda's such a scruff.

Gran's here to look after me. She's downstairs in the kitchen with our Matilda, making us all a cup of tea. Mum's had to go round to the Hall to try on aprons and suchlike, and to be shown where everything is.

Gran's my mum's mum. She's quite strict, but very kind, and always talks about 'when I was a lass'. She had quite a privileged upbringing, her dad being a Sedgewick. The Sedgewicks owned half of Barnsley at one time. They owned property for years, renting out shops and houses, all sorts of different places they had. They made a good living out of it, but it's nearly all gone now.

240

Gran's not keen on Mum working as a housemaid. I overheard her just now. "I don't know what the world's coming to, my daughter working for Lady Muck up there. I can't believe it, I can't."

I could tell Mum was upset. "Oh, Mum, Benny's pension pays a pittance. I've got to do something. It's either that or the factory, and I don't want to be working nights, not with our Beattie and Matilda to look after."

Poor Mum. She's got enough on her plate without all this, hasn't she? But I can understand Gran grumbling. I mean, she only wants the best for her children. And you should see her house. It's so beautiful, with big red carpets everywhere, and it's got an inside toilet and a proper fitted bath. When we go round there, I always manage to find another cupboard or a shelf or a tiny window that I've never seen before. It's like Aladdin's Cave.

We have to go up to Gran's house when the air-raid sirens go off. Anderson shelters have been built especially for us, just round the corner, brick with asbestos roofs. We watched the men building them, but they smell horrible and Mum won't go near them. Nor will Auntie Betty. So we all traipse up to Gran's and sit there while the planes fly overhead. We know the Jerries are going to bomb Sheffield, because that's where all the steel factories are. Steel's very important when you're fighting a war. After the planes have gone, we sit and sing songs and hymns until the All Clear sounds. Or play games, and Mum and Auntie Betty laugh and joke about the most stupid things. It's good fun most of the time, but then we suddenly remember why we're there, and what's happening to the people in Sheffield, and go all quiet, and feel terribly guilty. Sometimes we end up missing school the following morning. The rule is if the siren goes before midnight, then we go into school on time. But if it goes after midnight, then we go in at dinnertime. Our Barbara always prays for it to go after midnight and why, I don't know. I'm always so tired.

Gran just brought me up my tea. She chatted as I drank it. It was my opportunity to tell her how worried I've been about Mum. Trust Gran to make me feel better. "She'll be right as rain once she starts work - you'll see. Give her a few months or so. She just needs to feel her feet again, without your dad being there to hold her up. He did, you know. Always held her up, never let her down, not for an instant. And even though I don't approve of her having to go and work there, it may just be the making of her. She'll have other things to occupy her mind, you wait and see. Mind, though, she'll never forget your dad. She'll always miss him being there for her. And I'm sure you will too, my darling. But remember this. He's up there in Heaven, watching out for all of you. You know that, don't you?"

Tears fell into my cup, and I felt I was drowning in them, like Alice in Wonderland. But I nodded and tried to smile. Gran always makes me feel better.

Sometimes, Diary, when I'm sitting here writing, I do wonder what'll become of us all.

Saturday, November 29th

Mum's coming shopping with us today because after the Co-op we're going straight to the Memorial Hall. We're going to meet these evacuees Mrs Cooke's told us about - the woman and her daughter. I feel really nervous. What if they're not very nice? Surely they will be. Surely they'll be so grateful to get away from the bombing in London that they'll be exceptionally, exceedingly nice. I do hope so.

It was terrible, really awful. The place, I mean. Children with brown name tags fastened through the buttonholes on their coats, and gas masks tethered around their necks in battered cardboard boxes. Like Farmer Gillingham's cattle going to market, only much, much sadder.

I'm glad I'm writing this diary. I feel sometimes as if there's a massive screwed-up ball of paper inside my heart. But then, when I've written everything down, it's like I've pulled the paper out and flattened it, allowing me to see it for what it really is. And it's not always as bad as it first seems. Obviously, it doesn't help with really big things - nothing in the world can make them go away. But it does seem to help with all the little things. Mrs Cooke was right about diaries. They really do help.

Mrs Bellhouse and Mary Bellhouse are the names of our evacuees. Mrs Bellhouse is not at all like her name, so I must assume it suits her husband better. If a Bell House (if such a thing exists) were anything like the Bell Room at Chapel, then it would be a friendly, chatty, well-rounded individual. Not so Mrs

242

Bellhouse, who's thin, with crinkly hands that make her look ninety, though Mum thinks she must be about thirty. And she never smiles. But then, I suppose she doesn't have much to smile about.

Mary Bellhouse is just as thin, with long straggly hair and a pale face, but she does smile sometimes. She clings onto her mother's crinkly hand as if it was made of ice and might melt away at any moment. She's five. I quite like Mary.

Mum and our Matilda are downstairs with them now. I'm up here clearing my room, or supposed to be, ready for Matilda to move into.

Uncle John and Auntie Betty have been round to help move the bed out of Mum's room and into mine. Me and our Matilda are sharing Mum's big bed in my room, Mum is having my bed in her room, Mrs Bellhouse is going to sleep on the put-you-up – the one that used to be in the parlour downstairs - and Mary will have Matilda's bed, both of them in Matilda's room. What a palaver!

Dad always used to say that. "What a palaver!" I can just see him now, sitting there in the kitchen after work, mug of tea in hand to wet his thirst, three spoonfuls of sugar in it (our teaspoons are worn down at the ends, the amount of stirring he had to do), chatting about the men at the pit. He'd smell of soap and always have his clean shirt sleeves rolled up just so. His hair would still be wet from his bath, and there'd always be a tiny spot of black coal-dust in the corners of his eyes, waiting to be blinked out.

Mary Bellhouse is a real misery, just keeps crying all the time. She's lucky, though, because the other kids at the Memorial Hall haven't even got their mums with them. They're considered old enough to look after themselves. At least she's got her mum up here.

I suppose I'm not being very charitable, really. I don't know how I'd feel in her position. I did ask her if she wanted to come out to play, but she didn't want to. Apparently, she and Mrs Bellhouse were evacuated to Wales (Carmarthenshire) at the start of the war, but then the hostess's husband got killed and she had to move. That's why they've come to us. So they've not really been home for over a year now.

I do feel really sorry for them.

Sunday, November 30th

Me and our Matilda took Elizabeth and Baby Joan to Sunday school this morning. All dressed up, they were, in their pretty dresses. We were allowed. Mrs Daley, the Sunday school teacher, said as it was the last Sunday in November we could bring a toy. Our Sunday school teacher used to be Miss Robins. I liked her, but she went to work as a land girl when war broke out. Mrs Daley's nice though.

Mary Bellhouse came with us and brought her doll, too. But when Mrs Bellhouse went to go into chapel with the others, Mary wouldn't let go of her hand, so she had to come and sit with us in the Bell Room. There were a few other new faces there as well, other evacuees. They looked a bit scruffy, to my way of thinking. But when I told Mum afterwards, she said that some of them have had their houses bombed. It must be terrible, losing all your things like that. But at least they're still alive, aren't they?

I helped Mum make jam tarts after dinner. Gran gave us some of her home-made raspberry jam as a treat. We've only used the tiniest bit in each tart, but they still taste delicious.

The new people seem to have taken Mum's mind off Dad for a while. She's busying herself looking after them and making sure they're comfortable. Mrs Bellhouse doesn't seem to want to do much, though. You'd think she'd want to help Mum now she's got extra mouths to feed, but no, she just sits there drinking tea and seeing to Mary all the time. I hope once she's settled in, she's going to help out a bit more than this.

We went to put flowers on Dad's grave this afternoon. Mum wanted to, but I got this great big lump in my throat and felt poorly all over again. Our Matilda's joined Mary - they're both crying at the same time now. I think it's finally hit our Matilda that Dad's never going to come home. Not ever.

Monday, December 1st

School was brilliant. I had to sit next to this new boy. His name's Johnnie Whitaker, and he's one of the evacuees.

My face already wet with tears, I gasped. Johnnie Whitaker was my grandfather, Grandma Beattie's husband. Eagerly, I read on.

He's such a laugh. But he doesn't say it like that. We say laff and he says larrff. He's got bright blue eyes and the cheeky grin people have when they think they can do anything they want and get away with it. You can hardly tell what he's saying, half the time, the way he speaks. Cockney, Mrs Cooke calls it. He's from Battersea, that's London. His brother Michael's in our Matilda's class. Mary and some other evacuees are in there with them. We've only got two extra girls and three boys, including Johnnie. The girls seem all right, a bit quiet. But I suppose I would be too.

It was very, very cold today. Mum got the cod liver oil and malt out, a spoonful each. Yuk! She says there might be some snow coming. That would be brilliant! I love snow! She started work today, all smart in her new white apron. Mrs Bellhouse looked after us when she'd gone. Well, she was supposed to. What she actually did was stand round with an overcoat on over her nightie, shouting orders. "Get your breakfast! Get dressed! Look sharp!"

That was just to us, though. Not her precious Mary.

Barbara and Jack called round for us before school and we took Mary with us. She doesn't say much, and what she does say is smothered in this London accent, not Cockney like Johnnie's. Different. Posher. "Our house is near a big park. We've got five bedrooms and two telephones."

I don't believe her for a minute. No-one has telephones in their houses. Well, except for Doctors and suchlike, people who really need them. I think she was just showing off to make herself feel better, but Jack believes her, or pretends to. "Wow! Two telephones? In the 'ouse?"

Mrs Cooke was busy organising the new children into the right classes. Not difficult that, there's only two. Miss Jennings is the infant teacher. She's ever so nice. Big and jolly. She used to bring iced buns for us when I was in her class. She doesn't now though, because of rationing.

We had English this morning, Maths this afternoon. But it was freezing, even though Mr Slater, the caretaker, kept shovelling more coal onto the fires. We were allowed to sit in our coats. English was about Jane Eyre by Charlotte Bronte. She came from Yorkshire, too, and she was ten like me. We had to read the first chapter, then answer questions about it. Poor Jane. I'd hate to have lived in those days. Mrs Cooke says Jane was an orphan. I'd hate to be an orphan. But, imagine, if anything was to happen to Mum, then me and our Matilda would be orphans. I can't bear even to think about it.

The questions we had to answer were easy. Johnnie didn't think so, though. He kept looking at my answers. When I moved my notebook away, he just grinned and carried on. Until Mrs Cooke caught him. "I do understand you've come through a lot to be with us, Johnnie Whitaker. Nevertheless, I would appreciate it if you would act with decorum in the classroom, and not copy other people's work.'

So, what did he go and say?

"Sorry, Mrs Cooke. I just needed to make sure your writing was the same as ours. I mean, the way you all talk is different, see."

"It's our accent that's different, Johnnie, not our words. So please do as I ask, or I'm afraid I shall have to move you to sit on your own."

"Yes, Mrs Cooke."

That settles it. Johnnie Whitaker is now, officially, the naughty boy of the class. I still like him, though.

After Maths, we rehearsed our Nativity play. We're performing it at the Memorial Hall. Mrs Cooke's had to invent more angels and sheep for the new children to play. I'm playing the Angel Gabriel. I have to learn some words, but not too many, thank goodness. Most of the play is made up of songs, with Mrs Cooke playing the piano. They've some really lovely voices in our school.

We got home to find Mrs Bellhouse fast asleep in the parlour, her feet up on the sofa, and the radio on really loud. It's a good job we're not terraced like our Barbara's. We're used to Mum being there when we get in from school, with hot tea and toast and dripping, so I made tea and toast for us and Mary. But I'm not happy. I think Mrs Bellhouse is taking advantage. I won't say anything to Mum though, until she's settled into her new job. But it's not fair, is it?

Mum likes her job, even though she looked exhausted when she got home.

"It's really beautiful, and so many rooms! Lady Winstanley is lovely, too. Irish, she is, very ladylike. I'm to meet her little girl tomorrow. She's called Victoria. She's about your age, Matilda."

Our Matilda was awestruck. *"Is she going to my school?"*

Mum shook her head. *"No, dear. She has a governess every morning to teach her lessons, and then goes riding in the afternoons. So you'll probably never meet her, I'm afraid."*

"Come on, Mum," I said. *"Sit down and I'll make you a nice cuppa. And then me and Matilda will make us all something to eat."*

"Thank you, Beattie. But it's Matilda and I - don't forget your grammar."

I'm always saying that – me and Matilda. It sounds friendlier, somehow. But just to make Mum happy ...

I went back to Bible Class today. It's getting really dark at night now, and it's difficult to see, what with all the blackouts. If you don't black out your window these days, Grandad comes along and shouts at you. *"Let's 'ave them lights out!"*

We have to make sure the Jerries don't know there's a village down here, so they don't drop their bombs on us.

Grandad's in the Home Guard. Well, officially. If I'm honest, though, it's more often than not Gran who comes along and checks everyone's all right. The Home Guard is there to look after things while the men are at war, and to make sure we're all obeying the rules so we're safe.

Bible Class was all about Paul and the Corinthians today. At least Paul wasn't preaching to the already converted, which Uncle John says is a complete waste of time. Uncle John won't go to chapel. I agree with him to a certain extent, although it is nice to go to Sunday school and see everyone. Except Mrs Tripp. Do you know what she did last year? Mum found some lice in my hair. Thin black things they were - she pulled one off to show me. It makes me itch just to think about it. She poured vinegar all over my head after school on the Friday because it kills the lice and nits overnight. Nits are a kind of baby lice, before they hatch out. On the Saturday she combed through my hair with a comb to remove the nits, but I didn't wash my hair until the Sunday night, just to make sure. So when I got to Sunday School Mrs Tripp could smell vinegar on me. She pulled a face, the most awful face you've ever seen in your life, and looked straight at me. *"Have you been washing in vinegar? I can smell vinegar on you."* She must have known I had nits. I've never been so embarrassed in all my life.

247

She's supposed to be a lady of charity. Wouldn't you think she'd have kept quiet, even if she could smell it?

Me and our Barbara were frightened out of our lives tonight, on the way home from the Bell Room. I'm scared even to write it down, it was so terrifying.

We were passing St John's, the big Parish church, and we heard a voice in the graveyard. We're both certain, absolutely, definitely, that we heard a voice – low and haunting. But we could hardly see a thing. There was no moon, so it was really really dark, but we could just about make out the silhouette of the church, the awful dark gravestones, and the shape of the tall trees behind them. Barbara's first impulse was to shine her torch over the wall into the deep shadows of the gravestones, but it only throws the tiniest beam of light. You're not allowed to have proper torches. They have to have little covers over them with slits in, so the Jerries can't see us. But we couldn't see anything either. We tried to believe that the sound was the wind, or even our imagination. But then, we heard it again. A low moan.

I've never been so terrified in my whole life. My insides flew up into the air and turned themselves upside down. "Come on, Barbara! Run!"

We scarpered, running all the way home, only stopping when we reached the end of our street, out of breath.

I've not dared tell Mum.

Tuesday, December 2nd

It didn't snow, like Mum said it would. Just icy cold, with Jack Frost at the windows and along the walls all the way into school.

Not much happened today, but I think Mum must have had a word with Mrs Bellhouse about lazing around all the time. Because when we came home from school, there was a pot of hot tea on the table and Mrs Bellhouse was standing there in the kitchen waiting for us, with one of Mum's pinnies on. I didn't like that, her wearing Mum's pinny. I don't think Matilda did, either. She went very quiet on me, until the toast arrived on the table, of course.

At lunchtime today, we formed a class gang. It's all very exciting. 'The Churchill Chums', we're calling ourselves. We met behind the boys' toilet block, even though it's not that pretty round there - a bit smelly, to tell the truth.

Usually, when it's playtime, me and our Barbara meet up outside the classroom, just where the chimney is. If you snuggle up to the wall in the wintertime, you can feel the heat from the fire. But we have to keep our gang a secret, so we're meeting behind the toilet block. There's me, our Barbara, Judy Cottingham, Sydney Bates, and Johnnie. It was Johnnie's idea. We're going to beat Hitler. We're going to show him what for, and get all our men back home again.

I got ten out of ten for my spellings today. Johnnie got five. He obviously wasn't copying me this time.

Thursday, December 4th

I've been yawning my head off all day. Mrs Cooke said she could see my tonsils.

None of us got any sleep last night. The sirens went at quarter past nine, exactly. Me, Matilda and Mary were all in bed, fast asleep, so Mum had to wake us up, which is never easy. "Come on, you lot - look sharp - get your coat on. Old Hitler's up there.'

We knew the planes would be going over us, but we weren't a bit frightened, just traipsed off down to Gran's in our overcoats. We sit with the blackouts up at the windows, so there's no light showing. What a night, though. The All Clear didn't sound until five o'clock, but by then we were all much too awake to go to sleep.

But now I'm exhausted. We did go to school, but only for the afternoon. Poor old Bertie Willie Coughdrop didn't stand a chance trying to teach us our eight times tables. I think he was yawning nearly as much as we were!

It's quite good fun really, staying up all night. We get to do things we don't normally do. Gran makes us hot milk to drink, and we get to have biscuits or buns. And Uncle John plays cards with us. Our favourite at the moment is Newmarket, and Grandad gives us a few raisins to bet with – a real treat because they're hard to get. Mum disapproves of all that, though, saying it's teaching us gambling. But at least it keeps us occupied. Because if we were to stop and think about what's going on over in Sheffield, we'd be in tears, I'm sure we would.

Last night, we took our own game to play with. It's what Mum and Dad used to play when she visited him in hospital. A friend of

Dad's gave it him after he'd been to America and played it over there. He must have been a rich friend, going all the way to America and back. The game's called Monopoly and it's really good. You have to buy bits of London, and you charge people if they land on your property, and you can land in jail if you're not careful. I'd never heard of some of the places before, but apparently they really do exist. I'd love to go to London some day, too. Uncle John won. Me and our Matilda went bankrupt. It's a really good game.

So that's it. I've decided. I'm going to work really hard at school, train to be a nurse, and then I'm off to London. After the war's finished. Well, I wouldn't go there nowadays, not on your nelly. I'll take Mum and Matilda and Gyp with me, too.

Mrs Bellhouse made tea for us again - we had toast and dripping, and cake. Mrs Bellhouse actually made a cake. According to Mary, she always made cake down in London. It was quite nice, not as nice as Mum's, but all right. She had to use grated carrots instead of raisins, but that's the war for you.

Saturday, December 6th

The milk lady, Mrs Gillingham, came to collect the milk money this morning. She comes every Saturday morning. She's Farmer Gillingham's wife and they have a horse that pulls the milk-cart. He's called Topper and I often stop to stroke his mane. He can look fierce when he's a mind to, but he's really an old softie at heart. This morning I was walking Gyp up to the farm when I heard Mrs Gillingham talking to Mrs O'Mara, who lives up our street. Their conversation was like nothing I've ever heard before:

Mrs O'Mara: "It was just after her Alf died, you know. Doors was shutting all by themselves. Cupboards opening and closing all of their own accord. The mop, that had stood in the corner there for years, wouldn't stay still no longer. Kept falling over, it did. All by itself. And the dog - well, he wouldn't stay in that kitchen for love nor money."

Mrs Gillingham: "You don't say! Well, I must admit, I have heard of such things before. But poor Mrs Brown. She must have been beside herself. So what did she do, then?"

Mrs O'Mara: "Well, it's obvious the house was haunted. Her old Alf mustn't have wanted to leave the place. Local Vicar was called in, but he couldn't do nothing, nothing at all. So she moved out. Told the landlord she was going and off she went. Not heard hide nor hair of her since. God's honest truth."

I didn't hear any more. I was stroking Topper's mane while they were talking, then pretended to pull our Gyp out of some weeds at the roadside, but I couldn't carry on with that for too long. It would have been too obvious. But it did set me to thinking about that sound in the churchyard. It wasn't meant for me, was it? It wasn't Dad, was it?

We were allowed to go to the chippy last night. Me, Matilda and Barbara. Mum was feeling flush after working all week, so we got to have fish and chips for supper. They were delicious. We have to take our own newspaper to the shop these days, but because we didn't have any (Mum doesn't buy them any more – says they're not worth it because they're only four pages long), Barbara took theirs. Which was really good, because we could look at pictures of Clark Gable and Maureen O'Hara. She is just so glamorous. Barbara says she's going to have her hair like that when she grows up.

Sunday, December 7th

Today was a terrible day. After Sunday school, we went round to Gran's for dinner. Auntie Betty and Uncle John were there with Barbara and Jack. We left Mrs Bellhouse and Mary in our house because Mum says they need to be on their own sometimes.

But after dinner (sausage and mash and APPLE CRUMBLE!!!), it seemed as if all we did was listen to the radio. They were talking about an attack on some place called Pearl Harbour. It's an island somewhere in Hawaii, which is part of America. The strange thing is it wasn't Germany who attacked them. It was Japan. For some reason, Japan is siding with the Jerries. How can they? I don't really understand it all, but Uncle John seems quite pleased about the whole thing. He says America will help us fight the Jerries now. "That'll hot things up a bit. This war'll be over by Christmas, just thee mark my words." Uncle John talks like that all the time. A lot of the men around here do.

I suppose if Uncle John is right (and he usually is, Mum says), then maybe today wasn't such a terrible day after all.

251

Tuesday, December 9th

Mrs Cooke says I'm to learn my lines by next Monday's rehearsal, or there'll be trouble. Oh dear.

Bible Class last night was quite good fun. Some of the new evacuees were there, including Johnnie Whitaker and his brother. We made decorations for the Christmas tree. I made an angel. I coloured him all in yellow, apart from the face. The face was black, with big green eyes. When Mrs Daley asked why I'd painted the face black, I told her. You see, I wanted the angel to be my Dad. I thought Mrs Daley would say something, but she didn't. If my Dad's an angel in Heaven, then I'm glad. I wouldn't want him to be a nothing. I don't want him to be just a dead thing. I want him to be a something.

Wednesday, December 10th

We had our second meeting of the Churchill Chums today, after dinner. Mince again. Our Barbara and Johnnie came up with a brilliant plan. Johnnie says Britain and America declared war on Japan yesterday, because of the bombing on Sunday. He says what we need to do is raise money so we can send it to Winston Churchill, then he can send it to America, and they can use it to fight the Jerries and Japan. And then hopefully Johnnie's Dad can come back home, because that's all Johnnie really wants. Then, when the war's over, he and Michael can go back home to their Mum in Battersea. All we have to do now is think of a way to do it.

It's really awkward, sharing with your little sister. I try to be kind and thoughtful, remembering what Mum says about helping the war effort. But, really. Diary, if you had to pick up your sister's dirty knickers and socks every time you walked into the room, how would you feel? They're disgusting!

My eyes strained to read the next sentence. The writing was nearly illegible, a pencil let loose in the dark.

It's bedtime, and I'm trying to sleep. But I've just had an idea. We could collect old clothes and make them into blankets to send to the soldiers. That would help them win the war.

252

CHAPTER 27

ENID clapped her hands delightedly. 'It's lovely, Mattie, just right. Thank you.'

'It does look good, doesn't it?' I replied. 'Even though it's hard work, it does give me a wonderful feeling when it's all finished.'

I'd covered the walls in fresh cream paper, apart from the matt burgundy damask that now embellished the fireplace, and the coving and picture rails were a fresh, buttery silk.

'We should open a bottle of wine to celebrate,' she enthused. 'I've got one in the fridge, left over from Christmas.'

'It's only half past eleven. But if we get cleared up now, I'll call back tomorrow for a little celebration. It'll cheer me up; I'm seeing my solicitor first thing.'

She looked around. 'Pity I have to move, isn't it?'

Genevieve curled up into a ball on the hearth. Why did I always have the feeling she was watching me?

'If you want me to, I'll come and do up your new house, or apartment, or whatever it is you buy. No need to ask. And you don't have to pay - I'll just fit it in around my other work.'

Warm tears filled her eyes. 'You are good to me. What would I ever have done without you?'

'If it wasn't for you and your friends, I'd never, ever have thought about setting up in business. And then where would I have been when Rob left? So we'll have less of that, if you don't mind.'

'I have lots of friends, you know. Good friends, lovely friends. And they're here, every one of them, to help out whenever you need them.'

She looked at me, her eyes trying to tell me something.

'Sorry, Enid,' I stammered, rolling up pieces of spare wallpaper. 'I don't quite know what you mean.'

'It's nothing to be afraid of, my dear.' Taking my hand, she led me to the sofa, nodding at me to sit beside her. 'There is something I need to explain.'

'What?'

She sighed deeply, bracing herself. 'Mattie, I'm not just a Romany. I'm a Wiccan. Do you know what that is?'

I shook my head warily. 'No ...'

'In layman terms, I'm a white witch.'

Slightly relieved, I smiled awkwardly. 'Oh. Okay ...'

'Really. My herbs, my oils, Genevieve, my familiar – they're all here for a reason. I perform witchcraft, Mattie, but only good witchcraft. We believe strictly in the law of three, that anything we do or send out, whether good or bad, will return to us threefold. It's a religion, close to the law of Karma and its consequences.'

'Wow.' I stared into her warm eyes nervously. 'But what *exactly* do you do?'

'We use our own energies. We worship nature. We meditate, bending the laws of nature to suit our needs, raising and channelling the energy that is within us to harmonise with nature. It just takes a little practice. I – I've not told you before because I didn't want to scare you.'

'Wow. Amazing, Enid.'

I didn't really know what else to say. And all this time I'd thought I was helping out a little old lady.

'The thing is, Mattie, we're here to help. That's all I want to say. I didn't want to introduce you to my friends and then you find out we're all members of a coven.'

I stood up quickly. 'Now that *does* sound scary.'

'You see?'

I sat down. 'Okay. I can see you're serious about all this, and if you're not causing any harm …'

Relief lit her face. 'Thank you, Mattie. I just felt you should know. My friends are all wonderful people, and I wouldn't want them to scare you away. Goodness knows what you'd find in their kitchens.'

I giggled nervously. 'As long as they put the dead rats away before I arrive, I'll be fine.'

Smiling, the golden flecks of her eyes glowed like burnished copper. 'Let's have a little tea party to celebrate finishing. Bring Thomas straight round from school tomorrow, and I'll bake us a cake and we'll have sandwiches and sausage rolls. What do you think?'

*

That evening I finally managed to begin work on the food cupboards in the kitchen – a job that had been nagging all through my recuperation. Old tins, jars of pickle, sticky bags of raisins, all needed tidying out so I could wipe down the shelves. Working with warm soapy water and a dishcloth, I scrubbed away, feeling happy, fulfilled, my work on Enid's house the panacea to all my problems. I really had discovered a hidden talent, found such enormous satisfaction and independence.

Then the phone rang; it was Andrew.

'How are you?' I asked.

'Fine - I'm fine. You?'

'Okay. I'm just cleaning out the kitchen cupboards. They were desperate.'

'Great. You can come and do mine.' His voice was smooth, controlled, but I could tell he was nervous. 'Sorry to disturb you, Mattie. It's just - I wondered whether you'd like to go out somewhere one night - you know, to talk? I know it's difficult, with Thomas and all that, but …'

I felt sick, not wanting to let him down, but not wanting to say yes.

'I - I can't. There's no-one to babysit at the moment. Becca usually offers, but she's just got back with her husband and I don't want to impose. And - and I don't know whether it's a good idea, anyway. Sorry.'

'Oh. Okay.'

His disappointment twisted at my heart. 'I really am sorry. I think what I really mean to say is, could we just be friends, just until I know where I want to go? I'm in a mess just now. I don't know whether I'm ready for all this. Despite what happened on Tuesday.'

'Oh.' He sighed heavily.

'I'm sorry, Andrew.'

'Okay, Mattie. Just friends, then.'

*

I couldn't sleep. Tossing and turning, I worried about what the solicitor would say in the morning, considered the possible pros and cons of Enid's revelation (how many wiccans are out there, for instance?), went over and over my conversation with Andrew, and allowed my concerns over paperwork for 'Matilda's Decorating' to gnaw at me.

Finally sitting up, I switched on the bedside lamp. It was two twenty-five, and I'd not slept a wink. Tiptoeing out of bed, I opened my wardrobe door, pulled out the bag containing Grandma Beattie's diary, and curled quickly back beneath the duvet.

Thursday, December 11th

What a fantastic idea! All my best ideas happen when I'm half asleep.

So I ordered a Churchill Chums meeting. Johnnie was really enthusiastic about my idea, and Judy had some of her own. "We could collect other things too, things people usually throw out. We could 'Make Do and Mend'. Paint old bottles and sell them as flower vases at the Christmas Fair, or bake buns and things, or make decorations for the tree."

Judy's quite creative like that. She looks really creative – curly blonde hair and dimples. Sydney laughed at her, though. "What's the point in making flower vases when we're all growing vegetables? No-one'll have any flowers to put in them!"

I had to think quickly, Judy's the sensitive type. "Well – they'll look pretty. If we paint pretty flowers onto the outside they won't need to put flowers in, will they?"

257

She threw me a look of gratitude, but then our Barbara had to put her twopennorth's worth in. "What happens to all the money we make - how will we know where to send it?"

Johnnie knew exactly what to do. "We send it to the Houses of Parliament. They'll get it to Churchill and he'll use it to help finish the war."

We were full of ideas, all of us. Some ideas were a little crazy, some completely impractical, considering we're in the middle of a war. But one thing we did agree on, and we'll have to be quick-sharp about it, and that's to ask for a stall at the Christmas Fair, a week on Saturday. It's held every year, without fail. Or, as Johnnie put it, come Hitler or no Hitler. I don't know where he gets these sayings from, I really don't. He keeps calling me 'his most beautiful girl' as well, which makes me really embarrassed. And there's this little tune he hums. I've never heard it before, but it's so catchy I've found it whizzing round my head. Just when I'm trying to concentrate really hard on something, there it is. Very annoying. He could do with humming his times tables instead of silly tunes, anyway.

Some great news! Lady Winstanley's daughter, Victoria, it's her birthday soon. And she wants me and our Matilda to go to the Hall for a tea party. I can't believe it!

Friday, December 12th

Not written much today. Been learning my lines ready for rehearsal on Monday. I <u>think</u> I know them. Night night, Diary.

Saturday, December 13th

Mr Standen does make me laugh. Even though he and Mrs Standen have been running the shop for years now, he still stands behind her when she's using the scales, as if she doesn't know what she's doing. Just because she's a woman. I mean, today she was weighing the butter for Mrs Russell. There are seven children and her in that house of theirs. That's quite a lot of butter, all added up. A great big chunk of slippery, slimy grease. You wonder why we eat it really. But it does taste nice.

258

Well, Mr Standen was fussing round like Gertie the goose. "Add it up again, Mrs Standen, please. Don't want to leave ourselves short, now do we?"

I'm sure he doesn't call her Mrs Standen at home. Her real name's Joan. I know because I've heard Mum talking about her to Auntie Betty, about Mr and Mrs Standen wanting a family and not being able to have one. I don't know why they can't have one. Maybe the Government needs them to work in the shop all the time, so they don't have time for a family. Although Mum says it's up to God whether they have one or not.

I can't believe it! Mrs Bellhouse has started digging over the garden, even though the soil is rock solid. She's going to plant potatoes, carrots, parsnips and beans. She says she grew vegetables and suchlike with her father when she was little, so she knows what she's doing. It's good, because Mum will never have the time now and it means Uncle John won't have to help us out so much any more.

Cousin Barbara came round after dinner, saying she had a secret and didn't want our Matilda and Mary to know. Of course, that intrigued them even more than if she'd never said anything, so we had a row about us going without them. To be honest, I'd rather have stayed home. It's freezing out there!

Anyway, the secret wasn't very much, just about a meeting with the Churchill Chums near the allotments. The meeting was really good. We all decided that, after Chapel tomorrow, we're going to call round the village and collect salvage, bits of paper, tin, string, rags, whatever can be used again. If there's anything we can't use for the Christmas Fair, Johnnie will take it to Mrs Cooke's house so she can take it to WVS lady. It will all get used for the war effort. Nothing's to be wasted.

I had an idea too. A raffle. If we can get Mr Standen and some other people to donate food and suchlike. Our Barbara suggested collecting the donations at the same time as the salvage collection, kind of killing two birds with one stone.

I've just about warmed up from the meeting. My feet were like icicles! I got the hot shelf from the oven and wrapped it in a towel, so I can put my feet on it without burning them. Mum puts one into our beds at night to warm them up for us. We have to

259

remember to take them downstairs in the morning ready for dinner to be made, and are we in trouble if we forget. Oh, boy!

Sunday, December 14th

Been really, really busy today. When I collected the Missionary money this morning, I told everyone about our raffle and the salvage collection. Just so they'd be ready when we called round later. Everyone agreed to help out, even old misery, Mr Carpenter.

Sunday school was all right. Mrs Tripp was there with her red velvet bag. I didn't collect as much money today, probably because it's nearly Christmas and people are saving up. But I'll still get my prize in June. Last time I got a little badge with a painting of the sun on it, all pinks and oranges. I think it's supposed to signify Africa.

After dinner we went knocking on people's doors. I let Matilda and Mary come with me. For three reasons: 1. It let Mum have some peace. 2. I thought people might give more if they saw two little 'uns in the doorway. 3. They were very insistent.

Fitzackerley Street was by far the best street. Mr and Mrs Standen were really generous. Three tins of peaches they gave me. Tinned peaches are like gold dust around here. But the best bit was we got a quarter of Sharps toffees to share! Couldn't believe it. Delicious, they were.

Monday, December 15th

There was an air-raid practice today. We have to pretend the sirens have gone off, stop whatever we're doing, grab our gas masks, and run home as fast as we can. The school doesn't have air-raid shelters. Most of us live near enough to get to our shelters at home. There's an Anderson shelter in the school field, but only for a couple of the children and the teachers, because they have to stay behind and make sure everyone's gone home. There's never been a real air-raid while we've been at school, but we still need to practice, don't we? Between you and me, Diary, I think if we were attacked we'd be so terrified we wouldn't be able to run for tuppence.

After the practice, we had Bertie for Maths. We've never done algebra before. He says it's a way of substituting a letter for an unknown quantity, then working out what the unknown quantity should be. Some of us didn't understand it at all. But I quite enjoyed it because it's a bit like solving a puzzle. After lunch, we had a dress rehearsal. It's the real thing on Thursday. Scary.

Wednesday, December 17th
We met up at our Barbara's after school yesterday with our salvage and some painting stuff, scissors and suchlike. Johnnie brought along Dr Benson's little hacksaw and a bradawl, and he made some really good things. He's really good with his hands, wants to be a carpenter when he grows up.

So tonight we've worked really hard, finishing everything off. We've made: glass flower pots, wooden labels for plants, painted decorations made from wood, tiny cushions made from red gingham, and little red-ribboned bows, all for the Christmas tree. Let's hope we make lots of money.

We've still loads of old clothing left, so we've decided to leave it until after Christmas, then make blankets for the soldiers.

I had a really weird dream last night. Although it didn't feel like a dream at the time. It was Dad. I saw Dad standing beside me. Just standing there, not saying a word. I've not seen him standing up like that in ages – it looked strange. I just wish it had been real, and that the stupid accident had been the dream.

Thursday, December 18th
Johnnie and Michael didn't come into school today. I wonder if they've got this tummy bug that's going round. Poor things.

Winston Churchill's making it the law that unmarried women between 20 and 30 have to go and help with the war. I don't know if that affects any of our family. Cousin Alice is only just 16, and all the other women are married. I shouldn't think Churchill would send women to get killed anyway, would he?

The nativity play was wonderful, though a bit scary at times. I remembered every single one of my lines, and our Matilda looked very cute. She was a lamb, with a pink nose, tiny little ears and a woolly tail. Mum was welling up on the front row, she was so proud. Wish Dad could have been there.

Friday, December 19th

Last day at school - really excited about Christmas, but then Mrs Cooke went and told us why Johnnie and Michael never came to school yesterday. Their Mum's up from London because their Dad's been killed in France. The rotten, horrible, awful Jerries! I just wish Hitler would go and get himself killed, that's what I wish! Poor Johnnie. I can't believe it. Does this mean he'll have to go back home with his mum? I will miss him.

The new National Service Act means we're going to lose Miss Jennings from school. She's going nursing. Mrs Cooke was really upset in Assembly this morning, what with this and Johnnie and Michael and all. It looks as if we're going to have Bertie Willie Coughdrop teaching the juniors and Mrs Cooke teaching the infants. Will life ever be the same again?

Saturday, December 20th

We went to see Johnnie and his mum this morning, to say how sorry we are. Mum took some biscuits she made last night, specially. She wrapped them in paper and tied them all up with a pretty red ribbon. But poor Mrs Whitaker just burst into tears when she gave them to her.

Johnnie and Michael have been living with Dr Benson and his wife. They're really kind, and have asked Mrs Whitaker if she'd like to stay there for Christmas. I think that's really nice of them, she's in such a state. Her whole world must have exploded. You can see she's trying her best to make polite conversation with everyone, but she looks like she wants to curl into a ball and roll away somewhere. She's already as thin as a rake, looks like she's not eaten in months. Worried about Mr Whitaker, I should think, being over there in the thick of everything. She was right to worry. It's dreadful. Mum says if she does stay up here for Christmas she'll be in the best place. Dr and Mrs Benson will look after her and make sure she's eating properly. Hopefully she will stay, because that means Johnnie and Michael won't have to go home just yet. But I wish their Dad hadn't died. I know what it feels like, losing your Dad.

The Christmas Fair was brilliant. Barbara and Judy went along early to set up our stall. Mum and Matilda stopped for a cuppa

262

and a chat with Mrs Cooke. I wish they hadn't done that – it felt as if they were talking about me! But we sold absolutely everything, made £4 10s exactly. After we'd added in the money from the raffle, it made £10 12s 6d altogether. Brilliant - I can hardly believe it. Johnnie will be so happy when he hears. It'll be like paying the Jerries back for what they've done to his Dad. We'll beat them yet.

We went to Victoria Winstanley's birthday party after the Christmas Fair. I really didn't feel like going, not after seeing Mrs Whitaker all upset like that, but it was nice to see where Mum works. It's posh. Their windows don't have to be crossed with tape like ours (it's in case we get bombed, so the glass doesn't explode). No, their windows already have crosses on them, made out of lead, Mum says. The windows are really tall and beautiful, and look out onto lovely green lawns and vegetable gardens, all laid out like a strange kind of chessboard.

Lady Winstanley took us on a tour of the Hall when we first arrived. She's very regal – she was obviously born to become a Lady, but she's only called that because she married Lord Winstanley. The corridors in the Hall are so long it's no wonder they've got servants. They need someone to keep them clean.

We had pork sandwiches and chocolate biscuits and strawberry jelly and ice cream and a very small pink and white iced cake. Delicious. Helen Platt was there from Sunday school, because her mum works in the kitchens at the Hall. But no boys. I like boys though. They're always much more fun than girls, I think. Except for our Barbara, of course.

Victoria has the most wonderful playroom. It's next door to her bedroom – there's a door connecting the two rooms. The playroom is full of toys, and there are even more in her bedroom. I've never seen anything like it. There's a small sewing machine, a big black typewriter, a navy blue and silver doll's pram, the most gigantic rocking horse – I bet you could get six children onto it – and loads and loads of jigsaw puzzles and storybooks. She is so lucky.

Mum says, though, she bets Victoria would much rather have a little sister or brother to play with than all those toys put together. But because Lord Winstanley is away fighting the war, that might not be for a while yet. I wouldn't mind not having a sister though, if I had all those toys - especially the rocking horse.

Though I suppose it probably isn't that much fun if you don't have someone else to play with.

Victoria seemed a bit spoilt, to my way of thinking. When we played games – pass the parcel, hunt the doorknob and suchlike, she didn't like it because I kept winning. I suppose she's not used to another child winning. And she's probably a bit sad, too, because she must miss her dad if he's away all the time.

I placed this page behind the others, but was surprised to find the next page had not been written by Beattie's pen. It had been typed. The reason soon became obvious.

Thursday, December 25th

Christmas Day today!!!!!!!!!!!

I got a   typewriter!

This is the first page of my di ary in type writing. I'm a bot slow, and I know I'm not very good yet, but I'll soin learn.

Mum says she found my diary when we moved Matilda in   to my room. So she got this typewriter especially for me. It   's an old onw she bought from Mr Standen. It's beautiful. The best present ever!!!!!!!!!!!!!!!

I'm worried n ow, though. How much of m y diary has Mum read? I need to find a new hiding-place. The fit tted cupboard is no good any more, even though my scho olbag's always in front of it. That's the trouble when you shar e your room with someone else. Nothing's ever private. And now ev ery time I write something up, I'm going to have to take the paper out of the ty pewriter and hide it.

But I do love my new typewriter.

Matilda got a purple teddy bear with a pale blu e ribbon round its neck. She loves it. And some ch ocolates. How Mum got them, I'll never know.

Mary got a new baaby doll. She's got fair curly hair, and her name is Diana. Mary says she got a new doll's pram last

Christmas, but she's had to leave it with her Granny. That upset her a bit. But she's up here an d safe, isn't she?

Me and Matilda ma de Mum a card and a photograph frame out of red velve t and cardboard. We did it all at schoool, so it was a complete surprise. She's over the moon, and has put a picture of Dad into the fr ame. It was taaken at Uncle John's wedding. I'd forgotten how very handsome Dad was.

I hope Johnnie is hav ving a nice Christmas. He told me weeks ago that all he wanted for Chri stmas was his Dad to come home. So he probably isn't having a nice time at all.

Friday, December 26th

Well, we've nearly h ad a white Christmas. It snowed last night. Just a couple of inches, but it looks so beautiful. Fresh and pure, as if it coul d wipe away all thhe sadness around us. Wouldn't that be good? As if, when the snow disappears, everything goes back to the way it was. You know, Dad home and Johnnie's dad bac k home. And no war. I hate the war. I could kill Hitler. Mum says I'm n ot to become bitter and twisted, but how can I be anythi ng else?

Mum said we co uld go and call for Johnnie and Michael if we liked. And David Benson. We did, but then our Matilda got upset when Michael threw a snowball at her. She went back home, so we called on our Barbara and went to the fa rm to play. Farmer Gillingham doesn't mind us playing on his field if it's snowed, because we can't do that much da mage. I found a piece of old sheeting to play with, hidden under the hedge. There was an old ring caught up in it too, a very thin, shiny gold one.

"Finders, keepers!" I shouted.

So I've kept it. Well, if it was important to anyone, they wouldn't have left it there, would they?

Me and our Barbara wer e the first to try out the sheet on the snow. I pulled while she sat on it. It's only a slight hill, but if you run fast enough you can go really quickly. Then

Johnnie and Michael grabbed hold of it whil;e me and Barb
ara sat on it, holding on like glue. We had the most famtastic
time, with our Barbara screaming and giggling like mad. My
bottom's a bit bruised now.

Tuesday, December 30th

Yesterday was the worst day. I still can't believe it's
happened.

Mum was at work, so Mrs Bellhouse told me and our
Matilda to go out and play. She said she didn't want us
around the house, that she and Mary needed to listen to the
radio, see what was happening in London and suchlike. So
we went to Auntie Betty's to play with Barbara and Jack.
And - I left our Gyp at home because she doesn't like the
snow. She's only got little legs and it's too cold for her. I am
so, so, so stupid!

I can hardly type this. Our Gyp got run over. Mrs
Bellhouse, that rotten horrible beast of a woman! We should
never have let her into our house. She sent our Gyp outside
for no reason, no reason at all. And on her own. Gyp's never
had much road sense. We always watch her when she's out,
always shut the gate so she can't get onto the road. And Mrs
Bellhouse knows she doesn't like the snow.

Maureen O'Hara from up the street saw the whole thing.
A great big lorry, it was. Hardly any lorries drive through
our village. Why did it have to be there, and why then? Poor
Gyp – she never stood a chance.

We're burying her in the garden this afternoon. But I just
can't stop crying, and my head feels so heavy, like there's a
bomb in there ready to explode.

Mum's told Mrs Bellhouse and Mary to go. "Back to
London, where you came from."

They're packing now. I feel sorry for Mary, really. I
mean, it wasn't her fault, was it?

Wednesday, December 31st

New Year's Eve.

Let's wish that 1942 is a better year than this one. It has to be, it can't get much worse.

We're all meeting at the Memorial Hall tonight. Johnnie Whitaker has asked me for a dance, but I think I'm too young for all that kind of stuff. He keeps saying he's going to marry me when he's grown up. Ha! I'm not ever going to get married. I'm going to be a nurse, a good nurse - I've told him that. But he'll soon get a wife, he's got that charm about him. I do like it, though, when he calls me his most beautiful girl.

Mrs Bellhouse and Mary left today. Mrs Cooke's arranged for them to stay with her until a new billet's been arranged. It'll most likely be back in Wales, she says. Mum says Mrs Bellhouse is really sorry about letting Gyp out. But she says if she can't look after a dog properly, how can she trust her to look after me and our Matilda?

We're going to stay at Gran's house in future, while Mum's out at work.

My typing seems to be getting much better.

Thursday January 1st 1942

Very tired today. We stayed up until one o'clock this morning. I don't know how our Matilda did it! It was all very exciting, though. There was food to eat – don't know where it all came from, mind – I think Uncle John had something to do with it. And lots of singing and dancing.

Mum was crying this morning, though. She said she can't believe she's starting the New Year without Dad. For once, she didn't seem to mind me catching her crying. Well, let's face it - I've seen enough of it around, and I've done my fair share as well. It seems to be the norm around here at the moment. And it was nice to be able to give her a great big cuddle. It made me feel better too.

Twenty-six countries signed the Declaration of the United Nations today, an agreement between all the people who are on our side, fighting the Jerries. Let's hope it works, and really soon.

CHAPTER 28

THE sitting room smelt of flowers. A heavy, sweet scent that took me straight back to Grandma Beattie's funeral. A posy of white lilies on the coffin, the delicate fragrance of the long-stemmed yellow roses Mum had given me to place beside them.

The Yellow Rose of Texas ...

Silent tears filled my eyes, but I brushed them away.

'Mattie, love, are you alright?' Enid took my arm, leading me to the sofa. 'Thomas, you run into the kitchen, darling. There's sausage rolls if you want one. I won't be a minute.'

Thomas ran out excitedly, Genevieve at his feet.

'Sorry, Enid - the smell in here. It just took me back, that's all.'

'Goodness, Mattie, I'm sorry if it's upset you. Yes, it is a bit strong. I wanted to get rid of the paint smell. It's just a bit of coriander seed and jasmine. Sorry if it's upset you.'

'No, no, it's okay.'

She sat beside me, taking my hand. 'What was it? What did it remind you of?'

'Just a funeral. Silly, really.'

'It's not silly. The sense of smell is powerful. Highly linked to the memory, it is. It goes into the emotional parts of the brain, whereas words and suchlike go into the thinking parts.' She paused, patting my hand. 'Was it your grandma's funeral?'

Confused, I nodded. 'How did you know about that?'

She blushed. 'You mentioned her once, that's all. I know you were close.'

I nodded. 'Yes, we were very close.'

'But look, we're here to celebrate, aren't we? So let's drink a toast to your grandma. I've got some Pinot Grigio in the kitchen. I bought it for when my Carol and Richard came over, but we never got round to drinking it.'

We found Thomas with a sausage roll in one hand, a ham sandwich in the other.

Enid smiled. 'I hope you like my sausage rolls, Thomas. I put in some fresh coriander and parsley to liven them up a bit.'

He swallowed quickly. 'They're yummy.'

Pulling the wine from the fridge, Enid poured smooth liquid into two tall glasses.

'So here's to you and your new business. And to your grandma.'

'Thank you, Enid. And here's to the sale of your beautiful house.'

Lifting our glasses, we clinked them together.

'You've got Peggy Fleming's place next, haven't you?' she asked. 'She's been telling me all about it.'

I smiled. 'I know. I can't wait to get started.'

'Well, you've done a marvellous job here. Thank you so much, Mattie. Although I will be sorry to leave.'

'Don't be upset, Enid. You've got some wonderful memories, you know. And they'll never leave you. They're up here - in your head. Forever.'

*

Dad rang just as we were eating dinner.

'Just ringing to see how you went on this morning at Freeman's.'

'It was okay. All very sad, though. I just wish it wasn't happening.'

'Oh, Mattie ...'

'Sorry.' I swallowed my tears. 'I'm keeping the house, the furniture, the car, everything, really. Rob's to get the business and the van. They're going to work out who owes what and take it from there. We're to have joint custody of Thomas, giving Rob alternate weekends.'

'And is that alright? For Thomas, I mean?'

'It has to be, doesn't it? If he saw Rob every weekend, then I wouldn't see much of him, would I? I know he's here with me through the week, but he's either at school or in bed, bless him.'

'Well, just make sure he's okay, love. He's going to miss his father, you know, even if he doesn't say so. You need to make sure he doesn't keep it all bottled up. That's when the trouble starts.'

'I know. You're right. And he's the last person who should be hurt by all this. Rob's the culprit. But then,

I'm partly to blame for marrying him in the first place. I should have stayed on at uni, like Mum said.'

'Mattie love, don't go blaming yourself. It's not your fault Rob couldn't keep his trousers on. And you're doing the best you can for Thomas. He'll be fine, you wait and see.'

*

Eager to continue with Grandma Beattie's diary, I washed up, switched off the hall light, and settled down with a large glass of wine.

But then the doorbell rang. Typical. I opened the door gingerly.

'Andrew ...'

'Hi, Mattie.' He smiled shyly, his eyes deep saucers of green. 'Sorry to drop in unannounced. It's just - I had to see you.'

'No, it's fine.' I welcomed him in and closed the door, my heart thumping. 'I was just going to settle down with a good book.'

'I won't keep you long, then.'

'It's okay. Come on, I'll put the kettle on.'

'Mattie ...' He took my hand suddenly. 'I just needed to say something.'

I stared into his soft eyes, didn't pull away, couldn't resist. 'Yes?'

'That wasn't just a one night stand on Tuesday, you know. I love you. And I want you.'

I tried to say something, anything, but my mouth was too dry.

'Mattie?' He was gripping both hands now.

I looked down. 'I - I'm not sure. I need to think. I'm still married. It's too soon. And there's Thomas. It's just all been so sudden, hasn't it?'

'Not for me, it hasn't.'

I looked up. His face was a soft pillow I wanted to rest my head against. Safe. Secure.

'I just don't want to do anything rash. There are other people to think about.'

'There's yourself to think about.'

'I know.'

Dejected, he let go of me, running a hand through his dark hair. 'Sorry, I don't know what I was thinking, barging in like this. Look, have a think about it. I know it's too soon. I know you need time. It's just ...'

'Sorry ...'

'No. Don't be.' Without warning, he took my face into his hands and kissed me softly. A feather of a kiss, a brushstroke. A lifetime. 'There. Sorry. Again. I'll wait.'

He left then, quickly, unceremoniously, closing the car door and driving away.

Back inside the house, with pictures of myself, Rob and Thomas along the wall, I felt nothing but guilt. Except - except for a tiny space deep inside. A space that was no longer a space, but was full, contented. Complete.

My mind in turmoil, I took a long, hot shower. If only he had waited. If only *we* had waited. But why couldn't we wait now? Why couldn't we give it six months, then try again? But I already knew the answer. Because there'd always be the feeling of guilt. Because Thomas needed to know I'd really cared for Rob, and hadn't fallen for someone else as soon as his back was turned.

Even though it was only nine o'clock, I curled up in bed with my glass of wine, pulled Grandma Beattie's diary out of the bag and stretched out, my back against the pillow.

Saturday, January 3rd

Lady Winstanley had some bad news for Mum. She's had enough of the war here and is going back home to her family in Ireland. Mum's distraught. Can things get any worse? Now she'll have to go and work at the glass factory, the very place she's been trying to avoid.

The Churchill Chums met this afternoon. I let our Matilda come along this time, because Mum was at work and Gran was looking after us. Matilda was very excited because it's usually all top secret. We didn't do much, just mooched around in the allotments for an hour or so. It was too cold and we weren't in the mood for doing anything except talk. About the war, about our Mums and Dads. Poor Judy's dad is missing. He's in the RAF, an engineer of some kind. Her mum thinks he had to go flying over Germany and that's where he'll be, hopefully in a camp of some kind. At least he's not dead.

Monday, January 5th

I was looking forward to going back to school, but Miss Jennings wasn't there, so Mrs Cooke had her class and Bertie Willie Coughdrop had to read the last chapter of Jane Eyre to us. It's a really good story, but he doesn't read it half as well as Mrs Cooke. She always brings it to life, makes it real, even though the words are quite old-fashioned. I think Bertie finds it boring. It's a love story and I don't think Bertie's ever been married, so maybe he doesn't understand it.

Just got back from Bible Class. There were noises in the churchyard again. Our Barbara thinks it may be smugglers or something, but I think she's been reading too many stories. Maybe we should ask someone about it?

Friday, January 9th

It was Dad's birthday today.

We laid two red roses on his grave. Mum got Mr Standen to get them especially. She cried and cried.

So did me and our Matilda.

But I found in the end that I wasn't just crying for Dad. I was crying for our Gyp too, and for Johnnie's dad. For everyone. Everything.

Saturday, January 10th

It's six in the morning and I'm awake already. So's Matilda. She's pestering me right now, while I'm trying to write.

We ended up fighting. Until Mum came in and told us off for waking her up. I don't know - little sisters!

We're going to the Co-op for Mum today, then going to Gran's. Grandad's planning on a few games of Newmarket with us. It's really good fun, because he's got this bag of big juicy raisins to bet with and they're delicious. Let's see who wins.

This afternoon me and the Churchill Chums, of which our Matilda is now an honorary member, are going to make blankets out of the rags we've collected. They're not much good for making into clothes anyway, too raggedy. So we'll stitch all the best bits together to make huge sheets. And if we sew two of them together round the edges, we can stuff them with bits of the really horrible rags to make nice warm blankets. It's lucky Johnnie and Michael are staying with Dr Benson and his wife, because they're letting us use their old outhouse. It's massive, with an enormous table, which is just what we need. It was a Doctor's waiting room a long time ago, which is why he bought the house, apparently. But he has his own surgery now, near the Memorial Hall.

Grandad won! He won five games out of seven, but he gave me and our Matilda his raisins. They're really difficult to get in the shops nowadays and these are some they've had in the house for ages. But, as he says, "Once they're gone, they're gone. Isn't that right, Beattie?" I just hope this stupid war ends quickly, then we can get back to normal. It seems sometimes as if this is normal, though, it's been going on for so long.

The first blanket is coming along nicely, and Mrs Benson's lovely. She's shown us how to use her old sewing machine, so it will make it all a lot quicker. It's so exciting, and I can't wait for the first one to be finished.

Sunday, January 11th

Today is going to be a good day. Me and our Matilda are making dinner for Mum, then washing up afterwards. I think we'll make Stuffed Potatoes. I saw the recipe in a book at school and thought she might like it. I hope Mum likes it, and we're making her favourite pudding – gingerbread and custard.

There was a bit more money in the Missionary bag today. I think people are getting over the expense of Christmas. Not that there was that much to buy anyway, really.

Sunday school was quite exciting. Rosie and Tom Collins's dad walked in, right in the middle of prayers. He's home on leave and couldn't wait to see them. The looks on their faces, it was like Christmas all over again. I don't think Mrs Daley minded them missing a bit of Sunday school.

Mum loved our stuffed potatoes, although we burnt them a bit. But at least it put a smile on her face. She said if Dad's watching from Heaven he would be very proud of his two girls.

After dinner, we met up with the Churchill Chums at Dr Benson's. David Benson came to help out, too. Churchill Chums is getting bigger all the time.

Johnnie, Sydney and David cut up scraps to use as filling and Matilda helped sort through them. She found some really horrible stuff. Yuk! Old ladies knickers, for instance. They were huge! And quite disgusting. I don't think we'll be using them. Mrs Benson and Mrs Whitaker made us all tea and cake. Lovely. I think we got the sheet a bit sticky, to be honest, but I don't think the soldiers will mind. They just need something to keep them warm.

Mum seems a bit chirpier tonight and there's more colour in her cheeks. She went round to see Gran and Grandad while we were out, so they must have cheered her up a bit. I'm glad.

Tuesday, January 13th

We've got snow! I'm so excited, I'm typing this before I go to school. We're setting off early so we can make snowballs.

School was fantastic, although my fingers were so cold when we arrived I couldn't write anything for ages. And my gloves are still soaking wet. They're in front of the fire downstairs right now. But we had the most fantastic time. It's ten inches deep in some places. I put a snowball down Matilda's neck, which I really regretted because she did the same to me. It was freeeeeeeezing!

Mum's got a job at the glass factory. She starts on Monday, so me and our Matilda will have to go along to Gran's when we get in from school. Mum will have to work nights sometimes, so Cousin Alice is going to come and sleep here with us. I wonder if she minds not sleeping in her own bed. I know I would.

Mrs Whitaker's going back to London this weekend - she's going to live with her parents until the war's over. Hopefully that will be really soon. Johnnie and Michael are staying up here at Dr Benson's because it's too dangerous in London and the schools are all closed anyway. Yippee! Mum asked if I'd like to invite them all for tea on Saturday before Mrs Whitaker goes home. I'll ask Johnnie when I see him tomorrow.

Wednesday, January 15th

Someone's stolen our coal! Mum's really, really upset.

We used to get our coal free when Dad was working down the pit. I used to love watching the great big truck parked outside our coal shed, and the man opening up the back to let the coal fall out in a great black, dusty heap. Sometimes I'd get much too close and cough and splutter, and Mum would shoo me away into the kitchen. Now, of course, we don't get free coal, so other miners let us have their leftover coal cheap. Mum pays a bit towards the six shillings delivery charge and Uncle John helps her bring it round to our house in his wheelbarrow.

So whoever stole our coal mustn't know my mum, that she has to get her coal cheap from other people. They obviously think she gets it for nothing. I think they need their heads looking at.

Mum's come home just now, though, with a great big smile on her face. Lady Winstanley's sending her butler round with a barrowful of coal, just to see us through. Well, she won't be needing it soon anyway, will she? Mum says it's really kind of her. She's also letting Mum come home early on Saturday to arrange the tea party. She is a nice lady.

But what I want to know is - who stole our coal?

I asked Johnnie about coming round for tea, and he's asking his mum tonight. He doesn't know whether she'll come, though, because she's still very upset over everything. But I said if my mum can't understand how Mrs Whitaker is feeling, then no-one can. It's true, isn't it?

Thursday, January 16th

Johnnie's mum said yes, they'd love to come for tea on Saturday.

Saturday, January 18th

Me and Matilda went to the Co-op this morning, as usual. We managed to get all the stuff we needed for our tea party. We even got fresh eggs from Uncle John.

Mum got home from work, complete with the butler, who carried on delivering coal to us all afternoon, and some beautiful red velvet curtains, the likes of which you've never seen. Lady Winstanley also sent me and Matilda two bedspreads, pale pink and so beautifully soft and fluffy I can't even begin to describe them. But then we all gathered ourselves together, set to, and made: Egg and cress sandwiches. Cheese sandwiches. Fruit scones. Jam tarts. Treacle Tart. Cups of tea.

Me and Matilda made the jam tarts all by ourselves. It was really good fun.

The food was delicious and Mum and Mrs Whitaker had a good old laugh, despite Mum being a bit upset at having said goodbye to Lady Winstanley and Victoria. Us kids were laughing, too, at some of the things Mrs Whitaker came out with.

"Mrs Baxter," she said.

"Please, call me Hattie," said Mum.

"Thank you. And I'm Maureen."

"What a lovely name. Like the actress. So modern."

"Thank you. But what I was going to say was I do love the colour of your house. So unusual."

Excited beyond belief, I gasped out loud. Did this mean what I thought it meant? What *was* the colour of Grandma Beattie's house? I read on.

"Thank you. It was Benny's father who painted it, years ago. His favourite colour. And we've never had the heart to change it. Or the time."

"Oh, I know what it's like with children to look after. Our Johnnie, when he was little - oh, the trouble we had."

Johnnie moaned at that, which must have been really quite difficult as he was stuffing his mouth with an egg sandwich at the time.

I moaned too. Wouldn't she ever mention the actual colour of their house?

279

Mrs Whitaker smiled. "He's a good boy now, though. Aren't you, Johnnie?"

He nodded, despite me being there. He forgets I'm in school with him every day.

She continued, "When he was little - only eleven months old, mind you - he crawled into the kitchen, opened the cupboard door, pulled down a bag of flour from the shelf, and emptied the lot - all over the floor. I ask you! I only realised when our cat, Josephine, came outside where I was hanging out the washing. She was black, but, poor thing, she'd turned pure white. Covered in flour, she was. She looked like she should have been in that advert for Waifs and Strays. Not something we should laugh about, I know, because it's such a waste, but, really, it was so funny."

I think it's the stress they've been under, Mrs Whitaker and Mum, that made them fall about so much, because they just couldn't stop laughing. I didn't think it was that funny. Matilda rolled her eyes at the ceiling. Me and Michael shrugged at each other and carried on eating, while Johnnie turned bright red with embarrassment. But in a way it was nice to see them laughing so much. They've been through such a lot.

Sunday, January 19th

A sad day - Mrs Whitaker went back to London. We all said our goodbyes, and she promised to write. Mum was quite emotional, and said she'll visit once the war is over. When will that be, though? They said it would be Christmas, and here we are - the middle of January. It will all have been for nothing anyway. What's the point of returning to normal? It will never be normal, not with Dad gone. It will never, ever, be normal again.

We went to Dr Benson's afterwards. Mrs Benson made us tea and cake again, and I think it must have got our brain cells going, because we suddenly realised that our idea of stuffing the sheets with bits of material wouldn't work. It would all just fall to the bottom and stay there. So, what we're going to do is make a third sheet of thicker material - it doesn't have to look pretty, and we could even use those old knickers if necessary, and sew it in between the other two sheets. That should add some warmth. Anything to help the soldiers win the war and stop all this fighting.

CHAPTER 29

THOMAS ran to the front door. 'It's Becca, Mummy - and Chloe!'

I rushed through from the kitchen. 'Come on, I'll put the kettle on.'

Becca grinned, her shaggy faux fur gilet making her sizeable bump even bigger.

'Sorry to drop in unexpectedly. Alan's got a conference all weekend - in Plymouth of all places - and the weather's so grotty, and I couldn't stand the thought of staying in the house a minute longer, so I thought ...'

'There's no need to apologise, Becca. You're always welcome. It's quite fortuitous, anyway - I've just had Annie on the phone. We need to get organised with this jumble sale.'

'Brilliant. That should be fun.'

'Excuse the mess. I've been finishing off Enid's house, so there's not been much time for cleaning and stuff.' I offered the biscuit tin to Thomas. 'Here, take a biscuit or two. And I've got fairy cakes in the freezer.'

He took four biscuits, two for Chloe. 'We're going upstairs to play.'

'Be good.'

They scampered upstairs like two hungry monkeys.

I offered the tin to Becca. 'Here. You're eating for two, so you'll probably need six - they're tiny.'

She placed a biscuit to her mouth with long, delicate fingers. 'And don't mention eating for two. It feels like three, actually.'

'You look brilliant, Becca. Blooming. So don't tell me you're not the happiest person in the world right now.'

A gleam of starlight entered her eyes. 'You seem particularly chirpy yourself this morning. You've not made up with Rob or anything, have you?'

'No, I have not,' I retorted. 'And I wouldn't take him back if he was the last rat on earth.'

'What is it, then? You met someone else?'

'Just what do you think I am? I'm still a married woman, for goodness' sake.' But my cheeks were burning violently, so I busied myself making coffee and hot chocolate, their delicious scent filling the room.

'Why are you blushing, then?' she continued.

'I'm not.' I pulled milk from the fridge.

She shrugged. 'Okay, if you want to keep it a secret, I quite understand.'

'There's nothing to keep secret. So stop it. Come on, let's go and get comfy.'

We trundled into the sitting room while I searched my mind for a quick change of subject.

Sighing heavily, Becca sat down. 'That's better. I can't cope with those trendy kitchen stools, not at the moment.'

'I know,' I agreed.

'Now then - this little secret of yours. You do know you can tell Auntie Becca all about it, don't you?'

'We need to discuss the jumble sale, Becca. It's only a few weeks away, and I did offer to help.'

'I'm not wrong though, am I? There's something different. Come on, you can tell me, I'm a housewife.'

'Becca, please don't joke. There's nothing wrong - nothing at all.'

'I didn't say there was anything wrong, did I? I said there's something different. Come on Mattie, spill the beans. Please.'

'Becca – stop. There's nothing wrong. And all this has made me forget the cakes.'

I escaped to the kitchen. Searching the freezer for the box of fairy cakes, I welcomed the cool air as it brushed against my cheeks.

But she was there, behind me. 'It *is* a man, isn't it?'

I had no choice but to nod my head.

'How wonderful.' Delighted, she clapped her hands.

'What?' I turned, bewildered. 'How can you say that? I'm still married! I - I've ...'

'You've what?'

'Nothing.'

Turning back to the freezer, I would have pushed my head inside if there'd been room.

'What were you going to say?' Her voice became a whisper, silent and still. 'That you've committed adultery?'

'Oh - Becca.' Utterly ashamed now, sad tears filled my eyes.

'No. You haven't.' She hugged me. 'How can you even think of such a thing after what Rob's done to you? I think it's wonderful, marvellous, that you've found someone else.'

Moving away, I slammed shut the freezer door, loosened the lid on the box, and placed it inside the microwave. Pressing the buttons furiously, I turned back, whispering through clenched teeth.

'But Rob's the absolute scum of the earth. Don't you see? He gave up everything for a romp with a tart! I'm not like that. I don't want that - Thomas growing up with one uncle after another. He needs stability. *I* want stability. So how can you say it's wonderful, Becca? Because now *I'm* the scum of the earth.'

Taking a deep breath, she went to look out of the window. 'Talking of scum, Mattie - I've seen the two of them together.'

'What?'

She turned. 'Rob and Sonia. In the park of all places. Actually, Chloe saw them before I did.'

'The park? What were they doing in the park?'

'Walking. Holding hands and walking.'

'Walking?' I felt suddenly sick. 'Holding hands and walking?'

'Mm.'

'How old do they think they are, for God's sake? Holding hands in the park, like lovesick teenagers?'

'Weird, isn't it? Like he's going through a midlife crisis - but early.'

'You can say that again. Bastard.'

'You're right. He definitely is. But you've found someone who isn't. Hopefully. So, come on, tell all. Are you madly in love?'

My heart still, my mind as quiet as a snowstorm at midnight, I looked my friend straight in the eye.

'Yes. Yes, I am. I think so.'

'And is it serious - I mean, is he serious?'

'Yes, he is. He wants to be. The problem is - I don't think he's in a position to be serious. It's just - oh, I don't know, Becca.'

Taking my arm, she led me back to the sitting room. 'Come on, sit down - our coffee's getting cold. We'll sort out the cakes later.'

'Becca,' I moaned, resisting.

'No, really - I insist.'

She closed the door quietly. 'So, my darling, how long has it been going on? Who is he, and why can't he be serious? Not married, is he?'

'No, he's not.' I shook my head in despair. 'He's lovely, he really is - everything I could possibly want. But - I don't think he's ready. I don't think *I'm* ready. Not yet. Maybe in a year or two. I need to get Rob out of my system first. I know to some people I might seem all cool, calm and collected, but I still can't believe what he's done, can't get it into my head somehow. I must be in denial or something. I get two cups out for coffee, three plates out for dinner, I keep thinking he'll walk through that door and ...' Blinking back sudden tears, I looked away.

'I'm so sorry, Mattie.'

'Don't be. It's my own silly fault. I should just accept it, get on with my life.'

'Hey, don't forget I've been there. It's not easy. In fact, it's bloody hard, so don't go beating yourself up. It's his fault, not yours. He did the dirty on you. He walked out. He's the one who's not coming back. You, my angel, have done nothing - nothing at all.'

'You're right. And you know what, Becca? I'm going to be strong from now on. No more tears, no more wishing he was back, no more waiting for the phone to ring. It's over. I'm going to be Mattie Payton. Strong, reliable, stunning.' I grinned. 'But - that doesn't mean I have to jump into the arms of the first man to come along.'

'It sounds like you already have.'

'I know, I know. And it was a big gargantuan mistake. He's really lovely, but I need to stand on my own two feet. I need to *know* I can stand on my own two feet. Do you know what I'm trying to say?'

'I think so. You're obviously a stronger person than I am. I was totally, utterly lost without Alan.'

'I'm not stronger, but I need to be. That's the point. I have to know I don't need anyone else – not Rob or Andr ...'

'Andrew? Is that his name? Andrew?' She smiled, her very own *Becca* smile - clever, cunning, knowing. 'Not Andrew from Haringey's?'

Woefully, I nodded.

She clapped her hands gleefully. 'How wonderful. Is he gorgeous? Intelligent? Got his own mansion?'

'Yes. All of them. Well, apart from the mansion. But I don't know - it's just - I can't see him settling down, somehow.'

'Why ever not?'

'He's happy with his own life. Work, expensive holidays, ridiculously posh cars. He even teaches yoga in the evenings. He has a full life, and I can't see me and Thomas fitting in anywhere - you know?'

'Surely that's up to him to decide. Have you asked?'

*

Mum rang later. Clutching the phone, I was perched on the bottom step.

'Talking of books, Mum, I've been reading Grandma Beattie's diary. You have to read it. It's brilliant. Fascinating. There's so much detail - all about the war, the rations, the stuff they had to put up with. She even talks about Grandad. Did you know they met each other when she was only ten? Isn't that a wonderful love story?'

'I know. He came up from Battersea as an evacuee, didn't he? He'd tell us about it when we were kids, about how his dad died in the war, and how his mum came to live with Gran afterwards and helped bring up Grandma Beattie and Auntie Matilda until the war ended. Even after they moved back to Battersea, they all remained great friends.'

'Really?'

'It's a lovely story.'

'Wow.' I couldn't wait to finish it.

'So how are you doing anyway, love? You've got your first real customer lined up, haven't you?'

'Actually, I'm feeling a bit nervous about it, worried about doing everything wrong. She wants me to choose the colours for her - which is okay. But what if I choose something she absolutely hates? I mean, Enid was pretty easy-going, didn't mind what I picked.'

'Mattie, you've got good taste like me. Anyway, you can always get a couple of paint testers or paper samples first.'

'That's the trouble. I'll be spending half my time going backwards and forwards to the shops if I'm not careful. I suppose I'd have to take her with me if absolutely necessary.'

'Good idea. That's my girl.'

CHAPTER 30

I pinned a shiny new poster onto the sodden wood of a telegraph pole. *Folksbury C of E School's Jolly Jumble Sale.* Bright balloons decorated the edge in an explosion of colour.

'How did you get these done so quickly?' I asked Becca.

Behind us, the streets were deserted. Only the peal of bells welcoming people to Church and the noise of traffic in the distance could be heard.

She passed me another drawing pin. 'Alan did them for me at work. He's a sweetie, isn't he?'

'They're very professional.'

'Thank you. I designed them.'

I wasn't a bit surprised. 'Well done, they're brilliant.'

'What did you expect? Just because I'm thirty-two weeks' pregnant and have been out of the workplace …'

'I know, I know. Sorry. I didn't mean it the way it sounded. Don't be so sensitive. Must be the hormones. Come on, I know a good place just outside the veg shop. There are always loads of posters there.'

We continued onto the High Street and walked past Haringey's, its Georgian windows full of coloured photos, the great red door smiling encouragement to passing trade.

'How's it going with Andrew, then?' asked Becca. 'Have you seen him again since - you know?'

'He came round on Friday night.'

'And?'

'I think he said he'd give me time, he'll wait for me.'

'You *think* he said he'd give you time? What kind of answer is that? I need a definitive answer, Mattie. You can't just leave me wondering.' She stopped to catch her breath, the baby pressing upon her lungs.

'Sorry, but that's how it is, I'm afraid. Everything left uncertain. I don't know what I want. He doesn't know what I want either, really. It's a mess, Becca, a total mess. Maybe if it had happened in a couple of years' time.'

I felt suddenly depressed, a forgotten apple at the bottom of the basket.

She nodded quietly. 'You need to get Rob out of your system first. I don't know – men. Well, I suppose you'll be seeing him at work this week. That might help you decide, to see if you can just be friends.'

'We are friends, that's the point. Good friends. And I feel as if I've spoilt it all now.'

We'd reached the greengrocers' shop. The door was closed, the old wheelbarrow locked inside. 'Anyway, I'm handing in my notice.'

'What?' she exploded. 'Are you mad? You're a single mother. What will you live on?'

'We'll be fine. It doesn't pay that much anyway, and Rob will start paying maintenance soon – his business is picking up. And I'll get tax credits and so on. And when the sale of Grandma Beattie's house has gone through, I'll be able to pay off the mortgage. Anyway, I start my new business this week. Once I get cracking, I'll be raking it in.'

'I hope you do, Mattie.' She sighed heavily. 'Actually, I quite fancy getting my own teeth stuck into something like that. You don't fancy a partner, do you? I could be a sleeping partner at first, just until this little one's a bit older.' She rubbed her bump. 'I've plenty to invest, if you need it.'

The answer to my wildest dreams. I practically leapt at her.

'Are you sure? That would be just fantastic. Unbelievable. Not just the money, I'm fine with that. But you'd be solving one of my biggest problems.'

'What?'

'I need someone to help with the design side of things?'

*

I placed *Jodhpur and the Pirates* onto the bedside table.

'That was a good story, wasn't it?' I stroked Thomas's curls as he lay in bed, Blue Bear tucked under one arm. 'You had a nice day, darling?'

He nodded sleepily.

'You were okay being left with Chloe?'

292

'It was good. We played soldiers.'

I giggled. 'Didn't she mind playing soldiers?'

'Course not. We had to pretend a lot, though. I've never been a soldier. I've only seen one on the telly, so I don't know what they do, really.'

'Well, they have to learn how to be a soldier, too. They have to be able to survive in the wild and look after their guns and things. Then if there's a war, they go and defend their country. They have to be *very* brave.'

'I could have been a soldier, you know, but they wouldn't let me. I had to stay at home and work. But I didn't like it - it was all dark and scary ...'

Dark clouds filled his eyes. An icy shiver ran down my spine, but I shook it away. Thomas had always been afraid of the dark, but this had never been mentioned before.

'Well, maybe you had to do something much more important than being a soldier. But any work is good work, isn't it?'

'Yes, Mummy.'

I needed to change the subject, and quickly. 'What kind of work would you like to do when you grow up?'

He grinned. 'An ice cream man. I could drive a big van like Daddy's.'

'Ha!' I laughed. 'You'd eat all the profits.'

'I wouldn't. I'd make lots and lots of money.'

'Well, it makes a change from an estate agent, I suppose.' I kissed his tiny nose. 'Night-night, darling. Sweet dreams.'

'And Blue Bear, Mummy.'

'And Blue Bear. Night-night, Blue Bear.' I kissed him, too.

'You never founded Jeremy Bear, did you, Mummy?'

'Sorry, darling. I've looked everywhere. But don't you worry about him. He'll be having a wonderful time, wherever he is. He's that kind of bear.'

*

Confused, I searched one more time for Jeremy Bear, couldn't understand where on earth he'd got to. I'd never once seen Thomas take him out of the house. In any event, he would surely have brought him back. Frustrated, I switched on the TV as background noise, stretched out along the sofa, and pulled out the diary.

Monday, January 20th

I can't believe it. Johnnie is absolutely, totally, utterly selfish! I hate him! He was given a quarter of boiled sweets by Mrs Standen this morning. Just for nothing. Great big red ones, rhubarb ones. He only went in for a couple of pencils for Mrs Benson, and came out with them. Lord knows where she got them from. And he didn't share one with me, or our Matilda - just his precious Michael. I can't believe it. It's the last time I let him look at my spellings, I can tell you.

We had to recite our eight times tables today. Bertie was in a foul mood, and I wasn't much better. So between us we just about messed up the day for everyone. It was as if a thick black cloud had descended over the classroom. Gloom and doom. Well, what is there to be happy about these days? All we hear about is death and destruction.

The milk was frozen too. Me and David Benson are milk monitors this week, and Bertie forgot to tell us to bring it into class so it could defrost. We couldn't drink it until this afternoon, so were hungry all morning. Dinner was nice though – cauliflower cheese.

Mum started at the glass factory today, so me and Matilda went to Gran's after school, then had Bible class. We studied the first chapter of the Bible. Genesis – the beginning of time. It was a bit confusing. I've never really read the Old Testament before, not properly. What interested me, though, was it looks as if God created the birds and animals to be companions rather than to be eaten. It says He created herbs and trees for us to eat. Does that mean we shouldn't be eating all our lovely animals and fish? Except Gertie, of course. She should definitely be eaten.

Mum said she enjoyed her first day at the factory, but she looked very tired. We had tea at Gran's, so Mum didn't have to cook. I've offered to make tea sometimes and Mum says that's okay, but only until I get to big school.

Tuesday, January 31st

Bertie Willie Coughdrop was in a much better mood today. And Johnnie. He said sorry for not giving out his sweets. I'm trying to understand. It's hard being generous these days - there's not much to go round, is there?

After school, we went straight round to David Benson's. And the MOST EXCITING THING happened! Our Matilda was sorting through the old clothes and she found an old letter. It had been folded up really small, so would have been easy to miss, but our Matilda's tiny fingers found it in the corner of a pocket.

It's dated 19th June 1930 and begins 'Dear Joan …' and it's a love letter! But we can't make out who wrote it. The writing's really bad and the signature's even worse. I wonder who it is, and who's Joan? The only Joan I know of is Mrs Standen, but I can't imagine anyone writing a love letter to her, especially one like this, anyway. It's really romantic. He says he misses her so much, can't understand why she won't leave her husband and go away with him, he will love her for the rest of his life, why has she rejected him? … etc, etc, etc. Johnnie wasn't half pulling a face, but I think it's really sad. I wonder who it's from. It can only be from someone we know.

Anyway, I've made everyone swear to keep the letter a secret until we know a bit more about it. I might ask Mum if she knows anything. But isn't it exciting?

Saturday, January 25th
One month since Christmas Day. It seems like ages. We've been to the Co-op as usual. Nothing exciting, although I did have a good look at Mrs Standen's face. It's long, with a hard nose and a mouth like a straight brown line. She's got straight brown hair, too. The only nice bit of her face is her dimples when she smiles. But she's much too busy to smile. No, the letter definitely won't have been written to her – she's not exactly the romantic type. I think it must have been written to someone like Cousin Alice, sweet and pretty. Although our Barbara thinks it was probably someone like Maureen O'Hara, all beautiful and fiery.

Cousin Alice called round this afternoon. She's going to be staying with us when Mum works nights this week. I'm dreading it. The thought of her having to stay up all night, then having to sleep during the day when the sun's up - poor Mum.

Me and Matilda cleaned the parlour and our bedrooms (yes, we're back in our old rooms again) while Mum was making dinner. It was my idea, and I had to bully Matilda, but she did it. In the end.

When the Churchill Chums met up as usual, I asked if everyone minded me telling Mum about the love letter, and they agreed it was a good idea. But if she doesn't know who wrote it, then I don't know what I'll do with it. I can't just throw it away, can I?

It was freezing in the outhouse today. We were supposed to be spending more than a couple of hours there, and even though Mrs Benson brought in hot tea and biscuits, we still left at four on the dot. Brrr! We managed to finish the latest blanket though, so that's five so far. Johnnie says once we've made ten, we'll take them to Mrs Wright at the WVS so she can send them on. Can't wait!

I've asked Mum about the letter. The only Joan she knows is Mrs Standen, but she can't see it being her either. She thinks maybe the letter was written by someone we know, but never posted. I suppose that is possible. But still, I want to know – who is it?

Sunday, January 26th

It was so cold in the Bell room today. I had on my thickest liberty bodice, even though it's nearly small enough to fit our Matilda, and was still cold. I keep expecting it to snow, but Mum says it's too cold to snow. How come it's too cold to snow - surely that's when it does snow? Anyway, Mrs Daley helped us keep warm by playing hide and seek. We were allowed to run around the yard at the back of the chapel. It's a good place - there are lots of little nooks and crannies. Plenty of trees too, although you've got to be quite slim to hide behind them. Our Barbara wasn't too successful - much too easy to spot. But then, as Grandad says, she's got a bit of meat on her. Her red hair doesn't help. But hide and seek did warm us up, and we had great fun. I think it got Mrs Daley into a bit of trouble though – I saw the look on Mrs Tripp's face after she'd finished counting all the Missionary money. I think she cares more about the children in Africa than she does about us children in England.

I showed Mum the love letter after dinner at Gran's. Which is really, really fortunate, because Gran knew all about it. "If I'm right, and I'll bet I am, pound to a shilling, then it's old Bob Carpenter's written that letter. Now, you don't go saying anything, mind." She shook her finger at me - her nails scare me a bit because they're so long and hard.

I nodded solemnly, swearing not to breathe a word to anyone. Luckily, our Matilda was playing with her doll in the kitchen.

But Mum shook her head disapprovingly. "Before we go off down that road and start any rumours, Beattie – do you know if any of you collected rags from Mr Carpenter?"

I recalled that Sunday when I'd called for my missionary money and he'd handed me an old potato sack full of stuff. It had a horrible musty smell, as if there were mouldy green goblins hiding inside. I assumed at the time it was the bag that had been kept somewhere damp, but it could have been the clothing as well - which made sense if this letter had been stuck in a pocket for over ten years.

I nodded. "I did. I collected a sackful of stuff from him."

Gran folded her arms knowingly. "There you go then. And old Bob Carpenter did have a bit of a fling with Joan Standen, you know."

Me and Mum just sat there, aghast. We'd never have thought it in a month of Sundays. Mr Carpenter and Mrs Standen!

"Nothing inappropriate, mind. As far as I know, anyway." Gran talked as if I understood what she was talking about. I nodded as if I did understand what she was talking about.

"He wanted her to leave her 'usband. But, bless her, even though he's a sour old coot, she never did. Swore in her wedding vows to stay with him, and so she has. An' old Bob never got over it."

Mum crossed her arms questioningly. "So that's why he bosses her around so much, is it?"

"Who?"

"Harry Standen."

"Well, yes. Maybe. I don't know, do I? That'd be suggesting he found out about it, wouldn't it?"

My mind was working overtime. "Maybe he did find out about it, and that's why she didn't go! Maybe he stopped her before she had chance to meet up with Mr Carpenter!"

Mum smiled. "You just leave that imagination of yours at home, young lady. Truth is, we don't really know what happened, do we?"

But wouldn't we like to find out! Mr Carpenter and Mrs Standen! Well, I never!

Monday, January 27th

The day I've been dreading - Mum on nights. But then it wasn't so bad after all. Mum had made us our favourite when we got home from school – toast and Gran's homemade raspberry jam. She's made a bed of the put-you-up in the parlour for Cousin Alice to sleep in. I'm not looking forward to waking up in the morning and Mum not being here, though.

Bible Class was okay, but freezing cold. I do wish it would snow.

Me and our Barbara ran all the way home – no noises in the churchyard tonight. Too cold for ghosts, Barbara said.

Tuesday, January 28th

Got up to Cousin Alice making breakfast this morning. It was really good of her, although I don't think she'd slept very well. She looked pale and sad. She probably misses her own bed - I know I would.

At least Mum was here to say goodnight to us. But then after she'd gone, I lay in bed worrying about her. And that Mr Young, the foreman. He's horrible - stands there with a ciggie hanging from his mouth, staring. Some of the girls who work there hang around the factory gates, swearing and shouting, which isn't nice. Gran says they're up to no good, and I shouldn't take notice. We're not really allowed up near the factory, but we have to walk past if ever we go to the shoe shop. The Co-op doesn't sell shoes now, so we have to go to White's in Swinton when we need a pair. Cousin Alice works there. That's how she gets all her lovely shoes. The ones she's got now are really nice, all black and shiny, and I wouldn't mind them when she's finished with them. But Mum says she'll stop growing soon, so her shoes will last her until they're all worn out. Pity, that. But if my feet grow before the next coupon comes, Mrs Cooke can measure my feet for me, so Mum gets extra coupons and I get the next size up. My shoes are never as pretty as Cousin Alice's, though.

It's been a month since our Gyp died. I went to her little grave before school and whispered a prayer. I do miss her.

Thursday, January 30th

Stewed rhubarb for dinner today. Yum!

Afterwards I told the Churchill Chums about the love letter and that I'd be returning it to the rightful owner, but I didn't say any more than that. Our Barbara and Johnnie were like cats on a hot tin roof, they were so anxious for me to reveal my secret. But I've sworn to Gran I won't tell a soul. And I won't.

Mum was up and dressed when we got in from school. She's finding it difficult to sleep during the daytime, but says she'll get used to it.

We should have had a 'sew and go' tonight, but me and Matilda wanted to stay home with Mum, so we made tea instead. Potato stew with tiny bits of bacon (it's all there was) and carrot in it. Mum said it was lovely. Then left-over jam pudding.

Saturday, February 1st

It was Cousin Alice's final night at our house this week. Mum's working 'Afters' next week which means going to Gran's after school, then Gran coming here to stay with us until Mum gets home. It can all get a bit confusing. One of these days I'm going to end up at Gran's when I should be coming straight home.

It's nice having Mum at home all day, even though she spent the morning in bed. Me and Matilda went to the Co-op. Grandad's put a big basket onto the front of my bike, so I can push the food home instead of carrying it all. It's much easier. We had to be really quiet putting it away in the pantry though, so as not to wake Mum.

This afternoon I'm taking the love letter back to old Mr Carpenter. I don't know what I'll say and I'm getting really nervous, but it has to be done.

Just got back. I was shaking like a leaf when I knocked on Mr Carpenter's door, but then when he opened it I felt really brave and gave him the letter.

"I think this is yours, Mr Carpenter. I found it in your trouser pocket – you know, the ones you gave us for the appeal."

Taking it with his long fingers, his nails all dirty and broken, he opened it slowly and carefully, lifting his glasses up to his forehead so he could read it, like Grandad does. He stared at it, then looked at me, his face white, his down-turned trout mouth a strange shade of blue. But I was no longer brave, I just wanted to run. Far away.

Then the strangest thing happened. His face broke into a huge grin, with tears streaming down his face. He motioned for me to go inside, into the depths of his dirty, grimy kitchen, where his few halfpennies lay in wait for my collection.

But I shook my head vigorously, my heart beating crazily. "I have to go now. Bye, Mr Carpenter - sorry!"

I ran home for all I was worth.

Sunday, February 2nd

I didn't call for Mr Carpenter's missionary money today. I hope the little African children don't miss it. And I don't think Mrs Tripp will notice a couple of halfpennies, do you?

Mum must have got her energy back, because she made us clear out all our bedroom cupboards and drawers. I found something I'd completely forgotten about – the plaster cast from when I broke my arm. Disgusting, it was. I threw it away. I don't know why I kept it in the first place.

301

Shocked, I couldn't believe what I was seeing. Hadn't Thomas mentioned a child breaking her arm, on the train up to Jenny's? Was this diary trying to tell me something? Was Grandma Beattie trying to tell me something? Swallowing hard, I stilled my racing thoughts, and continued to read.

Monday, February 3rd

Mum's on Afters, so we went to Gran's for tea – mince, which we'd already had at school. And jam sponge, which was delicious.

Bible Class – we've finally found out what the noises in the churchyard are. Cousin Alice and a boy! We can't believe it! Up to no good, kissing and whispering and all that. They caught us looking over the wall at them with Barbara's torch, so we scarpered quickly. Well, they should have been more careful. Sat on a gravestone, they were. Some people have no respect.

But at least it wasn't a ghost.

CHAPTER 31

PULLING her very own clown face, Emma pulled on her headset. 'Hello, Mrs Witheringham - Emma here. How can I help?'

I grinned, returning to my work, to the mailing list I was trawling through. The next name on the list wanted a four-bedroomed detached property for anything up to two hundred thousand. They'll be lucky, I thought. Checking through the list, I matched other requirements to new properties on the market, emailing each client in turn. A tedious task, but necessary, any one of them a potential buyer.

Emma finished her call and groaned loudly. 'She's chasing up the survey, but it's with Taylor Harvey. They always take ages anyway, and now they're having problems with the tenants. Trust it to be them. Trust it to be them *and* Mrs Witheringham. She'll be on the phone every day now - you watch.'

I grinned. 'I'm just glad she's got your name and not mine.'

'I'd have given her yours, but you're only here two days a week, damn it.'

'And not for long, either.'

'What?'

'I'm leaving.'

She stopped typing. 'What? What do you mean, you're leaving?'

'In two weeks.'

Her face was an autumn sunflower, drab and drooping. 'Mattie, you can't. You've only been here since September.'

'I emailed Head Office first thing. I've decided to run my business full-time. And you know what? I can't wait.'

'I'll miss you.'

'You can still come and visit, you know.'

'I know, but it won't be the same.'

'I'm sorry. But you'll be welcome any time. I'll make buns, especially.'

'You're definitely staying in that house then? Not selling up?'

'I'm buying Rob out. It's not fair on Thomas otherwise. It would be too much if we had to move house on top of everything else.'

'Wise decision, I'd say. As long as we know where to come when …' Smiling now, she winked at me knowingly.

'When what?' I asked, perturbed.

'Nothing.' She resumed typing.

'Emma?'

She grinned cheekily. 'Get any Valentine cards today?'

Thoughts of the beautiful, beribboned card I'd received filled my thoughts, and I blushed hotly.

'Why?'

'Nothing,' and she returned to her work.

'Come on, what do you know?' I screwed up the paper I'd been using for notes and threw it at her. 'Tell me!'

She looked up. 'You tell *me* first.'

'Emma!' I was genuinely annoyed now.

'Okay, okay. I know that Andrew is desperately in love with you. I know he will *probably* have sent you a Valentine card.'

'Do you now?'

'Yes.'

I stared keenly. 'And is that all you know?'

'Yes. Why?'

CHAPTER 32

TUESDAY, nearly Thomas's bedtime. The house was quiet apart from the tick-tock of the hall clock and the radio murmuring quietly in the kitchen.

Yawning loudly, Thomas stretched out his arms. 'Mummy, can I sleep in your bed tonight?'

I picked up his toys from the sitting room floor, placing them inside the toybox.

'You know I'm no good at sleeping when you're there. You wriggle too much. And I've loads of work to do tomorrow, so mustn't be tired. Will you help tidy up, please?'

'Okay.' Picking up a book and a few Lego bricks from the floor, he threw them into the box. 'What work have you got?'

'You know we don't put books in there.' I pulled it out. 'What's wrong, darling?'

'But Mummy, I won't wriggle - promise.'

'No, Thomas.' Taking hold of his hand, I guided him upstairs. 'Maybe at the weekend, when I'm not working. We'll see.'

'Thank you.' He bounced onto his bed. 'It'll be fun, won't it?'

'If you say so.' Pulling off his tee-shirt and trousers, I walked him to the bathroom.

'But Mummy, the doorbell's ringing.'

'Oh, who can that be at this time of night?'

'I'll get it …'

'Thomas!'

But he'd already flown downstairs. Sprinting after him, I pulled him back, unlocked the front door and peered into the darkness.

'Hi, Mattie.'

'Andrew.' I opened the door. 'Come on in.'

'Thank you.' But then he spotted Thomas behind me, still in vest and boxers. 'Sorry, is it bedtime?'

'It's okay.' I closed the door behind him. 'It's actually bathtime, but it can wait, we'll do it in the morning. Thomas, why don't you go get your pyjamas on, then you can come and see Andrew for a few minutes?'

He ran upstairs. Turning back, I caught a flutter of flowers behind Andrew's back. Confused, dazed, I looked up as he pulled out a glorious bouquet of roses, lilies, and freesia.

'I understand you've handed in your notice, and I just wanted to say sorry. It is my fault, after all. So could I please talk you out of it?'

I accepted the bouquet, its fragile scent wrapping itself around me.

'Thank you, they're gorgeous. Thank you for the card too. It was beautiful.' I waved towards the kitchen. 'Come on through.'

He removed his soft corduroy jacket. 'Lovely house.'

I filled the kettle. 'It's going to be all mine soon. I'll be able to do whatever I like with it. Not that I'll have much time, I'll be too busy doing up everyone else's. Coffee?'

'Um, tea, please. Thanks.' Perching himself onto a barstool, he stretched out his legs. 'How was your day at work, then? Pleased to be leaving?'

I met his eyes for the first time.

'Andrew, I had to - you know that. I couldn't continue, not after - after ...'

He sighed heavily. 'I know I shouldn't say this, Mattie. But it was the most beautiful, wonderful thing that's ever happened to me. Please don't regret it.'

'It's just - I feel so guilty. I am still married, you know.' I busied myself making tea. 'But then, we've been over this a thousand times already.'

'I'm still not sure I believe you. I'm not sure you believe yourself. Just tell me again - tell me you didn't feel something - something absolutely breathtaking ...'

'You know I did. It was very special, and you're a lovely man. But - I need time. Rob - he's still here, in my mind. You can't expect me to forget him so easily - we've been together a long time. We had everything ...'

'But I can give you that. I can give you everything, and more. And I can give you time. As much as you need.'

I shook my head. 'No, I'm sorry. It wouldn't work. I could keep you hanging on forever. We'd end up resenting one another.'

I looked at him. For some kind of understanding, some kind of agreement. But there was nothing. Nothing but adoration. Love, lust, a glimmer of hope.

'I would never, ever resent you.' He pulled me to him, gently, seductively, his hands on mine, and there was that feeling again, that weird sense of déjà vu. 'Just watch my lips. I love you. Always have. It sounds corny, but there's no other way of saying it. I've had this thing for you ever since the day we met, in the training room at Head Office. You remember? I've always loved you, and I always will.' He smiled awkwardly. 'I do, however, have one regret. And that is that I moved too quickly. I wanted to give you more time, you know that. I *should* have given you more time but - it just happened - I couldn't help myself. Is that such a terrible sin?'

'It was a sin, Andrew.' Trembling slightly, afraid of giving in, afraid of this utter and complete adoration, I pulled away. 'But it was *my* sin. Nothing to do with you. And I'm sorry if I've hurt you, but I - I don't want to have to depend on anyone ever again. I need to know I can support myself and Thomas. I suppose I'm feeling fragile. I need to know that if divorce ever happened to me again, I'd be okay. I won't always have my parents round to bale me out, you know.'

Curving his arms around my waist, he turned my face up to his, our faces nearly touching. 'Mattie, you won't ever ...'

But a sudden noise made me turn.

'Thomas ...!'

'Mummy?' He watched as we pulled away. 'Do I have to clean my teeth as well?'

Shocked, embarrassed, I inhaled deeply. 'Thomas – I – I tell you what. Let's wait until Andrew's had his cup of tea, shall we?'

'But can't Andrew help, Mummy?' He pulled hard on Andrew's hand. 'You can read my story.'

'Andrew's a very busy man - he doesn't have time for bedtime stories.'

But Andrew had already knelt down.

'Tell you what, Thomas, old chap. If it's alright with your mum, you go upstairs, tidy your room and find your book for me, then I'll follow you up. How about that?'

'Ye –es!' He looked at me. 'That alright, Mummy?'

'I suppose so.'

'Thank you.' He ran off.

'Is that okay, Mattie? I don't want to push in where I'm not wanted.'

'You've promised him. You can't really back out now, can you?'

But my imagination was sprouting wings, wondering what kind of father Andrew would make, what kind of husband he'd be. But not with me as his wife. It really was much too soon. And anyway, he deserved a better wife, his own children. Not a second-hand family, picked up like clothes at a jumble sale.

*

Laughing, Thomas fell onto his pillow in delight; Andrew was extremely good at mimicry.

'The drama club at uni,' he explained, winking.

'Might have guessed,' I said.

He continued. 'So Theo the Cat, along with his hat, turned out of the light, the very bright light. He went back down the tunnel, the shape of a funnel. He went home to his bed, his very red bed. He went to sleep, a very deep sleep. And do you know what? Even though Isabella Mouse visited Theo the Cat's house again and again, he never ever saw her. For Isabella Mouse had learned her lesson. And why do you think that was? It was because ...'

'Isabella Mouse was a very clever mouse!' shouted Thomas, gleefully.

'That's right - Isabella Mouse was a very clever mouse.'

'Let me see - let me see!' Thomas pulled at the book.

Andrew smiled at me, a smile like warm sunshine at breakfast. I grinned, pleased we could still be friends.

'How about we look at it tomorrow, Thomas?' I said. 'It's already way past your bedtime. Come on, time to go to sleep.'

Downstairs, Andrew picked up his jacket reluctantly.

'Right, I'll be on my way. Sorry about earlier.'

'It's alright.' I smiled sadly. 'I'm sorry too, for everything. It's just - it's not the right time, is it? I'm not ready for another relationship. I feel as if I led you on, and I'm sorry, it should never have happened.'

'Never, ever, say that. It should have happened, and it did.' He smiled, his eyes creasing attractively, seductively. 'And if you should ever want it to happen again - well, you know where to find me.'

I giggled. 'Don't.'

'No. Seriously.'

He looked into my eyes so tenderly I could hardly breathe, their vibrant green forcing a fierce energy through me. My body wanting, my mind refusing, I turned away, desperate to end this conversation, this torture.

'I - I told you. The answer's no. Please don't make me feel worse than I already do.'

'I'll get home.' His disappointment was raw, like cold, sharp metal. 'I just thought I might try and persuade you into staying on at Haringey's. You're a good worker, we'll miss you.'

'But I need to start afresh, run my own business, be my own person.'

'I understand. Although we'll stay friends, won't we, stay in touch?'

'Of course.' I followed him to the door. 'Thomas has taken a shine to you, you know. Thanks for reading to him.'

'It was a pleasure. Any time.'

'And thank you for the flowers. They're beautiful.'

The cold night air sank into me as I watched him leave. The typical bachelor. Driving off in his brand new Alfa Romeo, shiny and black.

*

Hours later, and I still couldn't switch off. My mind had been spinning all evening, round and round, up and down, backwards and forwards. One minute I was convinced I'd made the right decision, the next minute I wasn't. He had said he'd give me time. But how much time? How much would I need? It could be years.

Tired, confused, I crawled up to bed, turning gratefully to the pages of Grandma Beattie's diary.

Wednesday, February 5th

Bertie Willie Coughdrop lost his teeth again today. He must be coming down with a cold. There's a lot of it about. Mum says people aren't getting their vitamins (as she shoves another spoonful of cod liver oil and malt down our throats)! Yuk!

The Churchill Chums have been working like nobody's business. We've finished the last blanket. Yippee! Mrs Cooke wants to arrange for us to take them to the WVS. It's all so exciting. Can't wait.

Saturday, February 8th

Freezing today. Jack Frost was at the windows and it looked really Christmassy when we walked to the Co-op. Mum came with us today. A good job too, because all I could do was stare at Mrs Standen the whole time. She stood chatting to Mum, so I got a really good look. I was trying to imagine her kissing Mr Carpenter and wondering how she must have looked all those years ago. I tried to imagine them both with big smiles on their faces, eyes dewy with happiness. It was really quite difficult, because they look so miserable nowadays. What a pity. What a waste of two lives.

We're getting our new coupon books this week. Soap's to be rationed. Soap! Mum can hardly believe it. Nor can I. There'll be a few smelly people around. Shaving soap isn't going to be rationed, though, which I think is quite silly. I mean, what does it matter if a man can't have a shave? But it does matter if we can't have a wash.

Sunday, February 9th

A bit of a shock today. Our Barbara came round really early to tell us. Uncle John got called out in the middle of the night. Someone's gone into the river and drowned himself. It's a young man and they think it's to do with him not wanting to be called up. Apparently, there's been a bit of that going on up and down the country. Isn't it awful? We don't know who he is yet, but I feel sorry for his family already. The war makes people do such dreadful things.

I called on Mr Carpenter this week to collect his money, hoping he'd had chance to calm down. He gave me tuppence! And a big smile, patting me on the head. Do you think he's trying to bribe me or something? I just said "Thanks", and ran off. Then Mr and Mrs Standen gave me their money AND a quarter of aniseed balls. Maybe they know something too.

We met up at the Benson's afterwards. Our blankets look wonderful. We've chosen much the best bits of fabric for the top bits. They look like proper patchwork quilts. I just hope they do some good and keep the soldiers warm enough.

Monday, February 10th

Mum came home from work with the most dreadful news. It's all round the factory, everywhere. It's Cousin Alice's sweetheart who's drowned himself. Paul Whiting. Can you believe it? Terrible, awful, news. His Dad's a Fire Chief, been down in London, helping them out. It was because Paul didn't want to go to war and fight that he threw himself into the river. You can't blame him, though – he's only seventeen. Though I suppose when you've got to defend your country …

Mum says he could have become a conscientious objector, although they do get ridiculed. But it's better than drowning yourself. His poor mother.

Tuesday, February 11th

Cousin Alice is in pieces, off work poorly. Our Barbara's says she'd no idea Paul was so worried about joining up. His birthday's soon, so he's been expecting his call-up papers any day. Poor Alice.

I can't begin to imagine what it must feel like to be told to go and fight, to get killed, to live in trenches of mud and water, freezing cold and frightened. But if I had to fight to save my country from being taken over by those awful, cruel

Jerries, then I think I would. I'm going to be a nurse anyway, so I might end up on the front line if the war's still on. I do hope it isn't - we've had enough already.

Utterly exhausted now, I pushed the diary onto the bedside table and fell into a dreamless, bottomless sleep.

CHAPTER 33

I was amazed at the queue of people snaking down the road into the Memorial Hall, twenty pence coins like nuggets of gold in their hands, their admission fee to the jumble sale. Pushing my way through, I passed yet another battered cardboard box to Annie at the door.

'That's it - the last of the lot.'

'Cheers, Mattie. You coming in now?'

'I'll just lock the car. It's going to be busy. Good job we left the kids at Sally's - they'd have been running riot.'

Our bric-a-brac stall was one of many filling the huge room. The remnants of people's lives, children's clothes now too small, and various mad impulse buys had created mountains of unwanted treasure. I helped Annie empty the box. Old curtains, duvet covers and pillowcases were wrapped around a small table lamp, a green glass bauble at its base. She studied it carefully.

'Not a bad lamp, that. Nice shade, too. If it doesn't sell, we'll Ebay it.'

She made room for it on the table.

'It will,' I replied. 'Have you seen all the traders out there? You can tell them a mile off.'

'I know, but it's good for business. Anyway, thanks Mattie, you've been fantastic. You and Becca are stars. All the advertising you've done, I don't know how you did it.'

'Well practised. Becca designed the posters. She's very arty, you know. In fact, she's thinking of joining me in my new decorating business, once the baby's old enough.'

She smiled. 'Is that you then, Matilda's Decorating? I did wonder. I saw the ad in the Parish magazine. It really caught my eye, like something out of an old newspaper.'

'It was my dad who thought up the idea - a kind of land army girl.'

'Clever dad.'

'He's been fantastic. Bought me a new car, helped with the VAT and the accounts. I honestly don't know what I'd have done without him.'

Becca interrupted us with two mugs of tea.

'Here we are - nourishment before the onslaught. They're queuing right back to the vicarage.'

*

The jumble sale was a huge success, only a few piles of clothing, some old ornaments, and the acrid smell of stale sweat remaining. Annie stepped up to the stage, holding out a bunch of blue plastic bags, her voice loud and clear.

317

'Here we go, everybody. You need to leave enough room at the top for knotting, so don't overfill. The rag and bone man will collect them later. And there's fresh tea and biscuits in the kitchen for everyone.'

I gulped down a huge mugful, the bright orange sticker advertising my position as Helper now a crumpled ball of sunshine against my black hoodie.

'I needed this,' I murmured. 'Thirsty work.'

'It's been worth it, though,' Annie agreed. 'Alison reckons we've made about seven hundred, and there's Ebay and the rag and bone man yet.'

I waved my empty mug at her. 'I need to get a move on. I've got Thomas to pick up. Where do the sacks go?'

'In the corridor, beside the toilets.'

Quickly filling two bags with clothing, I carried them along the corridor. But as I turned the corner, I found Becca, both hands gripping her back, her face contorted, white with fear. Dropping the bags, I ran to her.

'What's wrong, Becca?'

'I don't know. The baby.'

*

The nurse smiled benevolently, showing me the way to the drinks machine.

'There you are.'

Her Irish accent was soothing, calming, but she looked tired and drawn, causing me to wonder how many hours she'd worked, how many she still had left. I smiled at her appreciatively.

'Thank you, I'll be fine now.'

'We'll let you know when there's any news. Mr Bradbury's on his way - he's having to pick the little girl up from a neighbour's.'

'He's been working away. My phone call must have been a bit of a shock.'

'All will be well. Baby will wait a bit longer, I'm sure of it.'

I frowned. 'It will be alright, won't it, it's not too early?'

'They'll both be fine,' she smiled, small dimples lighting up her fatigue. 'Don't you go worrying yourself now.'

*

I'd had to ring Rob. Someone had to pick up Thomas from Sally's while I took Becca to hospital, and there was no-one else to ask. But the thought of meeting that Sonia, of having to go to that house to collect Thomas …

My headlights created a steady pool of light. Seeing the sign for Back Lane on the left, I turned, drove a couple of metres, and stopped. The radio was playing an old number. *Three Times a Lady*. Lionel Ritchie. Switching on the interior light, I flicked down the vanity mirror, pulled out my lip gloss and painted my lips, rubbing a little into my cheeks. My eyes were pink and swollen from too little sleep, so I blinked to soothe them, stroking back my long, dark lashes with my fingers.

My heart was thudding violently, a beating drum against my ears, and I felt sick. Driving on, however, I parked my shiny new people-carrier outside his house, a beautiful chocolate-box cottage. A tall streetlamp threw an orange glow onto the neatly-laid garden.

319

Small shrubs lined the path, the space around them dark and solid.

My nerves were like taut guitar strings. My hands gripped the leather of the steering wheel, afraid to let go. I tried to swallow but couldn't, my throat too dry. I wasn't sure I could do this.

'Shit.'

Intuitively, I took a deep gulp of air, holding it safe within my lungs. Closing my eyes, I released it to a count of two, concentrating on the point just beneath my nose where the breath enters and leaves. Breathing in again to three, I released it on a count of four. Just as the book says. My head began to clear, my grip loosened, and I opened my eyes. To see a solitary snowflake, a tiny ball of kitten fur, falling to the windscreen. I watched as it disappeared into nothing.

Then I heard a voice, a warm whisper.

Go on girl, you can do this. You can do anything if you've a mind to …

Wrapping itself around me like the arms of an angel, the ancient scent of Grandma Beattie's apple blossom perfume suddenly filled the car. Sweet and haunting. And even though I knew it was just my imagination, suddenly I felt refreshed, strong, ready to go.

Locking the car, I pushed open the wrought iron gate, determination gritting my teeth. The garden lay as quiet as death. A cluster of copper jam-pans filled with soil sat below the name on the wall. *The Old Bakery*. A brass doorbell was hewn into the stone. Pressing it, I shivered.

But there it was again, louder this time. Grandma Beattie, her blunt Yorkshire accent urging, insistent.

Go on girl, you can do this. You can do anything if you've a mind to ...

The door opened suddenly, light flooding the path behind me. I squinted at the silhouette anxiously. But it was only Rob.

'I've come to pick up Thomas.'

'What?' His voice came at me, low, stern, reprimanding. 'You do know what time it is, Mattie? He's in bed for goodness' sake. Couldn't you have left it 'til the morning? Couldn't it have waited?'

Tears threatened; I'd forgotten he could be like this. But I was desperate to see my son, to hold him tight.

I shook my head. 'No. No, it couldn't have waited. It was good of you to take him in, last minute and everything, but he needs to come home now.'

'Okay. Fine.' He beckoned me in. 'But you can go and wake him yourself.'

'Thank you.'

I stepped inside, following him through the tiny lobby, my nose wrinkling at the scent of an overwhelming and - no doubt - expensive perfume. But intermingled was the odour of stale nicotine. It reminded me of overheated, stinking wheelie bins in the sunshine.

'Up here.'

He led me upstairs, each stair newly carpeted, its deep pile springing back at me. Reaching the top, however, Rob turned suddenly, forcing me to steady myself. Our bodies touched briefly and a sudden desire, born of familiarity, swept over me. Then vanished. I could never, ever, have trusted him again. If it hadn't been Sonia, it would have been someone else.

I held tightly onto the banister.

'You alright?' His face was a blank canvas.

'Fine.'

He hadn't felt the same thing then. No. It really was dead.

Over.

'You sure about this, Mattie?' He looked at me oddly. 'I don't mind bringing him home in the morning, you know.'

'No - thank you. I'll be okay.'

'Fine.' He indicated an open door to the left. 'In here. We - I - left the door open for him. He fell asleep watching the telly and I carried him up.'

I allowed my eyes to adjust to the darkness. Thomas lay curled upon the bed, his arms around Blue Bear, the duvet kicked away. Leaning over him, I stroked his curls.

'Thomas. Thomas, darling, Mummy's here. I've come to take you home.'

'Mummy.' He rolled onto his back, one arm stretching out. 'I dreamed 'bout that lady in Nannie's summer-house. It was the nice lady in the rain.'

'What?' Tired, confused, I dismissed his words hastily. 'Thomas, come on, wake up.'

He opened his eyes. 'Mummy.'

I went to pick him up, but Rob intercepted. 'Here, let me.' Picking him up easily, he waited patiently while I collected his shoes and socks. 'Come on, let's get him into the car.'

But as I turned to leave, my eyes now fully adjusted, I caught sight of a teddy bear on the shelf, its tiny claws reaching into the darkness like talons. Sharp. Vicious. Malevolent.

Jeremy Bear.

Anger rose through me like a rush of bile. But I bit my tongue. No, I thought. Now is not the time. Here is not the place.

But then - the sudden realisation. Jeremy Bear had been missing since before Christmas. Rob must have been planning to leave even then. The CD's missing from the drawer - he must have taken them too. So that's why he let us go to Edinburgh without him. To give him time to collect all his old stuff.

The utter, total, bastard!

I felt sick. Pushing past him, I flew downstairs, staggered through the acrid fog of stale scent and cigarettes, and rushed through the door. The cold air welcomed me like a friend - fresh and pure - a white stag in the moonlight. I breathed in deeply, waiting. But as I waited, I realised I hadn't seen Sonia.

Where is she? What does she look like? Is she prettier than me? Is she better in bed - is that it? Is that it, Rob?

I turned, watching furtively as he came downstairs. But I found no answer. I probably never would find out, would never know. But in the light of the lobby I saw for the first time the face of - a man. A man capable of stealing from his own child. A man able to go behind my back. A new man. A new Rob. Not my Rob. Not the Rob I'd adored, the Rob who always made me laugh, the Rob who, even when we were still saving for a home together, would come home with a treat, a chocolate, a flower gleaned from a customer, even just a bar of soap or a silly pen. But the thought had always been there. I'd always known he was thinking about me. That he cared.

Not any more.

'There you go,' he said, placing Thomas into his car seat.

'Thanks.' I closed the door quickly and smiled. 'Sorry to drop him on you like that.'

'Don't worry about it - it was good to see him. Any time.'

I was sure I detected a hint of regret, a sadness, a realisation of what he was missing, had already missed. As if reading my mind, he smoothly changed the subject.

'How's Becca, anyway? Is everything okay?'

'She's fine. It's just - the baby's quite early. He's not due until mid-April.'

'Well, I hope it goes well for her.' He patted the roof of my new car, admiring the scripted navy blue lettering. 'Matilda's Decorating. Very nice. Business doing well, is it?'

'Stunningly, thank you. I don't seem to have enough hours in the day sometimes. But I make sure Thomas comes first. Always.'

There was a pause, awkward, nasty, so I continued hastily.

'Becca's coming into partnership with me. A sleeping partner at first, but it should be amazing, once we get going.' Smiling, to convince him how very happy I was, that I no longer needed him, I opened the driver's door. 'Thanks again for looking after Thomas. Good night, Rob.'

I climbed in, turned the key, changed into first gear.

And drove away.

CHAPTER 34

EMMA'S voice filled the room. 'Good morning - Haringey's. Emma speaking.'

I waved to gain her attention. 'Coffee?'

She nodded. 'Yes, Mr MacPherson, we have the plans here for anyone who wants to see them. Pop in any time.'

The kitchen was chilly; it was still early, the first day of March. My last day as an employee. I switched on the kettle and waited for it to boil, pulling my fingers lazily through my hair. But the act, usually so mundane, in this place flooded me with memories. Misty, half-forgotten memories. Had it only been three weeks? Andrew stroking my hair, kissing my lips, lifting me tenderly onto the ice cold table. A quiver of passion ran through me.

'How's that coffee coming along?' Emma had sneaked up quietly.

I was pulled dramatically from my vision, Andrew's face becoming Emma's. 'Emma.'

She stared. 'You okay?'

'Fine. I can't believe today's my last day.'

She placed a brown paper bag onto the table. 'Thought we should celebrate.'

I smiled. 'Oh, Emma, I'm going to miss you.'

'You silly. We'll still see each other. I'll keep you filled in on all the goss, and you can show off your sparkling diamonds.'

'Sparkling diamonds? Which sparkling diamonds are they, then?'

'You know, when you meet that gorgeous millionaire.'

'Oh yes, I'd forgotten about that.' Laughing, I shook my head slowly. 'No, if I'm to have sparkling diamonds, I'll buy them myself. I'm independent now, free as a bird.'

'That's the spirit.' She opened the bag. 'But before you fly off into the sunset, how about some deliciously gooey chocolate cake and sparkling wine?'

'That sounds amazing, but just a glassful. We're driving out to Becca's after school to see little Jacob. He's out of his incubator now, so should be coming home any day soon.'

'Oh, that's sweet.'

'Anyway, should we be drinking wine at work? I mean, I know they can't sack me now, but …'

'Don't worry, it's only a small bottle. We can always hide it. And Andrew's in Grantham today - I checked his diary. He's not been in much at all just lately, been a bit kind of mopey for some reason.'

She stared at me questioningly, her eyebrows lifting, her eyes huge saucers of milky blue.

'Hey, it's nothing to do with me. Come on, let's open that wine.'

We'd only just finished eating when the bell clanged noisily.

'Enid!' I rushed forward, holding the door for her. 'How lovely.'

She smiled, her warm eyes shining like fireflies. 'Well, couldn't let your last day go by without some sort of celebration, now could we?' She nodded to Emma. 'Nice to meet you, my dear.'

'Enid,' I said. 'Meet Emma. Emma, meet Enid. Would you like a coffee, Enid? We're just about ready for one ourselves.'

'That would be lovely. I've made a cake, as a kind of celebration.'

'Thank you, Enid. But Emma's brought cake in ...'

Emma interrupted. 'But it wasn't homemade, just Tesco's own.'

I grinned. 'I'm going to get fat.'

'Don't worry, you'll run it off,' said Enid. 'You young ones always do.'

Leaning forward, she pulled a large plastic box out of her bag. Removing the lid cautiously, she revealed a small square cake iced in white. *Matilda's Decorating* was written in pale blue, the whole thing finished off with a ribbon of the same colour.

'Thank you, Enid. It's beautiful.'

I kissed her cheek, which was warm and soft, smelling of baby powder and lavender.

'I just thought we'd celebrate your new business. All very exciting, isn't it?'

'It was your idea, though. Thank you so much.'

'It's me who should be thanking you. I'd never have sold my house so soon without all your help.'

'It's a beautiful house. It just needed a touch-up here and there, that's all.'

'I've put down a deposit on one of those apartments, you know - the new ones just round the corner from Josie's. Smashing it is, all fresh and new. There'll be less cleaning to do, less looking after.' She sighed. 'But I will miss my garden. I like a bit of gardening, although it does do my back in sometimes.'

I grinned as a thought struck me. 'You can come and help us with ours, if you like. I don't seem to get the time these days.'

'Really?' Her face lit up. 'Could I grow some herbs as well?'

I nodded. 'On one condition, though.'

'What's that?'

I picked up her empty shopping bag from my desk, allowing it to hang there.

'That day - do you remember - when you first came in here, when I first met you? You practically waddled in, this bag was so heavy. And I've often wondered what you had inside. What was it?'

Her face took on the impishness of a small child. 'Potatoes. I'd just been to Peggy Fleming's. We had a good natter, we did, I remember. But, yes, it was potatoes. You know how I love my jackets.'

*

Thomas, his face a picture of delight, his perfect teeth made imperfect by the loose tooth threatening to fall out at any moment, bounced up and down on his bed, a toy car clutched in his hand.

328

'Thomas, stop that now. It's bathtime.' I caught hold of his hand.

'Okay.'

He jumped down, the duvet crumpling onto the floor beside him. I picked it up, placed it onto the bed, and sat down.

'Thomas, we need to talk about Jeremy Bear. Did you see him at Daddy's new house?'

He nodded miserably. 'Yes.'

I took him onto my knee. 'I'm sorry, darling.'

'It's okay.'

I kissed his forehead. 'But at least you know where he is now.'

'Yes.'

'And you know Daddy will look after him, don't you?'

He nodded again. 'Yes, Mummy.'

I looked round his room suddenly, at the pine chest of drawers, the wardrobe, the bookcase.

'I've been thinking about rearranging things in here. That wardrobe, for a start. It might look nicer away from the window, let more light into the room.'

'No, Mummy!' Suddenly still, he stared at me anxiously. 'You can't.'

'It's only the wardrobe, darling. It would look so much better.'

'No, Mummy, you mustn't lift heavy things. Becca said so.'

'Mm?' Bewildered at first, I then recalled our conversation at the hospital. 'No, Thomas. She only said you couldn't lift heavy things if - if you're having a baby ...'

Inexplicably, I stumbled over the words.

'Is Becca's baby alright?' He jumped down from my knee. 'Why is he in that bator thing?'

'It's called an incubator.' But my mind was spinning. There was something wrong here, something I needed to concentrate on. But I kept my attention on Thomas. 'He's only in there until he grows a bit stronger, darling. He was born too early, but he's fine. He's a very healthy little boy.'

'That's okay, then.' He looked up thoughtfully. 'Mummy?'

'Yes?'

'Can I play with my car, very quickly - before bathtime?'

Suddenly, my mind cleared and I grasped hold of what it had been trying to tell me, what my son had been trying to say. Shaken, I stared in disbelief. My period! It should have been last Friday. Why hadn't I realised?

'No. No, darling.' My stomach churned, I felt suddenly sick. 'Maybe in the morning, we'll play with it in the morning.'

Andrew! No precautions whatsoever! How could I …?

Unless I was just late. It had happened before, a couple of times, when I'd been under a lot of stress. Yes, that was it; I'd been doing too much. But I'd pick up a test tomorrow. Just to be sure.

*

My mind was an ocean of swirling waves, bashing and thrashing against the rocks, over and over and over again, through centuries of time. Tossing and turning my way past midnight, I finally gave in. Climbing out of bed, I pulled out Grandma Beattie's diary.

Enthralled by the childhood antics of my beloved grandmother, I was eager to finish it. Yet, at the same time, I wasn't.

Saturday, February 15th

We didn't go to the Co-op today. Mum went instead. We had to take our blankets to Mrs Wright at the WVS. Mrs Cooke took us there on the bus. Me, our Barbara, Judy, Johnnie and Sydney, as the five original gang members, carried two blankets each, all rolled up with string. Our Matilda, David and Michael tagged along with us.

Mrs Wright was fascinated by the Churchill Gang. I was a bit nervous about meeting her at first, but she was nice. Her house smells a bit of mildew, but she was really friendly, with a big bust and a huge smile. She'd made us buns with white icing on the top. Delicious, and we had cups of tea as well.

She asked how we'd formed our gang and Johnnie (of course!) was the first to speak up.

"We wanted to do something for the war effort. Everyone else seemed to be doing things, but us kids were left out of it all."

She beamed at him. "Very commendable. I am most impressed, most impressed indeed." She offered him another bun, but he grabbed at it so quickly he nearly knocked the plate out of her hand. He remembered to say thank you, though.

Mrs Wright turned to our Matilda, the smallest of us all, and offered her the plate too. "And you, my dear - you're Beattie's sister, aren't you? Why did you want to help with the war effort?"

She grabbed a bun, and smiled her very best smile, the one that makes her eyes crinkle up just a little too much. "Well, I wanted to help all the daddies come home. I wanted to make everyone feel better. And then, when we got some peaches and toffees from Mr and Mrs Standen ..."

I interrupted before she said something she shouldn't. "We were collecting for the Christmas Fair, and the local Co-op gave us some things to use in the tombola."

"How lovely." Rubbing her hands together, she stood up. She really does have a large bust – the rest of her doesn't seem to fit in with it somehow. "Well, I must say, these quilts will be very much appreciated by our men in France. You have some wonderful children at St Mark's School, Mrs Cooke. They are a credit to you."

Mrs Cooke beamed. "Thank you. Yes, I think so too. They are children to be proud of. But they have suffered too …"

She went on to tell her about our fathers and suchlike, and they both fussed over us for what seemed like ages, until it was time to come home.

We had a lovely day and it's nice to think our hard work is going to be put to such good use. I'm really tired now, and am going to fall asleep if I don't get to bed soon. Matilda's already asleep.

Sunday, February 16th

I felt very brave today, I don't know why. I suddenly took it into my head to speak to old Mr Carpenter about the letter. My heart was thumping like mad, but I just knew I had to put him out of his misery.

I knocked on his door as usual, and as usual he rummaged around in his kitchen until he'd found a tuppenny bit. But this time I shook my head at him.

"Mr Carpenter, you don't have to give me lots of money all the time. I won't tell anyone about the letter and no-one else knows except my mum and Gran. And she knew already. So please don't keep giving me all your money, because you might need it yourself one day."

He smiled, patting my head. "Thank you, Beattie, you're a very kind girl. It all happened a long time ago, and there's not really very much to tell, but one day, maybe, I'll tell you. One day, when I'm feeling a bit stronger."

I panicked then. "You feeling all right, Mr Carpenter?"

"I'm fine. Just a bit tired, still getting over the shock of that letter turning up after all these years. I never sent it, you see. I wrote it, but I never had the nerve to send it. I was a coward. All those years, lost." His eyes, old and tired, filled with sorry tears. "So, Beattie," he said, "if you've learnt anything at all from this letter, it's to never be afraid to take what you truly want. Forge ahead, and be strong. Don't be a coward like me."

"Yes, Mr Carpenter. And I'm sorry the letter upset you. But I really won't tell anyone - promise." He looked a bit doubtful, so I said, "You can trust me."

He nodded. "I know I can, Beattie, you're a good girl. But, here, take the tuppence. I'm sure the African children can do more with it than I can." He pushed it into my hand.

"Thank you, Mr Carpenter - if you're sure."

But I'll always remember those words. Forge ahead. Be strong.

Monday, February 17th

The strange thing is, the Churchill Chums was supposed to be a secret gang. But now the whole world knows about it. I suppose it couldn't stay secret for long. Mrs Cooke announced in Assembly that we'd all been heroes and that we should stand up and be applauded. I went bright red and felt proud all at the same time. And then she said the most wonderful thing – that we should all, the whole school, collect scraps and old clothes from our neighbours and bring them to school, so that the older ones can use their sewing lessons to make blankets. We never do anything useful in our sewing lessons, just a bit of cross-stitch really. But now we'll be able to make lots and lots of blankets for our soldiers. I'm filling up now, just thinking about it.

In Bible Class we discussed the importance of Easter and why Jesus had to die for us. It's all right believing in miracles, but what I want to know is, why don't they happen in real life? Why do people die even when you don't want them to, even when you pray really, really hard?

Tuesday, February 18th

Cousin Alice is suffering really badly. It was the funeral yesterday. She looked terrible this morning, as if she'd been awake half the night. And I'm sure she brought up her breakfast. I could smell it when I went out to the lav. Poor thing. I didn't know what to say, so I just asked if she was all right and would she like me to make her a cup of tea. She just shook her head. It must be terrible, what she's going through. And she's only young yet.

I paused, wondering if Cousin Alice might be pregnant. Suddenly a rush of memory flooded me as I remembered that day - the day of the snow, the day Andrew and I made love, the vision of the churchyard, the dark, the cold, the sense of déjà vu I'd experienced. I trembled suddenly, the most ridiculous thought entering my mind. Was the vision I'd had, the churchyard, the trees, anything to do with Cousin Alice and Paul Whiting? Is it pure coincidence that Andrew is such a gentle soul, believing in the power of yoga and meditation, and Paul Whiting was a pacifist, willing to die for his beliefs? Was the déjà vu I'd experienced anything to do with Cousin Alice? Could my yoga-teaching lover possibly be the reincarnation of Paul Whiting?

Ridiculous. Shrugging the thought away, I yawned sleepily, and continued.

Mum was on nights again last night. I don't really mind nights now because Mum's here to tuck us in before she goes to work, we see her before we go to school, and she's

334

awake when we get home. So she's really only working while we're asleep. And even though she always looks washed out after nights, she seems quite cheerful and says she enjoys the company.

The Churchill Chums had a quick meeting after dinner (mince again) to discuss our next project. We want to raise some money, so we can give it to the WVS. Me, Barbara and Judy were full of ideas, but the boys were messing about too much to have a serious conversation, pretending to be Commies and shooting each other. I don't know. Boys will be boys.

Thursday, February 20th

There's something going on. I caught Mum dashing back into the house just as we got home from school. She'd been to Auntie Mary's, she said, for a natter. But she looked flustered, and a bit secretive. There was something else too, in those lovely blue eyes. Concern, I think. She must be worried about Cousin Alice, I suppose. She does look very poorly, not at all the lovely girl with the big blue eyes and bright red lips she used to be. I suppose that's what death does to you. Takes away everything good and replaces it with everything bad. If you let it.

School was all right, although Johnnie got told off again for knocking his milk off the desk. What a waste. But he can't seem to sit still for two minutes these days. He says he's over-excited because his Mum's coming up next week. I helped him mop up.

Friday, February 21st

Spelling test today. I got 24 out of 25. I spelt forty wrong, with a 'u'. Well, I'll remember that next time, won't I? Johnnie got 16 correct. Which isn't bad for him.

After dinner, two American pilots came into school to talk to us all. One of them was very good-looking, with lovely blue eyes and wavy hair. Anyway, they came to tell us they were touring the area, visiting schools and hospitals, trying to cheer everyone up, make us all feel better. They're up here for a few weeks, before going back down south to fly with the RAF. They said more and more Americans are coming over to Britain to fight the Jerries - it all sounds very exciting!

Mr Holt (Bertie) let us go home early. Yippee!

Saturday, February 22nd

Half-term at last! I do like school, but it's good being at home for a while, isn't it?

We went to the Co-op with Mum and Mrs Standen had saved us some liver. They don't get it in very often, but when they do it goes like wildfire. I hope this means we won't have to take that horrible Parish's Chemical Food this week.

I'm going to carry on with Mrs Bellhouse's vegetable patch. She dug it over for us, ready for planting, so all I need to do now is plant some seeds. I've taken our veg peelings over to Uncle John's house today. He mixes them with corn for the hens and geese, then gives us eggs in return. And he's promised to find some seeds for me to plant - can't wait to get started.

Sunday, February 23rd

Really icy today. I slipped over twice, and it hurt - a lot! I collected quite a bit of missionary money, though. I think everyone felt sorry for me, out in the cold. Even Mrs Tripp managed a smile, especially when I told her about our frozen lav. Mum has to pour boiling water down it when we need to flush. What a palaver!

CHAPTER 35

I'D had my fill of introspective musing, of unveiling the stone plinth of my marriage, my life - of running from one subject to another. Now I'd seen Rob for what he truly was, maybe I could move on. And if I were sure Andrew wouldn't lament relinquishing his bachelor status at the age of forty-one, maybe I could let him into my life. Might he be the Mr Rochester to my Jane, after all?

So Jenny's phone call announcing the birth of her twins was a welcome distraction, a wonderful distraction. Busy washing up, I waved my tea towel around excitedly.

'Whoo-hoo! I'm so happy for you, Jenny. A boy and a girl - how absolutely perfect is that?'

'We're bringing them home tomorrow. I'm just so excited.'

'How much do they weigh?'

'Iona Mackenzie is four and three-quarters pounds, and Hamish Duncan five and a half.'

'What beautiful names.'

'True Scottish names, they are.'

'So how is the mother?'

'She's only a wee lassie, but she did brilliantly.'

'Is she still okay about it, do you think?'

'Absolutely. She's determined she wants to get on with her own life now - no regrets. Oh, Mattie, you just can't imagine ...' Her voice broke into jagged pieces. 'Sorry, I just feel so very, very lucky. We've been through so much.'

'But it's all turned out right in the end, hasn't it?'

'Incredible, isn't it? As if these babies are really meant to be mine.'

'They are meant to be yours, silly. And no-one could love them more.'

*

It wasn't long before I was in bed, having had a long soak in the bath, a face pack and a manicure. My nails were suffering from my new-found career, but it was definitely worth it; I loved every minute.

So, tired, excited, my skin soft and glowing, I climbed into bed. Eager to switch off, my mind a shopping trolley of loose, unrelated articles, I picked up the last few pages of Grandma Beattie's diary.

Tuesday, February 25th

Much warmer today. A beautiful day. Mrs Whitaker has come up from London to visit Johnnie and Michael for a few days.

Me, Matilda and Barbara played near the allotments and Judy brought her doll, Millie, in her pram. I took Elizabeth and Matilda took baby Joan and we played at shops. It was good fun, especially when we pretended there was a burglar who stole our shopping. Judy was the burglar and I had to leave our babies with Matilda so I could chase her. We all went back to Gran's for tea – mince and mash with carrots, then jam sponge. Judy's mum came for her at 6 o'clock, then Gran came to sleep on the put-you-up at our house because Mum was on Afters. It was good fun having Judy round to play.

Wednesday, February 26th

Well! Found out what all the secrecy's been about. Cousin Alice. She's getting married. To that Mr Young, the foreman at the factory. How can she MARRY him? He's REALLY horrible. Our Barbara says she's going to have a baby, and that she's having to marry him because the father of the baby is the boy who's killed himself. But I don't think that can be right. If it was, then Mum would have told me, wouldn't she?

So I asked her, and yes, Cousin Alice is having a baby, but because Paul's not here to marry her, she's got to marry someone else. Mr Young offered, so she's said yes. Mum says Uncle Jonathan knows Mr Young quite well and asked him if he would. Poor Alice. What a state to be in. And she's only just lost Paul, the boy she really loves.

Mum's told me how they get babies. She saw our Matilda up to bed, then came back downstairs and made a big thing out of me being a big girl now, and all that. Then she told me. And I'm definitely not going to get married! It's disgusting! Yuk! How can people do that?

At least we've got a wedding to look forward to. And Mum says Cousin Alice has a really pretty frock I can wear. At least it'll be better than that black one. And at least it won't be for a funeral.

Thursday, February 27th

We went down to the allotments today, me and our Barbara, and saw our first snowdrops. Pure and white.

Beautiful. I just can't wait for summer now. I love the scent of flowers, especially after the rain's fallen.

Auntie Betty's already told Barbara about how they make babies. She told her ages ago, she says, but she wasn't allowed to say anything. Which has made me really upset. I thought Barbara told me everything.

Mrs Whitaker came round for tea today. She brought a bottle of the wine Dr Benson gave her for Christmas. She and Mum are downstairs now, drinking it. I'm supposed to be tucked up in bed, but I've climbed out to write my diary. There's a lot of laughing going on down there. I only hope there's no air raid tonight, else they'll be wobbling down to Gran's! It's nice to hear Mum laughing, though.

Friday, February 28th

Mrs Whitaker was still here this morning. She slept on the put-you-up in the parlour. Mum says it was too late for her to be walking home on her own, and anyway she'd had far too much wine. I don't know – grownups! I never know what to make of them. If I'd drunk loads of wine, I'd never have heard the last of it. Mum got Uncle John to go round to Dr Benson's to tell them where she was. What they must have thought, I don't know.

We had the most wonderful morning, though. You won't believe what's happened. Well, after breakfast, Mrs Whitaker went back to Dr Benson's to get washed and changed, then came back here after dinner. She brought Johnnie and Michael with her. I thought they were coming round to play, but no. Apparently, Mum had asked them round specially. She had a surprise for us, all of us. And it's this – Mrs Whitaker is coming to live with us. She's going to look after me and our Matilda while Mum's at work, and she'll get to see Johnnie and Michael every single day. You can't imagine the look on Johnnie's face. And Michael just burst into tears, bless his cotton socks. Isn't that the most wonderful news? It does mean I've got to move back in with

Matilda, but I think I can put up with that if Mrs Whitaker's going to stay here.

I've just written it all down. And I still can't believe it.

Saturday, March 1st

Mrs Whitaker moved in this morning. She brought Mum a brand new felt hat - rose pink, to match the outside of our house. She bought it from the Co-op yesterday, a thank you present for letting her stay.

Sitting there, perched against my pillow, I read the sentence again. And again.

My God, I thought. My God …

It's lovely, the latest fashion, a tilt hat with fine netting across the front. She's only brought a small suitcase with her, but she's bringing a few more things next time she goes to London. She says she doesn't need very much. Which is a good thing really, because there's not that much space in our Matilda's room.

At the Co-op, Mrs Standen smiled at me really nicely, I don't know why. Unless Mr Carpenter's told her about the love letter. But then, he can't have because he never sent it. I wonder if he's told her about it now, though. It is a long time ago. Maybe he has. Maybe he wishes he had sent it. Maybe she wishes he'd sent it and that she'd gone off with him. Maybe I'll just never know.

Johnnie and Michael were here when their mum moved in. We played at Firemen (Michael's idea) while Mum showed Mrs Whitaker her new room. Uncle John was here too, to help with carrying stuff, and so of course our Barbara came round. We had a houseful! We played at shops again, selling beautiful dresses and smart suits with dinner jackets. Our Barbara goes to the pictures too much, I think.

CHAPTER 36

I poked my head around the sitting room door. 'Are we all ready to go?'

Mum was gazing into space. Dad peered over his *Sunday Telegraph*.

'We are,' he said. 'Young Thomas is still upstairs, though.'

'I'll give him a couple of minutes.'

Sitting down beside Mum, I gave her the Morrison's carrier bag containing Grandma Beattie's diary. 'Here, I've brought this down for you. I finished it last night.'

She pushed it away. 'Thanks, love, but I gave it you to keep.'

I stared at her meaningfully. 'I think you might want to read it, Mum.'

'Oh. Okay. Is it good, then?'

I grinned stupidly, a clown whose magic trick has worked against all the odds. 'It was rose pink.'

'What?'

'The house. It was rose pink, Mum.'

She snatched at the bag. 'You're joking!'

Folding away his newspaper, Dad shook his head in disbelief. 'Well. I never ...'

'I'm not joking,' I insisted. 'The last diary entry, first of March.'

Mum pulled out the papers excitedly. 'Damn, I've not got my glasses. You read it.'

I found the final page and laid it upon the coffee table.

'Saturday, March first. Mrs Whitaker moved in this morning. She brought Mum a brand new felt hat - rose pink, to match the outside of our house. She bought it from the Co-op yesterday, a thank you present for letting her stay. It's lovely – the latest fashion, a tilt hat with fine netting across the front.' I paused, a satisfied grin on my face. 'There, what do you think?'

Stunned, she shook her head slowly. 'I can't quite believe it, to tell you the truth.'

'There's more, though. When me and Thomas went up to Edinburgh to see Jenny, Thomas saw a pink house out of the window. Then he started talking about his 'little girl' breaking her arm. Well, Grandma Beattie talks about breaking her arm when she finds an old plaster-cast in her bedroom.'

Dad was still shaking his head. 'Really?'

'So, you think Grandma Beattie was one of Thomas's 'little girls'?' asked Mum.

'Yes. What I think is, if he's the reincarnation of anyone, it's Grandma Beattie's father, Benny. His death is the reason she started the diary.'

She beamed, coiffing her hair absentmindedly. 'Now, that would make sense, wouldn't it? He died so young.'

'And you know how scared of the dark Thomas is - remember when he locked himself inside Mrs Wilson's shed with the old flashlight? And how he loves Monopoly? Well, you told me Benny played it when he was in hospital all that time.'

'Yes.'

I looked at Dad. 'What do you think to reincarnation now, Dad?'

Never before had I seen my dad, my wonderful dad, so lost for words.

'I don't know, love,' he said finally. 'But you do have to wonder.'

'Well, you explain why we have all this. Nice housing, expensive food, a good education, while other people - even tiny children - have to live in poverty, or through the most horrendous wars? And only because of where they're born or the religion they're born into. Is that fair?'

'No, love,' he sympathised.

'Well, don't you think we should all be given the same chance in life? If not in this life, then surely in another one. Shouldn't we all be given the opportunity to develop our gifts and talents at some stage? I mean, children who die at birth or those born with disabilities should be given a second chance, shouldn't they? And all the young men being killed in wars - surely they should be allowed to have full lives, not just be cut off in their prime?'

'Well, Mattie,' he sighed. 'I'm afraid life isn't fair. It never was.'

344

'But look at Thomas,' said Mum. 'If he is my granddad reborn, then it all makes sense. He was so young when he died, why shouldn't he have another stab at life? I've read about reincarnation - well, bits - and we're all here to learn. The theory is that we can't learn everything we need to know in a single lifetime. So it makes sense to have more than one go, doesn't it? I know it all sounds a bit airy-fairy, Kenneth, but go on - you explain why Thomas talks about a pink house, and now we find out there was one. '

'Or how he can play Monopoly like a pro,' I said, my hands waving emphatically.

'Ah, well,' Mum sighed. 'I knew about them playing Monopoly, didn't I? He could have picked up something from me, I suppose.'

'Well now,' said Dad. 'That could explain everything, couldn't it, love? Maybe there's a bit of telepathy going on. Maybe he can read our thoughts.'

But Mum demurred. 'No. We didn't know the house was pink - we've only just picked it up from the diary. All I know is what Mum told me - that Grandma Hattie had to sell the cottage after the war, and that it had been left to her husband by his father, a well-to-do market gardener. That's about it, really.'

'Mum,' I asked. 'Did you ever hear anything about Alice - a cousin of Grandma Beattie's?'

'Is she in the diary, too? It does sound rather interesting.'

'What do you know about her?'

'Not a lot, really. She was the black sheep of the family. Got pregnant when she was sixteen. I think the baby's father was killed in the war, so it was arranged for her to marry someone much older. They had to in those days, you know; it was all frowned upon. But then she miscarried. All very sad, it was.'

'What happened to her after that, do you know?'

'Not much. I seem to remember Mum telling me she died quite young. She volunteered for the Army, got killed somewhere down near London.'

'Oh. that's awful. Not much of a life, was it?'

'Well, they do say she never got over the death of her child, or the father. Does this have something to do with the diary?'

'No. No, it's nothing. I was just interested.'

But a silver shiver crawled slowly down my spine. So, Cousin Alice died long before I was born. She and Paul, the boy who drowned, had been lovers in the churchyard, a churchyard with ice-cold gravestones, the silhouette of a church, and tall oak trees. The churchyard of my vision, I was sure. Could Andrew and I have been lovers before? Could he possibly be the reincarnation of Paul Whiting? No, that was quite ridiculous. But if Thomas *was* my grandfather, reborn, then why shouldn't Paul Whiting have been reborn? He died too soon, as well. But why Andrew, and why Thomas?

I suddenly remembered Thomas's dream - that night - when I picked him up from Rob's.

'I dreamed 'bout that lady in Nannie's summer-house. It was the nice lady in the rain ...'

I thought of all the times he'd picked up on things, known about things. Was he somehow communicating with Grandma Beattie? Was she dictating who goes where and what happens next? And was she the lady who rescued him in that awful November storm, when he saw the snowflake?

'You alright, Mattie love?' Dad pushed himself off the sofa. 'You look a shade pale. Can I get you something?'

'No - thanks, Dad. I'm fine.'

But my mind was working overtime. Had the shock of losing her father at so young an age caused Beattie to stay in touch with him, even though his soul was now Thomas's? And if that *were* the case, was Grandma Beattie looking after me too, returning me to my lost love, my darling Andrew? Somehow?

CHAPTER 37

MORNING sun filled the kitchen. Opening the back door, I filled my lungs with fresh, warm air. Thomas's blue trike was parked just across the entrance, ready to trip me up at any moment. I moved it to its place on the patio. Switching on the kettle, I made tea. Thomas's red and blue butterfly hung on the cupboard above me, drawn when I'd been at my lowest, my mind an unlit and bitterly cold hurricane lamp.

But suddenly, expertly, I was seeing it properly. For the very first time.

I stared, my mind springing open with the jerk of a jack-in-the-box.

Thomas was right. The picture wasn't *for* me. It was *of* me. The tiny chrysalis in the corner was me as I was then. The beautiful butterfly; this was me now. I'd spread my wings. I was free.

So what else did Thomas know? Had he pulled me into Haringey's that day so I took the job, so I met Enid? Did he leave his sweater on purpose at Mum's house, so I'd follow him into the orchard and hear Grandma Beattie? And what else had he done that I'd brushed to one side?

The worktop was littered with empty Easter egg boxes, their cartoon characters smiling up at me. An errant chocolate button lay melting in the sunshine. I picked it up, placing it inside my mouth, the tip of my tongue squashing its creamy softness against my teeth.

Funny, isn't it, I thought, how Easter Sunday jogs the memory? Just like Christmas. Mum shouting at me for getting chocolate on my dress before Sunday school, dabbing crazily with a wet dishcloth as I left the house. Then after Sunday school a visit to Grandma Beattie's, her apple blossom perfume, her shiny yellow tablecloth. And even more Easter eggs.

Opening the oven door, I pulled out the hot baking tray, basting the chickens, potatoes and onions. Droplets of hot oil bounced up and down, their circles of ochre swimming around. I carefully pushed the tray back, closed the oven door, and headed for the sitting room.

A buzz of voices filled the air.

'No,' Jenny was saying. 'It's easy, really. Chris sleeps in the guest room with Iona in the cot. She's quicker at feeding than Hamish. After all, he's the one who has to get up for work in the morning.'

'Not that it doesn't take me an hour to feed her, mind,' he replied.

'And I sleep in our room with Hamish. Then we swap over, so Chris gets our bed alternate nights.' She laughed happily. 'It works.'

Mum smiled. 'Well, I think you're both wonderful, taking on twins like this. Believe me, it's hard work with just the one baby to look after. I remember. Now, when our Mattie was born ...'

Dad stood up. 'Here, Mattie love, sit yourself down a minute.'

'Thanks - it's okay. I need to pop back for the tea.'

I knelt on the carpet, allowing myself to relax momentarily. Dreamily, I listened to the rattle of conversation, mused over the happiness of my friends, and gazed fondly at their new babies, fast asleep in their arms. Christopher with Hamish, Jenny with Iona, and Alan with Jacob.

Enid caught my gaze. 'You alright, Mattie?'

I blinked. 'Sorry, I didn't sleep too well last night. The amount of work I've had, you'd think I'd sleep like a log, wouldn't you?'

Mum sighed. 'It can take a lot to switch off, especially with accounts and things to do. You never really stop when you're self-employed. But you can overdo it, you know - just take care now.'

'I will.'

'You still doing up Beth's bungalow?' Enid asked.

'I am, and I'm having the most tremendous fun. I've chosen duck egg for the walls, and cream satin bedding. She loves it.'

Enid looked at me carefully. 'Well, be careful. We don't want any more accidents, now do we?'

Enid knew things too. Just like Thomas. She'd always known. If I'd not had that accident at her

350

house, I'd never have found out about Rob. If she hadn't suggested I set up in business, I'd still be earning a pittance at Haringey's. And how did she know about Grandma Beattie? I know for a fact I'd never mentioned her before that day – the day she'd been burning coriander seed and jasmine. Was there some kind of link between Enid and Grandma Beattie? The only one I could think of was Old Mrs Fleming – she lived in the same place as Grandma Beattie, went to the same school; there must be a connection. And she and Enid are obviously friends – she calls her Peggy. Did Enid walk through the bright red door of Haringey's for a reason?

But she was still talking. 'You'll have to come and do up my apartment when I've moved in. But I'll be paying you this time. They've only put paint on the walls, and I like a bit o' wallpaper.'

Iona began to cry loudly, her face alternating hues of pink and white.

'Mattie,' cried Jenny.

I shook myself into action. 'Yes?'

'Could I use your microwave and a towel? I've left ours at the hotel.'

'Of course.'

She followed me into the kitchen, a bag on one arm, Iona over her shoulder.

'You warm the milk,' I said.

I placed the baby over my shoulder, rubbing gently at her back, soothing her. But as Jenny pulled the bottle of formula from her bag, she discovered a large, padded envelope.

'Damn! Nearly forgot this. It's from Benjamin – he asked me to pass it on.'

Much later, after everyone had gone, I left my parents with Thomas and went up to my room. Inside Benjamin's envelope was a small paperback entitled *Your Child's Past Lives,* and a letter, handwritten.

Colinton
Edinburgh
Wednesday 20ᵗʰ April

Dear Mattie,

I do hope you and Thomas are well.

Jenny's said things haven't been going well in your personal life just lately, which I'm very sorry to hear. But I hope you and Thomas are settling down to a normal life again, and that each day brings its share of happiness.

I feel I should write to you in connection with our conversation on the train that day. To this end - and I hope you don't mind - I enclose a book you may find interesting. A particular chapter discusses the concept of reincarnation - I've marked it for you.

Opening the book, I found the relevant page, marked with a fluorescent green post-it note. Two paragraphs were highlighted:

The philosophy of reincarnation is thousands of years old. Now accepted by two thirds of the world's population, the belief is that our soul returns to a new body after death. Each life is progressive and is seen as the vehicle for lessons that need to be learned by each individual as he or she journeys towards perfection of the soul.

Whether or not you can accept this theory of past lives, it is a fact that every human being shares the same genetic heritage. All human life came out of East Africa millions of years ago. It may be, therefore, that young children can somehow dip into the well of this collective past experience. The psychotherapist Carl Jung called this the 'collective unconscious'. He suggested that apart from a personal consciousness, there also existed a racial or commercial consciousness. This contains every thought, every emotion, every piece of information that mankind has ever experienced or brought into being. Each individual is linked to the collective unconscious, drawing from it as well as adding to its huge matrix. So it may be that from this well we are able to draw up memories of lives bearing similarities with our own, or those of our ancestors ...

Reading through it again, I allowed my eyes to travel back to Benjamin's letter.

You may find the whole thing rather far-fetched, Mattie, but it is for you to make up your own mind. We each have our own path to travel, each of us on different paths, at different times.

If you ever need to talk - about Thomas - about anything - I'd be more than happy to hear from you. Free of charge, of course. As a friend.

Take great care of each other, and I hope our paths will cross again some day.

Kind regards,
Benjamin Bradstock.

I pushed the book and letter into my bedside drawer. I needed to run Thomas's bath, and there was his room to tidy after the onslaught of Chloe's visit. Perching on the bed, however, I allowed myself a little smile. Because if there *were* such a thing as reincarnation, and if Thomas *was* the reincarnation of my great grandfather, then who might this tiny life, this new being, inside me be? Would this child talk about a special house, too?

Or was this baby - the one I had so ached for - was this baby the one Alice and Paul should have had in their previous lifetime, the one she lost after his death?

But who had instigated this fulfilment of my dream? Could it have been Grandma Beattie? Did she know Rob was playing away? Did she know he'd never have given me another child? And did she plan everything from the moment Thomas pulled me through that great red door of Haringey's? Because it did seem as if the last few months of my life had been mapped out. As if everything had happened for a reason.

Overcome with emotion, warm tears filled my eyes. Tears of happiness, of wonder. Of fulfilment.

But through the window, something caught my eye. A glint of starlight, a swish of silver.

I turned. I watched. A single snowflake, pure and white, tumbled to earth.

Then the sweet scent of apple blossom filled the room, wrapping itself around me. Like the arms of an angel.

THE END

SEASALT AND MIDNIGHT

BRANDY

A Benjamin Bradstock Tale (2)

1

Enid Phelps

WE lived in Dorset at the time, in a small tumbledown village at the edge of the sea. We were only there six months while Dad, a plasterer by trade, worked on new houses for the council. Nice they were, with iron gates and shiny front doors.

The year was 1959. A year of firsts. The first Barbie doll (I got one for Christmas), the first Mini travelling the roads, the first hovercraft launched. Woodstock and the Moon Landing were still a long way off, ten years into the future.

Me, I was seven years old. Each day, after school had finished, I'd find Mum waiting for me in the playground. We'd walk home hand in hand, chatting away, the salt of the sea and the squawking of seagulls filling the air around us. On the way, we'd pass this beautiful old house. It was derelict, ramshackle, but I loved it. Standing at the corner of a lane leading down to the beach, it had its own plot of land and a driveway full of small white pebbles. I'd comment on how sad it looked, how it could do with pretty flowers in the garden and lace curtains up at the windows. I'd chat about it, dreaming that one day we'd live there, or that I'd grow up, get married, and move in.

Then one day, one gloriously sunny day, with the sky as blue as Mum's eyes and the sparkling waves roaring in my ears, I realised Mum thought I was making the whole thing up. She couldn't see the house. Not one bit of it. She was merely pretending to, filling in the details in her lovely cockney accent. But the details were all wrong. She wasn't describing the house I could see, with broad windows either side of a black front door, two enormous steps leading up, and flakes of old paint hanging from the eaves. No. The one she described had pretty window boxes, flowery curtains, and a navy-blue door with a shiny brass letterbox.

I remember looking up at her, to see if she was joking, to catch the amused smile on her face.

But no. She thought *I* was the one making it up.

I realised suddenly, my heart thumping, that the house wasn't really there. I checked. I got Sam, my brother, to come with me, pulling at his arm so he couldn't escape.

The house had a big garden, but there were no flowers, just long strands of grass dried brown by the sun. A huge apple tree guarded the entrance, its strong branches and tiny fruits hanging above the path enticingly. It seemed such a lovely old place, the kind that should have a family living there, with children running round and a sun-kissed gardener looking after it.

'What do you think to this old house, Sam? Isn't it lovely?'

He looked around. 'What house?'

'Sam, stop messing! This house here.' I waved towards it. 'This great big house here. You can't exactly miss it.'

'Enid, what you talking about?' He stared at me, his expression the same as the time he had a gobstopper stuck inside his cheek. 'There's nothing there, stupid! Just a bit of old land!

I let go of his arm to study his face properly, screwing up my eyes against the light.

'You can't see a house? A great big house with big, massive windows? Can't you see anything, anything at all?'

'Come on Enid, stop messing. Let's get back.'

Sam is five years older than me. He was my protector and my best friend, so I knew he was telling the truth.

I finally knew with absolute certainty that I could see the house, but no-one else could.

Alexandra is a British author whose work includes **Snowflakes and Apple Blossom** (1st Benjamin Bradstock Tale), **Seasalt and Midnight Brandy** (2nd Benjamin Bradstock Tale), **Stardust and Vanilla Spice** (3rd Benjamin Bradstock Tale), and **One Tiny Mistake**, an April Stanislavski Murder Mystery.

Snowflakes and Apple Blossom was shortlisted for the Writers' Village International Novel Award.
Seasalt and Midnight Brandy has been serialised on BBC Radio.

Alexandra is deeply involved in amateur dramatics and loves to tread the boards. She lives in the beautiful Peak District with her husband and twin sons.

Contact her on Twitter@Alexjord18, Facebook, or https://alexjordan1.wixsite.com/author

Printed in Great Britain
by Amazon